NORTH COUNTRY

BOOKS BY MATT BONDURANT

The Third Translation
The Wettest County in the World
The Night Swimmer
Oleander City
North Country

NORTH COUNTRY

MATT BONDURANT

Published in 2025 by Blackstone Publishing
Cover and book design by Kathryn Galloway English

Printed in the United States of America

First edition: 2025
ISBN 979-8-8748-0936-2
Fiction / Thrillers / Crime

Version 1

Blackstone Publishing
31 Mistletoe Rd.
Ashland, OR 97520

www.BlackstonePublishing.com

For the people of the North Country,
who welcomed me into their homes and garage beer fridges.

In memory of Ray Balestri, Bruce Butterfield, and Tara Marlowe.

Indeed terror is in all cases whatsoever, either more openly or latently the ruling principle of the sublime.

Edmund Burke,
A Philosophical Enquiry into the Origin of Our Ideas of the Sublime and Beautiful, 1757

Two children of the North Country, up before dawn.

Their spoons clinked in unison as they ate cereal in the kitchen. Upstairs, their parents and older brother are swaddled in heavy blankets, the windows black and rimmed with frost. In the mudroom, Kaiser gathered jackets, pants, gloves, and hats, whispered instructions, worked buttons and zippers, tied laces. His little sister, weak with sleep, slumped against the wall in her down parka.

Kaiser pulled the runner sled across the soybean field, creating fresh tracks on the unblemished snow. The sun was obscured by a scrim of gossamer clouds, the frozen surface of Lake Champlain glistening like the inside of an oyster shell. He bumped the sled onto the ice, and they headed northeast around the curve of Stony Point, toward Kelly Bay. Ahead are Fort Montgomery, the international border, and the white plains of Quebec.

Children of the North Country are not afraid of the frozen lake. A familiarity and ease with ice was instinctual, necessary. At the age of seven Kaiser already knew the foot-feel of strong ice, the way weak ice moved and buckled. He was familiar with the myriad ice-sounds, the squeak of frost bubbles, the crack of a fissure developing, the low rumble of shifting plates.

Near the border, Kaiser dropped the rope and rested before turning back. He could hear the faint metallic grind of the train coming up the coast from Coopersville, the sound of diesel engines, a car door slamming, a beleaguered dog barking at the morning light. His parents would be awake soon.

Then he saw it coming from a long way off, a blot on the Quebec side of the border, an immense dark shape sliding under the ice. He thought it was the shadow of an airplane, but as it moved closer, he could see the ice welling upward, rippling across the blunt leading edge. The bulging shape was several hundred feet long, angling toward them as if it knew they were there. Kaiser's body went rigid with incomprehension and fear. There was no time to run and nowhere to go. He looked back at his little sister sitting cross-legged on the sled, scarf wrapped across her face, just her eyes showing. He could tell that she was smiling.

Then it was under them. The ice rose up and Kaiser fell to his hands and knees, the next moment dropping and the sensation of weightlessness and the crashing of breaking ice and the shock of cold water on his skin. He was underwater in a thick soup of drifting dark and light shapes, a raging torrent of sound filling his ears, the pores of his skin dilating as the icy water burrowed into him. He clawed his way to the surface, struggling in the dark water filled with slush and angular shards of ice, his arms clumsy in his heavy coat. He got his forearms up over the edge of the hole, levering up his torso, sliding his legs out sideways, and then he was laying on the ice, gasping for breath. Everything was white and spangled with refracting light, the water on his eyelashes freezing as he rolled over onto his stomach, his pants and jacket already stiffening. His face was close against the ice, and through the mottled and warped prism he saw her, eyes wide open, her scarf fallen free from her face, her mouth open in an expression of incomprehension, two white palms pressed against the bottom of the ice, just inches away from his own hands. Everything focused into a singular keening sound, a high-pitched scream that seemed to explode from his body into the sky. There was a flurry of confusion, the clatter of broken ice, sloshing water, then a blank darkness settling over him.

He ran a high fever for two weeks. At night, Kaiser would wake and find his father upright in the chair by the bed, eyes shut tight, grimacing, the wind humming outside the window. He was tormented by dreams of his sister, transfixed and silent under a pale sheen of ice, her hands pawing at the translucent wall between them. Daylight was like being buried alive. Everything pressed in on him, filling his head so he couldn't parse out a single specific thought.

They never recovered her body. Kaiser never told anyone about the shadow under the ice.

Then one morning he joined his parents at the breakfast table. His father, who everyone called Kodiak, came up from the barn, stamping the snow off his boots into the doorway. When he saw the boy at the table he smiled, a sort of deliberate, grinding smile. The morning was bright, the sun through the window illuminating the table like a bonfire, and his mother watched him and his father eating with quiet, rapid motions. Kaiser didn't know yet that he would never step on the ice again. He didn't know that a part of him was lost.

PART I

The White House Office of National Drug Control Policy said that between 2003 and 2006 the amount of Ecstasy seized in the 10 Canadian border states went up almost 10 times. And they warned that in many cases the Canadian drug is being laced with methamphetamine, both to make it easier to produce and to make it more addictive as a way to keep customers coming back. "Canada is the major supplier of MDMA in the United States," said Barbara Wetherell, a spokeswoman for the Drug Enforcement Administration in Washington.

Wilson Ring,
Associated Press,
January 11, 2009

To make anything very terrible, obscurity seems in general to be necessary. When we know the full extent of any danger, when we can accustom our eyes to it, a great deal of the apprehension vanishes.

Edmund Burke,
A Philosophical Enquiry into the Origin of Our Ideas of the Sublime and Beautiful

The boy at the bottom of the lake opened his eyes and found his right hand had floated free again. He watched the hand, slightly luminescent, glowing like moonlight. His legs and torso were wedged under an enormous maple half-buried in the mud bottom. The sediment in the water burned his eyes as he squinted in the gloom, the surface far above a mirror of dark glass. He waited another hour then gave up, allowing his body to slide out and ascend into starlight.

Someone walking the woods along the western edge of the lake on that October night might have seen him emerging from the water, his forehead breaking the smooth black surface of the lake. They might have heard the slow plod of his steps as he waded to shore among the cattails and jimson weed. They might have seen him on the bank, shivering, as the wind pulled at the tops of the shadowy forest, the supple trunks of the trees wending, the air murmuring of windfall and bird alarm.

At daybreak, the boy was working his way to the hard road that led into town. He kept to the tree line until he made a filling station with an outside bathroom. He locked the door and took off his wet clothes and dried them the best he could with paper towels, wiping away mud and lake debris. He used his fingers to comb his hair.

Later he stood by the fence at the park, watching the other children. The people of the town became used to the sight of this disheveled boy lurking on the perimeter. The woods were believed to be filled with such boys, scrawny, dirty-necked youths who filtered through backyards and crouched behind the woodpile. Stories were told of boys floating on the surface of the lake, thousands of them, face up to the moon, their large eyes unblinking.

But there really was only the one boy, the one who has been here forever, the boy we see here now.

The Boy at the Bottom of the Lake &
Other Legends of the North Country,
Jean-Pierre Montour, 1936

KAISER

It was autumn when he returned. The barn still frost-white, wind-blasted boards curling at the ends, the staggered fence-lines loping over the hills. A single lighted window, his old bedroom, on the second floor of the house. Kaiser slung his service duffel over his shoulder and checked his watch, looked southwest at the Adirondack range, stretched out his arm and put his finger on a ragged peak. A moment later, a faint dot of light separated from the mountain, heading east like a drifting star, crossing the arc of the sky, passing over the lake and dropping behind the Green Mountains.

He made his way down the hall and into the dark kitchen. The house smelled like meatloaf, soap, and coffee, the familiar smells of his youth. The door to the basement was cracked, leaking yellow light across the floor. The faint murmur of his father's voice. Kaiser descended a few steps and ducked his head so he could see into the unfinished basement, the beams stuffed with pink rolls of insulation, the bare studs, the cement floor lined with cracks where the old house settled. Kodiak sat at a long table wearing headphones, both hands working the dials of the radio console. Nailed to the rafters over the table was a list of famous call signs: Juan Carlos, King of Spain—EAOJC, Barry Goldwater—K7UGA, Walter Cronkite—KBC6SD.

Chasing DX, he said into the old intercom-style microphone. Six point oh-four.

His father spun the dial with a practiced hand, settling on a new frequency.

Chasing DX, he said. Is anyone there?

When he was a boy, Kaiser and his father spent hours every week "chasing DX," seeking out remote broadcasts from all over the world. Their ham radio console was an old vacuum-tube model upgraded with a modern amplifier. A coil of cables snaking across the floor, 2,500 watts of output, an ICOM 735 HF two-way that could reach around the globe and back. Kaiser learned to swap out a twelve-point crystal tube when he was eight. When he was twelve, they built a receiver array on the mountain by the hunting cabin.

Every Monday morning, Kaiser and Kodiak huddled in the basement to listen to the Chinese number lady. They regularly tracked and logged several so-called tone stations, mysterious transmitters that produced regular tones, sounds, words, or numbers. Like the Buzz Station, channel S1 at 436.006, which played a constant buzz that only varied twice in over fifty years: once in 1945, and the other when the Berlin Wall came down. The Chinese number lady came out of S2 at 123.004 every Monday morning, a woman with a Chinese accent greeting them in English and then reading six numbers between one and twenty. She ended each broadcast with an enigmatic goodbye, different every time: *I hope these numbers were of use to you*, or *Please help these numbers find their way home*. Nobody knew who she was, where the broadcast came from, or who the numbers were for. Kodiak had been recording the Chinese number lady for decades, searching for variations, patterns, clues. Kaise''s older brother Bill had little interest, so it became the singular province of Kaiser and his father.

With ten seconds to go Kodiak pressed the record button and they slipped on their headphones. Kaiser would have a pencil and log notebook ready, his knees bobbing.

Good morning! Are you ready?

They listened to the numbers together every week from grade school to high school. Each time Kaiser shivered with anticipation. He knew that he would leave this place. As soon as he was able, he would leave everything and everyone behind.

Kaiser walked upstairs to his room. His sports trophies, medals, posters, and pictures, exactly as he left them. When he opened his top drawer, everything was still in place: a metal gyroscope, rolls of pennies, a Montreal Canadiens hockey puck. On the dresser, pictures of Kaiser in various sports uniforms, a grim-faced stripling on a spring afternoon. A picture with his little sister, arm and arm in a snowy field, when she was just three years old.

When he turned around, his mother was in the doorway in her bathrobe, her mouth open, holding out her hands.

He hadn't been home since 2002, more than five years ago. His parents spent several weeks thinking he had died in Afghanistan, then more than a year knowing he was alive but being unable to communicate with him. For much of that time, Kaiser had considered this moment, how it might go. But as his mother lurched forward to embrace him, falling into his arms, nothing happened the way he thought it would.

LECLAIR

The boys were hungry, so LeClair set the meeting for the Michigan stand by the marina. They sat at a picnic table and LeClair sipped a Diet Coke while Buck and Gary inhaled a couple Michigan dogs with fries and onion rings. The sailboats rocked in their slips, the stays rhythmically clinking. In a couple weeks, the marina would start hauling out the boats to be winterized as the lake began the long freeze.

The boys ate while LeClair watched them from behind his sunglasses. Buck and Gary had the thick, ropey musculature and blocky faces of all-American athletes, square-chinned with heavy brows. They wore matching polo shirts with the collars turned up, mirrored aviator sunglasses, blue parkas, khaki pants, and duck boots. They crammed the last of their hot dogs into their smooth faces, wiping meticulously with multiple napkins that LeClair handed them. Across the lake, the mountains sprawled in the mist. At this distance, there was a kind of sacred quality to the mountains that LeClair could appreciate. This was his preferred perspective. Close up, the topography of nature tended to crowd his perception, like some kind of fabled beast swimming in the periphery of all things.

LeClair was here to meet a man who owed him money. This was not something he would normally do. Normally, he would have made a call to the Lavoie brothers and within a couple hours a wad of cash would have dropped through the slot in the alley door of his house in town. But the Lavoie brothers were in Clinton County Correctional, which made everything difficult. There were a lot of people in the North Country who owed LeClair money. The college boys were good for many things, but stomping the anklebones of a junkie or a mother of two was not one of them. Too many connections, too much risk, and so LeClair kept them separate from these sorts of dealings; they were nice young men with bright futures. The Lavoie brothers had no such connections, no family, no bright future. They didn't even seem to have any acquaintances, other than LeClair.

A Buick sedan riddled with rust and salt stains pulled into the gravel parking lot and LeClair told the boys to go wait in the Escalade. They sauntered off, Gary getting behind the wheel and Buck sprawling in the back. The man in the Buick was named Gorman, a former Baptist preacher who owed LeClair for loans and back rent. Gorman occupied a double-wide in the heart of the massive trailer park west of town called Wiggletown, named for the way the trailers vibrated when the winds howled off the lake.

Gorman shuffled over to the picnic table. He wore an Ausable College Hockey sweatshirt straining over his bouldery gut, a box-hedge beard, his eyes marbled like a fatty cut of brisket. The man had been high as an albatross since 2001, when he lost his church due to charges of immoral behavior.

Pastor Gorman, LeClair said. Looking good.

Gorman frowned, wiped his nose, and slid onto the picnic table bench. He cleared his throat and pulled an envelope from his pocket.

Heard the Lavoie brothers are up at Clinton County.

So? LeClair said.

I got information, Gorman whispered, wiping his eyes with his thumbs.

Information worth nine grand?

More than that.

Gorman took a deep breath, gripped the table with both hands, bending his head down so his nose nearly touched the table.

A painting, he whispered. A rare one. He said it's something you'd want.

What? What the fuck are you talking about?

There's a guy, Gorman said, he works with the South Asian cartels. Up in Montreal.

Gorman stuck a hand in his jeans pocket, found something, held it up between forefinger and thumb. A small white pill, emblazoned with a blue Fleur-de-Lis. He set it on the table.

What's that?

Fleur-de-Lis. The stuff everybody wants. He's the source.

So? Why are you telling me this? I don't give a fuck about pills or any paintings in Montreal. What you should be worrying about is the money you owe me.

Gorman slid the envelope over to him. LeClair looked inside: a couple hundreds, a rumpled stack of ones. He stood up and pulled on his gloves.

I can't believe you called me out here for this.

They call him La Montagne, Gorman said. I'm just passing along the info. He's got this painting and he's looking for a special buyer. He told me to write it down. It's there in the envelope.

LeClair looked down, and between two ratty bills was a receipt from Yando's Big Market. Scrawled on the back: *J. M. W. Turner.*

A Turner? There was simply no way. It was so outlandish that it had to be bullshit.

I'll be sending someone by shortly, LeClair said. I suggest you pass the plate, Pastor. Take up a fucking collection.

It was the start of the hockey season, and the boys were having a pig roast at the fraternity house. LeClair rarely ventured near the house, especially after dark. The boys had made LeClair an honorary brother years ago, due to his charitable giving to the chapter and the fact that he provided desirable jobs. LeClair paid cash, and he paid well. Yes, you had to wear the uniform (windbreaker, khakis, duck boots), go to a lot of art shows, antique galleries, and lonely barns deep in the mountains to look at a dusty painting owned by an old man reeking of pig shit. You had to weather awkward meals where LeClair pushed food around his plate, watching you eat. You had to show up sober, clean, freshly scrubbed, hair neat, smelling nice. You had to walk two steps behind him carrying his leather valise, which contained flat, crisp packets of cash, legal papers and deeds, and occasionally a silver-plated .22 caliber pistol. But these were minor inconveniences. The job and its trappings were never commented on by their peers, for these young men also had that feral attitude that a certain set from privileged backgrounds attain with startlingly incongruity. Their hearts were gemstones fashioned for beauty and cruelty.

Gary turned south on Route 9 and they passed the old air force base, a set of stately buildings around a wide grassy oval, all of them shuttered with plywood. Packs of mountain wolves and stray dogs roamed the grounds and fought over territory, their baying echoing across the water all the way to Burlington. Across Route 9 to the west was the massive airstrip, large enough to land heavy Cold War–era bombers, the tarmac now ruptured by frost heaves, the control tower welded shut, the heavy blast windows in the observation deck spider-webbed, the computer decks stripped and empty.

Gary drove the Escalade through the sylvan college campus and around the gate that blocked access to fraternity row, pulling into LeClair's designated spot, which was marked with traffic cones on the front lawn. They walked through the entranceway and down the stairs, musky with stale beer, chewing tobacco, and the acrid smell of young men, out to the back lawn filled with students, and beyond a limpid, taupe-colored pond. LeClair stood on the deck overlooking the sprawl of young people dressed in wool sweaters and duck boots, listening to the gentle murmur of voices punctuated by peals of laughter. He experienced that forlorn and pleasant feeling of being a part and apart—a paradox of belonging.

His gaze was drawn to a small knot of people surrounding a young man he hadn't noticed before. He was using one hand to gesticulate, the other fist in the pocket of his khakis, duck boots, a starched oxford shirt, leaning back on his heels in an attitude of nonchalance and ease. LeClair's current shop manager, Troy, an earnest accounting major, delivered a gin and tonic and pulled pork sandwich on a paper plate. LeClair pointed and Troy mumbled: *Scotty Marin, sophomore.* LeClair decided that the set of this young man's brow was something noble, like the mark of an ancient lineage of high chieftains. This was someone he would like to have around.

The early years of Donnie LeClair's life had been a wasteland of aesthetic experiences, dominated by the brutal logic of farm life that characterized the North Country. LeClair and his brother Walt were born and raised on a farm just west of North Chazy, a broad, flat section bisected by the Saranac River. By the time Donnie was in junior high, he was helping his mother dust the living room as Walt and their father birthed a calf in the barn. Donnie was reading novels on the davenport on Saturday afternoons as Walt fished the lake. They accepted this as the natural order of things.

But it is also fair to say that Donnie never had any real friends or lovers during his school years. Walt took over the farm soon after high school when their parents passed away in quick succession (blood clot, pneumonia), and at seventeen Donnie went to SUNY Albany on an academic scholarship, studying art history.

The most profound experience of university life for LeClair was a young man on the swim team, an olive-skinned Jewish boy from Long Island. They ate lunch together on the windswept concrete plaza and at night they huddled under the sheets of his narrow dorm bed. This boy was slender and sleek like a seal, and LeClair came to know the musk of youth and chlorine, the faint taste of the chicken fingers he had for dinner. Holding his body in the darkness seemed like embracing a second self.

During this time LeClair also fell in love with landscape oil paintings, which would ultimately determine his life.

After his sophomore year, LeClair dropped out and returned to North Chazy to open an antique shop and manage the family's sprawling real estate holdings in the area. His parents had invested shrewdly, buying up seemingly undevelopable land and properties. Eventually, most of the gas stations and service centers on the northern reaches of the Northway from Lake George to the Canadian border paid rent to the LeClairs. While Walt tended to the farm, Donnie continued to buy up real estate. He owned a restaurant, the antique jewelry store, the pawnshop, nearly half the buildings in downtown North Chazy, as well as the largest trailer park in northern New York. And if you needed an off-the-books loan, Donnie was your man. The irony of his vocation was not lost on him. If he had to traffic in the unseemly side of North Country commerce in order to build his collection of beautiful art, then that was the arrangement he had made. He slept soundly most nights.

But it wasn't enough, and LeClair was fighting a losing battle with unpaid debts, rent, mortgages. He'd been quietly selling off lots and buildings to pay for his collection of paintings. Last month he bought an original J. F. Cropsey at auction for one hundred and fifty thousand dollars. He had standing bids on several other originals up for sale, totaling another half million, which he didn't have liquid assets to cover. And now, a Turner? Even if this Quebecois dealer existed and the painting was real—which he doubted—the price would surely be in the millions. Still its value to his collection would be immeasurable. The main gallery in his house was already crammed like a Tudor salon, frame-edge to frame-edge, but he recently renovated the spare bedroom to create a new gallery for special additions. He kept all this from Walt through creative bookkeeping, but the reality of his financial situation was a catastrophic mess. The only way out would be to liquidate large portions of his collection to repay his debts and return to solvency, and he sure as hell wasn't going to do that. He knew there would be an end to all this, but how that end would arrive was a mystery. The only way was forward.

Now he was aggrieved at the thought of trying to find someone to do debt collection. It was imperative that he get his hands on that money.

There were plenty of meatheads living in their parents' basement who would readily take cash to administer crunchy beatings, but finding someone who was unattached, dependable, and who knew how to keep their mouth shut was harder. The Lavoie brothers existed on the fringe of society, more feral than civilized, appearing only when requested and disappearing afterward. LeClair promised Walt years ago he would never use the fraternity boys for collection or for anything that might veer into the criminal. He saw himself as a genteel benefactor, someone who could introduce a bit of culture or practical business strategy into their otherwise manicured lives, someone who could dispense sage advice as well as pocket money. Yes, he made regular donations to the fraternity and supplied the funds for the new volleyball court behind the house, but this was an investment in a relationship; the boys were valuable to him in many ways, but perhaps most of all he cherished their regard for him. To the boys he was a patriarch of the North Country, a savvy businessman, a local operator. From Lake George up to Rouses Point, everybody knew Donnie LeClair: upstanding member of the community, a leading local philanthropist, a self-made man. The boys were proud of their allegiance to him.

The thought of all that outstanding debt scattered around the North Country made LeClair grind the gristly pork between his molars. He watched the young men and women on the lawn. Scotty Marin was describing something to a clutch of women, their smooth faces tilted in earnest attention. The wad of bread and meat went down his throat like a billiard ball. The only way to survive this world, LeClair thought, was to surround yourself with what you found beautiful.

Scotty Marin, he said. Let's bring him in.

Troy nodded, wiping barbeque sauce off a downy cheek.

Start him at the restaurant, LeClair said.

After an hour, LeClair had Gary and Buck take him back to his row house, a hulking brownstone next to his jewelry and antique shop in downtown North Chazy. The house was decorated in an Empire Period style, the walls a mad tapestry of paintings, nearly all of them landscapes. Most of the furnishings were holdovers from the previous owners, a wealthy county judge who designed and built the house in the late nineteenth century, including the heavy brass plates on the mantel, beveled glass windows, and double-lined velvet curtains.

His brother rarely ventured into town, but there was a room in the house that served as Walt's, tucked away in the back of the kitchen, with bare walls and linoleum floor, a solitary toilet, and a gun rack that held a level and a deer rifle. When Walt was there, he mostly stood around in his coveralls and cap, hands thrust in his pockets, looking like a sod farmer who happened to stumble into the wrong house.

LeClair fixed himself a gimlet and went into his study, the largest gallery in the house with fourteen-foot ceilings and forty-two landscape paintings of varying sizes covering the walls. He opened the stereo console and cued up a disc. LeClair had pulled the guts of the old radio out and installed a fifty-disc CD changer and new speakers. Bryan Ferry and Roxy Music's "These Foolish Things" drifted out of the console as LeClair addressed his paintings. His dog, a white standard poodle named The Constable, stood at his usual post in the northwest corner of the room, under the George Inness, *Early Autumn, Montclair.* In the last nine years, he had never seen The Constable laying down or sitting. He always stood, ramrod straight, motionless, following you with his wet eyes. LeClair reached in the ice bucket and side-armed a cube at the dog, skipping it between his legs and clattering along the floorboard. The Constable blinked at him, motionless.

LeClair finished his drink standing before his Tomás Sánchez painting, *Oír las aguas*—a cascading waterfall that poured into a pool framed by cliffs and stylized trees. The white sky and soft blues of the Sánchez calmed his blood. LeClair knew that his collection was uneven, lacking an aesthetic center. But he knew what he liked. For LeClair, the best works often seemed like an ancient oracle, delivering insight disconnected from the painting itself and difficult to decipher. They entered you mysteriously.

After a few minutes he walked down the hall to a smaller second gallery, this one reserved for J. M. W. Turner. An upholstered backless settee sat in the middle of the room, a large skylight directly overhead. He had several serviceable hand-painted reproductions: *Dido and Aeneas*, *East Cowes Castle*, *Venice, from the Porch of Madonna della Salute*, plus a few other copies. It was his favorite room in the house, and some days he spent hours in there, casting himself into these paintings.

He thought about Gorman and this *La Montagne* in Quebec. Just the possibility that a *real* Turner was out there, available for purchase, just across the border, suddenly made his collection seem pathetic, the colors muted, the dynamism faded. An original Turner was nearly impossible to find in a private collection. Despite his status in the UK—he was often discussed as the greatest British painter, and his *The Fighting Temeraire* won a BBC poll of the most beloved British paintings—J. M. W. Turner was relatively unknown to the American layperson. The majority of Turners were held at the Tate Britain, with just a scattering of paintings in the US, places like the Indianapolis Museum of Art, the Kimbell in Fort Worth, and the Yale Center for British Art. LeClair couldn't help but speculate on which Turner this man in Quebec might be holding. A minor work, no doubt. Early watercolors? The pre-European tour oils, like the richly dark *Fishermen at Sea*, 1796? Or the grand late period, when Turner sought the evocation of pure light? But how could a real Turner end up here? And how did they know *he* wanted it?

He lay down on the settee and stared up at the skylight, a wash of gray, a ripple of clouds. He took some deep breaths. Why were some driven to surround themselves with the crafted simulations of the real? Was the world just too much? Or was it not enough?

KAISER

Kaiser went to North Chazy and drove through the Ausable College campus with the windows down. Sitting at the stoplight at Main and Montpelier, he could hear music drifting from the windows of the dorms that lined the quad. A group of young women sat on a blanket while barefoot boys threw frisbees around the perimeter, savoring the last of the fall weather. The other side of the road was lined with crumbling Victorian mansions. Students sat on the slanted porches and drank beer out of red Solo cups. A whiff of pot smoke on the wind.

The town of North Chazy is a small postindustrial hamlet just south of the Canadian border, the last exit on the Route 87 Northway. In the middle of the last century a visitor would have found a bustling commercial district, anchored by the air force base that featured nuclear-capable B-47 Stratojets as part of the Strategic Air Command. The historical part of the city was called Frenchtown, made up of wedding-cake Victorians built before the war, outfitted with carriage houses and dumbwaiters. When the air force base closed in the early 1990s, North Chazy and the surrounding area accelerated its fall into obscurity and economic stagnation. The public beach closed, and the old cabins and campsites became hole-up sites for wandering mendicants and youths stricken with various addictions. The only real thriving industry left in the region was the supermax federal prison at Dannemora or the pet food processing plant in North Chazy. North Chazy, pronounced "Shay-zee," in the French manner, became a stock indicator for depression and incompetence. In 1998, the North Chazy Fire Department station house burned down, prompting a headline in the Albany paper: "*Crazy Chazy.*"

The saving grace of North Chazy was the presence of Ausable College, a private institution built in 1879 that brought twelve hundred wealthy young people into the community with all their attendant needs. The college covered a hundred acres of the south part of town, an array of blue-limestone buildings with red-tile roofs and the miniaturized athletic facilities of a Division III school. The reputation of the college was moderate compared to the private schools of New England, though the upper part of New York is decidedly *not* part of New England, as any Vermonter would tell you, and like many of the other lesser-known private schools it was a favorite dumping ground for rich kids who didn't have a shot at Harvard or Yale. If the students found the decrepit town a shocking cultural experience, they didn't show it. Rather they seemed to revel in the "authentic" nature of North Chazy and enjoyed the low rents and lax law enforcement. Everyone involved seemed fully aware that without the college's existence the town of North Chazy would slide into a level of insignificance that nobody wanted to consider. They were, in this sense, in it together.

The light turned green, and Kaiser was about to ease forward when he saw the flaring lights of a state trooper behind him. He pulled to the curb by the lawn, next to a pair of girls reading paperback novels on their stomachs. They watched through their giant sunglasses as the trooper got out and walked to the passenger side.

Bill took off his hat and stuck his head in the passenger window. Kaiser's older brother was like a young version of their father: squared head fastened by a tree-trunk neck to wide shoulders, a deep belly cavity, chest like a bear.

Was that necessary? Kaiser said.

Bill smirked and opened the door and got in, the car sagging under his girth.

Don't get your panties in a wad.

Bill surveyed the students, pausing on the pair of co-eds stretched out on the blanket.

You think any of these kids give a shit?

So, what's up?

Bill shrugged.

Nothing, man. Just want to say hello. It's been a long time.

He held out his hand and Kaiser shook it.

So what're you up to?

Need a job and place to live, Kaiser said.

I guess you gotta make money, Bill said. Hey, Betsy made all-county hockey.

No shit? That's great. How's Monica?

Fine, fine.

Bill lived in the woods just south of the neighboring town of Dannemora in an Adirondack-style log cabin that he built himself, a branch of the Ausable River running through the backyard. His daughter, Betsy, was a true athlete like her father, who was a dominant hockey player back in high school. Bill's wife, Monica, was a walleyed promotions manager for the New York state prison system with a penchant for cut-rate plastic surgery and fistfuls of behavioral modification drugs. Bill shifted in the seat, rearranging his utility belt. His shirt buttons looked like they were about to explode through the windshield. Bill's work as a state trooper kept him patrolling the Northway, cruising the several-hundred-mile stretch between Albany and the border, where civilization bled out and died. It was a notoriously dangerous stretch of road, dark and sparsely populated, and often traveled by people who were fleeing something.

Extra shifts are wearing me out, Bill said. Roadblocks, drug patrols. DEA set up a command post in Rouses Point. This place has changed.

He spread out his arms.

Our fair hometown. Isn't it lovely? You seen Sydney Beauchamp yet? You know she's got a kid, right?

Sydney Beauchamp was Kaiser's girlfriend during his senior year of high school. After graduation, she went to college downstate, and their relationship faded quickly.

She's back over in Dannemora, Bill said. She ended up with Phil Herring. You remember him?

Kaiser nodded. Phil Herring, the best hockey player to come out of North Chazy in twenty years, the sprawling man-child with a beard at fifteen, the alpha of the pack. Phil was not unlike many of the men Kaiser worked with in the various SOF detachments he was embedded with in Afghanistan.

On the lawn a Labrador puppy was barking furiously at a soccer ball kicked about by a couple guys in Birkenstocks and wool socks.

They married?

Nah, Bill said. They got a little girl, maybe two years old? I think Phil is still up in Canada doing junior hockey. Never got the call up.

Haven't seen much of anyone, Kaiser said. I guess I'm trying to lay low until I figure out what I'm doing.

Bill nodded sagely, watching a group of girls dangling bits of a bagel in their fingers, holding it just above the puppy's pink, snapping mouth.

What about Dad? Who's paying for the medical stuff?

Insurance, Bill said. At least some of it. His old job with the county. You gonna be there Thursday for the surgery?

Yeah, sure. What about the farm? Mom said the IRS is sending notices.

I'll take care of it, Bill said.

How?

Don't worry about it.

I want to help.

Are you kidding me with this shit?

Bill cocked his head, the same way their father did when he was about to read the truth to you out loud. The flesh around his neck bulged over his collar.

Where was this two years ago, Bill said, when Mom was fucking crying her eyes out?

Bill got out of the car and slammed the door. Kaiser could see his brother at twelve, at sixteen, fuming at some insult, real or imagined. Bill stalked to his cruiser, then stopped and came back and bent to the window.

Your muffler is hanging off this piece of shit, Bill said. I ought to write you a fucking ticket.

One afternoon back in 1990, Kaiser stood on the shore of the lake, the heart-shaped face in a down parka and wool cap, moon boots with lightning bolts on the sides. He was ten years old. Just offshore, his older brother Bill and a half-dozen other kids were skating with hockey sticks, weaving and slapping the puck through the goals marked by piles of discarded jackets. The crunch and squeak of blades on ice, the *whump* and shriek of a falling body. As the air warmed, the ice boomed and pinged, the sound like distant cannon fire, a handful of nickels dropped into a deep well.

Some people would insist that Kaiser physically changed after the tragedy, his face narrowing, chin becoming more pointed, his mouth drawing tight, his gray eyes always searching, unable to hold your gaze. In groups he stood out like a burning torch. Other children became frightened of him.

That evening Kaiser and Bill crouched in their snow fort at the edge of the woods, packing snowballs. Up the slope, the lights of the house blazed, the chimney trailing smoke. The night sky pulled tight to the rim of the world like an obsidian tent. The boys watched the heavy bombers take off from the air force base to the south.

Dad checked yesterday, Bill said. It's at least sixteen inches thick. He said that ice would support a semi.

The stars like heavy fistfuls of confetti. The distant whine of a snowmobile in King's Bay to the south. Soon his mother would call them to wash up for bedtime. They lay on their backs and Kaiser pointed out to his brother a faint mote of light that came over the mountains and arced overhead, silent, unhurried. A satellite. Ever since that morning on the ice with his sister, Kaiser could sense their courses and trajectory, predict when they would appear over the edge of the horizon. He knew their relative speed, orbital height, their elliptical orbit around the globe. In his bed at night, he saw their movements across the ceiling like ghostly spiderwebs. He saw them when he closed his eyes, in his dreams.

Another satellite, Bill said. Do it again.

In the morning, he dropped Kodiak at the hospital to be prepped for heart surgery that afternoon. His father didn't want him to wait around all day but told him to come back before they put him under.

He had a couple hours to kill before returning to the hospital, so after putting in applications at a couple restaurants, Kaiser parked in the court square and checked out nearby apartments. He settled on a cheap one-bedroom walk-up, then wandered over to the coffee shop, one of only a couple of businesses still alive on the square.

The Artful Dodger was a dark, cavernous place with steel furniture and masses of terrible student art crowding the walls, echoing with the tinny strains of 1980s techno-pop. A long counter ran the length of the room, black marble with globed displays of baked goods, coffee beans, biscotti. A single customer sat at one of the spindly tables, a middle-aged woman with a tight blond head of hair, poring over a stack of open books and a laptop displaying colorful charts. Sitting on a stool by the register was the only employee, a young woman wearing a halter-top hippie dress reading a book. When Kaiser approached, she lifted her head and smiled, marking her place in the book. She had long honey-colored hair, a dash of freckles across the bridge of her nose. Kaiser scrutinized the menu board.

What's the "Hard Times Special"?

She grabbed a short mug from a stack and placed it before him.

Small coffee, she said, black. No cream or sugar allowed, for fifty cents.

Kaiser stared at the mug on the counter.

It's from Dickens, she said.

Okay.

It's kind of our thing here. Like the name of the place?

Okay. I'll take it.

As she filled his cup Kaiser picked up some pamphlets from the stacks on the counter, advertising sled tours, kayaking, tantric meditation. The afternoon light blasted the large front windows, court square empty except for an old man trundling up the courthouse steps carrying a can of paint. The woman at the table raised her head and looked at him, her glasses reflecting the blue glow of her computer screen. She was maybe forty years old, wearing a simple blouse, jeans, and sandals. She gave Kaiser a slight smirk and turned back to her work.

Kaiser sat at one of the small tables. He sipped the coffee, bitter and strong, and realized that he didn't bring anything to read. He listened to the music awhile, tinny, spangling drums and keyboards, a man singing about a love he couldn't live down. He watched the woman tapping away at her charts, consulting the open books, a pen clutched between her even, white teeth.

The young barista sidled down toward his end of the counter, and when Kaiser looked at her, she cocked a hip and planted a hand, the other hand holding out the flopping paperback.

You went to North Chazy High.

Yeah, Kaiser says. A while back.

You're Tom Kaiser, right?

He nodded.

I've heard of you, she said. You went and like joined the army or something?

The halter top did wonderful things for her neck and arms. Did he know her? She was at least three or four years younger than him. She was waiting for him to say something. He drank his coffee. He didn't know where to look or what to say. He hadn't been here for more than forty-eight hours.

Well, anywaaaay, she said. Nice to meet you.

She turned and headed back down the counter. Kaiser exhaled.

What's your name?

Emerson, she said.

What're you reading?

Oh, this is for school. Sherwood Anderson? *Winesburg, Ohio*? Heard of it?

No.

It's a bit dark, but I like it. You read . . . books?

Some, Kaiser said. Mostly science.

Like what?

Aeronautics, astrophysics. Satellites.

Did you, like, get a degree in that or something?

No, I didn't go to college.

The woman at the table with the computer was packing up her equipment, shoving her books into a large canvas tote bag. The music switched to the plaintive tones of Yaz, "In My Room."

Well, Emerson said. Satellites. Cool.

She closed up her book and set it on counter, scanning the room, both hands on her hips. The door chime rang as the lady with the computer walked out the door into the sunlight. Kaiser lifted his coffee and realized it was empty. One of his military habits. He stood up and set the mug on the counter.

See you around, Emerson said.

Kaiser smiled, gave her a little wave. He could feel her watching him walk out.

Then he was standing outside blinking in the sunlight, a silver Range Rover easing around the block, driven by the lady with the computer, her face composed and serene as the big vehicle glided by. Kaiser looked at the sky above the courthouse, the fragments of clouds still and distant. Nothing moved.

Kaiser returned to the Clinton County Regional Hospital at just after five o'clock. His mother and brother were already in Kodiak's room, standing by the bedside, his mother holding the old man's hand. Kodiak was sitting up in the bed, a stack of pillows behind his back, his hospital gown gapped at the neck showing gray chest hair dotted with the white disks of the EKG monitor.

You bring me anything to eat? Kodiak said.

Good to see you, Kodiak, Kaiser said.

All I had today was a glass of digestive cleanser. Tasted like dog vomit.

They pulled in a couple extra chairs and passed a reasonable hour before Bill had to leave. The troopers were assisting with a DEA checkpoint on the Northway. When visiting hours were almost over, Janice kissed her husband and went to get a cup of coffee in the lobby. Kodiak sat back in bed, gazing at Kaiser, blinking long and slow.

Listen, buddy. I want you to check on my gear.

You'll be home soon, Kaiser said.

Just do me the favor. You been logging the transmissions?

Yeah.

Working the telemetry?

Not lately. You?

No new patterns or variances. Still drifting.

Kodiak vigorously rubbed his face and head with his palms. Talking about the Chinese number lady always got him a little frustrated. He tapped his chest with a forefinger and closed his eyes.

Can you believe that they're gonna put a pig valve in here? Somewhere there is a pig rooting around that has no idea what's coming. There's something else I wanna tell you, Tom. Just in case.

In case of what?

Kodiak opened his eyes.

In case I end up on the slab, son! This is no joke. They're gonna open me up from neck to navel.

You're gonna be fine, Kaiser said.

Couple things, Kodiak said. First, I've been listening to the numbers longer than you know. Before Korea. Started when I was on a listening station in Burma. That's where we first picked her up. I was with the Army Air Corp, and there was this British crew, SAS. They were monitoring a whole range of transmissions. The communists, all that bullshit. Nobody but your mother knows this.

Kodiak adjusted his sheets, smoothing the fold. He looked away.

Anyway, I want you to go over to the house and clear out my set. Take it over to your place.

Why?

It's time, Kodiak said. Can't let an old bastard like me fall asleep on it.

Pop.

Take a look around, son.

Kodiak gestured around the room. The wires off his chest trailed off under the bed, and at his feet a rack hung with bags of clear fluid. His EKG readings chirped steadily, an LED readout marking time in wavering green lines.

I swear to god, Kodiak said, if I come outta here and that set is still in the basement I'm gonna come after you.

All right, Kaiser said. Don't get so worked up.

His father closed his eyes, took a couple deep breaths, and pulled the sheets up to his neck.

I came back to help, Kaiser said. I'll take care of it.

When Kodiak opened his eyes, they were wet and shining and he reached over and turned off the bedside lamp.

I'm gonna sleep now.

Outside the window the parking lot shimmered. The temperature was dropping. The wan rain-light cast the room in negative, the bed a silver box and the old man a shadow tucked into a pocket.

I'm happy, Kodiak said, that someone is listening. Someone is going to be paying attention. And I'm glad that it's you.

Kaiser walked down to the lobby where his mother sat on a couch looking into the parking lot, the windows sparkling with rain. She knows, Kaiser thought.

She put her hand on his arm.

Are you going to be okay?

The hospital parking lot was nearly empty, only a few cars spaced widely apart. Kaiser knew that some of the owners of these cars would not be returning to drive them home. He smiled at his mother as best he could.

I'm fine, he said.

The next day Kodiak underwent a quadruple bypass operation. Janice spent the day huddled in the waiting room with her Bible. Kaiser brought her tea and sat with her. Bill checked in several times.

Your old man's got a heart like an elephant, the surgeon told Kaiser. He's got plenty left.

Four days later Kodiak was back home. The first thing he did was walk down the basement steps. It was all gone, nothing left of the radio set but the old signs hanging on the rafters, a faint dusty outline of the equipment on the table. He went back to the kitchen and embraced Janice where she stood at the kitchen sink, the two of them swaying there, holding on to each other.

EMERSON

She was due at her father's house for dinner, so Emerson stacked the dishwasher and wiped down the tables so she could leave the Artful Dodger right when Drummy came in at six. He arrived stoned and despondent as usual, steamed himself a glass of milk with honey, fired up *Construction Time Again* by Depeche Mode, and perched his bony hips on the stool by the register with the paper neatly folded to the crossword puzzle. Though he owned the place, Drummy dragged himself around the shop with the air of a disgruntled minimum-wage employee. Which is what Emerson actually was, though he did allow her to keep all the tips; all the coffee she could drink; and all the day-old bagels, cakes, and pastries she could stand.

The Artful Dodger drew a regular crowd of English and philosophy majors from the college, some townie goth kids, and members of the local AA chapter that met in the Methodist church basement down the street. Customers seemed to annoy Drummy, and Emerson was sure that he would prefer to have the place to himself. She had no idea how he was able to keep the place in business.

Emerson let herself out the back door into the short alley and unlocked her bicycle. Her father had kitted her out with a top-quality mountain bike, twelve gears, carbon fiber frame, climbing bars, three sets of tires for different conditions. Emerson was self-conscious about the bike. She was twenty-one years old and struggling with her personal philosophy of a disregard for material possessions.

It was Emerson's mother who wanted to name her after the famous philosopher and poet. Her father, Walt, didn't have anything to do with it. Her mother taught literature at the college, and one January night twenty-two years ago, a kindly, quiet local man pulled her car out of a snowbank along Route 9 near Ausable Forks. Emerson always assumed there was something about the rough-hewn qualities of Walt LeClair that attracted her mother, perhaps his placid personality, steadfastly determined and capable, like some kind of North Country Thoreau. They married the next year in Lake Placid. There was a picture of Emerson's mother on her wedding day wearing a crown of spruce and holly and dancing barefoot on the wood deck, Walt bashfully holding her outstretched hands, eyes locked on her, but his face slightly averted, like he was hanging on to a bonfire.

Emerson left her bike on the porch and stripped off her parka and boots in the mudroom, setting them under the old walnut pew Walt salvaged from an abandoned Lutheran church. In the dining room, he had laid out the china with white cloth napkins, the utensils crossed over the plates in the style of her grandparents. The fire was low, and Emerson added a stout log. Her father always kept the temperature about five degrees lower than was comfortable. Walt was in the kitchen, washing up the cooking pans in the sink, his shirtsleeves rolled up around his elbows, his hands red and shining from the hot water. He turned to her, a broad smile on his face. Her father was a man of few moods, and the most dependable was his delight in Emerson's company. With each passing year, Emerson became more aware of this, and she often thought of the teenage years when she found him so annoying and obtrusive that she wished to be anywhere else than in that house.

Are you hungry?

Of course.

You gonna spend the night?

Yes, Dad.

Walt had made stuffed peppers with brown rice, tomatoes, and beans, served with pickled beets he canned himself. Years ago, Walt wrote a letter to a restaurant cook he knew in Lake Placid, asking her for vegetarian recipes. Emerson told him he could just use the internet, but Walt never even used his email, using the computer only late at night when he would play an hour or two of solitaire. He hadn't altered a thing in the house since her mother died, as if it would be an affront to his wife's spirit. So in the last fifteen years the dishes, furniture, and other items in the house were slowly being whittled away by age and use. To Emerson, the house seemed emptier every time she came.

When he finished eating, Walt pushed his plate forward and put his elbows on the table, leaning his mouth on his hands.

How's school?

Great. I love Dr. Frederick's class. The reading list is fantastic.

And the coffee shop?

Good. Drummy is still all depressed and whatnot, but it's cool.

Your Uncle Donnie come in yet?

Nah. He would hate it. The art. And the people.

My brother does have very definite ideas about art.

He reminds me of Dr. Sterne, Emerson said. I'm in his art history class and it is all, like, clearly stuff that Uncle Donnie would like? Dr. Sterne's got a thing about late nineteenth-century English painters, especially Turner. He's pretty much obsessed.

Your uncle's going off the deep end with that stuff, Walt said. Spending a lot of money. And he's running out of room.

I think it's cool that he's so passionate about it, Emerson said. The other day I was actually telling him about Dr. Sterne. He's been working on a book about Turner for, like, years now. Anyway, they should hang out.

Walt put his knife and fork next to his plate. His knuckles were scabbed and bruised, and Emerson knew that he had likely spent the day busting his hands on a wrench, bringing to life the various machines that were necessary for the maintenance of this place.

It was always clear, Walt said, that my brother is a man who was born into the wrong life.

That's really sad.

Is it?

Would you want a different life? she asked. Are you living the life you want?

He smiled and took up his fork, stabbing a piece of green pepper.

I am one of the lucky few, he said. The exceptions. It isn't a question of *want*. I have the farm, this house, this food, and the most amazing daughter in the world. I am living precisely the life that I *should*.

Emerson's mother was a natural swimmer, and many of Emerson's memories involve her entering or exiting the water, her wet hair, the smell of the lake on her skin during the summer. Her mother was fond of swimming out to the island, alone. Walt couldn't swim, but it was their ritual to watch on the shore. Isle La Motte was about a half mile offshore, and she would clamber out on the beach and wave to them, always in an exaggerated fashion, and Emerson would laugh. But Walt was always uneasy, a tension in his body that she could sense even at that age.

There was never a satisfying explanation. Her mother was on the rocky shore of Isle La Motte, waving to Emerson, then she waded in and began the swim back, her stroke sure and even. The sky was cloudless and the air still, the water like a pond. Emerson remembers her father saying that you could skip a stone across the whole lake in that kind of weather. The temperature was dropping, maybe sixty degrees. She sat in her father's lap, and he held her hands to keep them warm. She was six years old.

At about the halfway point, when Emerson could discern the dark hair and angled elbows, the trailing white spray of her kick, her mother paused, looking at them from across the water. Then she disappeared.

After a few moments, her father began to tighten his grip on her hands, his body going rigid. She remembers feeling nothing at all other than the expectation that her mother would emerge, and the increasing pain as her father crushed her fingers, his knuckles shaking and white. She began to cry and pull at her hands, trying to free herself. He released her and walked to the lake edge. She remembered the way he stood, his square back, the hang of his work coat, the water lapping at the toes of his boots, the pearl-gray color of the stones. He said her name in a quiet but insistent voice. Then it was all shouting and crying and a paroxysm of fear and rage. Emerson doesn't remember anything after that.

What she did remember: The soft feel of her mother's skin, her forearms that she rested her cheek on while they were standing in the kitchen, her mother working at the sink. The feel of her delicate arm hair. Her hip bones, stomach, and waist that she lay across while they sat on the couch, the flickering blue light of the television. Her mother laughing and saying something to her father. She remembers the subtle tension of the skin around her neck and throat when she was being carried, addled by sleep, the slash of stars in the night sky and the sound of the screen door slapping shut. The give and texture of her skin when she pushed her nose and forehead into the nape of her neck, closing her eyes. She remembered the feel of her mother's hand as they walked down the lane to the lake.

That night in her old room Emerson lay on her bed reading *Winesburg, Ohio* in the cone of light from her bedside lamp. The window was open, and moths pattered on the screen. A brilliant green Luna moth the size of her hand pressed its furry abdomen toward the light. In the book, George Willard was walking through the night reciting what he felt were profound incantations. Soon he would be thrown to the ground in front of the woman he hoped to impress, enduring yet another humiliation. She turned out the light and lay on her back. As she closed her eyes, still thinking about George Willard, she began to see him as Tom Kaiser, the man who came into the Artful Dodger. Something about his pointed chin, the way he angled his head when he spoke to her. The way he held his mug when he considered her question. The flash of surprise on his face when he realized it was empty.

KAISER

One evening a couple weeks later, Kaiser came into the kitchen of the Stagecoach Restaurant, a large tray with six entrées balanced in one hand, the other holding a bowl of salad. Scotty Marin, another waiter, stood by the line talking to Marissa, the hostesses. Scotty was smiling, spinning a tray on his finger. He was enjoying his dexterous physicality, the prospect of a big night, a couple Fleur-de-Lis in the glovebox of the Audi, the party starting soon at the fraternity house, the basement filling with a herd of young women, many completely unprepared for what they would soon be asked to endure. Marissa was describing her fitness routine, which consisted of dextromethorphan capsules and two hours on the elliptical machine at the college gym, seven days a week.

Kaiser stepped between them, and the spinning tray on Scotty's finger wobbled and he had to awkwardly catch it with both hands. The salad plates, Kaiser said. Where are they?

What?

It's your job, your *side-work*, Kaiser said. The salad plates.

He could tell Scotty was not used to being challenged like this. But Kaiser was doing four hundred push-ups and sit-ups a day; he was six-three in his boots, a taut two hundred pounds. In public places, every man was acutely aware of his presence. When he looked people in the eyes, especially close up, it seemed to inspire some deep thinking on their part, considering the choices that had led them to this moment. Kaiser didn't know that Scotty Marin had the job at the Stagecoach Restaurant as a cover for his business distributing Canadian weed to the student body of the college. Scotty's father was one of the richest and most influential men in Albany, a state legislator and successful lawyer who also believed everyone ought to be gainfully employed. Scotty was bright enough to understand that by performing this minor function, the job at the restaurant, the lease on the Audi would be renewed, his sixteen-hundred-square-foot condo on the lake would receive weekly cleaning service, the powerboat and pair of Jet Skis at the end of the dock would be serviced, gassed, and then in October they would be winterized and stored, replaced with a set of 800 cc high-performance snowmobiles, or "sleds" in North Country parlance, always in blue and gold, his fraternity colors.

The head line cook stopped saucing a plate of ravioli to watch and listen, and the other cooks followed suit. The head cook was an enormous, rangy fellow named Sebastian, a good three inches taller than Kaiser, with a shaved head, heavy Teutonic profile, and a metal halo-immobilizer screwed onto his head due to a disastrous motorcycle escapade on the Northway. Sebastian paused, saucepan in one hand and ladle in the other, dripping red sauce on the floor. The halo had four vertical bars connected by two rows of horizontal rods that gridded his face like a barbarian chieftain. This made head gestures impossible, and gave him a kind of sinister inscrutability.

Whatever, man, Scotty said, trying to reengage Marissa.

But Kaiser stepped between them again.

Get the plates, he said. *Now.*

Scotty slung his tray on the line. He held up both middle fingers, inches away from Kaiser's face.

Fuck! You!

The tips of his fingers touched Kaiser's nose. Kaiser's face remained composed, and he blinked once. Twice.

Then he pulled his hands from under the tray and salad bowl, letting them fall, and before they hit the floor, he had one of Scotty's middle fingers in his fist, twisting it hard. His other hand grabbed the boy's polo shirt at the collar and with a downward swipe ripped it open down the front. Scotty shrieked in alarm and spun around trying to relieve the pressure on his finger, and Kaiser forced it up his back into a chicken wing, his forearm jammed against the back of Scotty's neck, and frog-marched him across the kitchen, the other waiters and busboys scattering before them. Kaiser jammed Scotty's face against the white-tile wall and rubbed it back and forth, his teeth bared, hissing in the boy's ear:

Just do the fucking *plates*!

A couple of the busboys grabbed his arms and Kaiser let him go, Scotty cupping his hands to catch the blood, his nose already tumescent and purpling. The back of his neck was splotchy and his shoulders shook. Sebastian fingered one of the bolts around his forehead and let out a nervous laugh. On the wall there was a bloody smear like a child's finger painting.

I'm good, Kaiser said. I'm done.

He stepped back and they let him go. Marissa led Scotty away through the side door, trying to stem the blood with the remnants of his shirt. The manager came into the kitchen, his arms held out in disbelief.

What the hell? Guys?

Kaiser stood above his tray of food and salad, all smashed on the floor, the kitchen silent except the hiss and pump of the dishwasher.

Somebody want to tell me what the fuck is going on?

Then Sebastian whacked his ladle on the counter and the cooks began to work their orders again, dropping wads of pasta in steaming water, hot oil spitting in a pan with slices garlic skittering around the edge, plating medallions of chicken in wine sauce. Kaiser stood there looking at the food on the floor. He could be brought up on assault charges, and with his military record, he would be in some serious trouble. This was a shocking failure on his part, the impulsiveness, the loss of control. Something was happening to him. He bent down and began to clean up the mess, but the septuagenarian Russian dishwasher was there with a bus tray and waved him off, giving him a flinty hint of smile. Scotty Marin was not universally liked. Kaiser dropped his apron on the counter and walked out the door.

He had about four hundred dollars in cash. He would go with a public defender, keep his mouth shut, and ride it out. There was no point calling his brother. Bill would find out soon enough. Kaiser took a quick hot shower and attended to his toilet with rigor, figuring this would the last chance for a few days, scrubbing himself with soap and a pumice stone, shaving, clipping nails, flossing teeth. He changed into jeans and a T-shirt and packed a small bag of essentials and sat in his armchair waiting for the police to arrive. He had a half gallon of Bacardi in the freezer, but it wouldn't help his case if they took him into custody stinking drunk. He sat in the armchair and lit a Benson & Hedges 100.

Power cords snaked across the floor and under the table in the middle of the living room, stacked with Kodiak's radio equipment. One set of cords ran up the wall and out the window to a small antennae array that Kaiser bolted to the outside window frame. A heavy number eight size conductor funneled into a hole in the drywall to the water pipes for a ground. He stared at the pulsing light of the receiver, the yellow haze of the tuning dials like small sunsets.

Earlier he stopped at the pawnshop to hock a couple things and the shop manager, Zane, who knew Kaiser's dad from way back, loaned him a .357 Ruger, a massive black thing, and a box of 158 Grain Flat Points.

Gotta protect yourself, Zane said. Every man needs his own protection nowadays.

Zane was giving him good deals, so he took the pistol and didn't say anything. He was indifferent to guns despite the three years he spent carrying and firing an assortment of firearms. The feel of an HK MP5 cinched across his chest, the stock against his bicep, finger riding along the trigger guard was as natural as shoes on his feet. But he didn't miss it. He kept the .357 in the glovebox of his Volkswagen.

Kaiser passed the time waiting for the cops doing push-ups, sit-ups, and reading Carl Sagan. Around two in the morning he poured himself a tall rum and Coke and lit a B&H and opened the window, checking the clamps and attachments that held the antennae. A small, paved lot lay behind his building, then a row of dog-eared houses and the feed plant railyard. The lines of boxcars stood silent and atop the grain silo the American flag hung limp, a cloud of insects and bats funneling in the cone of the spotlight. Beyond this the moonlit eye of Lake Champlain and the Green Mountains of Vermont.

In the bedroom, his mattress was on the floor, a couple cardboard boxes for his clothes, a reading lamp by the bed. He sat in the bed with his back against the wall, the sheets wadded under his legs, the moon glowing on the dusty wooden floors. He listened to the skitter of rodents, watched the blank walls, the dark slot of the bathroom door. When he finally slept, he dreamed about the lake when he was young, running across the ice toward the shore that receded before him, the ice seeming to never end.

The cops never came. To his surprise, Kaiser wasn't even fired. When he came back to the Stagecoach the next day, everyone seemed to pretend that nothing happened. Now the hostesses always gave him the best sections and the cooks started shooting his entrées across the shelf when he walked in the door, everything hot and looking nice. Scotty Marin had quit, and no one spoke of him again.

A week later, the phone calls started. Always the same woman, threatening him with mysterious violence. When she called him at work for the third time, she said the sheriff's deputy was going to do him unpleasant physical harm. He was on the kitchen extension by the dish station, the middle of the dinner shift and the place was steaming with cooks and waiters shouting at each other. Kaiser held the phone to his ear with his shoulder and used his free hand to arrange the glasses on his tray. Next to him, the old Russian ran scalding water over sauce-encrusted plates, holding a set of them in his fat hand like playing cards before flicking them into the steel block of the industrial washer.

We will find you, the woman was saying. You understand?

Her voice was stable, almost monotone, graveled with a background of cigarettes and brown liquor, but with an educated lilt that suggested elite schools and a chalet on Lake Placid.

Find me? Kaiser said. You called me here. You know where I am right *now*.

The cooks, a slumped line of heavily tattooed and pierced young men, watched Kaiser as they prepped lasagna plates and slid cast-iron trays of frozen stuffed shells under the giant broilers. The ice in his drinks was melting fast and he needed to check his tables.

Look, Kaiser said, you know where I am. You keep calling me, but nothing happens. How about I give you my home number and you can threaten me there?

Kaiser was dragging the kitchen mats out into the alley when Sebastian, the head line cook, asked him for a lift home. He barely fit in the Volkswagen with his massive halo-head. The metal frame was bolted into his collarbones and had four screws threaded into his skull. Sebastian idly turned a squeaky bolt on his halo with his fingers as they headed toward downtown North Chazy. He stunk like sausage and sour cheese.

You must be one desperate dude, Sebastian said. I sure as hell wouldn't come back to this shithole.

So why are you still here?

Sebastian gave a neck bolt a contemplative twist.

Good fucking question. Cray-zee Chazy.

Friday night, and the streetlights were spangled jewels through the windshield as Kaiser drove past the strip mall and Price Chopper, the parking lots wadded with dirty piles of snow, moving into the light under the overpass to the Northway. Sebastian started describing the motorcycle accident that put him in the halo.

So, I'm doing like ninety-five, Sebastian said, rolling hard on some righteous Quebecois. Some of that stuff that is clearly cut with a bit too much speed or acid or something, know what I mean?

Quebecois?

The Fleur-de-Lis. E. *Ecstasy.* That rare shit. Aren't you from here?

It's been a long time.

Anyway, Sebastian said, I'm on the Northway and the needle is tapped out, the bike is just screaming and I'm hanging on to the handlebars, and I swear it's like my legs are flapping in the wind like fucking laundry. And then . . . well, it happened.

What?

Just lost it, man, Sebastian said. The lines on the road got all crossed up and I remember thinking, fuck—I have got to put this thing *down*, you know? Like, I didn't even know what my bike *was*, or how to control it. Like it was some kind of alien machine, something I couldn't even *comprehend*, know what I'm saying? So I went down, slid down the shoulder for about fifty yards—I still got a handful of gravel in my ass—and hit the guardrail. Woke up in the ditch. Fucked my neck all up.

How long till you get it off?

Sebastian cracked his window, maneuvered his halo-head, and spat. He reached for the stereo knob and turned up the volume.

I dig this song.

General Public. "Tenderness."

Yeah, Sebastian said. Solid. Man, I may never get this thing off. Might be a fucking android for the rest of my sorry-ass life. Turn here.

As they crossed the tracks by the feed plant, a bondo-scabbed cargo van roared out of the parking lot behind them, swerving on the road, then accelerating alongside. Kaiser knew that it was a crew of Russians from the second shift at the plant, just off work and likely knuckle deep in vodka and whatever other shit they hammered their brains with to forget what they had just endured for the last nine hours. Kaiser used to see the Russians years ago swimming in the lake in the city park, their pale, doughy bodies laced with homemade tattoos made with borax and coat-hangers heated over kitchen ranges. At the next light, the cargo van pulled alongside him, and Sebastian cranked his body around to look. They had the sliding door open and a handful of shaved heads fisting bottles crowded the opening.

Watch this.

Sebastian cranked down the window and extended his long bony middle fingers.

Fuck off, you communist motherfuckers!

The light changed and the van careened in front of them, slowing for the next light, and when it turned red, they locked up the brakes and a group of Russians tumbled out the door, strutting back to Kaiser's car, thumping their chests.

Oh shit, Sebastian muttered, rolling up the window.

Kaiser looked at him for a moment, then reached over and opened the glove compartment. The Russians were outside his window shouting incomprehensible oaths, one man stripping off his shirt. Kaiser pulled the .357 out, snapped it open to check the load, then rolled down his window halfway. The first angry face crammed in, razor stubble and saliva, and Kaiser poked the barrel of the pistol hard into his cheek.

Отвали!

The Russian went wide-eyed and backed out of the window, his hands raised. His companions moving quickly back to the van and diving inside. Kaiser let them drive off, then put the pistol back in the glove compartment. Sebastian stared at him.

You speak Russian?

Not really, Kaiser said, and that thing isn't even mine.

Sure, man.

Kaiser pulled through the intersection, bumping across the last set of train tracks, and headed east, the streets empty and windswept. The windows were fogging up and he turned up the defrost.

You can just let me out by the Dry Dock, Sebastian said.

I've never done that before, Kaiser says.

Pull a gun on someone?

No. Well, yeah. And the other thing. The thing with Scotty Marin. That's not who I am.

I know who you are, Sebastian said. I grew up here too, bro.

Sebastian wiped his forehead with the back of his hand and twisted in his halo, the bolts pulling at the skin on his forehead.

This is good, Sebastian said. Just anywhere.

Kaiser brought the Volkswagen to the curb and Sebastian levered his long body out the door and onto the sidewalk.

Hey, Kaiser said. Do me a favor and don't say anything about . . .

Yeah, bro. We're cool.

In his apartment, Kaiser filled a pint glass with ice and poured it full of rum, adding a splash of Coke and a wedge of lime. After a few drinks, he put his head down on the table and was unconscious almost immediately.

He was dreaming of an even surface of pure white. He was wearing boots, a coat, scarf, all soaking wet, and he was running toward a shore that he couldn't see. He turned and looking over his shoulder saw the dark slash of water, the hole in the ice. Then the lake seemed to bulge, like the curve of space-time around some large mass, gravity shifting, and passing underneath the ice a shadow the size of a whale moved under him.

He awoke to a ringing phone.

Yeah?

You shouldn't have touched him, the woman said.

Kaiser hung up the phone and got up and went to the freezer for some rum. His head ached and the dream unnerved him. It was a version of the dream he used to have often. It was happening more since he returned home. The phone began ringing again. He picked it up.

Just tell me where and when, goddamn it!

Getting right down to business. I like it.

A man's voice this time.

Who's this?

This is your employer.

Who?

I own the Stagecoach. Donnie LeClair. I want to speak with you about the incident with Scotty Marin.

Kaiser sat down at the desk and ran a hand through his hair.

Okay.

I want you to come over here, LeClair said. Tonight.

The restaurant?

Go to your living room window.

Kaiser walked to the window and pulled up the blind. The window looked down on the southeast side of court square. Snowflakes were drifting in the light above the door of a large Victorian row house next to the antique shop. *LeClair Fine Jewelry and Antiques.*

North Chazy is a small town, LeClair said. But we can help each other. Go look in your closet.

Kaiser opened his closet and found it full of clothes. New clothes, suit jackets, pants, shirts, an array of shoes, socks, undershirts stacked on the shelves. Kaiser flipped through the rack. Expensive clothes.

I guess you didn't know, LeClair said. I am also your landlord.

What's all this for? Kaiser said.

I want you to come over here, right now. And put on something nice.

LeClair hung up and Kaiser searched the room, trying to determine what else had been disturbed, but everything seemed in order. He checked the window again, the antique store sign swaying in the snowy wind, the stars winking out above the lake. He went to the closet and flipped through a few things, then selected a dark shirt, a pair of black jeans, a long overcoat, a cashmere scarf.

LeClair's door was answered by Alejandro, a thin, leathery man in a giant rag-wool sweater. He was barefoot and shivering, and when Kaiser stepped into the vestibule, he shut the door quickly. He eyed Kaiser, taking in the clothes.

I *knew* those would fit, he said.

He led Kaiser down a hallway that was painted a deep garnet, the walls covered in paintings of all sizes, most with elaborate, gilt-edged frames. Landscapes. Alejandro paused before a heavy door, knocked once, then entered.

It was a large room, high ceilings, heavy drapes covering the windows and the furniture made from ornately carved dark wood. A small, middle-aged bald man sat behind a desk. Another man in grease-stained coveralls and a ball cap stood off in one corner. The walls of the room were covered in more paintings, arranged without any discernable pattern that Kaiser could detect. All landscapes. The man behind the desk stood and came around to shake his hand.

Mr. Kaiser. Donnie LeClair.

He ran his fingers along the soft leather lapel of the overcoat.

This suits you, he said. Drink?

Alejandro went to the sideboard and took up a silver cocktail shaker set. Kaiser sat in a low armchair with slender jungle cats carved into the armrests. The flat faces of the paintings felt like being watched by a hundred disembodied eyes. Alejandro handed him a martini glass with a sugared rim.

I know you are a rum man, LeClair said. But in this house, we drink gin.

Kaiser took a sip. A gimlet, tangy with lime.

So, Scotty Marin, LeClair said.

LeClair picked up a piece of paper on his desk.

Felony assault, two counts. Now it's gone. No charges, no civil suit, nothing. Why would I do that?

I don't know, Kaiser said. Does it have something to do with these clothes?

Forget about the restaurant and Scotty Marin, LeClair said. I have a new job for you. And not many men have a thirty-inch waist and a forty-two-inch chest, so yes, you will wear the clothes that I had tailored for you.

Kaiser took a long sip of his drink, finishing it off. The man in the coveralls was watching him, his hands in his pockets. This was so absurd that he considered for the second time that perhaps he was still dreaming. He set the thin rim of the glass against his teeth and bit down. It crunched off neatly in his mouth. He turned to the side and discreetly spit the glass into his hand and stuffed it in his pocket.

Would you like to hear what I'm offering?

Kaiser nodded. He felt around with his tongue for glass shards.

So let's say, LeClair began, I have some problems that I need taken care of . . .

It's collection, the man in the coveralls said.

Yes, LeClair said, collection. Have you heard of the Lavoie brothers?

Alejandro gave him a fresh gimlet and took the broken glass from his hand, giving him a disapproving look.

These are *French crystal*! he whispered.

Well, LeClair said, the brothers are currently serving . . . what is it?

Three months, the man in the coveralls said.

That's my brother, Walt, by the way, LeClair said. The Lavoies are indisposed. So we need someone to fill in.

LeClair opened up a small wooden box on his desk and took out an envelope. He tossed it to Kaiser, then got up and walked around the desk. He was slight of build and wearing a plum-colored V-neck sweater and antique jeweled rings on several fingers. His top teeth were small and rode on his bottom lip like funhouse piano keys. He seemed awfully excited. Kaiser felt like he was acting a part in some kind of elaborate play. It must have been Sebastian, Kaiser thought. He must have run his mouth about the Russians and the gun.

I know you need money, LeClair said, and in this town, there aren't many options. It's either the prison or the feed plant, and I can't see you doing either of those things.

LeClair handed him a sheet of paper with a list of names and addresses.

We'll start you at 10 percent.

Ten percent?

Of what you collect, Walt said.

Correct, LeClair said. You keep 10 percent of what you collect. You start tomorrow.

Kaiser shook his head, then noticed that he was still holding the envelope. He looked inside. A neat stack of one-hundred-dollar bills.

So, LeClair said, what's with all that radio equipment?

Kaiser looked for someplace to set his glass. Nobody moved. He felt like he should stand up and walk out of there, but the money was still in his hand.

Shortwave radio, Kaiser said.

Kaiser held out his glass for Alejandro to take, but instead the Spaniard gave the shaker another swirl and topped off his gimlet.

You oughta start carrying that gun, LeClair said.

I don't have a gun, Kaiser said.

C'mon. The gun Zane gave you. Who do you think owns the pawnshop? Do I need to explain that to you as well?

Kaiser stood up. He was holding the paper with the names and the envelopes of money in one hand, his cocktail in another.

You *know* these people, LeClair said. You are from here. You do what you need to do. If there's no money, take anything of value. These are all final calls. You will not come back later.

Kaiser walked to the door and Alejandro scrambled to open it for him. He was still holding the money and the glass, his arms held out like he was going to embrace someone.

That night Kaiser drove out to the public boat ramp and watched the wide fingers of shimmering ice stretching out into the lake. In a couple weeks the ice would be solid, and the North Country would settle into the long six months of winter. The clouds were thinning out and satellites began to emerge like timid insects, crossing in delicate arcs overhead, spelling out their dark instructions in the sky. He could feel the mad rush of the planet spinning through the dark.

SYDNEY & PHIL

The Dannemora wall followed Sydney Beauchamp everywhere. It hung in front of her like a film negative, a shape overlaid on the world as she warmed up a pan of chicken in the kitchen, her daughter, Juliet, on her hip, when Sydney stood in the bathroom brushing her teeth, or when she sat in the living room watching TV while Juliet napped. She could see it through the floor, as if the wall was burrowing under the house, holding her in the palm of its hand.

At night the wall loomed over her sleep like a ghostly sentinel. Her right hand lay draped across the crib by the bed, Juliet holding on to a finger. Sydney would wake in the darkness, her arm lying prostrate, white and sparkling with numbness. She repeated the Lord's Prayer, murmuring the words out loud so they might fall upon her daughter.

Her job at the Department of Social Services didn't usually start until ten, so she had long, languid breakfasts, drinking cups of black coffee and reading the newspaper, Juliet sitting in her high chair, scrambling to corral Cheerios. It was December, and the lake was already half frozen, the snowplows thundering down the highway at night.

Juliet's father, Phil, was coming back, again, and Sydney couldn't decide if she was happy.

If you want the house, you can have it, his sister said in the letter. *I don't want anything to do with it.* There was a set of keys in the envelope. Phil Herring stood in the kitchen of his apartment in Selkirk, Manitoba, his hockey bag slung over his shoulder. The coach always wrung them out with speed drills after a loss, and Phil was exhausted. He blinked away the sweat that trickled into his eyes and made his scabs burn. *Dannemora.*

The wall was sixty-two feet high. Twelve feet thick at the base and eight at the top, painted white, and when the plows pushed boulders of muddy snow against the base, the wall seemed to rise from the snow like some kind of surreal arctic nightmare. Every four hundred feet a turreted guardhouse with black-trimmed vertical windows. In the summer months, the guards often kept them angled open, a single rifle barrel protruding from a dark square eye.

The wall filled the front windows of the house that Phil grew up in. The Dannemora prison is the largest high-security prison in New York, housing twenty-nine hundred inmates with several hundred guards and administrative personnel. The blunt face of the wall rose up just across the two-lane Cook Street, stretching in both directions for a quarter mile so the entire southern portion of the town lay in shadow. Standing in the kitchen, you could see just a sliver of sky above the wall. Phil thought of his father, sipping his coffee standing by the door in his polyester blues, listening, his eyes flicking over the guard towers. As a young boy, before he ventured beyond the town limits, Phil believed that there was no part of the world that was not under the wall.

He died in the main yard, his sister wrote, *a stroke. That's what two packs and a quart of Crown a day will get you. Whatever you do, Phil, don't go work at that fucking prison.*

Phil dropped his bag on the floor and opened the fridge. A rack of Labatt, old takeout boxes, open tins of tuna, tubs of yogurt. Phil knew it was likely the end for him at Selkirk anyway. Unless he knocked out the starting line of the Portage Terriers next week, he was done.

Phil had built a career around solid hockey skills and his ability to get a firm grip of jersey and to take hard punches and return them until the other man gave in. This was his third stint in Canadian Junior Hockey, each contract lasting about two years. His particular set of skills was always in demand. He was known as a guy who held on, who wouldn't let go until it was done.

Phil drank his beer and considered his options. He had nine hundred bucks in his bank account, a couple trash bags of clothes and gear. He walked into the bathroom, where he stripped down and examined his face. His right eye was ringed with glove burns where the winger poked him in the face a couple times before Phil got him down. But what really bothered him was the split ear. Last week the massive defenseman for Winnipeg, a Canuck named Halle, pinned his face to the ice and pummeled him with straight rights. Phil couldn't feel much pain, as both of his ears were already distorted pillows of cartilage and scar tissue, but he felt a kind of psychic ache at the sight of the bloody ear. He reached up and held both his ears in his blunt fingers. His ears would never heal; never again return to anything close to normal. For the first time they seemed to him a marker, an obvious tattoo of his failures.

After Halle got off him and skated away to the penalty box Phil lay on the ice, listening to the click and grind of metal on ice. A woman in the scant crowd howled in mock concern, calling him by name. He felt like he could lie there for a long time. But the horn sounded, referees crowded around, and so he got to all fours, fingers searching his face and neck for loose pieces of flesh, then gathered himself and left the ice.

In the bathroom, Phil touched the long purpling bruise shape of an eggplant that wrapped around the base of his skull.

Dannemora. Sydney, waiting. No. Sydney was waiting, but not necessarily for *him*.

Juliet. His daughter. There was only the muscle memory of her tiny, frail torso in his hands. He held out his arms as if he was holding a baby, shaking his head at himself in the mirror—*you fucking fool*—and he could feel it precisely, as if a ghost child lay in his arms.

Phil got in the shower and ran the water hot. It wouldn't be hard. He would surprise her with something nice.

My dad left me the old house on Cook Street, Phil said on the phone. All paid for.

That's great, Sydney said. I mean, I'm sorry about your dad.

Fuck that, Phil said. I couldn't care less.

Phil!

I can't wait to see you, he said. And Juliet.

I missed you, she said.

You have no idea, Syd. I'm so pumped to get the fuck out of here.

But are you gonna play again? Somewhere else?

Yeah, sure, Phil said. I mean, we'll see.

Sydney's first appointment was with a member of the Trombley clan, an extended family of Frenchtown ruffians whose DSS file filled a twelve-tab dossier folder the thickness of a phone book. Callie Trombley, divorced and widowed, and her nine-year-old son, Dylan. Callie was a stubborn, selfish woman with a drinking problem and a continuous cycle of mysterious illnesses. Syndey was assigned the Trombley case when Dylan showed up for school with a scorched ear; Callie had poured in hot melted butter as a home remedy for an earache.

Callie greeted her at the door wearing a bathrobe and a pair of CCM sweatpants. Dirty blond hair with dark roots, eyes permanently squinting as if searching in the dark. Callie Trombley was only in her early forties, but she had that hardened, weathered look of someone who had seen some things.

They talked about Dylan's progress in school. A smart kid, imaginative. He loved to build things with his hands, excelled in art class. His teachers all loved him, but it was like he barely knew any of his classmates. Then Sydney asked permission to do her usual inspection and walked around, poking her head into the many rooms of the crumbling grand old house while Callie watched *Maury* on television with a plastic Solo cup of warm vodka. Upstairs Dylan's bedroom was locked with a padlock, as usual. Callie said he didn't let anyone in there, not even her. He said he was doing something important. Sydney knew she would have to get access to the room. She didn't suspect Callie of anything, but still. Next visit she'd make it a priority.

They sat on the couch as Sydney sorted through her file, Callie coughing and complaining of chest pain. A half-dozen Solo cups on the coffee table with floating rafts of cigarette butts. Sydney reminded her of the medical vouchers the county provided, the network providers.

You should see someone about that cough and the chest pain, Sydney said.

Callie lit another menthol and pulled her robe together.

They won't do anything anyway.

Back in her car Sydney quickly filled out the report. She felt a small shiver of pride. These people deserved nothing but contempt, but the county and state refused to just let them go.

Please, God, help me help these people.

That evening, she told her roommate that Phil was coming back to town and that he wanted Sydney to move in with him. Brett sat at the small table in their kitchenette with a bottle of white wine and a shot glass. She was wearing hoop earrings and a black skirt, trying to talk Sydney into going out with her to the Green Room for ladies' night. She snorted and knocked back another shot of wine.

Are you kidding me?

Hey, that's not cool.

What? Move in with Phil? You really going to do it?

Sydney turned the water on a stack of dirty dishes in the sink. They lived in a modular home on the edge of town with a faux brick foundation and vinyl siding. Brett poured herself another shot of wine and licked her fingers. She was a striking dark-haired woman with a distracting sense about her face, a wildness in the eyes. They had gone to high school together in North Chazy, the queens of the most popular clique in school. Now Brett worked as a lab tech at Champlain Valley Regional Hospital, taking blood and urine samples.

I forgot to tell you, Brett said, guess who's working over at the Stagecoach?

Who?

Tom Kaiser. He's back in town.

Yeah, Sydney said. I heard.

Sydney still couldn't quite accept the reality of Kaiser being back. When he left to join the air force, he seemed unmoved about the dissolution of their relationship. She would have preferred outright cruelty to indifference. She sent letters to the various bases he was stationed, the addresses supplied by his parents, but after a few cryptic postcards, he stopped replying. He'd never said much anyway. Or that's how she tried to excuse it. He was a quiet, serious teenager. He rarely joked, and it was impossible to make him laugh. He refused to engage in small talk. He liked to read about astronomy, aviation, books that contained mathematical equations. But when he held you and said things, you believed him. He felt solid, *real.* When they kissed, Sydney could feel the blood pounding in his veins, and when they lay together, he clutched at her body like he was holding on for dear life. He was different from the others.

For several years after he left, Sydney harbored her affection for Kaiser like a battered pilot light—a small forge she nurtured and stoked with memories, some from their past together and some wholly imagined. She engaged in fantasies of their potential life together, which usually involved a desperate communication from Kaiser, a plea for Sydney to join him someplace like California, where they would wear flip-flops in winter as they walked sidewalks shaded with palm trees to a small cottage with a yard big enough for the kids to play ball. But it faded with time.

Brett shrugged and took a shot of wine.

So on Sunday, she said, we're taking Shelly out to get a makeover. To celebrate her stomach-stapling thing. She's lost like sixty pounds. You won't believe it. She's got an appointment at ten at Shear Madness and Nicky says he's blocked out the whole morning for her. Facial, mani, pedi, the works. Lauren and Tara are coming.

That'll be nice. I'm happy for her.

C'mon, Brett said, nudging the bottle across the table. Tonight. You gotta get out of here.

I can't. Juliet is already asleep.

We'll drop her at your mom's. She won't even wake up. We've done it before.

I'm not dressed or anything.

Please. Twenty minutes and you'll be killing every guy in the Green Room.

I don't feel like talking to people, Sydney said. That's what I do all day at work.

Bullshit. You talk to deranged cheewees all day. There's a difference.

I gotta work tomorrow, Sydney said, and with Phil coming . . . and I'm just not into the Green Room anymore. Too many college guys.

She turned back to the sink and began scrubbing a saucepan crusted with macaroni and cheese. Brett sat at the table, her face blank.

Are you mad? Sydney asked.

Brett shook the final drops of the bottle of wine into her glass. Outside the wind buffeted the walls of the trailer, causing the wood paneling to buckle.

Well, shit, Brett said. Sorta. You make me feel like. I don't know.

She drank the last of the wine and her face brightened.

I'm gonna borrow your windbreaker, Brett said. I don't wanna get my North Face all smoky in the bar.

Phil sent me the key, Sydney said. So I could get in and check the place out.

Brett stood up and put her cigarettes and lighter into her purse, checking her face in the small mirror by the front door.

I'm sorry, Sydney said. I know this is kind of short notice. I'll pay my rent next month anyway.

Brett stood framed by the foggy storm door, the lights from the highway moving like a delicate stream of fireflies through the trees. She had her hand on the door handle. In the gravel lot, her truck stood glowering in the darkness.

KAISER

The first address was on the outskirts of Wiggletown. *Walter Showker, 438 Lake Shore Drive. $4,800.* The house was a double-wide set up on bricks, some plastic picket fencing around the bottom to keep the opossums and skunks out. A kid's bike was chained to a rusted car axle in the weeds. A Christmas wreath hung on the door.

Kaiser was wearing the black Fendi overcoat, a muffler made of alpaca wool, supple leather boots dyed with vegetable oils. Why did LeClair want him to wear this stuff? He wasn't even there to see it. Did he just want to *imagine* Kaiser wearing the clothes? For his amusement? Kaiser decided that the outfits possibly helped with the task at hand, at least as a distraction. He had Zane's .357 snapped into a shoulder holster.

He knocked and after a moment he heard the trailer groan and shuffling feet. Kaiser stubbed out his Benson & Hedges 100 and put the butt in his pocket. These people owed money, he reminded himself. He was a legal representative of the lender, seeking due redress. He could make a lot of money in a few days if he did this right. And LeClair did fix the thing with Scotty Marin. An assault charge would put him back in prison. The door opened a crack and a woman with a tired face looked out at him.

Yeah?

I'm here to collect for Mr. LeClair.

She shook her head and spoke in a weary voice.

You'll have to come back later and talk to my husband.

I can't come back.

She was looking at his clothes. His wool pants were tapered at the ankle and his belt was tipped with silver birch leaves.

Well. Sorry. He's not here.

I need the money today, Kaiser said.

She shrugged and started to close the door, but Kaiser stuck his boot in and jacked the door open with his hand. She staggered back, her face blank with shock, and Kaiser walked inside the trailer. The place smelled like stagnant water and the sink was full of crusted dishes and moldering food. On the table, a dinner plate was festooned with a bouquet of cigarette butts. Crushed beer cans lined the windows, and tall stacks of newspapers littered the floor.

You better get out of here, she stammered, my husband will be back any minute!

Four thousand eight hundred, Kaiser said.

She gathered her bathrobe around her and ran a hand through her hair. She was barefoot, and when she glanced in the next room through the doorway Kaiser saw a small boy sitting on the floor watching a TV. He was shirtless, maybe six years old, his face about a foot from the screen. Kaiser looked around the kitchen, looking for anything of value. He walked into the other room with the boy and the TV. A queen-size bed filled the room, a snarl of sheets and blankets. The TV was new, and there was a DVD player. The boy finally looked up at him, his face blank. He had a faint crust of dried milk around his mouth, and he began to smile when Kaiser heard the unmistakable sound of claws on linoleum behind him, a large dog gearing up to take flight, and he reached in his coat and unsnapped the .357 as he spun around. Mrs. Showker had loosed a large black Rottweiler from the back room that cleared the kitchen in two bounds and launched itself at Kaiser, coming chest high. He got the gun out and pistol-whipped the animal in midair with a downward arcing swing. The dog smashed to the floor, knocking over an overflowing trash can. Mrs. Showker screamed. Kaiser turned to her, incredulous.

What the *hell* you do that for?

The dog got unsteadily to its feet, shaking its head, blood seeping out of its cracked skull, sniffed the spilled garbage and began greedily chomping on an empty package of bacon. Then the little boy was there, his face screwed up in anger or horror, tugging on the dog's collar, calling the dog's name, trying to pull him away from the garbage.

Max! Max, no!

Kaiser held the pistol up to the light. There were shards of bone and flecks on blood on the barrel. Mrs. Showker was crying and going through a drawer under the sink. She began pulling out wads of cash and throwing them on the table.

Listen, he said, I didn't want to do that.

Max! No!

Kaiser used the money from LeClair to buy a used laptop from Zane and cross-listed his records of the Chinese number lady with Kodiak's massive files. Kodiak identified her as Taiwanese because that was the best approximation of her accent. She somehow managed to bounce her signal off several satellite receptors, which made her location impossible to pinpoint exactly. They used the timing of her broadcasts and the principles of telemetry to determine that the signal was originating out of the South China Sea. Kodiak's theory was that she was transmitting from a ship, skirting around the coast and foraying occasionally into the Pacific, tactics to hide her location.

Kaiser often thought of the number lady standing at the rail of some rusted trawler, staring out into the gray waves with dark eyes, the sound of the teletype chattering out a new set of numbers down in the cabin. These stations were communicating with someone about something. Military intelligence experts assumed it was undercover operatives in foreign countries. The numbers were probably matched to some sort of scheduled key, or perhaps the key was contained in the message itself.

Whatever they were, Kaiser admired her tenacity, her refusal to quit. She couldn't know if anyone was out there listening, but she kept at it, transmitting into the vast darkness of radio subspace.

The next Monday he locked in his presets and double-checked the recording settings. Right on time, a set of tones, then:

Good morning! Are you ready?

Six. Fourteen. Nineteen. Eleven. Seven. Four.

May you be blessed with luck. The numbers will be your constant companion.

Kaiser sat in his parents' kitchen drinking coffee and reading a book by an English astrophysicist. His father was rooting through the fridge, his bathrobe hanging loose around his waist. Kodiak pulled out a carton of juice and drank, the light falling on the angry purple scar from his surgery, the thick black staples giving it the look of an enormous centipede crawling up the center of his chest. Since his open-heart surgery, Kodiak had been confined to the farm.

Birds, Kodiak said, shutting the fridge. It's like some kind of plague.

Kaiser looked up from his book. The fields below his parents' house were full of starlings, picking among the ridges of fallow earth. In the afternoons they packed the big naked oak in the back of the house, making an enormous racket. Kaiser bent to his book and tried once again to visually conceive of a Planck length, an incredibly small unit of subatomic measurement. The example comparison used was that if a single atom were the size of the earth, a Planck length would be approximately the size of a large tree. He pictured the oak, wearing a halo of black birds, perched on the expanding sphere of the earth.

The screen door slammed, and Kodiak was striding out into the backyard, wearing rubber duck boots and carrying an old shotgun by the barrel like it was a loaf of bread. Kaiser rose from his chair and went to the sink, watching the old man walking purposefully through the snow toward the great oak, pausing to break the gun and load the shells.

God no.

When Kaiser made the door, the old man was already sighting on the tree, sweeping the gun from side to side, as if he couldn't decide which portion of the branches laden with starlings to pepper with birdshot. Kaiser hit the ground at a full sprint, a full-throated yell, but Kodiak let go with both barrels, a deep *ka-thum* that shook the air, and the birds seemed to draw into themselves, an imploded swirl of ink, then bulging and expanding, the entire mass coming off the tree in every possible direction, swelling over the fields and the hard shining surface of the lake.

Kodiak dropped the gun awkwardly, took a step back, and turned to look at his son running toward him. He gave Kaiser a searching look, then slowly drawing back the lapels of his bathrobe he looked at his chest. The staples were split, a fissure nearly an inch wide, and Kaiser could see the wet slickness inside his father's chest, surprisingly black and purple at first, then vermilion as the blood came. Kodiak looked up in amazement. Behind him the birds began to coalesce, heading west toward the sun like a heavy band of smoke.

Kodiak began to say something, but the air hit his organs, and the pain seized him, and he fell to the ground.

He was dead before Kaiser reached him.

After graduating from high school, Kaiser enlisted in the air force. His mother cried at the kitchen table and his father slapped his gloves and stomped out the back door, heading for the barn. Kodiak graduated from Syracuse and wanted him to go to college. His dad had served in Korea as a communication technician and held a generally dim view of military service for reasons he never explained.

You'll be so far away, his mother said.

She pulled a wad of Kleenex out of her sleeve and dabbed her eyes. A plate on the table held the remains of a slice of marble cake, a set of coffee cups, cream, sugar, and a spoon. Through the window he could see his father trudging across the field, the hard afternoon light coming over the Adirondacks like sheets of burnished gold.

I'll be back soon, he said.

She sniffed and propped her cheek on her hand, elbow on the table, looking up at him.

You won't want to come back. And I don't blame you.

His girlfriend, Sydney Beauchamp, was going to college downstate. They had been dating for almost a year, but Kaiser still circled her like a wary coyote. He played the part of a high school boyfriend with an awkward reluctance. He felt like he was somehow compressed in a chamber that was too small, the ceiling too low. He didn't know how to explain to her that he felt he needed to strip away some part of himself like a tough coat of paint. Most of his high school classmates were destined to scratch out a living in the North Country, many working at the Dannemora supermax prison, a well-paid job with solid benefits. There wasn't much else. He wanted to get out, but he didn't have any money. He knew his parents would try to help him out, but they didn't have it either.

Kaiser hoped that in the air force, he would be able to study aviation, aeronautical engineering, astrophysics. He would learn the processes behind the magic of flight, the dynamic relationship between science and nature that allowed satellites to zip around the earth at thirty thousand miles an hour, how high-altitude bombers could pinpoint targets with laser-guided precision, how combustion and electronic pulses allowed massed blocks of steel to break the bonds of gravity, shed the thick gauze of atmosphere, and burst into the cold tranquility of space.

He arrived with a paper bag containing a turkey sandwich, a bottle of water, a paperback Carl Sagan book, and an extra pair of underwear and socks. The recruiting office was in a strip mall on the west side of Albany, next to a family fish restaurant. The recruiter blinked at the tall, fit young man before him. A hunk of quality rock, a snap recruit.

So why the air force?

I like space, Kaiser said.

Kaiser sat at a small desk filling out the paperwork. His jacket was folded across his lap, and he flipped through the stack of papers, filling in the boxes. The smell of fried perch hung in the air like a fog.

We got plenty of that, the recruiter said. Many of our bases are in big country, wide-open spaces. You need it for the big birds.

No, I mean space.

Kaiser pointed to the ceiling.

The recruiter sat back and tented his fingers.

You thinking about going to college? Getting a degree? If you wanna be an astronaut, it sorta works that way. We could help.

No, Kaiser said. I don't want to go *up* there. I just want to know how it works.

The recruiter watched a pack of children wearing disposable plastic bibs chasing each other on the sidewalk outside.

What about electronics? You familiar with radio equipment, anything like that?

My father and I are ham radio operators. Been doing it all my life.

Bingo. Welcome to the air force, son.

Kaiser was surprised when the recruiter handed him a bus ticket and told him to report to Lackland AFB in San Antonio, Texas, in four weeks. He had figured he'd be going right away.

Go do something fun, the recruiter said. Get some female attention.

Kaiser sat on the sidewalk of the strip mall and went through his wallet. He had sixty dollars and a credit card he'd never used before. His father told him it was only for emergencies. He did some calculations, then went to the bus station, cashed in his ticket to San Antonio for fifty-six dollars, then walked to the interstate and began hitchhiking.

He showered in coin-operated stalls in truck stops and slept in wooded areas. Near Memphis, a woman took him home after giving him a ride. She lived in a new suburban mansion built along a golf course. She had a head full of brassy blond hair, tired eyes, and her blouse was so tight the third button was gone, revealing a triangle of loose, tanned skin. They sat in chaise lounge chairs by the pool and drank glasses of chilled vodka with wedges of lemon and she talked about her ex-husband until she began to cry and stumbled inside the house. When Kaiser awoke, the sky was dark and the trees surrounding the pool glowed with green light, their long branches bending quietly toward the water.

It took him six days to get to Texas. He had thirty dollars left. Kaiser found a motel outside San Antonio and made a deal with the owner. For the next three weeks, he pushed the laundry carts out to the trucks, picked up loose trash in the parking lot, and watched the night desk from midnight to six in the morning. He bought a pound of baloney, a loaf of bread, mustard, and apples. He went for long runs and did sets of push-ups, sit-ups, and squat-thrusts in his room. At night he read Carl Sagan and washed his clothes in the bathtub. On the day of his induction into the air force, he used his final four dollars for a bus ticket to the base. He showed up in a T-shirt, jeans, and shoes, an envelope in his pocket that held his driver's license, blood donor card, and Social Security card. He had a single white handkerchief in his back pocket. His hands were empty.

After a couple days of processing, shuffling through rooms for paperwork, sensitivity training, and the issuing of gear, Kaiser's flight suited up for their first ABU five-mile training run. They assembled on the dusty parade ground, forty-five men and women in new starched camo, tactical ball caps, standard-issue leather boots. The TI was a tall, muscular Black man from Louisiana named Alcade who smoked Benson & Hedges. Many men in the flight, including Kaiser, took up this habit, as Alcade allowed smoke breaks during drill. When Alcade worked the lineup, he got in everybody's face and called them *stinking cunts*. This was June in Texas, and at seven in the morning it was already ninety degrees.

I'm gonna run you sorry motherfuckers into the ground!

Alcade keyed his watch, and they set out on the run, the TI setting a punishing pace, Kaiser trotting just behind him. At the marker for the final mile, he challenged them all to go as fast as they could and Kaiser took off, getting way out front, pounding away down the hard-packed dirt road. Alcade went after him but couldn't reel him in.

Get back here, motherfucker! Kaiser! Get back here!

Kaiser didn't stop until he got to the parade ground, and Alcade made him do extra calisthenics for an hour in the yard while the rest of the unit sat in the shade of the barracks. But Alcade left him alone after that, and two weeks into basic, Kaiser was targeted for special assignment. His overall physical stats were top 1 percent, ASVAB scores top in his flight, and during the SERE survival training week, he lay in a dry stream bed under a rotting log for forty-eight hours. He was the only one to escape detection during the exercise, emerging only when the all clear was signaled and the enraged trainers began combing the site with bullhorns.

Sydney wrote him letters telling stories of college classes and parties and young people living carefree and intellectually stimulating lives. Kaiser replied occasionally with a few sentences on a postcard. He didn't know how to express in words what he was going through.

After graduation, he was fast-tracked into the air combat controller program, part of a new Special Operations Forces Tactical Air Combat unit. Kaiser spent fifteen weeks at Keesler AFB, Mississippi, working on aircraft recognition, navigation, weather, communications, radar operation, the essentials of coordinating aeronautical interactions, and general air traffic control. Then he was sent to Fort Benning for static line airdrop training, three weeks of survival school at Fairchild AFB, Washington, then Pope Field, North Carolina, for thirteen weeks of Combat Control School, where he was in a classroom for six hours a day, then another six in the field with Army Rangers and Green Berets, learning GPS navigation, demolitions, fire support, SOFLAM laser acquisition marking, and coordinating close air support. Six months of Advanced Skills Training at Hulbert Field, Florida, then Free Fall Parachutist School at Fort Bragg, finishing with Combat Diving School in Panama City. At night in his bunk he read about kinematics, particle dynamics, gyro dynamics, and space vehicle motion.

The letters from Sydney stopped coming, and Kaiser was relieved. He still thought of her with a fondness that seemed strange to him, as if she were a relic of an antiquated past, framed in his memory by the mountains and the lake. He had let her go, because of something larger that drew him on like the relentless gravity of the stars, something that he could not name, but that he could see in his dreams. He could feel it in every bone, nerve, and tissue of his body.

Kaiser was on a carrier in the Persian Gulf on September 11, 2001, and within three weeks he was dropped into Afghanistan with a company of airborne Rangers and delivered to a squad from the Fifth Special Forces Group that was linking up with the Northern Alliance. He served one tour as an SFO-TACP attached to various special forces units and participated in multiple engagements.

Kaiser was held in a facility in Pakistan where he was court-martialed in July 2003, with a failed plea of Lack of Mental Responsibility. Then he was transferred to Fort Benning for another twenty-six months, some of that time spent in the psychiatric ward. Because of his otherwise exemplary combat record, in 2007 he was stripped of all tabs and given a general discharge without record. The army closed down the investigation and pulped the reports, consigning the incident to the dark places of redacted military history, a hole in his past that would never be acknowledged or known. When he was escorted off the base at Fort Benning, his hands were empty, again.

Half of North Chazy turned out for the funeral. Kodiak had been a regular substitute history teacher at the high school for more than thirty years, and there wasn't a family in town that didn't have at least one kid who'd sat through his lectures on the foresight of the founding fathers. Bill took care of most of the arrangements. The death of Kodiak's young daughter back in 1989 had marked the family with a kind of nobility only created by suffering, and this gave a suffocating solemnity to the proceedings.

Toward the end of the memorial service, Kaiser saw Sydney

Beauchamp in the back, standing alone in the overflow section. Her hair was longer, and she seemed thinner in the face, but she looked remarkably the same. She met Kaiser's eyes and nodded, a tightening of the lips.

The receiving line took more than hour and Kaiser shook hands with a hundred people, a strange grimace plastered on his face like a mask. His father was dead, his family and the entire community was mourning. He was thinking about Sydney. He wanted to talk to her, to hear her voice. Why now, after all these years? But when the receiving line finally ended, she wasn't there.

Afterward, Kaiser and his brother stood outside the wide door of the hay barn and drank from a bottle of Jameson as the hard chill of evening floated down from the mountains like a drifting blanket. The air was alive with the calls of feeder birds, and swallows darted in and out of the barn. Both men knew that the farm was already in arrears and would likely be sold barring some kind of miraculous financial intervention. The only value left was in the land, a hundred and ninety acres, about ten of which were low-lying lakefront. Bill had already taken out a second mortgage on his home and cleared out his 401(k). He estimated that if they came up with another twenty thousand, they could put it off another couple of years. They both knew the loss of the farm would be the final blow in a string of unearned tragedies from which their mother would never recover.

Don't tell Mom anything, Kaiser said. We'll get the money.

The morning after the funeral, he sat in front of his father's radio set. A glass of melted ice and a wedge of lime pooling on the table. He had the frequency dialed in tight, the crisp, steely hum of radio waves vibrating in his ears. His eyes were closed. In his mind he saw the concentric circles of radio subspace and all the celestial objects tracking blindly through the dark.

Then she spoke.

Greetings, friends! A new day is here!

Four, sixteen, thirteen, twelve, nine.

Hold the numbers close to your heart! I wish you good fortune in all things!

Kaiser gripped the table edge with both hands, trembling. The whoosh of radio silence. He rewound the recording and played it again.

Greetings, friends! A new day is here!

Four, sixteen, thirteen, twelve, nine.

Hold the numbers close to your heart! I wish you good fortune in all things!

The pattern had been stable, absolute. Six numbers between one and twenty. His father had recorded and checked every transmission.

He played it again. And again, writing down the numbers to be sure.

Five numbers. The first aberration in the code in fifty years.

Kaiser picked up his empty glass and threw it across the room.

LECLAIR

In the morning, LeClair stood at his kitchen counter and sprinkled a hard-boiled egg with salt while he read the *New York Times* arts section. The Constable stood at attention, watching with his glossy eyes. Alejandro came up the stairs, bringing the cold air with him, carrying a tray of takeout coffee from the Artful Dodger. LeClair wore a dark suit and a crisp oxford shirt, a pair of freshly buffed wing-tips, his Bulova watch. The door buzzer went off downstairs. The boys had arrived.

Gary eased the Escalade onto Market Street, a row of brick buildings that housed most of the lawyers in town, half of whom worked for LeClair is some capacity. A few cars muttered through the lakes of slush on the roads. Buck sipped from a carton of protein shake. His face was shining with moisture.

Why are you sweating?

Buck shrugged.

What're you wearing under your shirt? LeClair asked.

Rubber suit.

LeClair turned in his seat and regarded Gary in the back seat. He could see the edge of a black plastic garbage bag at his collar. His sweaty face an ashen hue. The day before at lunch Gary kept spitting into a plastic bottle and Buck only ate a pack of crackers, but LeClair had long since given up on deciphering the bizarre physical rituals of these young men.

What the hell are you two idiots doing?

Rip-off, Gary said.

What?

We're doing a rip-off. It's a bet.

Yeah, a contest, Buck said. To see who gets the most ripped? We got four weeks.

You know, you should be the judge, Gary said.

Yeah, since we both work for you and, like, you won't be bias? You could hold the money.

You mean I won't be bias*ed*, LeClair said.

Inside the offices of Larouche & Klein he arranged for his lawyer to apply a certified check of nine thousand dollars against the principal due on the Kaiser family farm, which would cover the back taxes and the fines that accrued. LeClair also had him prepare a legal challenge to the multiple liens on the property, citing personal hardship, death in the family, and veteran status. LeClair was pleased that Kaiser seemed to take it as a matter of course that LeClair would apply his payments directly to the mortgage and not short him. Now as LeClair sat in the lawyer's office, the wood paneling, Berber carpets, the air foggy with stale coffee, watching Klein tap away on his computer, he wondered if this trust was bound by some kind of fraternal understanding, two men of honor? Or if it was merely their shared knowledge that if LeClair screwed him in any way, Kaiser might kick in a window with a knife in his teeth one night while LeClair was watching Letterman in his tighty-whiteys?

The next stop was Montreal. He made inquiries about *La Montagne* through a business associate named Gerard, who had a cousin in Quebec City who worked with some Southeast Asian cartels. LeClair asked for a meeting, hinting at his desire to see the Turner painting and perhaps acquire it. To his surprise he almost immediately received a phone message, in French, saying the painting was in fact for sale, and giving him a time and place to meet. LeClair knew that if it *was* an original Turner, the asking price would likely be out of his league. Really, he just wanted to see the thing, to believe that it was real.

Most people in North Chazy preferred to cross the border on Route 9, the small way station with a single vestibule and often just one Canadian official and a handful of Americans, but LeClair liked the Northway crossing, with its banks of vestibules six lanes wide, the angular stone surfaces of the sprawling customs office buildings, the squads of uniformed men wielding assault rifles and mirrors on long sticks, the German shepherds straining in their harnesses, tongues lolling. It seemed both more cosmopolitan and dystopian, like a postapocalyptic voyage rather than simply crossing an imaginary international boundary.

He opened his valise and pulled out the boys' passports along with his own. He kept the passports of all the boys in a wall safe behind a decent copy of the *Shipwreck of the Minotaur.* He watched Gary pass the documents to the border agent, answering the rote questions like a professional. They'd been across more than twenty times in the last year. The agents didn't seem to care that the two young men were sweating like jungle animals on a zero-degree day in the North Country.

LeClair took the boys to lunch at Au Pied du Cochon, a gastropub on Chateaubriand Avenue in central Montreal, where you could get a pork chop the size of a dinner plate with ten-inch bone hanging off like a hammer handle. The cassoulet contained six types of meat and the house-made pâté was legendary. He ordered a plate of poutine for the table and a bottle of New Zealand Chardonnay on the recommendation of the sommelier. The place was crowded and noisy, LeClair and the boys sharing a long table with a set of Quebecois doctors and a young Japanese couple. Gary and Buck stared at the steaming pile of potatoes, gravy, and meat for a few moments, then after exchanging a look of agreement, they fell to, rip-off be dammed. LeClair sipped his wine and watched the boys mop up the poutine, their faces beaming with joy.

After lunch, LeClair slipped the boys a couple hundred Canadian and cut them loose in the old quarter by the Basilica, instructing them to pick him up in a couple hours. His meeting with Montagne was at three, and they requested he wait by the dock at the Parc du Bassin-Bonsecours. Gerard said they would make themselves known.

LeClair walked through the park of spindled birch trees and followed the icy path down to the river. The scent of fried dough drifted from the old quarter. A middle-aged woman sat on a bench doing some kind of knitting. LeClair leaned against the railing, watching a rolling tug negotiate the floating ice heading down the Saint Lawrence River. In the middle of the river was the Île Sainte-Hélène, a summertime tourist site, and the white bulge of the Biosphere de Montreal to the south.

He heard the crunch of snow and turned to see the woman on the bench crossing the path, a bag slung over her shoulder. She approached him, smiling, a knit toboggan cap, furry boots, long puffy black coat.

Bonjour, monsieur.

Bonjour.

She joined him at the rail and took a slip of paper with a picture on it out of her pocket and proceeded to shred it, letting the pieces fall into the river. Then she took out a cell phone and made a call.

Il est l à, she said.

She snapped the phone shut. A few seconds later, a rusty trawler steamed from behind the northern edge of Île Saint-Helene, smashing through the plates of ice. The woman lit a cigarette, gave LeClair a small nod, then walked away. The boat was barnacled with ice, the trawling arms and ropes frozen solid, the pilothouse shrouded in steam. A pair of Vietnamese men with ducktail haircuts and leather jackets stood at the rail, and they gestured to a hand-gate when the boat drew up flush with the quai, the captain gunning the engines in reverse.

Monsieur LeClair. *S'il vous plaît.*

They opened the gate for him and held out a hand. He stepped aboard and they led him back to the pilothouse, throwing open the pocket door. A portly man in a rubber smock, knee boots, and a wool cap stood at the console, spinning the wheel as the boat churned away from the pier. LeClair put a hand on the console to steady himself as the boat listed and rolled in its own wake.

La Montagne?

The pilot, with a bristly, porcine face, shook his head as he spun the boat around and pushed the throttle. The engine roared and the floor vibrated as the boat headed north toward Île Sainte-Hélène.

Non. Nous y serons en quelques minutes. It is short voyage.

They came along the west side of the island, passing under the Pilier du pont Jacques-Cartier and by the shuttered amusement park. The Ferris wheel was shrouded in sparkling ice, and a long roller coaster snaked down the length of the island. The boat coasted up to a metal floating pier just short of the north end and the Vietnamese men opened the door and gestured for him to debark. As soon as he stepped off, the boat motored away to the north. In the river channel, the wind howled, and the pier was slick with ice. At the end of the pier a path led through a stand of trees to a clearing where the terminus of the roller coaster crouched on its spindly support columns.

A figure separated itself from the support beams of the coaster, stepping out into the clearing. A man in a long coat, the faint sparkle of light on eyeglasses. As LeClair stood there squinting, he realized there were several men among the trees. He had expected a nice hotel suite, perhaps, maybe dinner, or an elegant office in a high-rise downtown. Not this. But what did he know about the habits of Canadian crime lords? He looked back across the river to the old city of Montreal. There was nowhere else to go. So holding his collar together at the neck, he made his way gingerly down the icy dock to the shore. This is how it begins, he thought.

They stood in the ankle-deep snow among the tall silver maples. Montagne had a shaved head, round wire glasses, gray stubble on his cheeks. He wore a heavy peacoat that he hunched down into like a European intellectual. Men stood around them in the background at different distances, hands in their coats, breath steaming. A man stepped forward with a flat leather case, cinched with buckles. He opened the case and held it out to LeClair.

A relatively small piece, thirty by thirty inches square with a simple unadorned frame. LeClair recognized it immediately.

Glaucus and Scylla, 1841. J. M. W. Turner. LeClair had seen this piece years ago at the Kimbell in Fort Worth. It was part of the famed "Villa Jaffe Paintings" collection: more than sixty works that had been in Nice, France, before they were seized by the Nazis in 1943. Reclamation of the paintings was still ongoing. A family in Texas received *Glaucus and Scylla* as part of the process, but numerous experts challenged the authenticity of the painting. It was rumored another painting was also in circulation, claiming to be the original.

LeClair knew the painting well. First exhibited at the Royal Academy in 1841, *Glaucus and Scylla* was a round composition, designed to be contained in a round frame, so the impression was of a burning, golden disk, with forms and shapes dissolving in a great wash of light. It represented an episode from Ovid's *Metamorphoses*, the myth of Glaucus and Scylla. A mottled sun left of center setting over a lake bordered with rocky peaks. In the foreground a limpid pool, and the torso of Glaucus with long seaweed hair holding out his arms to Scylla, who ran from him, looking back over her shoulder, a couple cherubs floating nearby, waving their arms, urging her to flee. There was the sense of a warning, but LeClair couldn't tell if it was coming from the hoary sea-god, or the fleeing woman. Or perhaps the figures were merely a distraction. Perhaps the message was emanating from the flat disk of yellow that cast the valley with a golden light, while at the same time seeming to take it away, pulling the light and the world with it. LeClair reached out and touched the frame. He wanted to hold it in his hands. He already believed it was real.

It is currently valued, Montagne said, by Christie's at five to seven million US. You can bring your representative to authenticate the painting if you wish.

Well, thought LeClair, it felt worth five million just to experience it, standing in wet shoes in a snowy forest. But there's no way he could come up with a quarter of that. Not without selling half their real estate assets, most of which were already significantly leveraged.

What about the painting in Texas? he said.

We are confident they are wrong, Montagne said. You are free to verify that as well.

How did you get this one? Where did it come from?

The end of the war was a . . . *période tumultueuse.* Many Nazis were looking for a way out of Europe. They were willing to trade nearly anything.

How much are you willing to sell it for?

It is not for sale.

Then what are we doing?

I am looking for someone, Montagne said, that can help me with a problem. It is a very special problem. If you can do this, I will give you the painting. Comme cadeau.

A gift? LeClair's heart leaped in his chest.

What Montagne wanted was a clear route across the Quebec border. He wanted to move a package. A hundred kilos, packed in large satchels.

Why not through the mountains? LeClair said. People run untaxed cigarettes and weed up there all the time.

This is a different kind of package, Montagne said. They don't care about those things. They care about this. And they are watching us.

LeClair looked around the woods. A man leaning against a tree was cradling a rifle in his arms. The island was quiet. Had he cleared the whole island just for this meeting? And who the hell told these Quebec gangsters that he was the man to arrange this? What did he know about finding clear routes across the border?

We lost three packages so far this year, Montagne said. This cost me beaucoup d'argent. Customers are waiting, so we have to do it plus gros. A hundred kilos is a difficult task, but splitting it up creates more risk.

Montagne shrugged, his face cracking open into a many-toothed smile.

They want to stop me, he said. But I plan to win.

He needed a way to avoid the surveillance detection systems of the US border; not just personnel and motion-detection cameras but also the aerial drones, tethered aerostat radar systems, low-orbit satellites. The Americans had put up a wall of technology to stop this kind of thing from entering the country. If LeClair could arrange this successfully, they would give him a small percentage, *plus* the painting. LeClair would come to Montreal while the drop was made, spend the evening with Montagne's associates, as a kind of assurance. A pleasant evening, Montagne assured him: hotel, dinner, drinks, some entertainment. The next day he goes home with the painting.

His cut would be two million dollars. LeClair did the rough math in his head; the total value of the package must be more than thirty million. He didn't bother to ask what was in it. *Fleur-de-Lis. The stuff everybody wants.*

If things go poorly, *si tu me trahis*, Montagne said. We will take everything from you.

LeClair didn't want to think about what this meant. Betrayal. *Everything.* He couldn't tell Walt about any of this.

A real Turner. His collection could finally have that centerpiece, the blank space filled. He couldn't miss this chance, because he wouldn't get another. And because LeClair had an idea.

The next day LeClair went to visit his brother. The two-story farmhouse stood in the center of a clearing with a gravel road trailing to a large cedar barn, silver with age, where Walt kept the farm equipment. The fields to the south that once held cattle now contained a forest of head-high fir trees. Buck drove LeClair and Gary around the house and parked in the gravel lot. Buck's face was a glossy patina of sweat. They were both wearing sunglasses and rubber suits under their clothes again. Gary wiped the back of his neck with a bandanna.

Christ, LeClair said. The sweating again?

The boys looked at him with their mirrored shades and shining faces.

Wipe your faces, for fuck's sake, LeClair said. You look like melting corpses. And you'll need to dry-clean those jackets. I'll be back in twenty minutes.

Can we get out of the car? Gary asked. Feelin' a little woozy.

Yes, LeClair said. Don't wander off.

They all got out and LeClair was handed the valise. The sound of an idling tractor motor in the barn broke the stillness of the afternoon. The boys leaned on the hood and adjusted their sunglasses, their breath trailing behind them like scarves. LeClair walked into the barn and paused to let his eyes adjust to the dim light, taking a sheaf of papers out of the valise. Walt was crouched by the front wheel of an aging Massey Ferguson with a crescent wrench. He was wearing the same stained tan coveralls that he wore every day. LeClair folded his arms and waited.

Why'd you bring those two fools out here? Walt said.

There was an auction in Ausable, LeClair said.

Walt shut the engine down and turned to face his younger brother. LeClair shifted, pushing the dusty straw underfoot.

Just what you need, Walt said, more paintings.

Gerard knows a guy in the Pentagon, LeClair said. Check this out.

He held out the papers in his hand. When it became clear that Walt wasn't going to take them, he began to read them aloud:

> *Kaiser, Thomas. Special Operations Air Combat Controller. Assigned to Vandenburg, California, Space and Missile Operations, then the 623rd Air and Space Operations Center in Hulbert, Florida, then at Fort Bragg, training with SOF units. Shipped to Afghanistan in 2001 with the Fifth Special Operations Forces, served one tour.*

Walt turned back to the tractor and reengaged his wrench. LeClair glanced over his shoulder, out the open door and across the snowy clearing toward the two handsome young men leaning on the hood of the Escalade. They were staring back at him, arms crossed over their chests, their sunglasses like the blank eyes of insects.

Walt, LeClair said. Gerard's guy at the Pentagon says that Kaiser's not listed on any of the official overseas manifests. His unit in Afghanistan had no name.

So what?

For the next three years he is just gone. Nothing. Then he turns up here a couple months ago.

So?

Well, I fixed the thing with Marin and now Kaiser *owes* us. But it goes deeper. Something happened over there. Whatever his dark secret is, whatever he did, doesn't matter. As long as he thinks we know.

LeClair could see his brother's back settle and relax. He slipped the wrench in his pocket and stood up.

I still don't see what this has to do with us.

Because we have over one hundred grand, LeClair said, in outstanding loans and rent! And some of those Wiggletown people are dangerous. Gorman is a menace. I'm done with those lunatics the Lavoie brothers. Kaiser cleared twelve grand, in *one* day. I think he can be our guy.

Walt checked his watch. LeClair knew that his brother found this tiresome.

So I'm going to make an investment, LeClair said. With his help I think we can get our books straightened out. I wanted to let you know before I start moving money around.

Walt frowned and shook his head. He pointed a greasy finger toward the Escalade parked in the field.

And them?

Not involved. Not at all.

Those boys, Walt said, will be the thing that brings you down. You and all your proclivities.

We've been through this, LeClair said.

I don't care, Walt said. It's foolish. A foolish weakness.

LeClair closed his eyes and took a long breath. He couldn't get into this argument again, not now. Walt would never understand the way he felt about the boys. He had never touched a single one of them, and he never would. The relationship was more meaningful than something as crude and momentary as sex.

The brothers stood looking at each other for a few moments. Then

Walt patted his pockets, cleared his throat, and walked past him out the door and into the sunlight.

I guess we'll see, he said over his shoulder.

Walt cut across the field toward the house, giving the Escalade a wide berth. Gary and Buck watched him go by and LeClair saw them smiling to each other and saying something. They were making a joke, something about his brother.

Buck took the valise and opened the door for him while Gary fired up the Escalade. LeClair wiped his forehead, prickly with sweat.

Back to the shop, he said.

Gary turned the car around, the tires crunching through the wet snow, and LeClair hit shuffle on the CD changer, bringing up "Oh Yeah" from *Flesh and Blood*. He knew the boys hated Bryan Ferry, but they were riddled with a variety of aesthetic failures. Also, he was paying them.

He called Kaiser, left a message for him to come by the shop tomorrow, he had an extra side-job.

Then he called the office of Dr. Laurence Sterne, assistant professor of art history at Ausable College, who his niece Emerson told him about. It went immediately to voicemail. LeClair asked him to come by his house tomorrow as well, for a consultation.

Listen, LeClair said to buck and Gary. If I ever catch one of you saying something about my brother, an insult, a joke, anything, you are fucking done. *Done.*

Sure, Gary said.

Walt's a cool dude, Buck said.

Buck pulled onto the hard road that led back toward North Chazy. Gary spat into his bottle.

Let's just keep it that way, LeClair said, okay? And maybe I'll judge your stupid contest.

Sweet!

That's awesome, bro. Thanks.

JANSKY & STERNE

By mid-December, several fishing shanties had gone under the ice, as well as a pickup truck, a pair of sleds, and an ATV piloted by a twelve-year-old boy. Three men and the boy were dead, including a North Chazy man who put away half a rack of Labatt before taking his sled out for a midnight screamer on the lake.

The danger didn't seem to matter. On her morning ski runs, Dr. Sue Jansky counted at least a half-dozen new shanties in the last week, crouched on the silent expanse of the lake between King Bay and Chazy Landing. Her core samples showed the ice to be more than twelve inches in most places, but there were always weak spots, shallows that created current eddies, hidden thermal vents pulsing deep heat from the bottom. And yet men drove out onto the ice in pickup trucks, parked a half dozen of them around a fishing shanty outfitted with a chugging generator, a pile of beer cans like a snowdrift under the porthole window. Everybody seemed to believe that the vagaries of the ice were like some kind of cosmic game, an elemental fate that could not be understood or avoided. But Dr. Jansky knew the ice was a scientific process. The various elements and conditions, even on a lake as large as Lake Champlain, could be accounted for and predicted.

Dr. Jansky skied along the rocky finger that shielded King Bay and then north toward Rouse's Point, North Chazy, and the Canadian border.

A tall, slender woman, with the muscular haunches of an endurance athlete, Dr. Jansky was forty-two years old, though with her steady churning stroke as she kicked across the ice, she looked more like a lithe teenage Olympian. She had a sixteen-mile loop finely calibrated in her head and she judged her deviation to be no more than a couple meters at most. She knew where the ice was safe and where the dark places waited.

Dr. Jansky was a geologist and climatologist at the college, specializing in limnology, or the study of lake formations. Using charts and satellite data along with current weather conditions, she carefully charted her courses before daybreak. When her husband Laurence came downstairs earlier that morning, yawning and searching for coffee, Dr. Jansky had the printer cranking out her route. Laurence read *The New York Times* while Dr. Jansky ate a bowl of granola and honey, poring over her map. Laurence poked her under the table with his toe.

I'm going into town this morning. To look at a painting. A consultation.

Dr. Jansky raised her head.

Consultation?

She said this with a sarcastic lilt that surprised them both. Laurence was embarrassed, going back to the *Times* with a rattle. Dr. Jansky's husband was a professor in the art history department, and though they had both been at the university for twelve years, Dr. Laurence Sterne was still an assistant professor, having failed to come up for tenure twice, mostly due to his inability to do anything with his ponderous book project on the work of J. M. W. Turner, titled *The Sun & the Sublime.* They both knew that "consulting" was ridiculous in this part of New York, unless you went across the border to Montreal.

Who is it? she asked.

Laurence set the paper down.

You know the antique store downtown? LeClair? He said he has something I have to see.

The same LeClair that owns Frenchtown? And the trailer parks? The slumlord?

Laurence shrugged, blowing on his coffee.

Paying gig?

Laurence sat back and ran a hand through his thick hair, smoothing it behind his ears. He was a man blessed with large, handsome facial features. Long arms. Wide palms.

Only one way to find out, he said.

Laurence smiled at the paper, and Dr. Jansky turned to her preparations.

The snow conditions were dry and light, so she got out her skis and applied some steel wool to the edges and a few swipes of number four wax. Since it was hovering just around twenty degrees she put on a silk one-piece under her Gore-Tex leggings and pullover Lycra storm parka, donning a wool toboggan, and her polarized goggles with the yellow lenses. She went through her stretching routine by the back door, pausing to drink from a thermos filled with Pedialyte and coconut water, which she cinched into the flat Ergo backpack with her core sampler, energy bars, signal flares, and several ocular devices. She checked her watch and set the chrono.

Laurence eyed her steadily, the paper lowered. Dr. Jansky went about her ministrations in such an unselfconscious manner and with intractable focus. He loved this about her.

Laurence first encountered Sue Jansky fourteen years ago at the University of Michigan. She was standing on the edge of a wooden deck at the graduate student association social event. It was a cool fall day, and she was the only person there wearing shorts, small, hip-hugging, khaki shorts. She had a glass of wine balanced in her long fingers. The planes of her face were angled like some kind of stealth aircraft.

Laurence worked his way closer into the knot of geology students. The scientists dominated the center of the deck, while the humanities students clumped under the eaves in the side yard, smoking cigarettes in a coolly intellectual manner. Laurence stood on the perimeter of Sue Jansky's circle as she talked about glaciers.

The forces at work, she was saying, are beyond any scale we can conceive of. The power to gouge out such vast tracks of earth and rock, to crush a million tons of solid rock into a paste that gets spread like butter, hardening smooth as glass.

She seemed to make eye contact with everyone at the party, all at once, her face in that curious tight-lipped smile, eyes almost flat, like a Renaissance Madonna.

The mass that cannot be stopped, she said. The most powerful force on earth.

Hope it works out, she said. I'll be back in a couple hours. Lunch?

Laurence nodded, and Dr. Jansky turned to the door. The wind was out of the south, blowing hard. It would snow heavily for most of the morning. The door gasped and then she was outside in the blowing cold, snapping into her bindings, a few more stretches and then with a pole plant she was off across the backyard and down the slope that led to the lake. Laurence watched from the window, admiring the lean muscles of her long arms and the ropey textures of her legs as she planted and skated across the snow like a woodland sprite. Dr. Jansky disappeared through a short stand of pines near the water's edge, then emerged, skating faster, her limbs dark and insect-like against the white ice, moving east toward Isle La Motte.

Laurence descended into the unfinished basement, retrieved his glass bong and a small wooden box he kept concealed behind the utility sink. He opened the small head-high window, and a sheet of drifting snow fell inside on the sill. Standing among stacked boxes of Dr. Jansky's notes, a half-finished wine rack, and an old tobacco cabinet that he intended one day to refurbish, Laurence took a pair of heavy, deeply drawn hits and stood with his eyes closed, listening to the soft pat of the snow outside, until his head thrummed and red shapes danced behind his eyelids. As usual, his thoughts turned toward *The Sun & the Sublime*, the stacks of draft copies on his desk upstairs, the dozens of computer files that contained the sprawling chapters, the long list of plates and illustrations. He took a last hit before placing the bong and the wooden box back behind the sink. He knew he was sufficiently high when the desire to look at something beautiful washed over him.

Laurence was familiar with LeClair's shop and had browsed there one afternoon as he waited for Sue to get out of class. As he parked on the court square, a woman in a long down coat staggered down the sidewalk with a small shivering dog on a leash. Nothing else moved save LeClair's sign swinging in the blowing wind. The address he was given was for LeClair's residence, the row house next door to the shop.

A Hispanic man in a sweater answered the door, cracking it and peering out at him, then pulling him quickly inside and shutting the door. The walls of the entranceway were painted a deep garnet, the floors polished oak, and Laurence was astonished at the number of paintings adorning the walls. In the style of the great chambers of Versailles, nearly every space on the narrow hallway was crammed with oil paintings in heavy gilded frames. Landscapes. The entranceway was mostly American, of the Hudson River school, disciples of Cole. Copies of Church, Kensett, Gifford. Broad vistas, misty lakes, gorges in the Catskills and the craggy peaks of the Adirondacks. Exceptional copies, Laurence noted. Down the hall the nineteenth-century American prevailed, moving into Luminism and the Dusseldorf school. Laurence stopped in front of a Cropsey, *Fisherman's House, Greenwood Lake*, 1877, peering at it closely. He stepped back and crossed his arms, frowning.

Mr. LeClair, Alejandro said, is waiting in the main gallery.

The Cropsey was either the best copy Laurence had ever seen, or it was the original. But he had seen it himself six years ago in the Spanierman Gallery in New York City. How could it possibly have found its way here, in North Chazy?

The main gallery was even more crammed with paintings, branching out into French, English, a couple Spanish. Laurence was aware of Mr. LeClair walking toward him from behind a desk, a little man with a gleaming round dome and a V-neck sweater, shaking his hand and gesturing to a seat. Laurence fell into the chair, craning his neck, scanning the room. Alejandro poured him a cocktail out of a gleaming silver shaker set, and Laurence picked up the martini glass and took two large swallows of ice-cold gin.

There will be plenty of time, LeClair was saying, to take it all in.

The Cropsey, Laurence gasped.

He put the glass down on a small tray next to the chair, coughed, and wiped his tearing eyes. LeClair returned to his chair behind a massive oak desk that seemed to bulge and flex its muscular forelegs. He had a half-dozen rings on his fingers. Alejandro folded himself into a love seat, tucking his bare feet under his legs like a small waterbird. The window behind Alejandro looked out into a brick alley filling with snow.

The Cropsey, Laurence managed to croak again.

Yes, LeClair said. You noticed.

How?

I've got something better than that to show you, LeClair said. Something you are *really* going to love.

When Dr. Jansky rounded the point, the snowfall was deepening, now falling straight down, and she let herself glide to a stop. She crouched and slipped off her pack. Peeling off her gloves, she ate an energy bar and drank some coconut water.

She was massaging her calves when she noticed a shot of light, straight north on the Canadian side. Something silver, winking through the mist of snow. She stood up, wiping off her goggles. Again, a flash of light, low on the ice. She slipped a set of compact binoculars out of her pack and aimed it at the winking light. A snowmobile, racing across the ice, coming straight at her, maybe a mile off. Her first thought was visibility. Make myself large, some movement and color. Looking through the binoculars again, she could see the driver was wearing a backpack, a tall rooster tail of snow and ice spraying behind him.

Then a dark shape the size of a passenger jet suddenly flashed under her feet, heading north. As it passed beneath her, the ice rose, bulging like the back of a surfacing whale. Her knees buckled and she fell onto the ice, dropping the binoculars. With a crunch and reverberating groan, the ice subsided, sagging back to its original plane. The dark shadow was gone. Her first thought was that the whiteout and her exertions were causing some kind vertigo, but the ice had *lifted*. The sled was now a roaring buzz and she could see it a half mile off and coming hard, directly at her. Dr. Jansky got to her feet, her legs shaky and fatigued, and raised her hands above her head, waving.

Hey, she whispered. It's me.

A hundred meters away the rear of the sled jackknifed skyward, the engine roaring as it formed a gentle parabola in the snowy air. Then the sharp crunch and clatter as machine and rider dove neatly headfirst into the ice, disappearing.

Laurence carried a fresh cocktail, sloshing it on his sleeve as he followed LeClair down the dark hall cluttered with paintings.

First, LeClair said, you need to agree to an oath of secrecy. You'll be well compensated, of course.

They paused and LeClair drew aside a set of heavy garnet curtains. The window opened up on a small interior courtyard, a crooked Japanese maple ringed with stones, a wrought-iron bench. A man in a black coat sat on this bench, his back to the window, the snow drifting into the courtyard and forming an even layer on his coat and uncovered head. His shoulders were squared and broad, his hands in his lap. LeClair tapped lightly on the glass.

If you tell anyone what you see today, he said, this man . . .

He tapped on the glass again.

This man will come for you.

The snow fell flat in the windless brick courtyard, giving it the look of an underwater window, a drifting sea of white, the black figure in the center suspended, weightless.

What?

Another tap on the glass, lightly, as if not to disturb the man in the black coat.

He will come for you, LeClair said, and your wife. You don't want this. Do you understand?

Cold air came through the antique windowpanes and Laurence shivered. He was familiar with what was often called the ecstatic experience of art, the delicious fear of the sublime. What he felt as he watched the man sitting silently in the courtyard was something more elemental and harrowing, the blunt instrument of terror.

They piled into the Escalade, cocktails in hand, and headed for the border. A sweaty young man, a college student likely, was driving. He wore a blue windbreaker and mirrored sunglasses, and didn't say a word the entire trip. LeClair was excitable and glib, talking to him about Turner, about oil paintings, landscapes, Hudson River school, French impressionists. Laurence was still dazed, more than slightly drunk and still high as a bat. He tried to respond, but he was still thinking about LeClair's gallery, the Cropsey, and how he ended up in this car, with this man who had just threatened him and his wife. And who was going to pay him ten thousand dollars to look at a painting. Ten thousand!

An hour later they were passing along the canal in the Little Burgundy section of Montreal, towering luxury apartments on the left side facing the water, the balconies tufted with snow. They entered a parking garage, circling deep underground. After entering a code, LeClair and Sterne took an elevator up to the top floor. LeClair paused before a massive double door near the end of the hall.

Do you understand what we are doing here? Our arrangement.

No, Laurence thought. I do not understand. He had a sense of the deal, that this man wanted his expertise on a painting. But why? Why am *I* here?

Yes, Laurence said.

The door opened and they entered a studio awash with natural light funneled in from skylights, the walls gallery white and with simple pale wooden floors. On the wall facing him was a small painting, about a foot square, in a simple black frame. Laurence stepped to the painting.

A dazzling swatch of light emerged from the upper third, illuminating figures transposed on rocks in the foreground. Mountain peaks rising up to the right, and just below center, a dark hole of smoke in a haze of rust and blood. The primary figure was a naked young woman in flight, turning in a backward glance. To her right a pair of cherubs floated, as if coaxing her onward. Just above the hole a pair of outstretched hands and a dark face gazed at the woman as she fled.

Laurence stepped up close, his face inches from the canvas. The brushstrokes, the layering unmistakable. The color. He felt a hand on his shoulder.

There is a family, LeClair said, a wealthy family, in Texas, who right now is looking at the same painting.

Laurence put his hands on the wall. He knew he was in a room in Montreal, Quebec. But he didn't feel like he was anywhere.

Glaucus and Scylla, Laurence said. From Ovid's *Metamorphoses*. 1841. It's in the Kimbell, in Fort Worth. This is a Turner.

It *was* in the Kimbell, LeClair said, and then it was returned to the Berrellez family. But the painting that the Berellezes are looking at is a copy. Or so I've been told. I need you to certify that the painting in Fort Worth is a fake, and *this* is the original.

Laurence felt like he wanted to cough, to spit, but there was nothing in his throat. He had a short chapter devoted to *Glaucus and Scylla* in his book, in the section titled "Myths, Legends, & the Anthropomorphic Landscape."

There are professional appraisers, Laurence said.

I'm in a hurry, LeClair said. You're the only expert on Turner for a hundred miles. And I want someone close. Someone that I can reach.

Nearly twenty years earlier, Laurence Sterne sat in dark amphitheater among a sea of students, gazing at a series of images projected on a screen. Dr. Rosen, a small man in a sweater-vest, intoned nasally at the podium.

Glaucus and Scylla, Dr. Rosen said. A tale of unrequited love and blind rage. Ovid described Scylla as a nymph of great beauty, who bathed in a silver pool. And Glaucus, a homely fisherman who was transformed into a minor sea-god. One day he catches sight of her and, as so often happens in these tales, is instantly smitten. And, of course, she was horrified and fled from him.

Laurence held a pen to an empty page of his notebook.

Glaucus went to Circe, Dr. Rosen said, the great sorceress of the *Odyssey*, for help. But Circe fell in love with Glaucus, and because he was unable to shake his love of Scylla, Circe went to the pool where Scylla bathed and poisoned the waters. When Scylla entered the water, she was transformed into a hideous monster. It's a common theme in ancient mythology: how jealousy and rage combine to create a deadly cocktail of vengeance. The gods, they lash out, like children.

Dr. Rosen switched to a slide of a tentacled monster snatching a sailor off the deck of a masted sailing ship.

Wolf heads and serpents sprouted from Scylla's waist. She was unable to stop the heads from devouring victims that happened to sail by.

He flipped back to the *Glaucus and Scylla* slide.

Consider for a moment the choice that Turner has made here, what to represent.

Dr. Rosen turned and addressed the image with open arms.

The heartbroken old god in his grief. The moment of realization. She is lost to him forever.

Laurence found that he was panting with effort, like a dog. There was a small man in a cashmere sweater beside him, watching his face. LeClair. There were other people in the room, someone was standing behind them, but he never got a clear look at anybody. He was *avoiding* looking at anybody. Laurence thought about the framed window where a man sat in a courtyard filling with snow.

Dr. Sterne, LeClair said. Do you need some time? Do you want to take it off the wall? I have some optical tools, if you would like.

Laurence took a deep breath.

No, he said. I mean yes. It does. It is.

Dr. Jansky scrambled toward the hole in the ice. About twenty meters away, she stopped and assembled her small hand auger and applied the bit. When she pulled the sample there was more than fourteen inches of ice. This ice would support a school bus. The water in the hole was dark like an open mouth and the dropping snowflakes blinked out on its surface. There was something floating in the water, rounded and black. Dr. Jansky stretched herself out in spread-eagle fashion to flatten out her weight and with a ski pole extended in her hand she inched toward the dark slot. He could be unconscious, she thought, the shock of the cold water and the wreck may have knocked him out. If she got him out in a few minutes, he might be revived without brain damage. It must have been some kind of thermal anomaly, she was thinking, a giant pressure bubble, an enormous pocket of bottom gas releasing all at once. But despite the complexities and movements of large ice formations, pressure bubbles, friction melt, migrations, stacking, and quick-thaw breakups, that didn't explain that enormous shadow under the ice, the path it seemed to take, the speed it traveled, how it zeroed in on the sled driver. The sheer *size* of it! Dr. Jansky had never seen or heard of anything like this.

Dr. Jansky extended the ski pole toward the humped figure. She glanced back at her scrawling track through the snow, where her skis stood upright in an X formation. At first, she thought it was the back of the driver floating on his stomach, but it was crisscrossed with bungee cords and Dr. Jansky realized it was the backpack. Which meant the driver, if he was still strapped in, would be submerged, hanging face down in the water. She knew he must be drowned by now, his blood thickened, muscles stiffening with ice crystals, the constriction of hypothermic rage pushing organic material into shock, then necrotic defeat. She got the pole under one of the straps and pulled him to the edge, and getting into a seated position she pulled with both arms, until the backpack came up over the lip and onto the ice, the straps empty.

Dr. Jansky knew the depth in this area was around ninety feet, and she imagined him slowly descending through the darkness like an astronaut drifting to the planet surface. He would sink into the soft lunar landscape, passing through a dozen feet of heavy silt, the bottom worms finding him in seconds as he came to rest on their burrows. The sea lampreys and limpets would be there a few minutes later, the body quickly becoming a writhing mass of pale tendrils. This image made her gag, and she lay on the ice for a few minutes and retched. Her tears crystallized on her goggles, and she tore them off her face. Her distress embarrassed her. The bottom of Lake Champlain was littered with the picked-over carcasses of thousands of men, women, children. She knew this.

She cut away the bungees and ripped into the plastic cover of the backpack. Inside were rectangular packages about the size of a brick, wrapped in brown paper, and for a moment she considered the horrible waste of dying in this manner, a backpack of illegal goods across the border traded for a life, but then the booming started, a sound coming from far off but that quickly closed on her, thundering reverberations like cannon shots. It was a sound Dr. Jansky had not heard but still somehow knew, and she was on her feet, slipping on the ice, running toward her skis that stood like some undecipherable totem against the milky sky, and she screamed for her husband, Laurence, a wild cry that echoed in the stillness as the crashing ice began to break up underneath her.

Back in his Land Rover, Laurence took the envelope out of his pocket and flipped through the money. The air in the cab got close and hot and Laurence paused to struggle out of his jacket, sweat bursting on his brow. Ten thousand dollars. He would travel to Texas and view the painting in the Berrellez family house, just to verify it was fake. There would be another ten thousand waiting for him when he returned. The money wasn't what convinced him, as Laurence and Sue had fashioned a comfortable living from their university salaries and relatively modest lifestyle. No, it was because LeClair had promised him something better. This new line of consulting work could help him network and bolster the publication pitch for *The Sun & the Sublime.* Tenure at the college would follow. Best of all, he would have complete access to the *Glaucus and Scylla.*

Laurence tuned the radio to the local NPR station, but flipped to the classic rock station and turned up the final section of "Dazed and Confused," a song that reminded him of high school parties. He rifled the various crannies in the cab and found a roach in the center console. He lit it with trembling fingers, inhaled deeply, and closed his eyes.

It was nearly noon when Laurence turned into the driveway, which meant Sue would be showered and dressed, likely eating a bowl of brown rice and peas while she flipped through her email. He would burst through the door, and she would turn to him with that slim, enigmatic smile.

The house seemed illuminated from within, the colors of melon, tangerine, tea rose, rust, vermilion, and as Laurence came up the stairs, he felt what must have been love singing in his veins. He yanked off his jacket and gloves and threw them on the floor.

Sue! he yelled. You won't believe this. Sue!

He came into the kitchen and found it empty, the newspaper still scattered on the counter, the smell of stale coffee in the air. The back door area was bare, no skis or equipment, no small puddles of water on the floor from melting snow.

Sue!

The vibrating emotional chord in his chest went into an even higher key, and he began running his hands over things, rattling the coffeepot, the little box of keys and pens on the counter, the fruit bowl on the dining room table. Laurence looked down the darkened hallway to the bedroom and the office. He stood in the wash of light.

Sue!

KAISER

Kaiser sat in LeClair's study drinking a gimlet, surrounded by the gaping eyes of landscapes. LeClair was counting out the money at his desk. On the floor there was some stereo equipment, a portable safe, a powder-blue jewelry box, a motorcycle deed and keys, a DVD player and a TV. LeClair finished counting and worked his calculator. He seemed to be in a good mood, for some reason. He was talking about how Kaiser ought to get himself a partner.

Someone big and scary. Make your job a lot easier.

LeClair separated out the money, put it in an envelope, then held up an extra hundred-dollar bill.

Bonus for a great day, he said. Tell me about that shortwave radio. Is that what you were doing in the air force?

Kaiser looked at his drink, the smeared rim, sugar on one side. LeClair glanced at the sheet of paper, underlined something with his finger.

What do you know about low earth-orbit objects? How about drones?

Kaiser stared at him. He could see Alejandro out of the corner of his eye, his legs drawn up under him on the couch. LeClair went into his drawer, pulled out another packet of cash, and wrote a name and address on a slip of paper. He walked around to Kaiser and held it out to him.

Listen, LeClair said, I don't have to be a tactical air combat controller to know that your current equipment is antique bullshit. There's a man in Quebec, named Gerard. He'll set you up.

LeClair tucked the money and the slip of paper into the front pocket of Kaiser's shirt. He waved his hand at his paintings that covered the room.

You seem interested. You like art?

I think so.

Well, let's try, LeClair said. Tell me, what do you find to be beautiful in this life?

Beautiful?

Yes. What is beautiful to you?

Kaiser looked at him for a moment. *Beautiful*? He stepped forward and snapped the money out of LeClair's hand, then turned and walked down the hall and through the vestibule and out the front door into the snowy night, still gripping the cocktail glass, his face set like stone.

Janice dished up steaming hunks of Crock-Pot lasagna on the faded willow-pattern china and placed them before her sons. The table next to Kaiser's plate was spotted and ringed with water stains. His little sister had always insisted on sitting next to him. Kaiser used to cut her food, fill her glass, and at night he made sure she dunked her head fully under the water in the bath. They read together in the same big chair, Kaiser turning the pages of *Alexander and the Wind-Up Mouse*. He raised a fork of lasagna and blew on it to cool. His mother wiped a strand of hair off her forehead, her eyes glittering in the firelight.

Before Kaiser arrived, Bill picked through the woodpile out back and found some dry logs. Kodiak always liked to have the fire at his back while he ate, a holdover from his early days on the farm thawing out from morning chores. Bill was still in his uniform, just off his shift on the Northway, and he forked his lasagna quickly, using the beer to cool the hot noodles and sauce in his mouth. His hair was sandy gray at the temples, his face windburned pink. They ate in silence, as was their custom, just the crack of the fire and the clink and slurp of the lasagna,

Bill knocking his beer bottle down on the oak tabletop. Janice put her hands on their resting forearms.

So nice to have you both here.

Bill pushed his empty plate aside and drained his beer. He looked down the eye of the bottle as if examining a foreign instrument.

After dinner, Bill stood by the fire, making unneeded adjustments with the poker and talking about surge of drug traffic along the border. The main target was Quebecois MDMA, which had been pouring across the mountainous regions around the North Country. Federal agencies were putting together all the possible assets to stop it. The addition of drone fleets was significant, because unlike satellites they could get under the weather.

Some strong stuff going around, Bill said. Something they call Fleur-de-Lis. Makes people do crazy things.

Kaiser slouched in the deep pile of the overstuffed couch and stared out the black windows, his eyelids drooping. He kept waiting for Kodiak to emerge from the bathroom or to come in the back with an armload of wood, shrugging off his heavy coat, slapping at his cold arms.

The brothers walked out to their cars together after Janice was tucked in her spot on the couch with a tennis match on the TV. Bill opened the door to his cruiser and stretched, his back audibly popping.

So the accountant says the taxes are nearly paid up. You've been making payments?

Yeah.

Kaiser scanned the western horizon, the irregular peaks. He reflexively checked his watch and sorted the grid.

You ain't at the restaurant anymore?

No.

What're you doin' for money?

Working with Donnie LeClair. Debt collection. Outstanding rent, mostly.

Bill cocked his head, eyed him for a moment, laughed. He tossed his utility belt in the car and sat in the driver's seat.

Careful. Everybody knows LeClair has some shady shit going on.

At that moment a mote of blue light crested the peak to the south and traversed across the valley, moving quickly over the heads of the two brothers as they looked at each other, a glittering shard of night tailing away into the darkness.

Kaiser was sitting on a bench in the Washland Laundromat reading *The Demon-Haunted World*, his underwear and socks folded in neat stacks next to him. All of the clothes LeClair gave him were picked up each Monday by a laundry service, then returned the next day dry-cleaned and pressed, but LeClair didn't handle underwear and socks.

Deal with your own unmentionables, he said.

This was fine by Kaiser, but that meant he needed to do a load at Washland nearly every week as he only had six pairs of each. He liked to go in the early morning, before the laundromat was taken over by shrieking cheewees smoking menthols and carrying babies that looked boiled in seawater. It was quiet and empty in the morning, and the sun, when there was any, beamed through the large front window that looked out across Durkee Street and the narrow tributary of the Saranac River that wound through downtown. He liked to sit on the bench before the window and read Carl Sagan in that warm field of golden light. The experience was only diminished by the constant reek of vomit in the laundromat, as by late afternoon various local sots holed up there clutching their pints of vodka, napping under the benches or babbling about the innumerable injustices of their existence.

Kaiser was looking out over the sparkling creek, rimmed with ice, when Sydney walked by holding hands with a little girl. She happened to glance through the window just as he looked up and they both froze. The little girl cupped her hands to the frosty window.

Who's that?

Kaiser held up a hand. Sydney smiled and opened the door, pulling the little girl along.

Tom, she said.

She took his hand, then they embraced like awkward cousins. She picked up the little girl and perched her on her hip. The girl gazed at him with sleepy eyes.

This is Juliet.

Hello, Juliet.

Juliet held her nose.

Gross!

Let's go outside, Sydney said. It stinks in here.

Kaiser stacked his underwear and socks in a plastic bag and followed them out onto the bright sidewalk. Durkee Street was lined with cars passing through town, their tires making a shushing sound on the packed snow and ice. Kaiser slipped on a pair of aviator sunglasses and wound a merino wool scarf around his neck. He was wearing a black satin dress shirt, tapered wool slacks, and a long, charcoal cashmere coat. They walked down the street to the river. The Saranac River was only a few inches deep in most places, a rippled run over smooth stones that drained into the lake. The current was strong enough that it never fully froze, and the shoreline was rimmed with a clear crust of ice. In the summer months, the college students liked to float down the river in tubes, scraping their bottoms along the stones, dragging ice chests of beer through miniature rapids. Juliet stood on a picnic table by the river, tossing crusted hunks of snow into the water. Kaiser thanked Sydney for coming to his dad's funeral.

I sorta skipped out of the receiving line, she said. To be honest, I sorta freaked out.

I understand, he said.

I always liked Kodiak. Was he still tracking that radio thing, with the lady reading the numbers?

Yeah. More than fifty years.

Wow, she said. What happens now?

Kaiser tucked the trash bag of clean underwear under his arm, put his hands in his pockets. A frozen draft blew across the river, chilling his ankles. The Italian leather loafers didn't keep his feet warm. He shrugged.

I'm still tracking it.

Anything interesting happen?

Yeah, Kaiser said. It was always six numbers. After my father died it went to five.

Oh my god! Is that, like, a coincidence?

Maybe, Kaiser said. I don't know. How's it going with Phil?

Phil's okay. He's actually taking a break from hockey and moving back to Dannemora, his old house. His father passed away and left it to him. So we're moving out there . . .

Kaiser nodded.

She smiled and tugged on his scarf.

What's with these clothes? New look?

Sort of.

You're definitely the only dude in the North Country wearing stuff like this!

She crinkled up her face and laughed in that silent way he remembered from high school. The skin around her eyes was worn, but her color was bright and for a moment he saw her just as he had back then. It made him suddenly sad. There were a lot of things he wanted to tell her, things he should say.

We gotta go, Sydney said. Juliet is doing a puppet workshop at the library in a few minutes.

She started backing away from him, holding Sydney's hand.

We'll run into each other again soon, she said. Great seeing you, Tom.

They walked back up the sloping road to Durkee Street, Juliet skipping around the chunks of ice on the sidewalk, the morning sun casting them in silhouettes, paper cutouts against the white streets and the gray buildings of downtown. Kaiser stood there by the river, clutching his bag of underwear, shivering in his wet shoes. She was different. There was a quiet contentment to her. Her life was full.

When they reached Durkee Street the little girl turned and swung her arm overhead side to side, waving to him. Her thin, tinny voice echoed down the cold street.

Goodbye, Mr. Kaiser!

When Kaiser came into the Dry Dock the next evening, Sebastian was posted up at the bar threading chicken wings through the halo-cage on his head. The Dry Dock was a dead-end toilet bar, the jukebox all heavy-hitting classic rock, the pool table a giant ashtray, and nearly all of the regular clientele was noticeably pissed off. Despite this, it was popular with the students from the college who reveled in the "authentic" atmosphere. Kaiser ordered a Cuba libre.

I'm surprised this dump is still open, Kaiser said.

Yeah, Sebastian said. It's like my home.

Yeah, I knew some guys who practically lived here.

No man, I mean I *literally* live here. Percy, the owner? Couple months ago I went back in the kitchen and showed him how to make some righteous wings.

Sebastian pointed to his plate of half-eaten wings, lurid and steaming.

Now he lets me sleep on a cot in the back. Gets me out of my mom's place.

She doesn't care?

Fuck no. Too drunk to notice most of the time. I only go back around there to check on my little bro, Dylan.

Sebastian tried to wipe his mouth with a napkin. Kaiser pointed to some sauce on one of the vertical bars of his halo. At the other end of the room a few middle-aged women were laughing desperately, a pitcher of beer sloshing around on the table.

Dylan gets upset though, Sebastian said. When I don't come home.

How old is he?

Nine. Little stringy fucker. Different dad. When I get my shit together I'm gonna get him outta there.

The bartender brought Kaiser his drink and he squeezed the lime and took a deep pull. The jukebox was cranking AC/DC's "Back in Black."

Fucking A, man, Sebastian said, you must be the only dude in the North Country that drinks *rum*.

Kaiser felt a finger tap his shoulder blade and turned to see Emerson from the Artful Dodger. Her hair was pulled back and she was wearing another hippie-halter top, her bare shoulders shining in the dim light.

Hey.

He looked around as if to say: What are you doing *here*?

I'm here with some school friends, Emerson said. They love this place.

Behind her a table of prison guards from Dannemora were cranking their heads around to get a look at her ass, bottles of Labatt in their meaty fists.

Can't say I agree, she said. But whatever . . .

The wings, Sebastian said. *Are* the best in town.

Yeah, she said. I've heard that. But I don't eat meat, so . . .

Sebastain nodded sagely from the sternum, a set of short bows.

Vegetarian. Respect.

One of the bartenders came over, a skinny redheaded chap. Emerson lit up when she saw him and angled into the bar beside Kaiser.

'Scuse me, she said. Sorry.

The bartender bent over the bar, and they exchanged whispers. Sebastian stuck a drumstick in his mouth and rolled his eyes. Kaiser drained his glass and put in on the bar. The bartender hustled off down the bar.

Sorry, Emerson said. Jud's a good friend of mine.

She looked at Kaiser.

Anyway, she said. I guess I'd better get back to my friends over there.

Sebastian gnawed a wing, his eyes going back and forth between them.

Stop by the shop, she said. You know. If you wanna.

The bartender came back, and Kaiser raised his finger for another drink.

See you around, Emerson said, and twirled on her heel.

Sebastian sighed and flung a clean bone onto his plate in disgust.

Tha fuck is *wrong* with you, dude?

Kaiser watched Emerson walk back to three other girls perched at a tall table by the jukebox. They were all watching her, leaning over their beers. Maybe Sebastian is right, he thought. But what was he supposed to do? He didn't want to build new relationships in North Chazy. But that didn't mean he had to act like some kind of frigid asshole.

A group of young men came through the door. The first guy in was Scotty Marin, a ski parka and purple polo shirt, his collars popped. Three other guys with him, dressed in similar fashion. They joined a group near Emerson's table.

Hey, Sebastian said. What'd you wanna talk about?

I'll tell you in a minute, Kaiser said. Let's get out of here.

What?

Let's leave.

Dude. I just do not *understand* you.

Kaiser put some money on the bar and shepherded Sebastian through the room to the door. He hoped to slip behind them, but as they neared the table, Emerson raised her chin and gave Kaiser a tight little wave and Scotty turned to look. He smirked and slapped his buddy's arm. The nose had healed remarkably well.

Check out these two clowns, Scotty said.

Who's the giant fucking android?

That dude who used to cook at the Stagecoach, Scotty said.

Kaiser turned to Sebastian.

Used to?

Sebastian sniffed and drew himself up to his full height.

Didn't properly appreciate my culinary skills, man. Fuck that place.

Scotty's friends watched with expectant faces.

My cousin is looking for you, Scotty said. He's a cop. He's gonna fuck you up.

His posture was aggressive, putting one shoulder into Kaiser's path to the door. Kaiser was genuinely surprised at the audacity. He tried to calculate the gain for Scotty.

He can't be much of a cop, Kaiser said, if he can't find me in *this* town.

Fuck you, Scotty said. Fucking townie loser.

Behind Scotty he could see Emerson and her friends, watching with alarmed faces. Scotty's boys were changing the spacing of their arms, giving themselves room. Kaiser felt the rum singing in his veins. He was feeling quick and brutal.

You don't have to try and provoke me, Kaiser said. If you'll step outside, I'll break all your asses, one at a time.

Kaiser stepped forward and everyone shifted back. Scotty's eyes shifted side to side, trying to gauge the level of commitment of his pals. Kaiser put his finger up to Scotty's face, poked him hard in the nose, making him wince and twist away.

Starting with *you*.

Kaiser turned and walked to the door. Something was said behind him, an exchange between the boys and Sebastian, but he ignored it.

Outside it was deeply cold, his breath billowing in heavy gusts. Sebastian came through the door carrying their drinks. Through the window, Kaiser watched Scotty and his friends debating, but it didn't last long. They sat down and signaled for a waitress.

They ain't coming out, dude, Sebastian said.

He handed Kaiser his drink. In the bar, everyone had gone back to whatever they were doing. The girls at Emerson's table were still there, but Emerson was gone.

I gotta say, Sebastian said, I was definitely hoping homeboy was gonna throw down.

Sebastian tried to light a cigarette and walked to the corner to get out of the wind. Kaiser was still standing in front of the window, looking in, watching Scotty pour himself a beer from a pitcher.

Dude, Sebastian whispered hoarsely. C'mere. It's your girl.

Kaiser walked over and looked around the corner into the alley. There was a set of dumpsters and, on the steps by the back door, Emerson and Jud the bartender were sharing a joint. Emerson was leaning against the wall. He could tell by the way she leaned into Jud that they were very close. She was wearing sandals, her shoulders bare in the cold, and when she exhaled, she smiled, handed the joint back, and leaned her head back against the brick, and the single floodlight at the end of the alley made her hair beautiful and strange. He suddenly thought of LeClair and his landscapes, compositions of frozen life at a distance. *What do you find to be beautiful in this life?*

You okay, dude?

Kaiser took the cigarette from Sebastian and took a drag.

I'm good.

Sebastian nodded, a slight bow from the midsection, because it was all he could do.

That night Kaiser dreamed of his father standing on a field of ice in his bathrobe, holding a shotgun and aiming it at the sky. He was pivoting around, as if searching for a target. The sky was deep black and without any stars or moon. Kodiak doesn't fire, he just keeps jerking the gun around, trying to cover the entire horizon.

Can't you see them? Kodiak says. They're beautiful!

When he turns and the bathrobe gaps open Kaiser can see the wide slot in his father's chest, dark and wet and endless, filled with moving points of light.

It's beautiful, he says. Can't you see it?

EMERSON

The note on the door of the auditorium announced that Dr. Sterne's class was canceled. A group of students were in the hallway, and Emerson overheard them say that Dr. Sterne's wife, Dr. Jansky, had gone missing. A pair of girls showed up, and seeing the note, they pumped their fists *yes!* then clattered down the hall in a jangle of boots, purses, long down-filled coats. There were only a couple weeks of classes left before exams and the holiday break.

Emerson went outside and stood on the steps. The sun was bright, and lumps of dirty snow were scattered across the quad like small continents on a map. She wrapped her scarf around the lower half of her face and watched a boy chasing a piece of paper blowing toward Main Street. She was thinking about Dr. Sterne and his wife. She'd taken Dr. Jansky's Geology 101 course and spent the semester terrified of this woman who paced the front of the classroom with militant purpose. Dr. Jansky occasionally came to the Artful Dodger to grade papers, working with a pot of green tea for a couple hours before slipping out again. She was there the first time Kaiser walked in and chugged a hot coffee. A seasoned intelligence seemed to radiate from Dr. Jansky. She seemed an unlikely person to go missing.

Emerson took Dr. Sterne's Intro to Art History when she was a sophomore and enjoyed the course so much she signed up for his Art

History 201, Masters of European Art. Dr. Sterne zipped through a couple hundred years of Western art in a few weeks, landing on the nineteenth century around midterm, but they never moved forward in time after that. They did six weeks on J. M. W. Turner. Emerson loved his long, meandering disquisitions on Turner, the light-drenched slides washing over the auditorium full of sleepy undergrads, scenes of tragedy and triumph baking under a southern sun.

Dr. Sterne's office was in Cash Hall, one of the oldest buildings on campus. The walls of his narrow office were dominated by large prints of Turner and jammed bookshelves. His desk covered in papers, test booklets, stuffed folders, with an occasional book as a paperweight.

You have a perceptive eye, Dr. Sterne told her once.

She had come to talk about her term paper. She wrote a transcendentalist interpretation of Turner's *Snow Storm: Hannibal and His Army Crossing the Alps*, and had gotten an A–. He flipped through her paper quickly, his boots resting on the desk.

The conflation of Turner's rendering of alpine weather with the transcendental concept of the Oversoul is . . . a stretch. But still impressive.

Dr. Sterne put his hands together and gazed at an indeterminate spot on the floor, just to the left of Emerson's feet.

I want to say I appreciate your participation in class. Your attempts to link the work we're studying with other types of art. It takes imagination and courage.

He looked up at her, his soft eyebrows coming up, and something warm sparked in Emerson's chest.

Standing on the quad in the wind, she tried to imagine Dr. Sterne in his anxiety. In the North Country, people went missing often, usually showing up a couple days later at a cousin's house sleeping off a serious bender or trapped in Quebec without a passport. But not people like Dr. Jansky. Emerson imagined Dr. Sterne combing the countryside with police and dogs, wearing his heavy boots, wool scarf tight around his neck, little pink blotches of exertion in his cheeks as he clambered through a field, terrified of finding his wife's body.

Many of the student houses on Main Street had esoteric names from the long history of the college. The Cat House, the Steak House, the Graffiti House. Emerson's, for unknown reasons, was called the Slaughterhouse. Located across the street from the quad, it had a wraparound porch that listed to the left like the deck of ship. One tiny bathroom, a terrifying unfinished basement with a coal chute, and a large pot-growing operation in the attic run by the tall hippie girl in the room next to Emerson's. Another English major lived in the house, a pretentious twat named Matthew, who often stood on the porch in an old tweed blazer and smoked a pipe. A Filipino girl named Lynn on the first floor collected the rent and utility checks, and then there was Emerson's good friend Jud, who lived in a converted dayroom at the back of the house, where he spent most his time in his sleeping bag on the floor listening to electronic music.

Jud used to be a philosophy major, but now he devoted all his time to smoking weed, making music mixes, and working as a bartender at the Dry Dock. He was a freckled, slender boy, with an unruly mess of red hair that he sometimes twisted into white-boy dreads. Emerson liked hanging out with Jud because he was earnest and kind, without a trace of irony or sarcasm. Jud basically made two kinds of mixtapes: for parties, and for Emerson. His mixes for her were thinly disguised odes of longing and desire. She understood that Jud carried his heart around like a bird in a cage, hoping to proffer it to her. She had made her feelings clear, making a point to occasionally sleep with some douchebag—usually some clove-smoking, ponytailed, wanna-be-poet—so it wasn't as if she was deceiving anyone. Jud seemed happy, and the way she saw it, they were engaged in a mutually beneficial arrangement.

Emerson walked across the quad to Main Street, where the Slaughterhouse sat like a broken-down old dog. On the porch, Matthew the

English major was puffing on his pipe, staring at her. *Oh, god.* She turned up Main and walked up to court square and the Dodger. Hanging around Drummy wasn't normally good for lifting your spirits, but he was a disciplined reader of the newspaper and had an ear for local gossip.

She made herself a latte and put the question to him as he worked the crossword at the register. He pushed the newspaper across the counter. There was a front-page story below the fold: "College Professor Missing."

> An Ausable College professor has been missing since she left her house Monday morning on a cross-country skiing run. Dr. Ellen Jansky is a professor of geology, specializing in the study of lake formations, and she has been at the college since 1993. She reportedly routinely skied a route that took her northeast toward Kelly Bay then continuing north past Fort Montgomery near the international border. Her husband, Dr. Laurence Sterne, a professor of art history at the college, reported her as missing when he came home Monday afternoon and found she hadn't returned. The North Chazy police department is treating this as a missing persons situation and do not suspect foul play. Search parties following Dr. Jansky's route noted that there was evidence of several possible large ice breakups near the middle of the lake.

The snow was blowing again, slanting sideways in the wind. Two students silently played chess in a corner booth. Drummy tapped the crossword with his pen. Emerson rinsed out her glass in the sink and went in the back to put it in the washer. She kept seeing Dr. Jansky drifting weightlessly, descending through dark water. It was hot in the kitchen and Emerson unzipped her fleece and opened the back door. The slice of sky above the alley was white and expressionless.

SYDNEY & PHIL

As a boy, the wall seemed just another part of the landscape, like hills or a forest. Now, after being away for a few years, its giant face was a kind of massive intrusion that didn't match Phil's childhood memories. *It couldn't have been like this.*

The porch was bowed in the middle where the tread of human life had worn a trough to the door. North Country winters had blasted the clapboard walls gray white. The front windows were dark, and Phil instinctively looked to the attic gable window, as if he might glimpse his own angry face, twelve years old, glaring back at him. On the street, the plows pushed up a knobby wall of dirty snow about three feet high, which Phil vaulted, then waded through the snow to the porch. There was a wad of mail behind the screen door, a month's worth of hunting catalogs, credit card offers, supermarket flyers.

The furniture stood layered with dust. The sameness of the inside of the house was comforting, and unlike the wall, it seemed exactly like it was in his youth. *Yes, this is where I lived.* Every piece in the same position. There was a dark smudge on the ceiling directly above the kitchen table where his father sat and smoked cigarettes every day for more than forty years. Phil knew that there was another in the den above the recliner, an evolving murky shape that he watched grow and change as a child.

A dead cat lay stretched out in the corner, tongue lolling, hair matted flat. Phil dumped his bags and set about opening the windows to try air out the fetid cat stink and the other odor that could only be described as cigarettes and dying old man.

The first night in the house, Sydney locked herself in the bathroom, knelt on the chipped white tiles, and dry heaved into the toilet. Phil was asleep in the bedroom. She cried quietly for a few minutes, then using toilet paper she wiped down all the surfaces. She had been dreaming about Tom Kaiser walking the streets of North Chazy in a heavy snowfall. She drank a glass of water, settled herself on the edge of the bathtub, and began to pray for forgiveness and guidance.

Their homecoming hadn't gone the way she hoped. When she came to the door, Phil was sleeping on the couch, a half-empty twelve pack of Labatt on the coffee table, a takeout container of chicken wing bones on the floor, and a dead cat in the corner. The house stank like wing sauce and death. Phil jumped up and kissed her and gave her a big hug, but he didn't seem as excited to see Juliet. He didn't even offer to hold her until later when Sydney brought it up. He said he was afraid, that he wasn't sure if he knew how to do it.

As usual, he had bought Sydney gifts. A small flat-screen TV and some DVDs, movies that he knew she liked: *The Fisher King*, *Far and Away*, *The Last of the Mohicans*. And the complete set of the *Peanuts* movies.

For Juliet and this place, Phil said. Our new home.

Sydney had been in the house before, years ago, but now it seemed especially forlorn, and she found a new vein of sympathy for the boy that grew up here. Sydney's parents lived on the far end of the prison wall, a dozen blocks back to the south, in a solidly middle-class neighborhood with grass in the yards in the summer, houses covered in plastic siding, where kids rode their bikes until after twilight like pack animals. The top of the wall a distant mesa over the treetops.

When she came downstairs the next morning, Phil was spraying down the counters with bleach. He had a bag full of cleaning supplies on the table, a mop and bucket, another twelve pack in the fridge along with some ground beef and buns, and later they fried patties in the skillet. They ate them dry. Phil had forgotten to buy any condiments.

The North Chazy Elementary School had a spare office they kept empty for DSS to interview children during the school day. Sydney stopped by the school nearly every day to speak with her assigned kids. She hung up her coat and hat and drank a cup of coffee, reviewing the case file for Eileen and Bianca Leroux, ages five and seven. Their mother, Kara, was twenty-four years old, living with the kids' grandmother and working in the dairy cooler at Yando's Big Market. Sydney was assigned to their case last year when the girl's father, Saul, moved in with them, and the girls started showing up to school with suspicious marks on their bodies.

Saul was a couple years behind Sydney at North Chazy High School until he quit school and had three kids with two different mothers, including Eileen and Bianca. He managed to pick up contractor work occasionally, but when winter weather locked up construction projects, Saul mostly lurked in the basement with a bottle and his Xbox, playing long hours of *Grand Theft Auto.*

Sydney sat the girls on the futon couch in the office with a handful of jelly beans. She asked them to roll up their sleeves so she could inspect the skin on their arms, neck, and face more closely. The girls had decent color, solid weight, but the state of their hygiene and clothes needed documentation. Eileen was a voluble and lively kindergartner with a thin sheet of dishwater hair she kept pinned back in a simple ponytail. As she chewed the jelly beans and answered Sydney's questions, her knees bounced with manic energy. Bianca kept her straight hair parted in the middle, forming a curtain frame to her face.

Has your dad been home?

Yeah, Eileen said.

Do you have fun with your dad? Is he nice?

Yeah. He's funny sometimes.

Bianca?

She lowered her face and shook her head.

Does he get mad at you?

A little, Eileen said.

Does he yell at you?

Yeah. But not, like, *bad*. He gets mad at Bianca a lot though.

Sydney took subtle notes on her clipboard while maintaining a steady gaze at the girls. If they became aware that she was taking notes, they would likely either stop talking or launch into maddening defenses of their guardians, especially if they were being abused. The victim almost always expressed a powerful desire to stay with the locus of the abuse.

Why does he get mad at Bianca?

Um, when she bothers him, Eileen said. Like when he's playing *GTA* and she wants to sit in his lap. Stuff like that.

Does he yell? Or does he do anything else?

He makes lots of noise. Throws some things. He smashed the big ashtray against the wall. *Boom*!

Eileen made little wavy movements with her fingers to designate an explosion. Sydney put another handful of jelly beans into Eileen's lap.

Why did he do that?

Because Bianca died.

Bianca hissed something at her little sister. The knuckles of her fists were bone white. Outside the office a class was moving down the hall to the cafeteria, their shrill voices echoing. Sydney said nothing for a moment. She kept her face serene. She wrote the words on her clipboard with faint, small movements.

Bianca died.

What do you mean, Bianca died?

She died, Eileen said. He choked her and she died.

Sydney's hairline stung with perspiration. Eileen chewed a mouthful of jelly beans, still looking at Sydney. *Hold her gaze, don't let her go.*

You saw this happen? When she died?

Yeah. He was pretty mad. I was watching from the stairs.

Eileen tried to laugh, the small kind of fake laugh kids do when they desperately want something to be funny. Sydney took a quick glance at the clock. In the parking lot outside, a small boy trudged between parked cars, shielding his face from the howling wind with one bare hand.

Don't, Bianca hissed.

Tears began to roll down Bianca's face, and Sydney reached across and took hold of her trembling hands, still holding Eileen's gaze.

He choked her with his hands? Show me how.

Eileen put both her hands up around her neck, opened her eyes wide, then stuck out her tongue. Then she flopped her head to the side and closed her eyes. Sydney let herself exhale. This was a protection issue for certain, and a call for foster care intervention. They would have to do the notification visit with a police officer. Kara would be devastated, and she would never forgive Sydney for it. Eileen was now watching her sister, and her face was twisting up as she began to realize what she had done.

But it's okay, she whined. Because she's not dead! Right?

Her eyes filled with tears, her voice desperate, pleading.

She *was* dead, but then she came back to life!

The next day, Sydney laid out a stack of diapers and wipes on the changing table, filled two sippy cups in the fridge with milk, quartered a cup of grapes, and set out a bowl of animal crackers. Phil was picking at the wall paint in the kitchen. He was determined to repaint the whole interior.

If she gets wild, she said, there's also frozen yogurt in the freezer.

Juliet sat on the living room floor in a shaft of weak sunlight, playing with a cardboard box. Sydney slung her bag over her shoulder and paused at the door to watch her daughter.

She will put stuff in her mouth, she said.

Phil was spreading drop cloths around the base of the walls. He turned to look at her, his eyes squinting. He tore open a package of foam rollers.

I got it, Syd, he said. Have fun.

Brett came out of the double-wide and walked unsteadily to Sydney's car wearing oversized sunglasses. It was ten in the morning, and Sydney could tell she was still wearing last night's makeup.

Big night?

Brett took out a cigarette and held it in her lips, a lighter in her hand. She closed her eyes.

I'm still rolling, Brett said. Haven't slept.

You meet someone?

Oh yeah. He had the most amazing place. It was down nine, past the beach, one of those condos? It was all white and sleek and shit. Like something you'd see in Miami.

A college guy?

Oh, c'mon, Syd. Don't do that.

What?

They drove for a few blocks in silence. The first few years Sydney was back from college, she did a lot of partying with Brett and her old crew. Regular happy hours at the Monopole, the Last Resort, and the Dry Dock, a gang of her fellow DSS caseworkers cramming shitty margaritas down their throats in a desperate attempt to bury the emotional anguish. But it all just thinned her out, made her feel weaker, and when Juliet came along, she pretty much gave it up.

The streets were mostly deserted. A prison transport bus was pulled up to the main gate, a couple guards with clipboards conferring. Through the chicken-wire windows, they could see a single prisoner in the orange jumpsuit sitting in the last row of the bus, looking out the back window like a small child on his way to school.

Nicky had the closed sign on the door, but Sydney could see people moving behind the blinds. Inside Shear Madness, the only local beauty parlor in town, the girls were drinking mimosas, standing around Shelly, who was reclined in a chair while Nicky applied an exfoliating mask to her face. When they came in, Shelly smiled and sat up to embrace them, her mask cracking. Sydney was astonished at the transformation; Shelly was a dark-haired gal who was clearly designed to carry a fair bit of weight, broad shoulders and hips, big feet, just like everyone else in her large Greek family. Lauren and Tara gave Sydney hugs, and they exchanged the usual rote compliments. Lauren was an administrative assistant at the college, and Tara waited tables at night and cared for her six-year-old boy. When Brett took the bottle of vodka out of her purse their faces lit up. While the mask set, Nicky gave Shelly a manicure and pedicure.

Everybody was rolling, Brett said. We were all dancing. It was wild. There was this one guy, named Scotty? So hot. They were all wearing duck boots and these matching blue jackets? Anyway, we go to Scotty's condo on the lake and this place is like, tricked out. All white and low-slung furniture and stuff, like a supervillain. The floor was heated from underneath. Full bar. A lot of E, that good stuff that's hard to get. With the little flower on it? I was like, *oooh yeah.*

Tell me you didn't sleep with one of them, Lauren said.

Brett grimaced and topped off her glass with more orange juice.

No. I didn't. I messed around with this guy Scotty a bit, like in his room? He was pretty strange. We were wearing headphones the whole time.

Wait, *what*?

Yeah, he had this whole setup, Brett said. Two sets of headphones. It was like a ritual or something.

Oh my god, Lauren said. What kind of music?

Some kind of techno, Brett said. It was pretty intense.

Outside the sun fully cleared the prison wall, and condensation beaded on the front window. Sydney watched a guard in the west tower crank open his window and prop it open, his breath steaming in the air. Crude graffiti spotted the lower reaches of the wall, various tags by local boys, abstract shapes, short proclamations. Sydney stared at one that said *No Horizon.*

She suddenly thought of Juliet, back at the house with Phil. She checked her phone and debated calling, but the girls were laughing at something Shelly said so she put her phone away and took a sip of the warm vodka and orange juice. She watched these four women, all born and raised in the area like her, and suddenly felt like she didn't *believe* any of them. Lauren, a tall and stately woman, tried to laugh along, but Sydney could see in her eyes that she wasn't even present. Tara was watching Nicky work on Shelly's toes while fingering the tattoo that wound around her collarbone, the name of her little boy, Ethan, and a Bible verse. Tara hadn't been to church in ten years, and when Sydney tried to talk to her about it, she always claimed her Saturday-night shift kept her up too late.

A phrase intoned in her mind, a voice that wasn't her own, the voice of a young girl:

What will happen to us?

They went to the Bowl Mart because it was the only place serving beer and food at that hour. It was empty except for a group of old men at the bar and so they sat at a table and got pitchers of Labatt and an order of deluxe nachos. The lanes were shining, the polished floors reflecting the fluorescent strip lighting, and they poured the foaming beer into glasses and lit cigarettes. Shelly beamed, shifting her new body around on her chair. Nicky put a series of Madonna songs on the jukebox, and "True Blue" pumped through the empty bowling alley. Lauren drained her beer.

Have you run into Tom Kaiser?

Yeah, the other day, Sydney said. He was at the laundromat downtown. We just talked for a second. I went to his dad's funeral.

Oh my god, Tara said, Phil must be *pissed*. Does he know Kaiser's back?

I don't think so.

You'd better say something. What if he just runs into him on the street? Or finds out you talked to him?

Sydney drank some of her beer and watched her friends, drinking and smoking with a kind of manic desperation. She pretended to be dismissive, but in reality, she *was* afraid of what Phil might do. Or what Tom Kaiser might do. Some people said he did something terrible in

Afghanistan and was locked up in a secret government prison. She had a hard time believing that. The Tom Kaiser she knew always seemed at a distance, even when he held her in his arms. But he wasn't a terrible person. At the laundromat, he seemed startled to see her, but he still had that far-off look, that distant air about him. Tara topped off everyone's beers and the ashtray brimmed with butts stained with lipstick. Sydney felt like she was watching her friends from the other end of a long tunnel.

What will happen to us?

The voice rang out again and when she recognized it as her daughter, Juliet, years from now, older, sitting in a room very much like this one, Sydney had to turn her face away. Something from deep in her chest rolled out of her body like a convulsive shudder.

The nachos arrived, a tray of chips covered with ground beef, onions, and melted cheese. Shelly was piling chips and cheese on her plate. Brett snorted loudly, her arms folded over her chest, a belligerent look on her face.

Jesus fucking *Christ*, Shelly, Brett said. You trying to pack it right back on?

Nicky opened his mouth, and then covered it with his hand. Everyone went quiet, and Shelly stared down at her plate.

Brett, Lauren hissed, and then looked away.

"Borderline" was playing and one of the old men at the bar stood and did an awkward parody of a little hip-shimmy. Shelly pushed her chair back and rose slowly, her eyes glassy. She turned and wobbled unsteadily toward the bathroom. Sydney grabbed Brett's wrist.

Hey, she said. What's going on? What are you doing?

Brett turned to her and her face broke into an awful expression that Sydney had never seen before. Sydney stood and pulled her into an embrace.

It's okay, she said. It's okay.

I don't know, Brett whispered in her ear. I don't know what I'm doing.

Juliet stepped in the pan of paint. She looked down where her bare foot disappeared into the light blue pool, puzzled by this new development. She was wearing a long-sleeved cotton dress with green and white stripes. The top of her head a thin swirl of red blond, with patches of longer hair curling near her ears.

Shit.

Phil started looking for a place to put the dripping roller down. Then Juliet put her other foot in the paint pan and looked up at him. Her mother's eyes and mouth, and Phil's squashed nose. She would be tall, like her father. Juliet raised both her arms up, hands clenching and unclenching. This was the first time she had ever signaled that she wanted Phil to pick her up. He set the roller down and lifted her, her feet trailing paint across the floor and onto his shirt as he brought her to his shoulder. Juliet put her arms around his neck. Outside the prison entry buzzer sounded and the metallic ring of locks and hinges opening, the sound of diesel engine roaring by. The noon horn, two short tones, signaling the start of the midday exercise yard session. Phil wrapped his arms around her, squeezing her tiny torso. He could feel her lips moving silently on his skin below his ear.

Phil sat her on the edge of the kitchen sink to wash the paint off her feet. Juliet kicked at the water, holding a wad of his shirt in her first. He'd taped off one wall and gotten a dozen swathes of paint applied with the roller. That would have to be it until Sydney got back, he decided. Working the rabbit ears, he was able to tune in to a cooking show on the local PBS station. He sat on the couch with a beer while Juliet stood on the other side of the coffee table regarding him with a defiant gaze, handling a small pile of coins that Phil gave her to play with.

Earlier that day, a man named Fortier from the prison human resources department came to the door. After some rather unconvincing condolences for his father, Fortier offered him a job. Phil sifted through the papers that Fortier gave him, detailing the offer. They would bring him in as a Class 2 Correctional Officer, six weeks paid training, thirty dollars an hour with regular scaled advancement, forty-hour weeks, available overtime, union contract, full benefits. Half-pay retirement in twenty years. On a Post-it note, Fortier had written: *Just walk in Phil. We will take care of everything.*

The older Italian woman on the TV show ladled creamy sauce onto star-shaped pasta. Phil thought about his father in his prison blues and cap, staggering across the street in the morning, carrying his lunch pail, a cigarette jammed in his face. Then in the evenings passed out on the porch, a pint of Crown Royal in his lap, face locked in a pained grimace. When he slept, his father audibly ground his teeth, wearing the enamel down until the nerves were exposed. He had to get drunk to sleep through the agonizing pain. He looked like a man who was trapped in a world he didn't understand. Not me, Phil always said. That'll *never* be me. Juliet screeched and swiped all of the coins onto the floor. We should get this place really fixed up, Phil thought. Not just paint. Like a proper home.

Mommy? Juliet said.

Hire professionals. Landscaping. A swing set in back.

Mommy?

Juliet, Phil said, you probably don't really know who I am. But I want you to know something.

Juliet lunged for his beer and he wrestled it away and set it out of reach. She stomped a foot angrily and held out a fist. The floor shuddered as the pipes under the house opened their valves. He slid off the couch and sat on the floor.

So it's like this, Phil said. I feel one way on the inside. And another way on the outside.

He reached across the table and held her hands. They were warm and damp.

And I'm hoping maybe you love me, too, on the inside. Maybe it's a secret? When we hold hands like this, we can feel it.

Juliet was still, and just for a moment there was a flash over her face that was something like instant maturity, the light from the window falling on her just so, and Phil was able to see the young woman she would be, how she would look when she grew up, and *oh dear god* he thought his heart would shatter. She opened her mouth and began to laugh.

Phil dug out her snowsuit and boots and they spent the next hour floundering in the drifts below the porch, building small creatures with the damp snow under the eaves, a forest of icicles, a garden of crystalline wonders. Juliet never seemed to notice the impassive wall that kept the horizon a white mystery, how it loomed over them all.

KAISER

Kaiser was kicking in the door of a trailer, deep in the coiled innards of Wiggletown. Sebastian stood behind him in the yard, wearing a pair of wool Prada slacks that rode up over his leather motorcycle boots, and a wool suit jacket with the collars up. Kaiser lent him the clothes, but Sebastian couldn't wear the shirts because of his halo-head, so underneath he wore old T-shirt that said: *Catch and Release All Finless Brown Trout.* He'd been smoking blunts since breakfast.

The door was more solid than it looked, and Kaiser was getting tired. Inside a man named Gorman was screaming in a frantic, high-pitched voice.

Leave me alone! I'm warning you!

It was seven in the morning, and most of the residents of Wiggletown would not stir for several more hours. Kaiser kicked the door again. He turned to Sebastian.

You wanna do something here? Kaiser said. Or are you fucking useless?

Sebastian drew himself up to his full height.

I am a person of value, man. I'm a human being with skills and talents.

What?

You don't think I can do anything, Sebastian said. You probably don't even think I can *cook.*

Kaiser held out his arms, gesturing at the circle of ragged trailers, the muddy gravel road, the white trees.

Look around, you stupid sonofabitch. Do I look like I'm in a fucking position to judge anyone? About anything?

Sebastian shrugged, walked up the steps, and put his heavy boot through the middle of the door.

Now we're cooking! Kaiser said.

Then there was a deafening blast, and an explosion of wood splinters and Sebastian was launched backward off the steps. Kaiser was on one knee with his hands over his ears. He looked over to Sebastian, lying on his back, his head turned toward Kaiser, his eyes wide open. There was a slight blur to everything, trails coming off the points of Sebastian's halo, the tips of Kaiser's fingers as he snapped the .357 out of the shoulder holster. The front door had a star-shaped hole in it the size of a basketball. He stumbled around to the back of the trailer where he saw the naked backside of Gorman galloping through the tall grass, a duffel bag slung around his shoulders. Kaiser sighted the pistol, the hammer right down the middle of Gorman's back. He held it there as the preacher leaped like a deer into the woods at the base of the mountain.

Sebastian's T-shirt was torn away and a tight spread of quail-load peppered his midsection. He was awake and trying to look at his torso, but his head was wrenched at an odd angle, the bolt points in his skull twisted and bleeding. Kaiser ripped some sheets off the preacher's bed and wrapped him up and applied direct pressure with his hands, the blood bubbling between his fingers. Sebastian's eyes watered and he gasped, trying to reach his wounds with his fingers, but Kaiser batted them away.

You're good, Kaiser said. I got you.

They took Sebastian away in the ambulance, and Kaiser spent the next couple hours talking to the police. Gorman had several warrants, and he wouldn't get far, they said, especially with no clothes on. Kaiser sat on the front steps, hands cuffed behind his back. They were saying how lucky Sebastian was that the load in the gun wasn't something heavier, like buckshot or slugs. At that range it would have cut him in half. The dense weave of the high-quality Irish wool coat slowed the tiny shot considerably.

There was no mention of charges against Kaiser, and it seemed the officers believed that he was only collecting back rent on behalf of Mr. LeClair. They told him that there was a deputy who wanted to talk to him and after that they would let him go. Then everyone left.

The deputy led him around the trailer into the field behind. The sun had warmed the frozen stalks of grass that poked through the wet snow and the air smelled fresh and clean.

That's far enough, the deputy said. Turn around.

When Kaiser turned, the deputy shot him with two taser darts, one in his chest and the other sinking into his neck. The electric surge locked his head back and buckled his knees. He closed his eyes and everything went white, then several rolling waves of pain, as if his muscles were being folded up. Then it relaxed and Kaiser was on his knees, panting and gagging, saliva hanging from his mouth.

You better be more careful, the deputy said. Out of respect for your brother, I'm gonna take it easy.

He unsnapped his nightstick and with a short stroke he clipped Kaiser on the side of the head, dropping him face-first into the muddy snow. Then he removed the handcuffs.

Stay the fuck away from the Marin kid.

Kaiser blinked as blood ran into his eye. The frozen grass crackled in the wind, and it seemed like it was evening, the dimming tide of light, crimson spreading across the valley and mountains. He was thinking about Emerson, the way the light wrapped around her hair in that alley, the slope and curve of her neck. The silhouette of Sydney and Juliet on Durkee Street, waving in the morning light. He was thinking about how it all comes down to something so simple as a blow to the head, a missed signal, a falling satellite, a momentary failure.

That evening, he sat in front of Kodiak's humming radio set wearing his headphones. He was playing a composite of the number lady's broadcasts, tracking the satellite relays as she bounced the signal off the rim of the world. Maybe there were others, solitary listeners, spread over the planet. There had to be at least *one* person out there that the numbers were intended for.

Kaiser's ear throbbed and he had a tumescent nodule on his neck where the taser dart hit him. He was exhausted. The garble of voices and numbers swelled into a kind of white noise, and eventually he laid his head down on the table and fell asleep.

He dreamed he was a young boy, running, holding a rope tied to a sled that rattled behind him. A deep set of booming sounds from far off. An enormous black shape passed under him, and he stumbled and dropped the rope.

He awoke with a start, the headphones roaring with white noise. He threw them off and walked to the bathroom to rinse off his face. He fingered his ear, the bottom lobe nearly split. There was a crimson spray of Sebastian's blood across his shirt. The apartment building was dead quiet, just the creak of his own body weight on the floor.

Something beautiful.

He put on a jacket, snatched the wool blanket off his bed, and left the apartment.

Court square was still, the last bit of sun leaking over the westward side above the Artful Dodger. Kaiser zipped up his jacket and checked his watch. He looked at the sky, growing purple, the faint smoke of clouds trailing away over the lake. It was going to be a clear evening. He closed his eyes for a few moments and sorted the grid, the trajectories, the timing.

The coffee shop was empty except for Emerson, sitting on the stool by the register, reading a book. OMD's "Enola Gay" drifted through the shop. She looked up and watched him walk across the long room. It seemed like she was trying to decide whether she should smile.

Hi, he said.

Hi.

She looked at his ear, the dried blood in his hair. Her eyes crinkled with worry.

It's no big deal, he said.

Okay.

Hard Times Special, please.

She filled a mug with coffee and set it down in front of him. Kaiser picked it up and took a deep drink. It was rich and hot and tasted wonderful. He put the cup down and they looked at each other for a few moments. Emerson looked at the blanket rolled up under his arm. She put her book down, marking her page.

Is everything okay?

Would you like to see a satellite? he asked. Actually, two of them.

Sure.

He kept looking at her. He began to understand the depth and color of her eyes, and she did not look away. She smiled and cocked her head, waiting for the punchline.

Are you *serious*?

Yes, he said.

Where? How?

Right now. Will you come with me?

She looked around the shop, the dark front windows, then back at him.

Yes.

They walked out across the street and onto the lawn of the courthouse. He checked his watch again. RUDAK AO-30 would enter from the southeast just over the Artful Dodger, then thirteen seconds later, RUDAK AO-65, traveling a bit faster, would enter from the east, over the empty brick building where the variety store used to be. Kaiser laid out the blanket on the frozen grass. He lay down on one side.

Lie down here, he said. Hurry.

She lay down beside him, both of them staring up at the purpling sky. You have to let your eyes adjust, he said. Keep them wide open. Let them fill with light.

She was quiet and still, and he hoped that she wasn't afraid. He hoped she trusted him. After a moment he looked at his watch, then stretched out his arm and pointed to the top of the coffee shop.

That corner there, he said. Now.

The satellite, RUDAK AO-30 emerged, a faint blip of blue light, and it slowly moved north, a subtle flicker.

Oh my god, she said.

A satellite is more visible at dusk, he said, when there is light to reflect. Keep looking at it. You can see the parts of it, the solar array.

As their eyes adjusted the shape of it began to emerge, and as it moved overhead the fading sunlight caught more of the reflective surfaces, playing over the various protrusions, and the true artificiality of the thing became clear.

Now over there, Kaiser said, and pointed as another light emerged, RUDAK AO-65, slightly larger and faster. A satellite intersection was when two satellites enter the evening sky and intersect at an exact point. Of course they are at different orbital altitudes, so they don't collide, but considering the magnitude of the open expanse of sky, it is a remarkable occurrence.

When the trajectory became clear, Emerson gasped. Kaiser found himself amazed, once again, at these objects hurtling around the earth, propelled purely by gravity and initial momentum. Started with an initial push, then something elemental takes over. Something that would go on forever.

Sharing the experience created a feeling that was gratifying for reasons Kaiser didn't understand. He had watched a thousand satellites cross the sky. This felt different. Is this what I find beautiful?

The satellites arched across the sky, closing on each other. As they drew closer, she reached out and grabbed his hand and at the moment of intersection he felt her body stiffen, a sharp intake of breath, then she fell silent. They watched the satellites continue on and disappear over the roofs of their hometown. They lay there holding hands as the purple sky turned black and the pinpricks of stars burned through, the milky slash of the galaxy stretching over them.

The other soldiers slept, their heads lolling in concentric circles, spittle bubbling on their lips. The shuddering din of velocity and aerodynamics. A glowing red light at the door, the bay dimly lit by a strip of weak lights down the center aisle, a shaking crate of boy-killers in the dark. The Rangers were in two rows on either side of the fuselage, twenty-one men with chutes, gear, and weapons strapped across their fronts and their cargo pockets bulging with bullets, hypos, and chocolate. They had been in the air for three hours since they lifted off the sticky tarmac of a temporary field surrounded by bony black goats outside a city of minarets. The jerking drops of the plane rattled Kaiser's hip bones. He was in the aft section, just three spaces from the stick pusher, the only one in the gray fatigues and black helmet favored by SOF. He studied the face of the Ranger seated opposite, his face slack, eyes closed. A bubble of snot in one nostril that inflated and deflated as he snored. His name was Tucker, a Mormon kid from Wyoming, part of the QRF squad that was supposed to escort Kaiser to a forward operating unit. A tall, reedy blond kid, eyes a little too close together. During their training for the operation Tucker bunked with Kaiser, shadowed him in the field. Tucker carried books of poetry in his rucksack, and when they dug their "Ranger graves" he would wrap himself in his field poncho and read Larry Levis and Philip Levine poems by moonlight. Sometimes he read them aloud. Kaiser thought the poems were okay. He was going to be a writer, Tucker told Kaiser. He was going to write about the terrible things they were trained to do, about the weight they all carried. He was going to write beautiful books about the world of men. Kaiser thought this was okay too.

Eventually, the droning engines bored through Kaiser's frontal lobe until he felt adrift from the concerns of the future.

Then, like a dream interrupted, the jumpmaster was up and screaming and the entire unit stood as one and began the checking of lines, straps, tabs, ropes, then turning to their partner and going over his gear. Kaiser hooked himself to the static line while Tucker tugged at his chute apparatus, checking each connection. The plane began to bank, pulling steeply to the right and the parallel lines of men leaned with it, gripping the man in front of them with a hand on their pack straps. The red light was winking slowly, and the air crew cranked the door open, a dark slot of sky lit with brilliant slashes of white and red lights and roaring noise. The plane banked again, when suddenly a section of the floor in the center fragmented into a thousand metal particles that filled the air like a swarm of flies. The cold air howled from a rupture in the floor the size of a beach ball. Hot metal smoked and danced around their legs and there was the sudden pungent scent of bile and bowel movements. The man in front of Kaiser sagged, head nodding, and something slapped wetly on the floor. Tucker should have been behind him, but he was gone, lost in the mass of gear and limbs and weapons. The jumpmaster was howling in a voice that nobody heard, but the winking light by the door went green and the line shuffled forward, the gear bags between their legs enormous, distended scrotums, the men dropping into the darkness like drips from a faucet. Kaiser struggled to hold the man in front of him upright and shouted in his ear, *Hey, you okay, man?* his lips on the scruff of his shaved neck, the smell of burning skin, crotch-funk, and something sweet, but the man seemed to be fading into unconsciousness. A Ranger in the door stumbled and fell athwart the opening and got hung up with his upper body out in the rush of wind, the static line wrapped around his waist until the jumpmaster and an airman pried him from the grasp of physics and he slipped out into the night. Then Kaiser was at the door, and the jumpmaster, red-faced and heaving, a visage of focused madness, slapped his hands on the chest of the soldier Kaiser was supporting and heaved his inert body out the door. Then Kaiser was on the threshold and dropping into the dark, legs piked into a sitting hamstring stretch, and he turned over slowly once watching his own feet and then the crushing jerk as the static line ripped the chute and the three-point seizure at the crotch and the plane roared overhead, banking and arching heavenward like some kind of great smoking fish leaping from the water.

The trooper's bad exit messed up the timing and put some distance between the bulk of the drop and Kaiser and the couple men behind him. The AA streamed through their formation, the red balls of light in slow-moving streams, then wavering like dying birds and falling back to earth. The twist and creak of carabiners and tethers pulling at their sockets and underneath him the spread of black earth, sparkling with flares of light in every direction. *People trying to kill me*, he thought, and it seemed that he was going to land right among them. Except for Kaiser and a couple others, the chalk was falling into the drop zone just north of the darkened village. The wind was pushing Kaiser and his small group further down the slope from the village, and when they reached six hundred feet, the small arms fire started up and the tracer rounds sought out the falling men in the sky, bullets tumbling and snapping through the canopies and Kaiser clutched his straps and focused on the rushing swirl of ground. A Ranger to his right began to fire his weapon as they fell, and Kaiser screamed at him to stop but it was too late, and the fingers of light found him and his body shuddered in the harness as the tracer rounds ripped through him. Then it seemed everyone on the ground was firing at him, glad for the easy target, and parts of his body started to fall away, flesh and liquid drifting down like falling leaves, and his chute soared upward, spinning over and over, now weighted only by a small clump of what was once a man.

Kaiser released his gear bag, and it dropped and swung below him like a bell. He pitched his angle and flared and hit on his heels, running a few steps, then falling and turning over, securing his chute and bag and staying prone. The snap of small arms nearby, the distinct rattle of AK-47s and heavy antiaircraft cannons thundering and as the sound of the planes diminished he could hear the shouts and curses of men in several languages. They were too close to the village. Kaiser low-crawled to a position in a shallow drainage ditch, his heaving breath creating clouds of fine, silty dust that filled his ears, nostrils, and clumped in the corners of his eyes. It seemed they didn't know he was there, and Kaiser rolled onto his back and unclipped his HK MP5 from the harness, his fingers searching the smooth, greased weapon for the right indications, slapping the charging handle, thumbing the fire selector. Kaiser looked up and saw the sky full of stars, a concentration of light not only in the thick disk of the Milky Way but in every space of the sky. Points of white, blue, red, green, yellow, the entire spectrum of visible light all the way down to the horizon, the saw-toothed ridge of mountains in star-shadow.

The Rangers were there to deliver him to a squad of Green Berets bunkered deep in the folds of a mountain with Northern Alliance tribesman who needed a JTAC to coordinate airpower. But now he was alone and all the men in the village seemed to be focused on the bulk of the drop to the north. Kaiser flipped his night-vision goggles down and peered over the edge of the ditch, where the field was mixed terrain, dust and rock, rising up to the trees in uniform rows. Pale shapes intertwined with dozens of green forms moving and firing white flashes, men behind a wall, heads bobbing to fire and duck, at least a couple DSHK machine guns, several four-barreled ZSU-57s, maybe four hundred meters away. There were big flashes with repeated concussive reports and fountains of earth rose up in the drop zone and he knew they had turned the antiaircraft guns to the ground and were firing point blank at the Rangers.

He made an assessment. The cover was light and the A-10s were maybe ten minutes out. Apache gunships would be even better, but longer rendezvous. Kaiser unsnapped the MTS display from his chest and fired it up, extended the handheld antennae and the radio began searching for a signal. The MTS screen was spider-webbed, so he took another look at the fire teams and their positions and matched the coordinates to the map in his mind. His SOFLAM laser was in Tucker's gear bag, along with the GPS, but he could do it manually, with estimated coordinates. Kaiser could see some Rangers returning fire, the blue tracers going out, red coming in, but they were pinned down without cover and more men from the village were filtering through the orchard and down the drainage ditches and the Rangers would be flanked in a few minutes.

Valkyrie! Valkyrie!

A hoarse voice, shouting in the dark to his right. He could see a lanky green form coming toward him in a crouch, working around the rocks, the long M240 swinging from his chest. Tucker. Kaiser cupped his hands and shouted the response.

Valhalla! Valhalla!

Tucker paused, redirected, and came smartly to him, scooting down in the ditch and up against Kaiser in a jumble of bony knees and elbows. He had lost his gear bag and helmet, and his night vision was strapped around his bare head, his shock of blond hair and white teeth ethereal in the flashing dark. Kaiser raised his night-vision goggles and Tucker was grinning at him.

JTAC! Fuck yeah!

Who else is out there?

Man, I can't find anyone, he said. We might be *it*, bro.

Tucker snapped down the bipod on his M240 and set up his belt feed.

We gotta bring some of that fire over here or those guys are fucked.

I'm working on a signal, Kaiser said. Give me two minutes.

I only got three belts, Tucker said. Fucking Balestri has the rest and who knows where the fuck he is.

He squatted behind his weapon and checked the bolt. Then he looked over at Kaiser.

You'd better move away a bit, he said. Like a couple meters, at least.

We got assets in the air, Kaiser said. I'm waiting on a signal.

Kaiser unsnapped his SAT phone, the dim green light glowing. It was unsecured but quicker. Tucker smiled and turned away and sighted down range on the men in the orchard, one hand smoothing the belt, like he was petting a house cat.

Just wait a second!

Sorry, my man. *All the fucking way.*

Kaiser scooted to his left, behind a low boulder as Tucker opened up, stock jamming into his shoulder as he walked the tracers up the dirt slope and into the orchard, sweeping it across the trees. It only took a few seconds for the whole contingent to redirect their fire in his direction and suddenly the air was full of the snap and tumble of bullets, dust rising in clouds of smoke and splinters of rock and earth but Tucker kept going, switching the belt and pouring it on, his mouth in a toothy snarl, and in the muzzle flash his skull was illuminated like an x-ray, like naked bone with a shock of white hair, the barrel of the gun glowing red like a hot poker, the shaken dust rising off him as if a spectral form was leaving his body and floating heavenward. Then something large got in on it, the heavy machine guns and the antiaircraft, gouging out the earth around them and then they finally found him, heavy wet explosions tearing through his body, pieces of him flying off, and it seemed to Kaiser like some massive dark hammer was swinging out of the night sky and knocking slabs off the man, hacking away chunks of him until it was just a ragged torso behind the gun and then that was gone, too, in a red mist and Kaiser turned away and had his arms over his head, open mouth in the dirt, screaming without sound.

The introduction is always a set of three tones, and then the greeting: *Good morning! Are you ready?*

Kaiser brought a duffel bag into the hospital room at one in the morning, and Sebastian woke to see him unpacking a small bag of ice, a bottle of rum, a lime, knife, can of Coke, two glasses. A packet of B&H 100s. Kaiser sliced the limes on the windowsill and made two drinks, handed one to Sebastian, who blinked at it, still groggy. They redrilled his skull and he had a new halo-device on, cables hanging from the ceiling keeping him upright in bed. His torso was a swath of cotton bandages, his knobby shoulders and arms laced with poorly conceived tattoos. Kaiser took out a small audio recorder from the bag and set it on the bed by Sebastian's feet. He scratched at his swollen and crusty ear. My father is dead, Kaiser thought. All those hours, days, years that I gave away, all that time I spent in the dark.

Through the window the streetlights glimmered on the frosted panes, the slow whoosh of cars on the highway. Sebastian maneuvered the glass through his halo-head and the cables and took a big drink, pouring a considerable quantity down his chest. Kaiser lit them each a B&H 100 and pressed the play button.

Good morning! Are you ready?

There was an upward lilt to her voice, a hopeful tone.

Seven. Four. Eight.

Sebastian licked his lips and set the drink on the nightstand. His eyes were shining, motionless, and he folded his hands on his stomach. Cigarette ash drifting across the sheet. Something seemed to contract and gather itself in the room.

Sixteen.

Four numbers. Another number dropped.

The principles of telemetry can pinpoint the locations and trajectories of satellites. But those are just mathematical models, the theory of how things move and find one another. How to locate the transmitters, the initial parts of the equation? Those who beamed their signals into the sky to be caught and sprinkled upon the earth like electronic snowfall?

Please enjoy today's numbers with a full heart. Goodbye.

Sebastian grinned, a loose, wide, toothy smile, and Kaiser had to laugh. She would never be found. It would take a miracle to find any of us.

PART II

In every little thing there must be order, in the place where men work, in their clothes, in their thoughts. I myself must be orderly. I must learn that law. I must get myself into touch with something orderly and big that swings through the night like a star.

Sherwood Anderson,
Winesburg, Ohio

He saw God's foot upon the treadle of the loom; and therefore his shipmates called him mad.

Herman Melville,
Moby Dick

The boy spent his waking hours in the thrall of his confusing loneliness. There was no explanation for his birth into this life and it became clear long ago that he would never leave. When he dreamed under the skin of the lake, he only saw deep fields of black sky, dotted with moving motes of light.

As the weather turned cold, he often loitered on the public beach near a set of overturned metal canoes that served as a kind of gathering place for itinerant youth. When he lurked on the outskirts of this group he was never bothered, rarely noticed. He walked down the beach and along the rocky coast, sometimes along the railroad tracks. At night, he huddled under the pines and watched the lights from houses come on before returning to the lake. He had no memory of speaking to another person. But there was an absence, and he was aware of a sense of belonging to someone or something that was now gone.

When he grew tired, he filled his pockets with large

stones and waded out into the dark water. The dim, shaded world of the lake bottom, tree limbs, mud mounds, and the occasional rack of human effluence. The boy trudged through the silent drifts of silt like thigh-deep snow, the fine-grained mud billowing around his legs.

Then a single star separated from the firmament and began to descend, a splay of arms and legs. She was a thin woman, her short hair like a diaphanous halo as she drifted downward. He caught her in his arms and laid her gently on the lake bottom, smoothing the shocked expression from her face. He held her hand, stiff and cold, and closing his eyes he tried to imagine this life that lay before him as the body settled into the silt, the scuttling denizens of the deep moving toward their work.

The Boy at the Bottom of the Lake & Other Legends of the North Country,
Jean-Pierre Montour, 1936

KAISER

The Canadian border guard was standing in his shirtsleeves, holding a cigarette behind his back. Blowing flurries whisked the road from the east and the vestibule door was open, the inside lit with a warm yellow light. He raised the gate and waved Kaiser through. Three miles on Canadian two twenty-three, left on Rue Richelieu, another mile, then right on the unmarked gravel road that wound into thick woods.

The snow stopped by the time he arrived. The warehouse stood in a clearing by a stream, a high-roofed building of corrugated metal and surrounded by an eight-foot chain-link fence topped with coils of razor wire. Reaching behind his back, Kaiser snapped the collapsible baton into the quick-drop holster on his belt. He took a set of mirrored Ray-Ban aviators out of the case and arranged them on his face, pulling the looped arms neatly over his ears. LeClair had delivered a box of accessories to his apartment: belts, pocket squares, scarves, gloves, sunglasses. Kaiser laid the items out on his bed and taped the printed matrix LeClair provided next to his closet. The chart indicated which accessory belonged with which outfit. Kaiser appreciated the efficiency.

After slipping on his gloves, he stepped out of the car, leaving the engine running. There was a video camera mounted on the fence that had been repeatedly sprayed with high-gauge birdshot. The yard around the warehouse was smooth with white snow and completely empty.

A receiving cage around the front door like a prison entrance, with a mailbox affixed to the outside. A single window next to the door was covered with a metal shutter. The speaker crackled to life, and a raspy voice spoke to him.

Allo? Qui êtes-vous?

Kaiser buttoned the front of the leather Fendi trench coat, leaving the bottom two buttons undone, and closed his car door.

Mr. LeClair sent me, he said.

After a few moments of silence the speaker crackled again.

Je ne sais pas tout LeClair.

Kaiser reached into his jacket pocket and took out the piece of paper and held it up to the camera.

He told me to give you this.

The gate buzzed and disengaged. Kaiser walked into the yard. Another intercom on the cage snapped to life.

Do not be concerned, the voice said. Put your guns in the box.

Kaiser looked at the camera. The metal shutter on the window rattled up and he could see the silhouette of a man through the darkly tinted bulletproof glass.

Please, sir. It is precaution.

Kaiser shook his head.

The man sighed on the intercom.

Then we must wake La Herrisson.

The shape behind the glass moved away, and Kaiser heard the sharp rapping sound of pipe on concrete and shouting:

Eh! Réveillez vous salaud! Un homme de fantaisie avec une arme à feu ici! Mettez un pistolet sur la gorge!

The cage door opened, and Kaiser stepped inside and waited. The man returned to the window and picked up a cell phone, dialed a number, and held it to his ear. Kaiser stretched his fingers in the black leather driving gloves, admiring the delicate stitching. The man in the window put the phone down and bent forward to the microphone.

La Herrisson will ensure safety, he said. It is not the pleasant way.

The door to the warehouse swung open, and a compact man with a heavy beard dressed in blue coveralls stepped out of the doorway pointing a Luger at Kaiser's face. His eyes and forehead were creased with sun and cold, his beard and hair matted like some kind of demented woodland creature just woken from a nap. He pressed the thin barrel of the pistol into the side of Kaiser's neck.

You don't need to do that, Kaiser said.

La Herrisson grunted and pushed the barrel into his neck harder.

Kaiser looked at his face while he measured the distances. He thought about the slide and push of the heavy leather of the jacket, the snap on the baton holster nestled in the center of his lower back.

They walked inside a short hallway, where the man from the window was waiting, a fellow with a loose face wearing a rumpled brown suit and tie. A door to the left opened to an office with a desk and filing cabinets vomiting thick sheaves of yellowing papers, an antiquated computer set with multiple screens, closed circuit television monitors, an ashtray with the smoking end of a hand-rolled cigarette. At the end of the hall, a vertical sliding door was secured with an enormous padlock. The man held out his hand, and Kaiser handed him the slip of paper. He put into his pocket without looking at it.

My name is Gerard, he said. And this unfortunate fellow is La Herrisson. You have cash, yes?

When Kaiser reached into the interior pocket of the overcoat, La Herrisson grunted again and stabbed the barrel of the Luger hard into his neck. Kaiser slowly took out a tight roll of bills wrapped in a rubber band. La Herrisson reached for it, but Gerard stepped forward and snapped it out of Kaiser's hand. He pulled a nest of keys from his pocket, removed the padlock, and raised the door.

The main space of the warehouse was lined with steel shelves ten feet high, at least a dozen rows that receded into the darkness, all the shelves crowded with electronics equipment, computers, monitors, radios, satellite dishes, and bins of spare parts. The floor was littered with larger pieces, and immediately Kaiser stopped to stare at a trapezoidal device about the size of a riding lawnmower with metallic reflective panels and a twisted sprout of antennae on each end.

Ah, Gerard said, the Geoid-Sfera. 1976.

Kaiser began to move toward the satellite, but when La Herrisson jabbed the Luger into his neck again he paused. When he felt the gun pressure lessen on his skin, he shot his right hand back and seized La Herrisson's gun hand, pulling it over his shoulder. He rotated the arm, dropped to one knee, and using his shoulder as a fulcrum, cranked down and hyperextended the elbow, the joint separating with a wet crunch. La Herrisson shrieked and the Luger popped out of his hand, Kaiser snagging it out of the air before it hit the ground.

D'accord, d'accord, Gerard said, stepping between them.

Kaiser held the gun down and with his other hand, he snapped out the telescoping baton to its full length. La Herrisson knelt on the floor, clutching his arm.

There is no need, Gerard said. *D'accord.*

Kaiser checked the safety and put the Luger in his pocket. Gerard stood there with his hands out in a gesture of supplication. His suit was frayed at the sleeve ends and had deep sweat stains in the armpits. Kaiser waited until the thrumming of his blood calmed and he could hear more clearly, the only sound La Herrisson's labored breathing. He scanned the ceiling and walls of the room, checked the hallway, then knocked the tip of the baton against the floor to collapse it and tucked it back into the holster. He walked over to the satellite and pushed on a panel, which slid aside to reveal a small protruding nozzle housing a carbon-based laser light.

Kosmos-842, Kaiser said. This light allowed them to photograph the position relative to stars in three arc seconds.

You like Soviet technology? Gerard said. We have plenty. Military like this, KGB, ACM, other things.

La Herrisson groaned and rolled onto the ground, his face twisted in agony.

Happy shopping, Gerard said.

The Trombley home in Frenchtown was a relic of the early twentieth century, when North Chazy was a thriving way station in the chain of commerce extending north to the Saint Lawrence Seaway. Now the houses of Frenchtown mainly harbored widows, most of them air force wives, their husbands long dead from heart disease, cancer, diabetes, stroke. The widows now stood like silent sentinels through the afternoons, watching the interlopers who moved in during the last couple decades, drawn by the low rents. Many of the houses were cut into a warren of apartments or informal crash pads for squatters. The corner grocery began to sell singles of everything, food items slowly vanishing from the shelves until the store subsisted on alcohol, cigarettes, and a staggering amount of lottery tickets. The air force widows of Frenchtown watched the open-air drinking, the late-night shouting, the salty teenage girls with a baby on their hip sauntering down to the corner for another pack of smokes. The widows drew their curtains tighter each year, and as they made their tea in the evenings in their darkened rooms, they began to see the final truth that they had labored so long and so patiently to embrace.

Calliope Trombley answered the door in her bathrobe, holding a red Solo cup and smoking a cigarette.

Is Seb here?

Calliope gave him a long up-down look. He could tell that she was confused by the clothes. Kaiser had the Fendi overcoat on and the leather driving gloves. She shrugged and opened the door, bellowing *Seb!*

When Kaiser came down the basement stairs, Sebastian was stripped to the waist, sitting on a velvet-covered footstool in front of an antique vanity mirror, working a socket wrench on a bolt on a lower rod that was screwed into his collarbone. The doctors instructed Sebastian to not adjust his halo, but he said sometimes the thing felt loose and rattled his spine. The walls were open studs with fiberglass insulation, the cement floor mostly covered by a balding oriental carpet. A mattress up on cinder blocks, milk crate for a nightstand. A spatter of raised white welts across his chest and stomach where Gorman shot him.

What's up?

Up for trip into the mountains? Kaiser asked him. There's some money in it.

Collections?

Something else.

Sebastian grinned and twisted a bolt with a finger, testing for tightness.

I gotta make my little bro some lunch first.

Upstairs, his mother was banging around the kitchen, muttering to herself. In the mornings Sebastian was sometimes able to get her to eat a bit of eggs or toast, but most days Callie seemed to subsist on a diet of Parliaments and Bowman's Vodka. Sebastian maneuvered her away from the sink and to the table, where she sat smoking, watching Kaiser. She wore a single house slipper, her other bare foot blackened on the bottom, the calloused heel cracked. There were two clocks in the kitchen, both stopped at twenty minutes to nine. Sebastian was vigorously washing the small pile of dishes in the sink.

Dylan!

Feet pounded the stairs, and a skinny boy ran into the kitchen and hugged Sebastian. He saw Kaiser and stepped back.

This is Kaiser, Sebastian said. Buddy of mine.

'Sup.

'Sup.

Sebastian cleaned a pan and a couple plates and got a hunk of butter melting. He cut a small tomato into razor thin slices and grated a small pile of cheese. He dipped the bread into the pan and got it buttered on all sides, then assembled the sandwiches, Dylan watching intently at his elbow. His face was more rounded than Sebastian, his skin an olive tone, large eyes. Sebastian plucked a leaf off a basil plant growing in a jar on the windowsill, quickly diced it up and added it to the sandwich, giving it a press and flipping with a spatula. He slid one off onto a plate, sliced it, and handed it to his brother. Then he slid the other onto a plate and handed it to Kaiser. The whole process took less than three minutes.

Nice work, Kaiser said. Thanks.

Dylan sat next to his mom and chomped the sandwich. She gave him a sleepy smile, tousled his hair, then got up to go lay down on the couch in the living room.

Dylan's wicked smart in school, Sebastian said. Right, bro?

The boy nodded, his cheek bulging with sandwich, his limpid eyes watching Kaiser.

Kaiser here knows a lot about science and shit. You should ask him a question.

Dylan swallowed a large wad of sandwich and stared at Kaiser with his mouth open.

Is there any orange juice? Sebastian asked. Go get it. Drink it all.

It was near the end of the month, but the government assistance check wouldn't come for another week. Sebastian told Kaiser that his mother had a house visit with the DSS caseworker coming up. Which meant Callie was going to really let the place go to shit. She had determined that exhibitions of extreme need were the best way to keep the money coming. She got a partial rent waiver and three hundred sixty a month, just enough to keep her in Bowman's and Parliaments for about three and a half weeks.

I'm heading out, Sebastian said to Callie, shrugging on a baggy, multicolored hoodie.

Are you really going to wear that? Kaiser asked.

Dude. Now you're just being unkind.

Where ya goin'? Dylan said. He was hanging on the doorjamb with one hand, swinging his body back and forth.

We got a job, Sebastian said.

Doin' what?

Science.

Kaiser drove them up an old logging road climbing the eastern ridge of the Adirondacks, the back seat and trunk of the Volkswagen packed tight with a programmable dish receiver, amplifier console, PCM, telemeter with green screen, spare motherboard, laptop, and nearly a half mile of cable. This was still his father's land, and Kodiak had an old hunting cabin built up on a knoll, several thousand feet in elevation, where he and Kaiser set up their antennae array for their ham radio receivers. The antennae were fixed to a small wooden tower with an observation platform that afforded a view down into the Champlain Valley and across the Canadian border. Decades ago, Kodiak had rigged up a cable that tapped into the elevated power lines. But over the years the lines rotted, and they'd have to be replaced if Kaiser wanted to use the antennae.

It was LeClair's idea to track the satellite and aerial surveillance on the border to find a safe route for Montagne's package. But when Kaiser told him that with the right equipment he could also intercept telemetry, the instructions and communication between the aerial vehicle and whomever was controlling them, when he told them that he could *see what they see, know what they know*, LeClair liked this even better. He didn't blink when Kaiser requested ten grand for more equipment and cables from Gerard's warehouse.

We just need one clear window, LeClair said. Do what you need to do.

They unloaded the gear at the trailhead, and the two men trooped up the ridge, Sebastian with two spools of cable on a rod balanced across his shoulders, Kaiser carrying the dish and console his shoulder and another spool of cable. A half hour later, they reached the hunting cabin, a weathered old shack perched on a limestone outcropping. The air inside the cabin was stale and smelled of wood rot and copper wire. A set of bunks in one corner, a sink, the rest of the room dominated by a table and shelf units that housed old radio receivers, transmitters, cable, vacuum tubes, and other odds and ends.

Nice place, Sebastian said. Looks like the location of many a fond boyhood memory.

Your family have a camp?

Fuck no, Sebastian said. Closest thing to a camp we had was when my mother locked out me out of the house for the summer when I was sixteen. Caught me stealing her smokes for like the fifth time and was like, get the fuck *outta* here! I slept in an old canoe down at the public beach for a month. Good times. Mostly.

They dumped the gear and ran a fresh cable up to the antennae array perched just outside on a tall platform. The deep winds gusting down the mountain made the platform sway like the crow's nest on a schooner rounding the horn.

I'm going to need to secure this thing, Kaiser said. Ground anchors.

We gonna broadcast something?

We're gonna receive, Kaiser said.

Like those recordings you played in the hospital? That number lady?

This is for radio telemetry, Kaiser said. The instructions that are beamed to surveillance vehicles and the data they send back.

Like drones?

Kaiser shrugged.

It's just for fun.

Sure, sounds fun, bro.

Kaiser needed to run the cable from the power line across the ridge and to the high-voltage transmission tower. He hoped he remembered how Kodiak tapped into the line. Carrying the large spools of cable between them, they hiked toward the line of steel towers just behind a ridge to the west. When they reached the ridge, they were above the tree line and looked down into a steep valley of pine and beech dusted with snow, the metal power line towers staggered down the valley.

You hear that? Sebastian said.

There was a faint, high-pitched buzz, and Kaiser stretched out an arm to the north and pointed at a small shape nosing above the trees, like an insect perusing the foliage.

Ultralight, Kaiser said.

The aircraft came up along the eastern edge of the valley, keeping the power lines to his right, staying about halfway up the ridge.

He's coming over the border, Sebastian said. Dude's making a drop!

The ultralight came on about a hundred meters below them, and they could see the pilot in a black shell suit and goggles, and two hockey bags strapped next to him.

I told you, dude! Quebec Gold. Canadian weed.

The pilot passed their position and a few seconds later cut the bags loose. The hockey bags tumbled down through the trees, crashing through limbs and thumping on the frozen ground. The ultralight quickly banked into a U-turn, heading back to Canada. Kaiser got up and started walking down the hill.

The fuck you doing? Sebastian said.

Gonna hook up this cable, Kaiser said.

Right now? Somebody's coming to get those bags.

So let's be quick.

They got the cable down to the base of the tower, and Kaiser located the access panel and the small rectangular cut in the back that Kodiak had made with an acetylene torch. The lines were tagged with small bits of electrical tape in a configuration he recognized. Then they heard the sound of another type of small engine.

Sleds, Kaiser said. Just need a few minutes.

He worked the line along the cement base, securing it with zip ties, then ran it up the inside of one of the struts.

May want to get back, Kaiser said. In case I hooked this up wrong.

Sebastian scrambled up the hill and crouched behind a rocky outcropping. The sound of the sleds was distinct now, their engines roaring as the drivers gassed them up the mountain. Kaiser touched the naked wire to the contact and there was a hard gasp, like a can of soda opening, and the power cable convulsed like a snake, flopping over all the way up and over the ridge. Kaiser cupped his eyes and looked back toward the cabin.

What are you looking for?

Explosion, Kaiser said. But I think we're good.

He taped down the wires and close the panel. Then worked his way up the cable, covering it with snow and anchoring it with large rocks.

We have power.

He scrambled back up to the top of the ridge and took a pair of binoculars out of his pack. He focused on the logging road, and in a few seconds the first sled came into view, the driver standing up and looking side to side. The other two sleds came up the path behind him, all with matching blue and gold trim. The lead driver spotted the bags and came to a stop. He took off his helmet and got off the sled, the other two pulling up behind him, and the three of them went into the trees. All wearing the same blue jackets, khaki pants, aviator sunglasses. Kaiser recognized them as LeClair's boys, from the fraternity. Did he know they were out here picking up weed drops? Two of them heaved a bag onto their shoulders and started back to their sleds. Kaiser got a tight focus on the one without a bag, who stood looking toward the Canadian border.

Scotty Marin.

They got back to the cabin as dusk was falling. The cabin now had light and Kaiser fired up the space heater. He peeled off a couple hundred-dollar bills and handed them to Sebastian, who sat against the wall drinking a National Bohemian, his face shining with sweat.

Another penny in the bucket, Sebastian said. For my truck.

What?

A food truck, bro! Like, a mobile restaurant?

A food truck? Around here?

Fuck no! I'm thinking Austin, Texas. Maybe Florida. Just need about twenty grand. I know a guy who's got an old panel truck that I can retrofit.

Sebastian drained the can of beer and crushed it against one of his halo rods. Kaiser reached in the cooler and tossed him another.

Just me and Dylan, Sebastian said, on the road, fucking slinging chef-quality food out of a tricked-out truck, rollin' in the Texas sunshine, know what I'm sayin?

Calli won't mind?

Fuck no, Sebastian said. She'd be happy to have me gone.

You and Dylan?

Man, it's embarrassing, Sebastian said, but its abundantly clear to both of us the boy is better off with me than her. Me! The original android fuck up. But D's smart and loves to cook and we make a great team.

He pulled out a packet of B&H 100s and offered one to Kaiser, who took it with a raised eyebrow.

When you start smoking these?

Sebastian selected one of the long, slender cigarettes and put it in his mouth, the end resting on the nut of one of his halo bars. He flicked the lighter and got it burning. The nut was already scorched black.

It just fits, bro.

Kaiser got the board set up and set the dish to oscillate and receive, the small green screen attached to the motherboard registering the topography and scanning area. Kaiser pointed to a set of parallel dots.

These are tethered aerostat radar systems and ground sensor stations, he said. They can locate and track any kind of heat or movement signature.

How'd that ultralight get through?

They aren't really worried about small weed drops, Kaiser said. They are looking for other kinds of things.

Like what?

Higher value targets.

A few blinking blips began to migrate across the screen, moving in different directions.

What're those?

Sebastian was crouched behind him, slurping his beer.

Satellites.

Bullshit. No fucking way.

I'll show you.

They went out and they climbed up the ladder and squatted on the platform. The wind had died and the platform was relatively still so Kaiser screwed his Celestron 25x70 binoculars onto a collapsible tripod and arranged it facing east. He straightened his arm and put it about forty degrees from the horizon.

There, he said.

Sebastian got the binoculars lined up between his halo bars and it came into view, a short cylinder with antennae on one end, alarmingly close. A small machine hanging in the sky.

You gotta be fucking kidding me!

Kaiser repositioned tripod and the binoculars to a steeper angle, northeast. He crouched down and looking through them got it positioned.

That's USA 93.

Holy shit, Sebastian said. It's bigger! And the shape is different. It has wings? And it's hauling ass!

Solar array, Kaiser said. That's a government surveillance satellite.

It's watching us?

Not right now. It's a multispectral sensor, an Evolved Enhanced Crystal System. SLAR. Side Looking Airborne Radar.

What's it looking for?

Movement. Heat signatures. Traffic on the border. They have a variety of sensing equipment.

Sebastian sat back and looked at the sky.

So there's like satellites all over the place up there?

More than two thousand in orbit, Kaiser said. Mostly communication sats.

Bro, how do you know this?

Kaiser started slinging gear into his bag and climbing down the ladder. Everything was set; now he just needed time to get a large enough sample of the surveillance vehicles tasked over the border. Once he had the patterns he could find an open window.

Just a hobby, he said. Let's get out of here and get something to eat.

They stopped at Michigans Plus and sat in a Formica booth that shimmered with grease. Seb ordered four Michigan dogs, onion rings, and a Coke. Kaiser ordered two Michigans and water. It was after the dinner hour and the place was nearly empty. The waitress seemed annoyed they were there. Sebastian pounded a Michigan before Kaiser took a first bite.

You must've been hungry, Kaiser said.

The Michigan dog, Sebastian said, is a mysterious culinary invention. Nobody even knows where the fucking name comes from, but the balance of the fat content of the meat, the implied acid in the sauce—there is no tomato in here, you know that?—the density of the split-top bun, simple mustard and raw onion, and a nice snap to the casing, it just all works, you know?

He bit his second Michigan in half, chewing with a satisfied air. Kaiser lifted his Michigan and appraised the thing.

Pretty deep thoughts about a chili dog.

Sebastian propped an elbow on the table and thrust a long, bony finger at Kaiser.

You take that back.

You are weirdly serious about this, Kaiser said.

Yeah, motherfucker I'm serious!

Sebastian wiped his mouth and gave his vertical bars a quick rub with a napkin. The waitress flipped the open sign around and the cook was sitting on the curb outside smoking a cigarette. An elderly couple sat at a booth in the front, nursing cups of coffee, a half-finished Michigan in front of them. Kaiser checked his watch. He was thinking he should go by the Artful Dodger and talk to Emerson. He hadn't seen her since the satellite intersection on court square and probably owed her an explanation for his abrupt behavior. Dragging her out to look at a satellite intersection with no warning like that, probably looking like a maniac with Sebastian's blood on his shirt, his mind a frenzy of thoughts about the shooting, LeClair's proposition, all of it. Holding her hand as they lay in the grass. He didn't know what explanation he could give her.

It's all I know, Sebastian said. Food's the only thing I'm good at.

What're you going to do now? Another restaurant?

Sebastian sniffed and squirted ketchup on his plate.

Shit, man. I was thinking I'd keep working with you. The pay is better. And it's been, like, the most interesting shit I've done.

You got fucking *shot* working with me.

Yeah. True.

Since you've known me, Kaiser said, I assaulted a college kid, pulled a gun on some Russians, then got you shot. And today we illegally tapped into a high-voltage transmission tower.

And witnessed that weed pickup, Sebastian said.

Exactly, Kaiser said. Figured you'd want to stay the fuck away from me.

Sebastian plucked a giant onion ring and swirled it through a smear of ketchup.

Do you know who I *normally* hang out with? Charley White, Speedy, Little Nelson, the Larkin brothers? The guys I normally do shit with? You know what we do? Last summer we all took three hits of acid and Little Nelson jumped off the Champlain Bridge, sixty feet up, bare-assed naked. He had like a long tail of toilet paper stuck in his ass and we lit the end on fire right before he jumped. He got second degree burns all up his groin area. I think it may be the high point of Little Nelson's life. You know what I was doing that night I laid down my bike and fucked myself up? I was coming from Nick Larkin's house. We were playing *Halo* for like six hours, smoking a pile of shit weed, some of that Frenchy E, shotgunning beers. I'm so fucked up I need some food and Nick doesn't have shit in his house because his dad shows up every Friday morning and takes all the food out of the fucking cupboard and takes it back to Wiggletown. And that Fleur-de-Lis stuff makes you feel like *anything's* possible, you know? Like all the options are *open*. So I'm like fuck it and I'm on my bike, doing ninety down the Northway because I know I got a pan of egg noodles I made from scratch in the fridge. That's what I was doing when I fucking crippled my whole life.

Sebastian maneuvered the onion ring through his halo and folded it into his mouth, looking out the window at the snowy parking lot. Kaiser watched him as he chewed. Sebastian swallowed and tapped one of his vertical bars with a finger.

Which is what makes that shit dangerous, you know? That Fleur-de-Lis? It gives you *hope*.

Sebastian wiped the crumbs off his lips with a napkin.

Yeah, he said. But no. I'm *not* worried about hanging with you, even if I get shot again or some shit. Because, like, it's still way better than what I was doing before. I feel like I'm on the right side for once.

Kaiser picked up his Michigan and took a big bite. It was delicious, better than he remembered. Sebastian sat back and patted his stomach. Outside in the parking lot it was snowing harder, and the cook in his grease-spattered apron turned his face up and opened his mouth, catching snowflakes.

Kaiser dropped Sebastian back at his house around ten and drove back to his apartment. The Artful Dodger was glowing across the square, and he could see the silhouettes of customers in the front tables. He had new transmissions from the Chinese Number lady to compile and cross-reference before bed. His brother Bill had called twice but didn't leave messages, and Kaiser knew word had gotten back about Gorman and the deputy. He had no idea how he was going to explain to his brother how he ended up in that mess. He stood watching the light and shapes of the coffee shop for a few more minutes before going to the table and powering up Kodiak's set, the tubes humming as they warmed, the staticky crackle of subspace radio reaching out into the dark. He brushed the knobs with his fingertips, wiped the dust on the amplifier vents. The channel numbers nearly worn off by his father's fingers. He tapped the mic button.

Chasing DX, he said.

Chasing DX.

Is anyone there?

LECLAIR

LeClair was locking the jewelry cases on Saturday night when the gut-rusted Ford LTD pulled up outside the shop. He walked to the front door and pointed toward the alley. The LTD rocked with a throaty rumble, the transmission engaged, and it rolled away.

In the main gallery, LeClair mixed himself a gimlet and arranged the kindling in the fireplace. The Constable stood ramrod stiff under *Early Autumn, Montclair*, watching as LeClair crossed the room and sat in one of his tall leather wingbacks. The Lavoie brothers would sit in the alley for hours without complaint, cracking walnuts with their teeth, drinking Labatt, spitting in the floorboard. Waiting was one of their more refined skills. After he finished his cocktail, LeClair went down the hall to his office and took the Taurus PT-22 from his valise, reracking the clip. He took a banded stack of hundreds from the cash box and put them into an envelope that he tucked in an inside pocket. He then walked to the heavy iron door that led to the alley and pulled back the eye-slot.

The LTD rumbled in the alley, the windows dark and the headlights off. The alley entrance was one of the features of the Court Square house that LeClair loved, along with the hidden courtyard and the mirror-channeled skylights in the gallery rooms. The Lavoie brothers never came inside. He wouldn't allow it, with their shit-kicker boots and hockey-rink funk. LeClair slipped on a long black down coat, the sort that every citizen in Montreal wore in the winter, the pistol in the left-hand pocket, unlatched the deadbolts, and stepped out into the alley.

The driver's side door of the LTD opened and the little one, Jake, stepped out, wearing an old ski-jacket and toboggan cap. The churn and shriek of Led Zepplin's "Immigrant Song" echoed off the narrow alley walls. LeClair motioned to lower the volume and Jake ducked back in to turn it down before coming around the front of the car, approaching LeClair sideways, like a crab. Jake was the runt of the litter, the third triplet, and it almost seemed as if there was just barely enough living matter left to make a full-size human. But Jake was the one who made the decisions, who avoided jail time.

LeClair kept his hands in his pockets, fingering the cool metal of the pistol while Jake brushed snow off the hood with a bare hand. The passenger windows front and back started cranking down. The lumpy, meaty faces of Ty-Ty and Lorne, lopsided grins of mostly raw gums, cauliflower ears. Rink-rat faces.

Hey, Donnie, Ty-Ty said.

We're back, Lorne said. You miss us?

Out early, LeClair said. Congratulations.

Yeah, Jake said. Probation came through. The lawyer did good.

LeClair nodded. He kept the lawyer, an ex-assemblyman in Albany, on retainer for these kinds of things. He was paid through three different parties, impossible to trace back to LeClair and his holdings. So the Lavoie brothers were out after serving three months. He doubted it was for good behavior. They slurped from tall-boy cans and Ty-Ty hawked a lunger onto the snow.

Where did *you* sequester yourself, LeClair said to Jake, during the incarceration? Catch up on some reading?

Jake looked around. The damp plat of snowflakes on the windshield, the plaintive moan of Robert Plant.

Whaddya mean?

What did you do, LeClair said, while your brothers were in jail?

Jake's face blanked, mouth dropping a little, staring right at LeClair.

Nothin'.

Of course, LeClair said. A zen traveler searching for enlightenment. You guys got something to tell me?

Well, Ty-Ty said, we figured . . .

Yeah, said Lorne.

We come back to work, Jake said. Like we was before.

Yeah, Lorne said.

They all smiled bashfully, happy to be there on this bitterly cold night in an alley with him, and LeClair was struck with the thought that these demented mutts actually thought of their working arrangement as something pleasurable and satisfying. They actually had an emotional attachment to the act of dragging some poor fuck out of a trailer in Wiggletown and snapping his ribs at LeClair's behest.

Ah, LeClair said. I'm sorry, boys, but I no longer need your services.

They all remained frozen, still smiling at him for what seemed at least a minute. From across the square, LeClair could hear the faint sound of voices, the door to the Artful Dodger opening and closing. College kids drinking crappy cappuccinos and pretending to look at shit art.

I'm going in a different direction, LeClair said.

He pulled the envelope out of his pocket and held it out to Jake.

To help you celebrate the homecoming, he said. I'm sure your mother must be enchanted at the prospect of having you all around the house once again.

Jake looked at his brothers, who hung their heads out the car windows like a couple Labrador retrievers.

These fucks don't get it, LeClair thought, but then Jake turned back, and his face was all screwed up like someone poked him in the eye.

We never missed a job, Jake said. The boys never said *shit.*

I know, LeClair said. And I paid you well for that. If the situation changes, I know where to find you. Tuesday open ice at the rink? The Dry Dock on wing night?

We got other people calling us, Jake said. Some people in Montreal offering good money.

Excellent, LeClair said. I suggest you take it.

More silence and frozen expressions. LeClair gripped the .22, his forefinger circling the trigger. He stepped forward and held out the envelope.

It's almost Christmas, he said. Treat yourself. Have a beer. Another beer.

We don't wanna celebrate, Jake said. We want work.

Ty-Ty spat into the snow. Their faces had darkened. They were starting to figure it out. LeClair tossed the envelope of money on the hood of the car.

Good luck, fellas, LeClair said. See you around.

EMERSON

When she got back to the Slaughterhouse, the upstairs hallway was shimmering with Jud's techno, and Emerson remembered that she had promised to accompany him that night to a party. Jud rarely got DJ gigs, as his kind of dance parties were not especially popular in the North Country, where most people preferred the chugging hammer and anvil of classic rock to Jud's electronic beats and soaring anthems. She'd gone to parties with him before and generally enjoyed it, getting pleasantly baked and watching the frothing crowd lurch. But tonight was different, with the image of Dr. Jansky frozen in the deep of the lake, the poignant portrait of Dr. Sterne in his grief flashing through her mind.

The party was also on fraternity row, which was unpleasant. Though Emerson was not against the Greek system in general, she had found them to be philistines who seemed to care mostly about drinking and drugs. Her poetry workshop was half full of hungover frat boys wearing their hats low and turning in shit poems they wrote five minutes before class. Growing up in North Chazy, it was an obvious teenage townie goal to get into frat parties, and Emerson and her friends were no different. But she found the party rooms loud and crowded with red-faced meat-heads who tried to press their sweaty bodies against you on the dance floor. The general stench, a miasma of stale beer, chewing tobacco, cigarettes, urine, vomit, and sweat was powerful enough to make you choke. But hey, her friends were fond of pointing out, *free beer!*

At about nine thirty, Jud got his gear together and they rode their bikes across Main and through the darkened campus grounds.

I'm a little surprised, she said, that these guys like your kind of music.

Oh yeah, Jud said. These guys love it.

They glided down the wide sidewalk of Greek row, the houses in neat lines on their left. She knew that about forty people lived in each house, and they were outfitted with kitchens, formal rooms, a large party room, and various other secret nooks and crannies where they carried out whatever rituals they honored. They locked their bikes to the rack in the front yard. The fraternity coat of arms was painted on the large glass window in the front, and the Greek letters arched over the door. Emerson stopped, grabbing Jud by the arm.

I know these guys, she said. They work for my uncle. Down at the shop and stuff?

Jud smiled and twisted a knot of his unruly hair.

The best sound system on the row, he said, and the best E.

Yeah, but. They'll know who I am, right? Won't that be weird?

They don't know, Jud said. These guys don't pay attention to shit like that. And if they do know, they don't care.

A brother named Troy escorted them through the house and down the stairs to the party room. The walls were painted dark colors, giving the place the aspect of a subterranean cavern. A chest-high bar cut across one of the narrow ends of the room with the DJ booth tucked into a corner. There was a truck at the back door unloading a dozen kegs. In the booth, Jud powered up the gear and started cueing up his tracks and adjusting the mixing board. Troy brought them a frothy pitcher of beer and couple plastic cups, then handed Jud a small wax paper packet. Jud opened the packet and showed it to Emerson. Four small pills, each stamped with a blue Fleur-de-Lis.

Frenchy, Jud said. Nice. These are hard to get.

He poured them both a beer and they washed down a pill. A few minutes later Troy gave Jud a thumbs-up sign and Jud cued up some moderate techno. The lights went off save the door lights and their booth. By ten thirty, the dance floor was a throbbing, heaving mass of young people. It was clear to Emerson that many were rolling hard, dancing in that loose, unselfconscious fashion that signaled the end of concerns that extended beyond their fingertips. She had a quick bout of nausea gave Jud a look and patted her stomach, and he nodded, indicating that he too was about to take off. Almost right on cue, Jud's music took on an insistent, urgent quality. She smoothed her shirt and felt the electric crackle of her skin. Watching the crowd dance was strangely compelling. She picked out various people, a beautiful girl wearing a string of glow necklaces, a fat guy in the back bobbing with two cups of beer, the intricate moves of a slender brother in duck boots. Not bad, she thought, nudging Jud and giving him a smile.

When Jud put on New Order's "Bizarre Love Triangle" a group of about twenty sorority girls formed into lines and began to execute a fairly chaste choreographed routine. As the girls went through the steps, spinning in unison, their faces seemed lit with the freshness of youth. Emerson had always considered the Greek system of Ausable College as self-absorbed children of advantage, living out some kind of Disneyland rite of passage. But this display was pure joy. Jud was already lost, one hand clutching his headphones, the other working his syncopations on the mixer, his saucered pupils flickering in the leaping LED readouts.

When the next track came on, Emerson slipped out of the booth and joined the dancing. The full throaty power of the bass from the concert amplifiers hanging from the ceiling hit her like a wave. As she danced, it seemed like everyone in the room was trailing a static line, like an inverted fistful of balloons, a flock of kites, all of them attached by a shimmering tether that led upward through the ceiling and into the sky.

A couple hours later, Emerson was in the first-floor hallway, gulping water from the water fountain, her sweaty clothes pasted to her body. Her skin felt like an open window in a storm. The water fountain basin was half full of dip spit and cigarette butts. Then a young man took her elbow like a figure from an old movie, leading her away from the fountain. Emerson allowed herself to be led like a child through the bright hallway, the two of them going upstream through the mob of walleyed undergraduates. The young man was wearing a blue windbreaker, khakis, and duck boots. One of her uncle's boys. She did not get a clear look at his face, but he had the well-formed back half of a good looking individual, and Emerson felt the warm stirrings of desire. She was not beholden to anyone. They walked by a room full of people passing a tall glass bong, heavy gouts of a Bob Marley remix pounding through the doorway, then up two flights of stairs, the music and commotion beginning to diminish. The third level of the house was decidedly different; carpeting, for one, better lighting, and a muted atmosphere. Girls loitered in the hallway, every one of them giving Emerson a once over. All she could think about was that each one of them was a gorgeous example of womanhood, and she loved them all like sisters. Then she was standing before a water cooler, the young man who led her there proffering a paper cup. She brought the chilled liquid to her lips, swallowed. The most delicious water she'd ever known.

Thank you!

She looked at him with unabashed gratitude, and he smiled, even more beautiful than she had guessed, widely set blue eyes, cleft chin, hair tousled just so, like he stepped off a schooner at the Kennedy compound. But she'd seen him before. She knew this guy. *Scotty.* She was just about to say, *Hey, you were trying to get into a fight with Tom Kaiser at the Dry Dock*, when he slipped through a doorway hung with a thick curtain of red beads like a Moroccan hookah lounge. She checked her watch: 1:45 a.m. Nothing good ever happens after one in the morning, she often claimed to her friends who tried to drag her into cars and bars on moon-washed nights. Emerson normally opted to hoist herself onto her bike and weave back to the Slaughterhouse for a rigorous tooth brushing, a glass of water, and a satisfying pee, falling asleep with Dylan Thomas reciting "Fern Hill" in his boozy drawl on her record player. But on this night, she drank another cup of water, wiped the sweat from her neck and forehead, and followed the thump of music and men through the red beads, closing her eyes and stepping forward, letting the beads glide over her body like fingers. She felt the spinning dynamo of her heart.

There were more young men sitting in the room in addition to the one who led her there, all wearing blue windbreakers, khaki pants, and duck boots, their faces all turned to her, their eyes bright. More techno music, a plodding, doomed sort of dirge with a distinct melancholy timbre. The effect was so disarming and, well, *cute*, that Emerson couldn't help putting her hands to her mouth to stifle a laugh. Like most fraternity house rooms, it was all couches and seating area, beds hanging from the ceiling with heavy chains and shrouded with tapestry curtains, strings of Christmas lights circling the room in a kind of antic geometry. They all stood up, introducing themselves: *Cruz*, *Cool-Mite*, *Tripp*, *Stanton*. They lowered the music and offered her a flute of champagne from an enormous black bottle. She accepted the glass and sat on a couch next to the young man who brought her there.

I'm Scotty, he said.

He was even more beautiful close up, and she suddenly longed to touch him. I am on the hunt, she thought. This is something.

You wanna boost the roll? Scotty asked.

He opened a wooden box on the coffee table and took out a metallic cone with a wooden base, a few vials of weed, and a clear plastic bag with a tapered end and stem-valve. He put a bristly nugget in the top of the cone, attached the bag, and pushed a button. After a few moments the bag began to inflate and fill with creamy smoke. Scotty sealed the valve and removed the bag, handing it to Emerson.

Quebec Gold, Cruz said. The vaporizer draws out the flavors and purifies the smoke.

Scotty then opened an Altoids tin, full of pills adorned with blue, yellow, and red Fleur-de-Lis.

Or you could just have another, he said.

I don't think so, she said. Not sure I could handle it.

They passed the bag around, and Emerson had to admit it was quality weed and the vapor was cool and nuanced. But she didn't want to sit still, so Scotty offered to take her on a brief tour. He led her down the hall to a quiet, carpeted room covered with portraits of past members and group photos of the whole fraternity, a sea of faces in identical blue blazers and gold ties. At one end a sort of shrine was set up, an altar covered with blue silk with yellow borders, the symbols of a star and oil lamp. When she inspected some of the group photos it seemed each face beamed with a kind of youthful promise. They seemed happy. Another room held a group of miserable pledges sharing a pitcher of red-tinted beer and listening to an Elvis Costello song. They were scrawling something down on a pad of paper. An empty bottle of Tabasco sat on the coffee table next to the pitcher and as Emerson watched one of the boys took a gulp of his beer and retched painfully before returning to his pad and pen.

Elvis Costello's "Beyond Belief," Scotty said. They have to write down the lyrics. They drink till they get it right.

That seems cruel, Emerson said.

Another boy gagged and vomited smoothly into his empty cup. He set it on the table and poured himself a fresh one.

They are developing their power of perception, Scotty said. They have to overcome and focus. It's one of our core principles.

The next room held three more pledges sitting blindfolded on couches with their feet in buckets of water. An overdubbed remix of the first thirty seconds of Pink Floyd's "Money" was playing at an excruciating decibel level. Clanging coins and cash registers layered on top of each other. Emerson had never heard anything more horrid.

What's the principle here? she asked.

Scotty shrugged.

This one's just tradition.

As they walked down the hallway, Scotty refilled her glass from the champagne bottle. The girls were still leaning against the walls, clustered around doorways, as if they were waiting for someone to emerge, some thumbing their tiny Nokia phones. They seemed familiar, and Emerson recognized them as the group of girls that performed the dance to the New Order song downstairs some hours ago. The last room on the hall was lit with black lights and a slow-flashing strobe light set under an enormous block of ice. A channel had been carved into the ice and there was a table laden with pitchers full of neon yellow liquid, half-gallon bottles of vodka, cans of frozen concentrated lemonade, a liter of Mountain Dew. In the flickering gloom she could make out two young men on the couch, both of them naked save for a sock on their genitals. They slouched there with somber eyes, completely still. It struck Emerson as kind of sad, and then the boys on the couch seemed to stretch and flex like a funhouse mirror. She took a deep breath. Here comes the Quebec Gold, she thought. High. Hi. Hello. Walk right through it.

Hop Skip and Go Naked shots, Scotty said. Off the ice block. Want one?

Why are those guys naked?

That's Fondue and Carr, he said. This is their room.

Yeah, but why are they naked?

Another shrug.

It's just what they do. The free expression of creative will is one of the central tenants of our creed.

Scotty took her back to the other end of the hall and into a spare room that opened up onto a balcony overlooking the back lawn and the frozen pond. It was freezing out but the air felt amazing on her skin, her pores contracting, the cold in her lungs. Somehow her glass was empty again and Scotty topped her off, then flung the empty champagne bottle toward the pond, the bottle spinning slowly into the dark. Emerson thought about the night on court square with Kaiser, the satellite intersection, the quick panic as the two speeding elements moved toward collision. How he seemed to conjure them up with some kind of internal vision, bringing them into view with a touch of his fingertip. His hand when she grabbed it at the moment of intersection, the calm, dry feeling of it. She was pretty sure he had blood stains on his shirt, and his eyes definitely had the look of someone on the edge of something. He seemed afraid. But of what? Of her? What was with Kaiser, anyway? What was he doing here?

The champagne bottle fell onto the grass where it bounced and rolled to the water's edge. Emerson felt a subtle roll of revulsion, almost like vertigo. Her eyes were burning and her limbs felt heavy.

I think I need to go inside, she said.

Everything seemed darker inside, as if the lights had been lowered, and the hallway was empty. As Scotty led her down the hall, Emerson let her fingers trail along the walls covered with distorted images from a Dr. Seuss book, *Fox in Sox*. The Tweetle Beetle Bottle Battle. She looked at her watch and saw it was nearly three o'clock. She could hear the thump of heavy bass through the floor, the cries of people on the lower floors. Scotty unlocked a door and opened it. Darkness.

I should go find my friend Jud, she said. Downstairs.

She took a step, and her knee buckled. A wave rippled through her body and her mouth began to water. Scotty put his arm around her back and helped her up.

Sit down for second, he said.

He brought her into the room and set her down on a couch, then turned on a couple dim lights. Emerson sat very still. She *needed* to be still.

I think you should bring me a bowl or something she said. I might vomit.

Scotty reached into a mini-fridge and took out a chilled bottle of peach colored liquid and handed it to her.

Your electrolytes are low, he said.

She held the bottle in her hands. It looked inviting, delicious even, but she couldn't imagine drinking anything. Music was playing now, something low and electronic, then it cut out abruptly. The light was so dim she felt like she couldn't see anything beyond a small halo of light around her body, her forearms resting across her thighs, her legs together, the rise and fall of her stomach as she breathed. Her head felt full, like sounds were pushing to get out, and she realized her eyes were barely open. She tried to open them wide but couldn't seem to do it.

Scotty was sitting next to her wearing a set of headphones, with another set in his hands.

Put these on, he said.

Emerson felt his hands around her head, a sense of pressure, then the sound of something far off, like an approaching train in the distance, some kind of dark machinery traveling at high speed. He was holding her hands, looking at her like he expected her to say something. *He is beautiful and lonely,* she thought. She could see the overlaid image of patterns, moments, and incidents of his life, a vision of extraordinary beauty, placed over him like a shimmering schematic drawing of his origins. She knew that she was going to lay down with him, it seemed as inevitable as sleep. She wasn't afraid.

Suddenly the light amplified drastically, and she put her hands over her eyes. The headphones were taken off her head and she had the sense of other people in the room. There were six young women standing in a semicircle around her. Scotty was gone. The overhead light was hard and bright, and what had seemed just moments before like a mystical grotto now just looked like another fraternity house room: old couches, empty Solo cups, posters of Joy Division and the Cure.

I think I'm gonna be sick, Emerson said.

One of the girls placed a trash can between Emerson's knees while another girl sat next to her on the couch and snapping a hairband off her wrist expertly put Emerson's hair into a tight ponytail. Emerson leaned over the trash can, her mouth open and watering. These were the same girls she had seen loitering about the hallway earlier, the ones she'd seen down on the dance floor.

I'm sorry, she sputtered.

A girl sat on the other side of her and put an arm around her waist, her face close.

It's okay, the girl said, you're safe. My name is Stacy. We're the QRF. You're with the Zetas now.

Emerson gagged and vomited a torrent of watery bile into the trash can. When she was done, they wiped her face with a damp towel and when she could stand, they led her out into the hallway where Scotty was standing slumped against the wall, three Zetas standing around him. He ran his hand through his hair and smirked. Stanton, Cruz, Cool-Mite were just down the hall, watching.

We're going to take you to our safe area, Stacy said. If at any time you are not comfortable with what is happening, please tell us.

They led her down the hall and Emerson turned around to try and catch Scotty's eye, but he was surrounded by Zetas, one of them standing in front of him and pointing a finger in his face, speaking quietly. Scotty looked away, a smirk on his face. His fraternity brothers down the hall started to laugh until the Zetas turned around and they jumped back in their room like scolded children. The Zetas slipped a loose cotton hoodie on Emerson and ushered her out the front door, one on each arm, a phalanx of girls ahead clearing the way through the addled throng that was milling around the entrance.

The sky was lightening, a washed-out quality to the elms and gum trees along Greek row. The two girls at her side had her firmly by the elbow and it was like her feet were skimming across the ground. She felt much clearer after vomiting, but the helpless feeling in her limbs persisted, like her brain was sending signals to her arms and legs from millions of miles away. She closed her eyes for a moment and when she opened them, she was inside the Zeta house, Stacy and the others leading her into a room. The light was pleasing, and the furnishings spare but new looking: a pillowy couch and loveseat, a bed with a dark, gauzy canopy, the walls adorned with pictures. Landscapes. As she sat on the couch and lay back on the proffered pillow, she recognized some of the paintings from her uncle's collection. Hudson School. They seemed to pulse with life, trees shifting, water rushing. The distant tableaux, dramatic juxtapositions of scale, the enormity of nature at a remove.

Yes, she thought, I see it now. I should tell Uncle Donnie.

Stacy knelt on the floor by the couch and several other girls drew up ottomans and clustered around her. Someone covered her shoulders with a light blanket.

This is our safe room, Stacy said. It's custom-made with reinforced concrete block, wired with an automated security system. It's completely soundproof and fireproof. The door locks from the inside and can only be opened by two keys.

Stacy reached into her V-neck shirt and took out a small silver key on a chain.

The other key, she said, is held by another sister in a safe location off-campus. Climate controls are over there on the wall, along with lighting. We have a fridge here with drinks and snacks. The phone there gives you a direct line to our house manager downstairs, the police, and the campus women's counseling center. You can stay here as long as you like. Nobody will bother you.

Another girl leaned in and took her hand.

I'm Stephanie. I'm the house manager. If you need anything, just let me know.

You don't even know me, Emerson said.

Stacy nodded.

But we're all on the same team, she said. Right?

Yeah, Emerson said. I guess so.

What's your name?

Emerson LeClair.

Emerson *LeClair*?

The Zetas seemed puzzled as how to proceed with this information. This was something Emerson experienced with regularity.

As in Donnie LeClair?

Yeah.

Okay, but do you know what house you were at? That party?

Yeah.

Like, those guys *work* for LeClair?

I know, I know.

A couple of the girls widened their eyes and put their fingers in front of their mouths.

Oh, snap!

Damn!

That is fucked *up*!

We can talk about that later, Stacy said. Don't worry about those pencil-dick douchebags. You feel okay? You need anything? Herbal tea? Eye cream?

No, Emerson said. I think I might sleep. Too many . . . drugs.

Several of the girls rolled their eyes.

Tell me about it.

I'm rolling so hard I chewed through my fucking cheek!

Did you have the Frenchy?

I think so.

That stuff is *ridiculous.*

Okay, Stacy said, let's get out of here and let Emerson rest.

The bed there is nice, Stephanie said, the sheets are amazing. With the soundproof walls you can sleep awesome. That's what I usually do.

Emerson looked up at Stephanie, a pretty cat-eyed girl in a sleeveless blouse and tight jeans. She felt drained, her body heavy, like lying in the tub with the plug pulled and the water funneling out by your feet. Did something happen to her in Scotty's room? She didn't think so, but she also felt like she was missing time, like something was obscured. Her eyes were closing.

Yeah, Emerson said. Wait. What you *usually* do?

Stephanie blinked. A tight-lipped smile.

Yeah, she said. When it happens to me.

SYDNEY & PHIL

A few miles south of North Chazy, a small housing development was built for ranking officers at the air force base, a sheltered subdivision with wide streets and a small private beach. The Cliff Haven beach fronted a little half-moon bay with tall granite cliffs on the south side. A half-dozen dinghies, splintered and colored with algae and mold, lay face down on the sand, now covered with snow. Occasionally students from the college had bonfire parties on the beach, and because they generally buried their coals and policed their empties, nobody seemed to mind.

After church, Sydney took Juliet down to the beach to skate with Phil. Sydney felt Juliet was too young to skate, but she could not begrudge Phil these moments. When she came out of the bathroom, he was spooning oatmeal into Juliet's mouth, both of them grinning madly. Phil had put a heaping tablespoon of brown sugar in her bowl. Their relationship was deepening in important ways. But Phil wouldn't go to church with them. Nope, he said, never again.

Sydney and Phil attended the same Lutheran church growing up, though his family stopped going when his mother died, when Phil and his sister were just in grade school. Sydney couldn't understand how going to church, singing in the choir, participating in youth group, could be considered some kind of burden. For Sydney, the ritual and practice of church had a meditative quality. When she closed her eyes for prayer, she felt the numinous spirit of the prophets and the embracing arms of God, and when she left the building, Juliet skipping down the slushy sidewalk beside her, she felt renewed, almost reborn. Without church, she would have probably quit DSS a long time ago.

They sat on a log on the beach and laced up their skates. Juliet was wearing a furry white hat and matching scarf. Phil had bought her a new pair of white leather figure skates in Lake Placid. A handful of skaters executed loops and figure-eights across the ice, a teenage boy slapping at a frozen hunk of snow with a hockey stick. Juliet tiptoed out onto the ice, holding on to Phil's hand. He started skating backward, pulling her along, moving faster and in tighter circles, her face shining with joy. Just watching them reminded Sydney of how skilled and fluid Phil was, how he had such natural grace for a bulky guy. It was also clear to Sydney that he was done with professional hockey. She knew it was probably better that he stopped playing, especially as his main job seemed to be hitting other men in the face, but she was worried about what he would do when cut adrift. Since he'd been back, he'd only played pickup games a couple times, and every time Sydney brought it up, he just griped about stupid managers and crooked front office assholes and his incompetent teammates. Like everything else with Phil, it was never his fault; if he hadn't got screwed by the coach at Selkirk, if his teammates hadn't been assholes, he'd be playing in the NHL, easy. Nobody in that fucking league knows shit about hockey, he actually said to her. It didn't matter to Phil how accomplished or notable his superiors were; he had no faith in accumulated knowledge or wisdom. To him, all expertise came through some kind of natural intuition. Sydney had studied such personality types in her college psychology classes, and she knew that these people were destined for a lifetime of frustration and strife. But there was something in her heart that felt like love. She couldn't deny that. And there was Juliet.

The other skaters cleared out space as Phil skated backward faster and faster, holding on to Juliet's hands, the blades of his skates squeaking as he sliced across the ice, swiveling his ankles, knees, and hips, a giant grin on his unshaven face, their collective breath steaming behind them. The other skaters began to cheer and Juliet, barely hanging on, screamed for Sydney to *watch me, Momma, watch me, watch me!*

The Dannemora receiving gate was busy with deliveries and releases. Business is booming, Phil thought. It seemed remarkable that a guy with a high school degree and a half-dozen years of junior hockey could walk into a job paying that much. Each morning, he planned on walking across the street, but as the afternoon drew on, he kept drinking beer and puttering around the house, figuring he'd enjoy this brief bit of freedom. He'd earned it. He had a couple hundred left from his last hockey check. He'd spend some quality time with his daughter. The house was paid off and Sydney was covering groceries and utilities.

Fortier said they'd hold the position for a couple more weeks, but Phil couldn't bring himself to commit. His whole life he swore he'd never work at the prison, he'd never be like his old man. Maybe another job would come up.

They finished dinner and Phil washed the dishes in the sink, sipping a beer, Sydney preparing Juliet's bath. She was watching a PBS show about meerkats. When Sydney called down the hall Phil tucked the beer in his back pocket and picked up Juliet and carried her under his arm like a football, removing her shirt, socks, and pants. She had become accustomed to Phil handling, feeding, and bathing her. He put her in the tub and leaned against the sink as Sydney soaped up her hair. Juliet sat chest deep in the old chipped tub, her shoulders shining, a tiger-sponge in her fist.

I was thinking about some renovations, Phil said. Roland and LeChance are still in town. I can get them to do the floors cheap, maybe strip out some of this shitty drywall.

Let's not curse around Jules, okay?

Landscaping in the spring, Phil said. Get the yard looking good. May have to tear out the whole front porch.

Phil. You don't even have a job yet.

He finished his beer and tossed the can in the wastebasket.

Are you going in? she said. Across the street?

He looked in the mirror and rubbed his face. He didn't know what to say.

You told me a hundred times you'd never work there, and I get that. But maybe it'll be different for you. It's a steady job. You could do all the work on the house you keep talking about.

It's hard to explain, Phil said. It's like I'm part of this chain and I need to get loose of it.

I understand, Sydney said. And I'm not rushing you. I will support your decision. I just wish you'd talk to me about it. Talking about it will help.

You're doing that psychology crap on me again, Syd.

Phil! I'm not trying to *do* anything to you! You know that pisses me off.

Okay, okay, sorry. I just feel like this house isn't . . . good enough. For her. To grow up in a house like this just doesn't seem right. I guess that's all I can think about right now.

Sydney hoisted Juliet out of the tub and Phil caught her in a towel. As he rubbed her down, she made little high-pitched hooting noises. Sydney dried her hands.

You hear Tom Kaiser is back in town? she said.

Phil paused, a small flash of heat, then kept drying Juliet with the towel. He didn't really know Kaiser. But he knew something about him, mostly based on a series of things Sydney had said about him over the years. Once about three years ago she got drunk at the Dry Dock and they were reminiscing about old boyfriends and girlfriends and she brought up Kaiser and her eyes got all teary, right there at the bar. She said that he just disappeared without ever really telling her goodbye or breaking up or anything, silently slipping into the dark maw of the military. Phil knew that he had no rights to be salty about who Sydney was with before they were together. But he couldn't help carrying a thorny chip for Kaiser. He was a few years behind Phil at school, but he never played hockey for some reason. What kind of asshole from North Chazy doesn't play hockey?

What's he doing here?

I don't know, she said. I mean, he came back for his father, I think.

Phil ground his teeth. He'd heard about the funeral, how the whole county turned out. Phil's dad died right around the same time and didn't even have a funeral; he was cremated and shipped to his sister. Phil never even saw the ashes. He would've poured them in the street storm drain. Or maybe in the prison yard. Hell, skip the cremation—Phil would've dumped his carcass in the woods.

He came back for the funeral?

I think he was here before that, Sydney said. His dad had a heart condition or something.

I wouldn't mind running into him, Phil said.

Seriously?

What? The guy was a dick to you.

So long ago, she said.

Doesn't matter, Phil said.

Yes, it does. We are different people. Time matters.

South of North Chazy, Route 9 wound alongside the picturesque Ausable River, a narrow canyon with a torrent kept fast and cold by the mountain snowpack. The Ausable Bridge passed over dramatic cataracts that thundered through the hardest freezes of winter, and a few tourist motels were built along the river in the early postwar years for visitors to enjoy the falls. Then a decade ago the state bought the old motels to provide housing for convicted child molesters and other sexual offenders. Prohibitions against living within a certain distance from children created an impossible quandary for convicted felons: There was nowhere for them to live without violating the terms.

The only motel that was still inhabited in this manner was a place called the White Pines. The paint on the motel was relatively fresh, and the sign still standing, but the in-ground pool between the road and the parking lot was a frozen slab, thick with leaves and trash. Cars were scattered through the lot, most covered in hard pupas of snow and ice. Outside each room sat a folding chair and a coffee can for butts. Men sat outside their doorways in heavy coats, all of them smoking, one with a transistor radio playing old-time country tunes. Across the street the river ran fast over smooth pale stones as torn specters of fog drifted out of the pines.

The manager at Stewart's had called Sydney to say that her former client Braden Tullus had stopped showing up for work. Nobody had seen him for several days now. Braden was learning disabled and had a physically abusive father. At seventeen he went through a meth addiction that nearly killed him. Sydney got him through rehab, but a couple weeks after Braden turned eighteen, he got busted for statutory rape of a fifteen-year-old Wiggletown girl. There was another branch of DSS that dealt with adult offenders, another case worker, but Sydney thought she'd at least try to talk to him first.

Braden's door was slightly ajar, so Sydney knocked, calling his name. She saw the owl when she eased the door open. It was standing on the dresser next to the television, perched in a ring of wadded-up clothes, staring at her, its deep eyes ringed with a fringe of white gray. *What the hell?* Sydney opened the door, watching the bird. It remained completely motionless, its eyes fixed on her. A small drift of snow had formed where the door was cracked, and the room was ice-cold. The bed was in disarray and clothes littered the floor. A paper cup of coffee on the dresser, the lamp still on, a takeout carton of chicken wings on a chair. She stepped inside slowly, watching the owl. The place smelled like pine sap, vegetable rot, and a faint whiff of animal dung.

Braden, are you here? It's Sydney Beauchamp. From DSS?

Sydney gave the owl a wide berth and walked back to the bathroom area. If Braden had an accident or overdose, he was most likely in the bathroom. But the bathroom was empty except for the usual detritus of men living alone in decrepit conditions: a soda can holding a frayed toothbrush, a rusty razor in the sink that was ringed with hair and grime, a pair of dollar-store flip-flops, a scattering of prescription pill bottles on the toilet tank. Burn marks on the edge of the sink where cigarettes had been laid to rest. Sydney picked up a couple of the pill bottles and rattled them: all empty, save one with a small wad of tin foil inside. She opened it and unfolded the foil to reveal one small white pill emblazoned with a red Fleur-de-Lis.

Sydney looked at herself in the speckled mirror for a moment, her breath billowing around her. In the corner of the mirror, she saw the owl slowly rotate his furred head away from the door to gaze back at her.

When she came outside, Braden's neighbor was sitting in a folding chair smoking a cigarette.

Have you seen Braden? Emerson asked him. The guy who lives here?

He took a dramatic draw on his cigarette and exhaled, still staring at the river.

Nope.

Sydney thought of the paperwork required to report this absence, notifying the parole officer. She probably shouldn't have entered the room at all, especially if it was a crime scene.

There's an owl in there, she said. In his room.

Sydney didn't know why she said it. The man raised his eyebrows and smirked as if to say, *life comes at you fast, amigo.*

Any idea where he might have gone?

He squinted at the river, pinching his cigarette between his forefinger and thumb.

If he's gone off again, I'd say the base bridge would be a good start.

He turned and looked at her, a man with hooded eyes and deep creases around his mouth, skin the color of roasted meat, like he'd lived his life on a windswept rock staring into the sun.

I'm not a cop, she said. I'm with Social Services.

He nodded and drew on his cigarette.

You say there's an owl in there? he said. That's gotta mean *something.*

In the 1940s, the air force built a steel pedestrian walkway over the train tracks so people on the base could access the lake. On the lake side, the bridge was connected to a set of steps that led down to a wide concrete pier, a row of boat sheds, and a boat ramp. Since the base closure, the bridge and pier area became a favorite gathering spot for assorted miscreants, and the concrete pier was scorched with bonfire marks, littered with cigarette buts and crushed empties. Hardy squatters lived year around in the abandoned boat sheds, some running thriving businesses dealing in weed, meth, animal tranquilizers, assorted aerosols and huffers. The base bridge was where you went if you wanted to score, though you might just as likely get assaulted, and the location served as the backdrop to many tragic North Country anecdotes.

At the top of the stairs, Sydney could see a fire winking through the spindled trees, the acrid smoke of burning plastic and the low murmur of voices. A teenager in a dirty white parka sat on the top step smoking a cigarette and staring at a cell phone. He turned and appraised her as she approached.

Social Services, Sydney said. Just trying to find a guy.

The teenager shrugged and went back to his phone.

There were more than a dozen figures on the pier, most huddled around a bonfire. Some kids, teenagers and young twentysomethings, a couple older and decidedly hard-looking individuals, shrunk down in their coats, with the blasted eyes and splayed gait of an addict crossing uneven ground. A couple boys tried to execute skateboard tricks on the lumpy surface of the pier. The six metal sheds that once served as boathouses were scarred with graffiti and had open doorways covered with tarps and blankets. A young girl with pigtails and a puffy coat emerged from a shed and tossed a bag of trash on the fire. Everyone glanced over at Sydney as she came down the stairs and then looked away. She had brought a picture of Braden Tullus from her old file, but she knew if she tried to show it around no one would talk to her.

The blanket covering the doorway of one of the sheds swung open and three young men stepped out, their dress and general comportment immediately dissonant, as if the shed had disgorged aliens. Three boys from the college. All wearing blue parkas, khaki pants, duck boots, one carrying an empty hockey bag.

The college boys strode directly to the end of the pier, where three sleds were parked in a row on the ice, gleaming blue and gold trim. They slipped on gloves, helmets, and goggles, then got astride their machines, fired them up, and launched themselves across the lake in a loose V formation, accelerating fast to the center of the lake, then bending north to round Cumberland Head, toward North Chazy. Within twenty seconds they were gone from sight. Sydney noticed that nearly everyone else there was watching their departure as well. As soon as they were gone, people began queuing up at the boat shed.

Then she saw the boy, out on the edge of the pier, on his hands and knees with a couple other boys, working on something on the ground. No hat and a light coat, that's what did it. She wasn't supposed to intercede unless it was an official visit, and she wasn't due to see Callie Trombley for a week, but the sight of Dylan playing in the muddy snow at the bottom of the base bridge seemed like an exceptional case. The kid was nine years old.

When Sydney approached, the two other kids moved off like feral animals, but Dylan stayed, intent on shaping something with his bare hands. He had erected a series of squared shapes of snow and chunks of ice, sprouting small twigs, plastic strips, and drinking straws that all pointed in the same direction, a low angle out across the lake.

Dylan, she said. You remember me? It's Sydney.

Yeah, he said.

I'm gonna take you home. Okay?

Okay, he said.

He stood up and dusted snow off his pants, which were soaked through and smeared with mud. He flipped the hair out of his eyes with one hand, still not looking at her. She knew it would be bad for him to be seen leaving with a woman from DSS.

My car's on the road, she said. The black Subaru. Meet me there in ten minutes.

Okay.

You gonna come? You promise?

Yeah, I promise.

Phil spent the week repainting the house and watching Juliet while Sydney was at work. In the afternoons, before the sun dropped below the wall, he sat on the porch in his heavy coat and cracked beers as Juliet made snow angels in the drifts in the front yard. It was similar to what his old man used to do on his days off, when he would drink a pint of Crown and doze off on the porch with a burning cigarette in his hand, waking angrily to the hard chill of sundown, Phil and his sister already in bed. Nobody wanted to be outside when the shadow of the wall eclipsed the house in the evening.

Phil began to grasp the gravity of the wall was when he was a boy playing baseball in the summer, Dannemora Community Park, his Little Yankees squad sponsored by the New York Correctional Officers Association. It was a bright August day and Phil was pitching to a team from Rouse's Point that mostly shied away from his fastball. Phil's mother was sitting in the bleachers, smoking menthols, wearing a thin windbreaker and a scarf on her hair. Afterward she usually took him down to the dairy bar for a creamy.

In the fourth inning the other team still didn't have a hit. At the plate was a pigeon-toed kid in a giant batting helmet that kept slipping over his eyes.

Then a sharp *crack . . . crack crack crack* of a carbine from the direction of the prison. The faint sound of a whistle bleating repeatedly, the clang of metal. The players in the field straightened from their crouches, turning toward the wall.

Crack crack . . . crack.

The mothers began calling out to their boys on the field. Phil's mother was shaking out a menthol, lighting it with a pearl butane lighter. She was wearing a tan skirt and shoes the deep color of a ripe raspberry. The catcher and batter had run off and the umpire was jogging toward his car.

Crack.

Cars started up and gunned their engines, boys rattled away on bicycles, sawing back and forth on the handles. Phil took off his glove and ran to his mother.

When they got home, she locked the deadbolts, drew all the blinds, and got the .38 out of the closet and stuck it in the side-table drawer in the living room. His sister was at a friend's house, a half-dozen blocks south of the wall, and it was understood that she would be safer there. Phil and his mom sat on the sofa watching sitcoms, *Barney Miller*, *WKRP in Cincinnati*, his mother chain-smoking and drinking black coffee. Phil stirred his cherry Kool-Aid with his finger and watched the wall through a crack in the curtains. The receiving entrance was quiet, the chain-link cage empty, a yellow alarm light circling silently. The east tower had the windows covers opened, the thin black sticks of rifle barrels trained on the interior. He could hear the faint sounds of voices, shouting.

For the next couple days, everyone crackled with an edge, a flinty sensitivity. People avoided each other. But the damage had been done. They had seen the revelation in the dregs of their coffee cup, the dark specter of dissatisfactions and regrets that burned in the guts of every home in the shadow of the wall. In the hours and days after lockdowns and yard incidents is when most divorces were broached, when hidden thoughts and secret transgressions were aired, when the ponderous, mundane deceptions of family life were exposed. This was when people left. If you made it through those couple days, then all would return to normal. Everyone would go back to ignoring the wall.

On Tuesdays, the Ausable College ice arena had open pickup games with college players lined up against a mixed bag of older locals. Phil sorted out his gear and took the bus to the rink, hoping to work up a sweat and get his mind straight. The college players were decent; quick, agile players, but they were undersized and lacking in the ambidextrous ability necessary to play Division I or Canadian Junior Hockey. The older local players kept a case of Labatt on the bench. Phil usually skated at about 50 percent, passing off the puck and trying to set up his teammates. When the college guys started to get aggressive, he would turn it up a bit, using his speed to explode past the blue line and stickhandle his way to a quick shot.

Near the end of the first period, a college player chopped at his ankles, and when Phil took the puck behind the net, he launched himself into Phil's back, jamming him into the boards. Phil flipped the puck off to his wing and spun around.

What the *fuck*?

The kid gave him an insolent glare through the plexiglass of his helmet face shield. When they skated off for a line change, Phil saw the kid's teammates talking to him. He knew they were telling him not to fuck with a pro, but the fact that he was the most accomplished and skilled player on the ice felt like a point of embarrassment, a reminder of his failures to succeed at the next level. He sat on the bench and tried to enjoy the familiar and comforting aspects of the rink, the damp chill, the ancient scoreboard with painted bulbs and faulty clock, the warbling horn, the jostle of his teammates on the bench during line changes, the metronomic crack of the puck on wood, the crunch of a body into plexiglass. There was a kind of tension in the air when Phil had the puck, everyone watching. He knew they were all waiting for him to turn it up for at least a few moments so that they might get their shot against a professional-caliber player. But Phil couldn't shake the feeling that he shouldn't be here.

On his next shift, he intercepted the kid mid-ice, chopping into him with a hip check that sent him sprawling, spread-eagled, sliding into the zone. Phil followed his sliding body, using him as a screen, worked the stick handle to get the goalie to commit right and then roofed it with a quick backhand flip, the puck popping the goalie's water bottle on top of the net. His team hooted from the bench and Phil went over the wall and accepted a proffered Labatt, downing the can in one go as his teammates slapped his shin pads with their sticks. *Fuck yeah!*

Phil left after the second period. He was out of shape, already feeling the deep soreness that would develop over the next couple days. There was a cooler in the locker room, and Phil plucked a couple beers and drank them in the shower, leaning against the moldy tiles with the hot water on the back of his neck.

When he stepped outside, it was full dark and the wind off the lake razored through his coat. He could've got a ride with someone if he waited around, but he wanted to get home, so he slipped a wool cap over his damp hair and headed toward the bus station four blocks away. In the front row of the parking lot, a long black Audi sedan was idling. As Phil approached, the back door swung open and a man got out. He was wearing a wool topcoat over a suit, maybe sixty years old, a bristly flattop of steel-gray hair.

How you doin', Phil?

He proffered his hand and Phil took it, inspecting his face, trying to place him.

I used to watch you play, the man said, in the Canadian American cup series down in Lake Placid. I even caught a Selkirk game on TV when I was in Toronto. You did most of the third in the box after you beat that Swedish guy unconscious. Remember that one?

Phil nodded.

My name's Gene Marin. I'm down in Albany, just come up to visit my son. He was the guy you decked open ice before you roofed that lousy goalie.

Phil glanced back at the squat structure of the rink, the floodlights casting pools of light. At the far end of the parking lot an old LTD belched exhaust and the faint wail of Led Zepplin. Gene Marin had his head cocked, a grin on his face. Phil decided he must be a salesman of some kind.

Yeah, Phil said. He charged me in the boards. I figure he was asking for it.

Maybe, Gene Marin said. Seems a little unfair, though, doesn't it? You being an ex-pro? And him just a college kid? You being, what, twenty-seven, twenty-eight?

Thirty.

You think it's a good idea to knock around kids like that?

I don't consider a guy in college a *kid*.

Gene Marin laughed, a short, hard laugh. He slapped Phil on the arm.

I'm just fucking with you. I agree completely. Those little shits ask for it, especially my kid. I wish you would've hit him a couple more times! But listen, I want to talk to you about something. Hop in, I'll give you a ride home. Okay?

Talk about what?

A proposition, Gene Marin said. A job. A better job than the Dannemora prison. No disrespect.

Gene opened the back door of the Audi. The spacious back seat was black leather, and the driver was facing front, hands on the wheel, the dash glowing like the cockpit of a spaceship. Gene took a copper flask out of his overcoat and waggled it. Phil took it, unscrewed the top, and turned it up. Whiskey. It coursed through his bones and Phil felt the raw skin on his cheeks flame with blood. He wiped a film of sweat off his forehead with the inside of his forearm. Gene sat in the back seat, scooting over and gesturing to the driver. The trunk popped open with a meaty thunk.

C'mon, Phil. Chuck your bag in the trunk. Hear me out.

The LTD across the lot gunned its engine, a cloud of exhaust rolling out, the wailing intro of "Immigrant Song" still shrieking, like they had it on a loop. Phil looked up at the faint slash of stars over the lake. He felt the lactic acid pooling in his hamstrings, the dampness of his socks. Sydney at home, putting Juliet to bed in an unpainted room with cigarette smoke stains on the ceiling.

A ride home, at least, Gene Marin said.

He pulled a long wallet out of his coat and slipped out a couple bills.

Hundred dollars. Just to hear the deal.

Phil slung his bag into the open trunk and slammed it shut. He tossed the flask to Gene in the back seat, who fumbled the catch. Phil sat down heavily, the pressurized shocks sinking with his weight.

You got any beers?

While she waited for Dylan to emerge from the base bridge, Sydney cranked the heat up in the Subaru and dug out a packet of Juliet's peanut butter crackers. Dylan said he wasn't hungry, but he ate the whole pack before she got back to town. She could see the lines of dirt around his ears, the crusty fingernails, and she instructed him to take a hot bath first thing, and to give his mother the note she wrote out on the steering wheel.

> *Callie—I found Dylan at the Base Bridge today—you have got to keep him away from there and closer to home. If this happens again, I will be forced to do the report, and you'll get a visit from PROTECTIVE. I know you don't want that. I don't want that. Please, Callie.*
>
> *—Sydney Beauchamp,*
> *DSS*

Sydney headed to her mother's to pick up Juliet before heading to the church for Bible study. Epiphany Lutheran was an old blue-limestone structure with a bell tower covered by summer-ivy. The congregation had steadily shrunk each year, and Sydney missed the full narthex after church fellowship, the row of coffee urns, the plates of sliced pound cake, the animated talk. Now there was just the single coffeepot, a paper plate of store-bought cookies, and the thirty or so parishioners huddled around the table as if to create the impression of a crowd. Sydney dropped Juliet in the nursery room, where calcified old ladies sat in folding chairs with tumbling children at their feet.

The Bible study class sat in a circle of chairs in the choir room, about a dozen regulars, most of them over sixty. They were reading a passage from Jerimiah. Pastor Lyle sat back in his chair, arms crossed, and worried his mustache with one hand.

Call to me and I will answer you and will tell you great and hidden things that you have not known.

Sydney thought about telling him about the voice she heard that plaintive question: *What will happen to us*? The voice *did* seem real. What if it was from God?

The room was still, and their collective breathing, the wind coursing in and out of the weathered bodies, suddenly became deafening. Sydney closed her eyes.

When we pray, she thought, we send our messages into boundless space, into eternity. That's all we can do. Then we turn our hearts to the sky and wait.

KAISER

Kaiser trekked to the hunting cabin to check the readings and secure the tower. His backpack contained a sleeping bag, a couple apples, water, and a pint flask of rum with a splash of Coke and a squeeze of lime. Several loops of steel cable were strapped to the outside of the pack, along with metal stakes and a small sledgehammer. In his inside coat pocket was a thumb drive containing a program called Skygrabber. It was designed to steal music and other internet content, but with a bit of tweaking could be used to intercept air-to-ground telemetry transmissions. When Kaiser was in Afghanistan, several Taliban groups used the program to hack into US drones, breaking military encryption using twenty-year-old Hewlett-Packard desktops running off diesel generators deep in the caves of Tora Bora. It is a simple fact: The air-to-ground telemetry of drones isn't that difficult to intercept.

It was dark and raining pea-size ice pellets when he reached the cabin. He fired up the propane heater, which warmed the small room quickly. His intercept rig was bolted into an old plastic suitcase, a laptop, motherboard, extra screen for sensor area display, the small black box of the telemeter, with cables leading outside to the tower and the modified sensor array. Kaiser scrolled through the log for the last week and found a variety of intercepts, satellites and drones, their trajectories crisscrossing the border creating a hatch of green lines on the screen.

The government entities coordinating the surveillance tasking had to cover as much ground as possible while making it seem random, so the passes were difficult to anticipate. Of course there *was* a pattern, but it was clear to Kaiser that he would have to have a much larger sample to work out the formula. Hundreds, maybe thousands of runs. LeClair wanted to make his move in the next couple weeks. They needed a quick route, a way to get across and the package out of their hands in less than thirty minutes. Kaiser ruled out going through the mountains, too much logistic difficulty and impassible terrain. The border along the central plains, from Cornwall to Hemingford, was far too secure, with radar stations and ground-based heat sensing equipment that would pick up a sprinting rabbit in the night. Passing through the border stations was out of the question; Kaiser knew the sensing equipment they had there, including the dogs, were impossible to beat.

The lake was the most difficult to monitor, because the weather was unpredictable and more extreme due to lake effects. If they could time it with heavy weather, taking satellites out of the equation, and if Kaiser could hack the drones and avoid their sensors, they could send a single screamer on a sled across the ice. Gerard had a high-powered sled, custom outfitted by La Herrison, with a trailer attachment. The package would be 250 pounds, the size of a filing cabinet. If the drop site was close, they could have it across and out of their hands in thirty minutes.

Kaiser downloaded all the intercepted video recordings to the laptop and started the Skygrabber program. There was SLAR, IMINT, MASINT, multispectral sensors, thermal, and synthetic aperture radar that created three-dimensional landscape images. Once the Skygrabber program was silently crunching away on the encryption codes, Kaiser took the steel cable, hammer, and stakes outside to stabilize the sensor array.

The heavy sleet clattered in the trees like a rain of marbles. Kaiser put on ski goggles, tucked his chin into his coat, and trudged to the antennae tower, the faint light of LEDs from his instruments under the snapping tarp. The ladder was crusted with ice and the structure swayed as he climbed. At the top, he hooked the looped cable ends onto carabineers on each corner of the stand and dropped the other end to the ground. Then he climbed down and secured the cables to stakes that he drove into the ground, giving the stand four stable stays. Climbing back up, he wedged himself under the tarp to check the equipment, then sitting with his legs dangling over the edge he scanned the sky with his binoculars. The cloud cover was too heavy to spot anything, so he watched the faint lights of Point Au Roche, North Chazy, and Isle La Motte.

It just had to work *once.* Kaiser's cut would settle everything for the farm, with a lot left over. But was that it? Was that the reason he was doing this? The truth was he was feeling something that he'd hadn't felt for years, since Afghanistan. During his incarceration he spent almost three years without any access to gear, and while he could close his eyes wherever he was and work out the trajectories by time, memory, and intuition, it wasn't the same. Now he felt like he was tapping into the neural pathways of the universe. He could see the order, he understood the information. He was reading the mind of the gods.

Now he just needed a pilot for the sled. He needed a screamer.

I was racing sleds on Kings Bay, Sebastian said, when I was fucking nine years old!

They were sitting at the Dry Dock splitting a platter of chicken wings. Kaiser hadn't mentioned the need for a screamer, but Seb knew.

I've been across the lake a thousand times, Sebastian said. Across the border, down the fucking Ausable River. There ain't anything I can't do on a sled.

So?

Bro. Don't treat me like I'm stupid.

The redheaded bartender named Jud took away their empty glasses. The place was mostly deserted except for three guys playing pool in the back who kept putting money in the jukebox to play the same song, over and over. Sebastian had just woken up from his cot in the back room and was wearing a sweatshirt with cut off sleeves, jeans, and bare feet. He had shaved his head the day before, and his bare skull shone in the damp light.

What's the cut for the driver? Sebastian asked.

Not sure.

Well give me a fucking estimate, dude.

Jud came back with a fresh pair of Cuba Libres. Outside, cars whooshed down Route 9. Sebastian carefully squeezed his lime before stirring the drink, the same way Kaiser always did.

Maybe 50K?

Sebastian stopped stirring and turned his whole body on the stool toward Kaiser.

I'm the guy, he said. You know this. C'mon!

Sebastian rotated around to take in the rest of the bar, then lowered his voice.

We're partners, right? And I'm a fucking *master* on the sled!

Sebastian looked away out the frosted windows. His hand compulsively gripped his drink. He licked his lips.

C'mon, man, he said. I haven't complained about *squat* since we started. Getting shot. Fucking running cables across the mountains. Tracking fucking satellites. I never pried into your crazy shit. I know you already paid me for stuff, and I'm not saying you owe me. I'm asking you to help me out.

The crack of pool balls and a short curse. The door rasped open and slammed shut, the wave of cold air, an old man in a fur hat listing toward the bar. Kaiser checked his watch. He didn't have any other options. When Sebastian turned back to Kaiser his eyes were shining. He twisted one of his bolts with his thumb and forefinger.

I don't wanna die in this town, he said. And I don't want Dylan to either. You get me?

Yeah, Kaiser said. I do.

Sebastian rapped one of his vertical halo bars with his knuckles.

I even got a built-in fucking helmet!

Up on the tower, Kaiser drank deeply from the flask, the rum a shaft of fire down his chest, staring out at the roiling sky. Only four numbers left. The instruments hummed and clicked behind him, and in the blinding sheet of ice, Kaiser could almost see the radio waves, the pulses of electromagnetic radiation as they emanated from his outpost, spreading like the ripples from a pebble dropped in a pond, moving through the atmosphere and into space, beyond the planets and through the galaxy; radio transmissions, television shows, signal noises, the voice of his father calling into the black. They would go on, moving through space at the speed of light, becoming fainter and harder to detect as the inverse square law decrees, just ethereal threads and strands of human desire, projected into eternity. It was all still out there, every radio wave ever transmitted. It would never end.

In the cabin, Kaiser laid out the bedroll and got into his sleeping bag with the laptop on his chest to watch the collected video transmissions. There was plenty of synthetic aperture and thermal video, and he focused on these as they were the most direct evidence of what the drones and satellites were seeing. As he toggled through the screens of landscapes, the garish hues and blocky textures of the synthetic, and the fields of green littered with spots of reds and yellows on the thermal scopes, Kaiser noticed a repeated elliptical shape on the lake, just northeast of North Chazy, that straddled the border. An instrument malfunction? A barge? He triple-checked all the images. A dark, oblong shape, several hundred meters long. It wasn't weather, and radar imaging could penetrate water and ice. Was it something *under* the ice? The bottom of Lake Champlain was littered with shipwrecks, but the size was incredible.

Outside the pines creaked in the high winds. He marked the spot and took coordinates on multiple images, all the same. They couldn't see through it. None of the sensors could penetrate this dark place. Kaiser's pulse started throbbing in his temple. An anomaly. A blind spot.

A dark spot in the lake.

STERNE

Laurence Sterne woke up in the Rover with the engine running. He was parked in his garage, the door halfway open. His bong was between his feet, the apple-butter jar of Quebec Gold cradled in his lap, his crotch mysteriously damp. He was about twenty minutes late for his morning class. His briefcase was still in the back seat, so he put the truck in gear and headed toward campus.

The houses along Route 9 seemed to be burdened by a great weight, pressing down on them from the heavens. Laurence had watched these scenes from the car window a thousand times. The listing porches, sagging window frames, and fraying rooflines, a tin shed hammered to the side of a decrepit Victorian mansion and secured with tar paper and a staple gun. Mud yards with a squad of pit bull mixes staked to the ground. The hardpan ice on the roads, six inches deep and bluish like the ancient ice of high mountain glaciers. Sterne passed a yard sale, maybe, that had been going on for at least a month, items strewn about a snowy yard and piled on card tables, a couple guys sitting in lawn chairs with a cooler, a leathery woman on the stoop. A teenage boy on the road ahead of him on a handicapped scooter, bags of groceries tied to the front, the boy hunched over the handlebars squeezing out every last bit of speed. As Sterne passed the boy looked over and grinned with enlarged, black eyes.

When he got to the college parking lot, Sterne kept the Rover running and took a couple bong hits, listening to Joan Armatrading sing "I'm Lucky." *Track Record* was one of Sue's favorite albums. He pulled out the bowl stem and sucked in the cloud of floral smoke, exhaling out his window, watching the hunched forms of students walking to their classes, the ardent timbre of Armatrading's voice running through his heart like a lance of ice. How foolish could he be, imagining that these self-serving, spoiled bastards cared about him and his sorrows? There were grade point averages and transcripts and graduate school and résumés to build.

Sterne walked across the lawn, sloughing through the windblown snow in his loafers. He had his wool overcoat but no hat or scarf, and his face was raw from the wind. Inside the foyer there were dozens of students milling around, waiting to see if he was going to show up. He had told the dean he wanted to finish out the semester. He didn't know why. The students in the foyer followed him into the lecture hall. Sterne was sweating heavily now, and he shrugged off his coat. He was vaguely aware that final exams were supposed to happen sometime in the next week or so. He checked the front of his pants, the stain now just barely visible. The students filing into the hall had trailing forms, ghost-selves, and they seemed slowed down, like they were moving through liquid glass. After they were all inside, he flipped off the lights, went to the front of the room, and wrestled the laptop out of his briefcase. The only sound was the squeak of his soaked boots and the metallic clicks as the projector powered up. He checked his watch: The class was officially over in fifteen minutes. That would be just enough time. Sterne toggled through his presentation to get to the painting he wanted.

Sterne decided he would audit a limnology course at the University of Michigan. Sue Jansky was the TA. She never asked why a guy getting his PhD in art history would be auditing an undergraduate science class. But she knew. The second week they had a study date at the library, that led to an art history cocktail hour, and then an impromptu party at another grad student's house. His initial attraction was merely desire, as her physical being made him cringe with lust. Sterne had also run through all the available candidates for sexual congress in the art history graduate program, a procession of bug-eyed lunatics with a tendency for *Sturm und Drang* during sex and breakfast. But the smooth and authoritative confidence of Sue Jansky amplified his interest. She drew him like the invisible tides of gravity.

That evening at the party, after the whiskey shots and midnight wiffle ball and the shouting match over the moral hubris of Hudson River school painters, they were standing with about a dozen people in the galley kitchen, someone playing Simon & Garfunkel's *Live in Central Park* on the record player. Sterne was stoned, focusing his attention on a bowl of hummus and pita, when a cockroach the size of a mouse came from under the fridge, coming to a stop in the middle of the kitchen floor. Everyone froze. Sterne had a dripping triangle of pita halfway to his mouth. Sue Jansky stepped forward with both hands high in the air, one holding her sweating glass of gin and tonic, and drove the stake of her high heel squarely into the carapace of the creature, severing it into two equal parts. She stepped back and took a deep drink, meeting all of their gazes. Sterne licked a bit of hummus off his finger and placed his hand on the small of her back, feeling the warmth and power that radiated off her like the nuclear furnace of the stars.

They ended up kissing on the front porch with the light from the windows streaming over them, a dog in the yard across the street howling at the invisible river of scents in the midnight wind. Within a couple weeks, she had built a fortress in his heart.

Sterne tapped the button and Turner's masterpiece *Regulus* filled the room.

As a young boy, Sterne said, raising his voice, Turner was fond of staring at the sun. In his old age, he was afraid that he had damaged his eyesight by looking at the sun directly too often as a child. Turner was obsessed with the literal applications of the sun, how it supplied *and* stripped the world of color.

Sterne paused and coughed into his fist. The creak of seat bolts, forearms on desks, and the faintest scratching of pen nubs on paper. He could see them all looking at him. He flapped his arms.

Look at the goddamn painting! Not at *me*!

Sterne felt sweat gathering between his shoulder blades, and he caught a sudden whiff of his own body odor.

Regulus, Sterne said. We have the wash of light from left of center, the framing buildings in raked perspective, the ruins of the ancient city of Carthage. Turner worked the piece over a second time in 1837. A large hunk of flake white on his palette, working it into every conceivable crevice. So we are viewing the scene from the *perspective* of Regulus, a Roman general, captured and imprisoned by the Carthaginians.

Sterne began to pace the front of the room.

In 256 BC, Rome was at war with Carthage. The Carthaginians worshipped an ancient god named Moloch, who was fond of human sacrifice. They built an enormous cast-iron statue of Moloch. Groups of people could be placed on his hands and lifted with pulleys and chains and dumped down the open mouth and into the furnace in the idol's belly. On a regular basis, men, women, and children were consumed by Moloch. When Carthage was attacked by Rome, the priests declared that Moloch desired the sacrifice of the eldest sons of Carthage's noble families. It is said they all went willingly. It seemed to work because the Carthaginians used their elephants to crush the Roman legions, capturing many prisoners, including the general Regulus. All of the prisoners went into the mouth of Moloch, *except* for Regulus, who was sent back to Rome to deliver the terms of peace. He was made to swear to return to Carthage regardless of the reply, and he gave his word. So Regulus goes to the Roman Senate and explains what the Carthaginians expect in terms of tribute and surrender. Amazingly, he then urged the Romans *not* to accept the deal. The senators agreed.

Sterne paused, now standing in the dark off to the side of the projected painting, gazing at it as he spoke.

His family begged him, Sterne said. *Not* to go back. If Regulus returned to Carthage with the rejection, it would mean certain death or worse. But he gave his word, and so he went. The Carthaginians were enraged at the response from Rome. They threw Regulus into a dark pit, without any light, for several months. Then one morning they hauled him to the surface, strapped him to a board, and cut off his eyelids. They propped him up at the harbor facing east, to catch every ray of the blazing African sun as it rose over the Mediterranean.

Sterne was suddenly tired. He looked into the first rows of students and saw they were looking at him again, their eyes rounded, pens in hand. He swung his arm wildly.

Look at the fucking painting!

He recognized one young girl in the front row. She had taken his class before. Not an art history major, but a bright kid. She was gazing at the painting, hand roving over the notebook on her desk, taking blind notes. She had long, tangled hair, and the light from the projector seemed to make loose strands glow. Her gaze slowly turned to him, her eyes blinking, watery. Was she crying? He tapped a button to advance the slide, a block of text.

This is from Edmund Burke, Sterne said. *A Philosophical Enquiry into the Origin of Our Ideas of the Sublime and Beautiful.* You read this in September. Or you were supposed to. From part two, "Of the Passion Caused by the Sublime."

> The passion caused by the great and sublime in nature, when those causes operate most powerfully, is astonishment; and astonishment is that state of the soul, in which all its motions are suspended, with some degree of horror.

Pens scribbled furiously across paper and someone hacked out a long, tubercular cough in the deep darkness of the back of the hall. The girl in the front row. Emerson LeClair. That was her name. *Wait.* LeClair? He flipped the slide back to *Regulus.*

Regulus, he said, went blind and insane. Later the Romans put him in a barrel full of spikes and rolled him down a hill until he was dead. It is fair to say that Regulus was *astonished* by his experiences. *This* is what the painting captures, that moment of . . . astonishment.

Sterne leaned on the lectern with both hands. He could see the Turner's colors washing over his forearms and shirt. He stood there for what felt like a long time.

Then he raised his head, looking into the blue light of the projector, blind to the room.

This is the perspective of Regulus!

He was shouting, shaking the lectern with both hands.

Can you see what's there, in the light?

Can you see it?

LECLAIR

The boys scrubbed the house down for the rip-off competition. The party room was mopped, the floor drains cleared, the walls murals wiped, and the long bar polished. They had a small stage set up in the corner, a rigged spotlight, two kegs of Labatt Blue on ice, a bottle of baby oil, and Jane's Addiction wailing from the speakers. LeClair paused in the doorway until Troy could clear a path to the judge's seat, a blue velvet armchair from the chapter room set up on a dais of beer kegs and plywood near the back of the room, surrounded by police tape.

I'll take a gimlet, LeClair told Troy. A double.

The boys were hypercompetitive, LeClair knew that, but the lengths they went to in service of some bet or contest was absurd. LeClair had been at the house to judge a contest several years ago, a drinking contest between two brothers who played on the same line together on the college hockey team billed as "Vitte vs. Crouchet." LeClair sat on the same throne chair, with the competition taking place in the middle of the party room in a boxing ring created by empty kegs and toilet paper. Inside the ring, a table was lined with cups of beer and two trash cans at each end. A brother with his body painted with black and white stripes and wearing an adult diaper was the "referee" of the event. It was all quite amusing until the spectacle began, and Vitte and Crouchet began to chug beers at an alarming rate, punctuated by regular bouts of explosive vomiting. After the first five-minute round LeClair was nearly ill himself. The room stunk of stomach bile and sausage pizza—the pregame meal—and in the second round, after around sixteen cups of beer each, Vitte vomited so hard he bashed his upper lip into the rim of the metal trash can, drawing blood. A howl went up from the crowd but Vitte snatched another cup and turned it up, blood running down his chest. By the time the third round was over they had drunk twenty-four cups each, and the match came down to the judge's decision. LeClair figured Vitte probably drank at least a quart of his own blood based on what he was vomiting up in the last round, and so he decided in Vitte's favor, setting off a riot among the two camps of supporters, and LeClair had to be escorted out for safety. Enraged at the perceived injustice of the decision, Crouchet stormed out of the house and threw himself into the lake like some kind of despondent romantic poet.

They promised him the rip-off would not be nearly as violent. LeClair had completely forgotten he'd agreed to do it. He had just settled in with a glass of Bombay Sapphire on ice with sprigs of fresh mint, the Sunday *New York Times* arts section, and *Bête Noire* cued up on the CD changer when the alley buzzer went off. On the security cam, he saw a couple of the boys standing before the alley door, stamping their feet and blowing into their hands.

He was cultivating a delicate relationship. It was LeClair who bailed out the boys in the drunk tank, who set them up with his team of loosely affiliated lawyers, who fixed tickets at the courthouse, who made calls to the provost's office on behalf of a struggling brother who'd lost his way, and it was LeClair who on a couple occasions paid someone to keep their mouth shut (a professor, a winsome co-ed), or who dispatched the Lavoie brothers for a late-night mediation. In return he expected . . . what was it, exactly? Loyalty? Honesty? Truthfully it was something more like a bank of debts he was building, a depository for future requests. He *owned* them, nearly all of them, in some way or another. He would come down and judge the stupid contest, and in return they would come when he called. At least he hoped they would.

It was Troy waiting in the alley, along with the brother that caught LeClair's eye at the fall pig roast, the attractive lad Kaiser handled so roughly at the restaurant: Scotty Marin. They'd come to chauffeur LeClair down to the house in the Escalade.

It was the first time at LeClair's house for Scotty. They stood by the fire, their coats steaming. Scotty ran a hand through his gloriously tousled hair and surveyed the room.

This is incredible, Scotty said. I love landscapes.

Troy wiped off his glasses and accepted a mug of hot cider from Alejandro.

Since when?

Since I went to the Tate Britain, Scotty said, back in high school. My dad had business in London, and he brought me along. The Turner prize thing was going on, but I was really into the Pre-Raphaelites mostly.

LeClair was rinsing out his glass in the wet bar sink.

Anybody in particular?

Rossetti, Scotty said. Thomas Woolner is okay. I really like William Holman Hunt.

LeClair let them wait downstairs while he went up to change. What does one wear to judge a muscle contest at a frat house? He slipped on a lightweight wool suit, a French-blue tab collar, his waterproof chukkas. No cuff links. He sat on the edge of the bed and tied his boots. He would need drinks. More than a few.

The final meeting in Quebec with Montagne had gone well despite the strangeness of it all. This time they met in a busy café in Le Vieux, no minders or bodyguards or anyone else as far as Clair could tell. The spindly Quebecois looked even more like a prep-school headmaster than the czar of an international criminal syndicate. LeClair was reminded of a poster his college roommate had on his wall of the playwright Samuel Beckett, a flinty, stern visage that seemed born of hand-rolled cigarettes and obscure literary devices. Montagne agreed to the plan that LeClair outlined for him. It had to be done on the frozen lake. When Kaiser determined the right time, Montagne would set up the receiving crew on the New York side. LeClair would come to Montreal for the duration of the deal, enjoying a night of entertainment with some of Montagne's associates. When Montagne's people received the package, he would be free to return to North Chazy, with *Glaucus and Scylla* safely sealed in a carrying case and two million dollars in cash.

LeClair picked at his pistachio bombolini. He was trying to control his enthusiasm. He was already thinking about his escape from the North Country, the new life he would have. This was going to work, he could feel it.

Your niece at the *universite*, Montagne said. A student of literature? *Excellente.*

Montagne drained his espresso, smacking his lips in appreciation. LeClair stared at him. Montagne signaled for the check.

Remember, *mon ami*. Mistake, failure, there will be a cost. For me, and for you.

Troy drove the Escalade through town, heading south to the campus as Scotty Marin tried to banter with LeClair from the back seat.

I plan on owning my own business someday, Scotty said. Hopefully something diversified, like you. But right now, I'm, like, saving up, gathering capital.

Troy gripped the wheel and looked like he might puke. LeClair was solemn, thinking about Montagne. *Your niece at the universite.*

How long is this thing going to take? he asked.

Troy checked his watched as he turned down fraternity row.

One hour, tops. We'll have you back by eleven o'clock.

The undercard, a range of preliminary contests, lasted until eleven thirty. It seemed the brothers used the rip-off event as a sort of clearing house for assorted grievances, disputes of physical strength, and general differing opinions about the theoretical ends of human suffering. There were arm wrestling contests, a push-up contest, and a sort of hybrid-speed-eating contest involving chicken wings doused in some kind of vile sauce. The boundaries of the human body, LeClair thought. A dangerous frontier to explore.

LeClair sipped his third drink and watched a pair of young men standing bare-chested and with their feet duct-taped to the stage taking turns punching each other in the chest until one collapsed in agony. The brothers went wild, shoving and elbowing each other, a knot of bodies grappling on the beer-slick floor at LeClair's feet, the air thick with animal musk.

Finally, the music for the main event was cued up. Whenever the boys had a big event, contest, or pledge-hazing activity, it was always Black Sabbath's *Paranoid*, always starting off with the grinding, swooping guitars of "Iron Man," which they greeted with a chorus of banshee howls. Gary's entourage entered first, a troop of boys holding a sheet of plywood overhead, a wild-eyed Gary on top doing rapid-fire push-ups, wearing only a pair of black Lycra shorts, his body raining sweat as he thrust himself upward again and again like a fleshy piston. Buck's group entered from the opposite hallway door, a brother holding up a giant "world champion" belt, crafted rather meticulously, LeClair thought, including gilt filigree and stenciled lettering. Following was Buck in his rubber suit, hood up, doing a boxer's dance, bobbing, feinting, throwing jabs. Gary got into a crouch on the plywood, then launched himself like a bullfrog at the stage, doing a neat tuck and roll, leaping to his feet and throwing his shoulders back, fists clenched at his sides, the striated tendons in his neck popping like meat cables. *The Garden of Earthly Delights*, LeClair found himself thinking, and he shifted in his seat, putting his chin in his hand in a pose of studied nonchalance. Scotty Marin caught his eye and gave him a look like: *Now that's a spicy meatball, eh?*

Buck now reached the stage and squat-jumped into the air, shrieking like a man possessed, turning to the audience and unzipping the rubber suit top in one fluid motion and pulling it back from his shoulders, his head rolled back in ecstasy. LeClair nearly dropped his drink. Buck's gleaming torso was like a topographical map of a fabled, undiscovered country, his abdomen segmented like an alien exoskeleton, the neck and shoulders of the titan Atlas bending to his work. Somebody slapped an electronic timer on the stage. LeClair fumbled with the pad and pen provided him. He wrote "Gary" on one side of the page, "Buck" on the other. When he looked up Gary had his back to the crowd, pushing out his lats like butterfly wings, his buttocks clenched, one leg modeling the knotted ball of his calf muscle. Buck had his pants around his ankles, a green French-cut Speedo plastered over his straining crotch. He was looking hungrily at his opponent, brandishing an enormous hunting knife in one hand, his face set like he intended to do something carnal to him, some kind of unspeakable violation. Something rose in LeClair's throat. His vision dimmed, ringed with delicate, sparkling flashes of light.

LeClair dropped his drink to the floor, the glass popping silently in the wash of sound. He stood up, unsteady on his feet, and tried to step off the platform and fell, going down hard on one arm and knee, falling on his side into the lake of beer sludge. The boys rushed to him.

Alejandro had prepared the fireplace before he left for the evening. LeClair wadded up a piece of newspaper under the neatly stacked wood and threw lit matches at it while Scotty mixed them a round of drinks from the cart. When the kindling was crackling, LeClair stepped back and inspected the cuffs of his pants, sodden with beer and sweat. He gingerly took off his suit jacket, one sleeve smeared with floor grease and his elbow throbbing from his fall. The whole way home there was a litany of apologies and LeClair finally told the two boys to *shut the fuck up* and *take your shoes off if you are coming in*. Troy begged off for an economics exam in the morning.

LeClair was angry that he suffered such an ungainly exit. He was nearly fifty years old, an eccentric bachelor, a certified crank in North Chazy. What *was* he doing? He sat on the couch and Scotty handed him a gimlet, the rim of the glass expertly sugared and the color of the liquid indicating the correct ratio of gin to Rose's lime juice. Scotty sat down next to him and sighed, stretching out his legs, pointing his toes. Argyle socks. The yeasty scent of damp clothing, sweaty feet. LeClair used the remote to cue up *Flesh and Blood* on the CD player, put it on shuffle, and "Same Old Scene" swelled from the speakers. Scotty seemed restless, gulping his drink and standing up again. He took a turn about the room, slowing to look at LeClair's collection of Thomas Cole copies, stopping at *The Oxbow*, hip cocked in a classic contrapposto, his blue oxford shirt tight around the shoulders, hands thrust in the pockets of his khakis. LeClair turned up the music, and Scotty turned to give him a slight smile.

I don't want to hear any fucking comments, LeClair said.

I like Roxy Music! I mean, not a real fan of the early stuff, but anything after *For Your Pleasure* is pretty cool. I think Eddie Jobson was a *great* replacement for Eno.

LeClair sipped his drink. How many twenty-one-year-olds know the early discography of Roxy Music? The fire was pushing some heat around the room, but his damp pant legs and shirtsleeves made LeClair shiver.

You should get a shower, Scotty said. Put on some clean stuff. Make you feel better.

LeClair kept looking at *The Oxbow*. The promise of green hills, the placid length of water, and the menace of the coming storm. His drink was empty. He was shaking now, from cold or something else he couldn't tell.

He did feel better after a shower. When he came downstairs to turn off the lights and lock up, he found Scotty stretched out on the couch in the TV room, washed in the flickering black-and-white glow of *Sullivan's Travels*, the DVD that LeClair kept in the player. One foot rested on the ground, his hands crossed on his chest, his chin dropped and snoring lightly. LeClair stood over him for a few moments, watching the play of light on his noble face. The young man was determined, he had to give him that. *Youth.*

LeClair turned the TV off and went upstairs.

He was standing at the sink brushing his teeth when he heard a furtive knock on the bathroom door.

Scotty?

You mind if I take a shower too?

Really?

Yeah, I feel pretty gross.

LeClair opened the door. Scotty stood there with his oxford untucked, bare feet, rubbing the back of his head. A sleepy grin. LeClair checked his watch: 2:30 a.m.

Right now?

Yeah.

You know there's another shower downstairs.

Scotty started unbuttoning his shirt.

Yeah, but I'm right here and I'm tired as shit. Just take a minute.

He stripped off his oxford, dropping it to the floor. His chest was slender and sinewy, a small diamond-shaped tuft of chest hair, which surprised LeClair for a reason he could not define. Scotty started unbuckling his belt, and LeClair realized that the boy was going to strip down naked in front of him.

Towels are in there!

LeClair turned on the bedside lamp and sat on the bed staring at his feet. The shower came on and the shower curtain rattled, Scotty murmuring with satisfaction as he got in the hot water. The wind howled down the alley outside the window, funneling into the vortex of court square. It was officially the coldest winter in a decade, the entire lake solid, the ice up to two feet thick in the shallows. LeClair felt the mountains rising up outside the window, pressing in, the unknowable density.

He shucked off his robe, slipped into bed, and turned off the light. This way Scotty would finish and get dressed and leave, or at least go back downstairs. It would be even better if he was asleep. He closed his eyes and tried to slow his breathing.

Kaiser told him the only way to be sure was to wait for heavy weather. Precipitation would obscure all but drones or manned aerial and ground surveillance, and Kaiser would take care of those. He had a clear path, he said. They would send a screamer on a sled across the ice, and then by springtime LeClair planned to be sipping a gimlet on the veranda of a seventeenth-century villa outside Marseille with a view of a Roman aqueduct looping through the valley.

The shower shut off. The rip of the curtain. Wet feet on the tile, towel sounds. LeClair tried to slow his breathing again. Meditation, like a Himalayan ascetic, a cave-dwelling anchorite squatting in robes, following the nose of the wind. The door opened, and the creak of the floorboards. The gust of warm, moist air from the bathroom, and the smell of his shampoo, his soap.

Donnie?

Two more steps. LeClair kept his face relaxed, his breathing even.

Donnie?

Jesus fucking Christ, the boy was next to the bed! He wasn't going to leave. And *Donnie*?

LeClair cracked his eyes.

What?

You awake?

He turned his head and saw the silhouette of Scotty's body, still steaming from the shower, his shoulders bare. He had a towel around his waist. Scotty turned and sat on the bed, his hip nearly touching LeClair's shoulder. LeClair felt his body go numb. He couldn't move. Scotty placed a hand on LeClair's collarbone.

I want you to know how much I respect you, he said.

Scotty eased himself down on the bed, reclining on one elbow. LeClair could see the droplets of water that beaded on his arms and neck. The boy smelled like water and sky.

You're, like, a mentor to me.

Scotty eased the hand on LeClair's collarbone downward, sliding it under the blanket, moving lightly across his chest and belly. LeClair tightened up and twisted, raising his knees, a knot in his stomach.

What're you doing? he gasped.

Scotty put his other hand on the back of LeClair's neck, squeezing gently. His hands were strong and sure of their intentions. LeClair felt his body reacting in the old way.

I wanna show my appreciation, Scotty said. For all you've done for us, for me.

Scotty slipped his fingers under the waistband of LeClair's underwear, brushing pubic hair with the tips of his fingers. He smiled, a slight, brief smile, then his eyes went dark, and he slipped his hand around LeClair's straining cock. He leaned over and put his lips to LeClair's ear.

Is this what you want?

Leclair closed his eyes and groaned. He wanted to leap up, to scream, but he was pinioned to the bed by the heat in his groin. He began to pump his hips, grabbing handfuls of the sheets, breathing through gritted teeth.

Scotty stood up and took off his towel, then pulled the covers back and slid into the bed, pressing into LeClair with the full length of his warm body, looming over him in the near-dark.

Are you ready to begin?

EMERSON

Emerson sliced another stale bagel in the Artful Dodger kitchen. For the last two days, she tried to sleep off the residual hangover from her excursion to Scotty Marin's and the Zeta safe room. Mostly she wallowed in bed listening to Sarah McLachlan, trying to piece together the evening at the fraternity house. She remembered being in the room with Scotty, the headphones and music and her flipping stomach, the darkness and falling sensation like going into a deep sleep. Was this the same guy that Brett was talking about? Is this what these guys do? And then the Zetas were there. Was she missing some time? Did something happen between the darkness and headphones and when the Zetas barged in the room and liberated her? There was a strange memory of hands around her hips. Or was that just from dancing? What was it about the Fleur-de-Lis that made the night seem so charged with possibility? She had done plenty of Ecstasy before, but this was different. Why was she so willing to just let everything happen? How would Uncle Donnie react if he found out?

When she crossed court square that afternoon, she looked at the spot on the courthouse lawn where she had lain with Kaiser for the satellite intersection. It was a brief, astonishing experience, and when it was over, Kaiser had simply walked away. Emerson went back into the Dodger and sat on the couch for a few minutes, trying to hold the image of that delicate silver thread tracing across the sky. It was as if Kaiser conjured them out of the sky. She grabbed his hand as if she were a kid on a frightening ride, and he clutched her hand back.

As the bagels toasted, she pulled shots of espresso from the hulking Rapallo Astoria, a machine fitted in chrome with bronze trimmings, lever-style, that Drummy bought out of a van on Venice Beach in the '80s for three thousand dollars. It was temperamental and expensive to maintain, but the thing made legitimate espresso, deep, rich, with a custard-like crema. Emerson made herself a triple latte with a touch of almond, then spread the bagels with cream cheese and ate them standing at the prep table in the kitchen, "Joan of Arc" by OMD thumping out of the speakers. Court square was empty, the snow gleaming from a morning shower of sleet and going rose, peach, amber in the afternoon light. A state police sedan nosed into a spot at the courthouse.

On a weeknight they rarely had more than a dozen customers at a time, nondrinkers and potheads gathering to get jacked on caffeine and ogle the student paintings that Drummy hung on the wall. It seemed a point of pride to Drummy that he never sold a single work, and Emerson often thought he inflated the prices for this reason. Nobody in this town wanted to pay $600 for a mixed-media collage piece consisting of magazine pictures of air-brushed models and printed stills from plastic surgery videos.

After she ate, Emerson took his place at the register, and Drummy stalked through the kitchen to the alley to smoke a joint. After he was sufficiently high, he would light a cigarette and position himself at the Rapallo Astoria, meting out perfectly constructed shots of espresso, which Emerson would dump into pint glasses and douse with syrup and milk. Her copy of *Winesburg, Ohio*, the pages puffy with moisture and age, was still sitting next to the register. The term paper loomed, and she figured she'd better revisit George Willard and his blunted desires. She turned to "Tandy," the one story in the book that baffled her completely, when she noticed Kaiser sitting at a table bent over a book, a mug of coffee in hand. A stack of books on the table from the public library, with heavy, gray-toned fabric covers. He raised his head, blinked, head cocked slightly to the side like a Labrador, then stood up and stretched his back before picking up his mug and coming to the counter.

Refill, please.

He pushed the mug toward her. He was wearing a charcoal wool V-neck sweater, black jeans, motorcycle boots with silver buckles. Where the hell does he get these clothes? She poured his coffee.

Whaddya reading? she asked. Looks serious.

Lake formations, Kaiser said. Limnology. What about you?

Emerson put the mug down on the counter in front of him.

Still working on *Winesburg, Ohio*. New hobby?

He shrugged.

Just trying to learn stuff about the lake.

Oh, she said. Have you read Dr. Jansky's book?

I don't think so, Kaiser said. What's the title?

Uh, *The Shaping of Lake Champlain*, or something like that. I took a geology class from her last year. She is, like, obsessed with the lake. I mean, she was. You probably heard.

Heard what?

She's missing. Dr. Jansky went missing out on the ice.

When?

Last week? Cross-country skiing. Disappeared. Her husband teaches art history and I'm in his class right now, and, like, he's . . . not doing great.

Kaiser stared at her, his forehead all scrunched up. He seemed astonished by this news.

She went through?

Most likely, she said. Anyway, she's like the world's foremost expert on Lake Champlain. Or was. You wanna borrow her book? I have a copy back at my place.

When . . . how can I get it?

My roommate Jud will be coming by later and I'll tell him to bring it. I'll be done here at ten thirty? Come by then.

Okay. I appreciate it.

That'll be twenty-five cents, she said. No cream or sugar allowed.

Kaiser patted his back pockets, then dug a hand deep in his front pocket.

I'm afraid I don't have anything small.

He was eyeing the tip jar that had a small card taped to it that said: *Starving Student Seeking Useless Liberal Arts Degree.* Drummy was at the other end of the bar, leaning on the counter and smoking, his glazed eyes resting on a collage made of candy wrappers and diet pills, marked for sale at $700. Kaiser pulled a wad of cash out of his pocket and got a bill separated. A twenty. She popped open the register drawer. A couple singles, a roll of nickels, a dozen pennies.

Hey, Drummy, she said, c'mon, man? No change again?

Drummy took a long drag off his cigarette, then blew a perfect set of concentric smoke rings that ascended to the ceiling like a stack of blue halos. The military snare drum of OMD's "Maid of Orleans" rattled over a thumping bassline.

If Joan of Arc had a heart,
Would she give it as a gift?

Emerson looked back at Kaiser, who was staring at her blankly. He tucked the bill into the tip jar quickly, as if she might try and stop him.

Just keep the change.

He hoisted his mug and took a deep drink, then turned around, the cup still held at his chin. He stood there with his back to her. This was crazy. What was with this strange, emotionless older man who wore oddly fashionable clothes? Despite how old he was, and how good-looking, there was something hermetic about him, like he'd been living on a deserted island for the last decade.

He turned around, his mouth open.

I can bring the book in tomorrow, she said, if you like.

No, he said. I was just going to ask you where. Where specifically on the lake did Dr. Jansky go under?

I don't think they know for sure, Emerson said. They found tracks going north all the way up to the border, but not south.

She disappeared right around the border?

Seems like it.

Kaier stood there for a moment, mug still stalled by his sharp chin. Emerson could see a slight tremor move through him and the mug shook slightly as he put it to his lips and gulped the rest of it down. He put the cup on the counter.

I'll see you at ten thirty.

He quickly stowed his books in a shoulder bag, a supple leather cross-body piece that Emerson could tell was radically expensive and strode quickly out the door.

Why was it always so weird? Every time she ran into Kaiser something strange would happen, an awkward exchange, the scene at the Dry Dock, the bizarre satellite viewing invitation on court square. Drummy coughed, turned to the Rapallo Astoria and began rubbing the metal wands vigorously, stroking them with a damp rag like he was milking a cow.

Well done, he drawled out of the side of his mouth, cigarette dangling.

Oh, come on! she said. You just like his clothes.

No, Drummy said. That one's . . . *mysterious.* He's got a secret.

When Kaiser came back, Emerson presented him with *Unstoppable Force: The Glacial Formation of Lake Champlain* by Dr. Sue Jansky, published by the Princeton University Press in a blue jacket and gold lettering on the spine, a topographic map of the lake on the cover. He flipped it over to look at the author photo. Dr. Jansky was out on the lake, standing on the ice, her hands gripping ski poles, her face ruddy but her expression grim.

Then Emerson asked if he would give her a ride to a bonfire party down at Cliff Haven beach to celebrate the end of the semester. A couple girls from the student literary magazine had made her promise to show up.

Normally I would bike it, Emerson said, but they are saying a windchill of maybe negative ten tonight. So, you know . . .

A few minutes later, Kaiser was chiseling the ice off his windshield while Emerson sat in the Volkswagen listening to The English Beat's "Mirror in the Bathroom" and adjusting the heating vents. They coasted gingerly south on Route 9, passing the college and the old air force base. Kaiser wiped the condensation of their breath off the windshield. They were quiet, watching the spangled lights passing over the hood, the road a white sheet.

You should just park, Emerson said when they arrived. Come check out the party. What else are you gonna do?

I was hoping to start on this, Kaiser said, hefting the book.

C'mon. Should be a mixed crowd. You know, like, some townies? Maybe some people you know?

That isn't an incentive, he said. For me.

The street was lined with parked cars, and down the short gravel road through the trees Emerson could see the flickering glare of a bonfire. She put her hand on the door handle.

I was just thinking we could talk? she said. Hang out a bit?

Kaiser licked his lips.

Have one drink. My friend Tara is bringing a giant thermos of hot whiskey. It's pretty damn good, I'm not gonna lie.

I don't really drink whiskey, he said.

Emerson took the flask from the center console and inspected the words engraved in a looping hand.

Cher poisson, prepare par les Anges! Did you put this on here?

No, he said. I got it at a flea market in California.

You know what this means? In French?

No.

How long you had this?

About six years.

And all that time you *never* thought to look up what this means?

Kaiser licked his lips again, then wiped his mouth with the wrist of his jacket.

Something about poison, right?

Well, yeah, Emerson said. *Sweet poison, mixed by angels.* I've read this before. I think it's like Rimbaud or Verlaine or something. French Symbolist poets. Lovers.

She unscrewed the top and took a sniff.

Ugh! What *is* that?

Rum.

Rum? You must be the only dude in the North Country drinking rum.

So people say.

Well, bring your French Symbolist rum and walk down there with me. I don't want to go alone. Please?

Kaiser was wearing a long, supple calfskin overcoat, but Emerson could tell it wasn't exactly warm. He buttoned the top button and pulled the collar up as they stumbled down the gravel road toward the glowing light, the voices, laughter, the skunk-fruit smell of weed and burning cedar drifting through the woods. He was silent, the lower half of his face tucked into the folds of his coal-black cashmere scarf. Was this a bad idea? Would it look weird? She figured Jess and Amber from the magazine would totally dig him at least, since poets were attracted to all manner of eccentricity. The footing was uneven, and they jostled each other as they stepped through rutted ice and snow and Emerson took a pinch of his coat sleeve to steady herself.

There were maybe sixty people on the beach, mostly clustered around the bonfire. In the outer dark, small groups were marked by the trailing tips of cigarettes, lighters flaring and the face of a young woman, lit from underneath like a Vermeer, the stem of a pipe in her mouth. The reflected moon and starlight created night-shadows, faint silhouettes on the contours of wind-rippled snow. Nobody seemed to mind that Emerson had brought along an oddly dressed, nearly thirty-year-old man, since there were usually at least a few sketchy local-types hanging about the fringes of bonfire parties. Jess and Amber took to Kaiser immediately, plying him with hot whiskey, which he gamely drank out of a shared metal cup that hung from a chain attached to Jess's belt. The bonfire was roaring like a train in a tunnel, and they all stared at it, hollow-eyed, dumb with booze, smoke, and darkness.

Fire zombies, Jess said. I've spent half my life doing this.

Jess and Amber were dark-haired girls with black-framed glasses, progressive politics, red-trade feminists. Emerson knew that Jess had a dog-eared copy of Sylvia Plath somewhere on her person, Amber more likely Jeanette Winterson. They carried the banner at the front of the Take Back the Night parade on campus, and manned phone banks for North Country Public Radio and Hilary Clinton. But around Kaiser, they seemed to be regressing to flirty sorority girls, Emerson thought. Or perhaps, thinking of the Zetas and their safe room, at least a certain *kind* of sorority girl. As the cup was passed around, Kaiser's face loosened up, a slight smile on his lips as he stared at the leaping flames. A guy with a shaggy goatee in a bright blue Canadiens jacket handed Emerson a packed bowl and she took a hit before passing it to Kaiser, who passed it on to Amber. On the street up the hill the throaty rumble of a car, the whine of music.

Why do we like it? Jess said. Staring at fires. It's creepy.

It's pure energy, Emerson said. Released from the wood by a chemical process. We are watching plants give up their lives.

Whoa, the Canadiens jacket said, grabbing the bill of his ball cap. *Tight.*

Amber elbowed Kaiser.

What do you think? What's the attraction?

Kaiser smiled and looked up, the knob of his throat working. He pointed at the spill of the Milky Way.

Concentrated energy travels billions of miles in the form of light to hit the earth. It gets absorbed by organic matter, and when it burns that energy is released again. So this fire is actually the nuclear furnace of stars. The source of all matter. It's where we come from.

Canadiens jacket turned to Kaiser.

Bro, I don't know what you are smoking, but I *want* some of that shit!

The best part, Jess said, is that all this light energy traveled millions of years to reach earth and like ten feet from the ground some tree is like, *nah dude.*

The music behind them become louder, a car door opening. Emerson glanced back in the darkness toward the road where a pair of headlights glowed through the trees, vibrating. A high shriek and wail, repeating on a loop.

Kaiser is full of all kinds of tricks, Emerson said. This guy, like, knows where satellites are orbiting around the earth?

What?

Yeah, like he knows the trajectories and stuff. Probably show you one right now.

Emerson glanced at him as she finished saying this and the look on his face made her instantly regret it.

Really?

Cool!

No way. Show me one.

The dozen or so people around them were now all craning their necks, looking skyward, searching, turning back to Kaiser.

Amber clutched Kaiser's arm, her eyes narrowed, talking directly in his ear.

Dude, show me a fucking satellite!

Chill, Emerson said. He's not like some kind of circus act.

Kaiser pulled out his flask and turned it up even though it'd been empty for a while. He screwed the cap back on, pocketed it, raised his eyes and squinted into the dark. Emerson could hear the music behind them more clearly now. Led Zepplin. Some stupid townie attracted by the parked cars, surveying the scene. Some stupid townie like *her.*

Probably too dark now, Emerson said.

Too dark? What?

No, really, she said, it's much better to see them at twilight, like when the angle of the sunlight catches the metal and stuff? You can see the shiny parts, and then after a while they come, like, totally into focus.

That's crazy, Jess said. Is that true?

Kaiser nodded, staring out at the white expanse of the lake. After a moment, Emerson realized he was watching something, a handful of lights coming across the ice toward them. Then the engines were audible, the faint drone growing louder, and the entire party turned to look at the approaching snowmobiles. Five of them, running in a tight group, coming in fast, several of the sleds towing flat-bottomed aluminum dinghies poached from the North Chazy Marina.

The lead sled came racing in, the driver crouching, then letting go of the handlebars and standing on the seat, back straight, his arms raised in a T. He was wearing a black shell suit and helmet, and when the sled plowed into the snowdrifts at the lake edge he leaped over the handlebars, catapulted by the momentum a good twenty feet, kicking in slow revolutions like an Olympic long jumper. When he hit the ground, he rolled over once and came to his feet, arms outstretched like a gymnast sticking the dismount. The party erupted in cheers, everyone raising their drinks in salute, and when he pulled off his helmet Emerson saw it was the boy from the party, the boy who put the headphones on her. The boy who tried to pick a fight with Kaiser. Scotty Marin.

Scotty started slapping hands and doing bro hugs. The other riders dismounted and walked up the beach, save one, who remained on his sled, a big guy with his helmet visor down, engine idling. Emerson recognized Cool-Mite, Cruz, and Stanton, the boys from the frat house. She noticed Kaiser had slipped back, stepping out of the throng, and was now at the edge of the firelight behind her. He pulled the tall collar of his coat up, jammed his hands in his pockets, chin tucked in his scarf.

Scotty Marin addressed the crowd.

Listen up, people! We got a keg of Blue, Jager bombs, and lots of other goodies out on Crab Island. And a fire bigger than this one. Put your fucking hats on and get in!

Everybody cheered and people started moving toward the boats. Amber and Jess grabbed fistfuls of Emerson's coat.

Let's go!

Seriously?

C'mon, fuck it! Let's do it!

Emerson turned back to Kaiser, but he was standing even farther back in the shadows. He shook his head. She knew that he had some kind of problem with Scotty Marin.

I can't, she told the girls. Kaiser's my ride.

Oh, fuck that!

You can catch a ride with us!

She knew she wouldn't be able to convince them not to go, even if she told them about what happened with the Zetas, which she didn't want to do. But she certainly didn't want something like that to happen to Amber and Jess. The best thing would be to go, keep an eye on things. So, Emerson let herself be led away by her friends, miming to Kaiser that'd she'd catch a ride with them. She got in the back of one of the dinghies, sitting on Amber's lap. Jess got on the sled seat behind Scotty, wrapping her arms around his midsection, and Emerson logged this bit of stark irony in her mental Rolodex. Scotty gave Emerson a broad smile and a wink.

Then the boys were turning around and gunning the engines and they shot out across the frozen lake, jerking and swinging the dinghies behind them, the metal bottoms skittering across the ice. Clutching the gunwale, facing backward in the boat, Emerson saw Kaiser standing alone on the sand. The one guy who never got off his sled was turning around slowly in a broad arc in front of the beach, staring at Kaiser, before hitting the throttle and quickly catching up to the other sleds. Up ahead on Crab Island she could see flickers of light on the trees. Looking back as the New York shoreline diminished into the dark, she saw the silhouette of Kaiser in front of the fire, one hand raised, high over his shoulder, waving.

CHRISTMAS

Kaiser stomped through the crusty snow to the front door of the Trombley house carrying a pot of mashed potatoes. In the interior pockets of his wool-cashmere Ludlow jacket, he had a bottle of wine and a bottle of rum. Dylan swung the door open wearing holiday pajamas, skin-tight and frayed around the seams, green and white reindeer prancing against a red background.

Kaiser!

Hey, Dylan. Merry Christmas.

The house was rich with meaty scents and shuddered with kitchen activity. The floors had been swept and the surfaces wiped, and the TV in the den was playing the Peanuts Christmas Special. Dylan led him into the kitchen where Sebastian was whisking up a horseradish sauce, pausing to sprinkle in chopped scallions and salt. On the counter there was a bowl of kale greens tossed with bacon and Fuji apples, a sweet potato mousse, and fried polenta cakes with jalapeño and manchego cheese. Sebastian was wearing a chef coat, shorts, and bare feet, his halo sparkling with grease.

Man, I'm glad you made it, Sebastian said.

Kaiser eyed the beef tenderloin lying in a nest of heavy foil.

I brought a bucket of spuds.

Got butter in there? Salt?

Yeah.

Sour cream?

Ah, no.

Garlic?

No.

I'll fix it up in a sec, Sebastian said. Check out this protein here.

Sebastian poked the tenderloin with a finger.

This motherfucker is from the Lakeside Inn in Lake Placid. Buddy of mine is a sous chef and he nicked it for me. Six pounds, grass finished.

Kaiser could see Callie on the couch craning her neck to see who was there, so he stepped through the doorway into the living room.

Merry Christmas, Mrs. Trombley.

She gave him a dreamy smile and raised her red Solo cup. She was wearing a set of pajamas that matched Dylan's, equally tight and worn. On the TV screen Charlie Brown was giving his plaintive diatribe about the commercialization of Christmas.

She's all lit up with the nog, bro, Sebastian said behind him. She's been hitting it hard since noon. But Mom loves Christmas, right, Callie?

Callie raised her cup again, another sleepy grin.

Kaiser pulled out the wine bottle and set it on the coffee table.

I thought you might like this, he said. It's from New Zealand.

Callie lurched upright and seized the bottle, holding it up to the light, inspecting the label closely. She nodded sagely, then began trying to twist the top off the bottle.

I think you're gonna need a corkscrew, Kaiser said.

Callie picked up her Solo cup and dumped the dregs of her eggnog into the overflowing ashtray. She held the cup and bottle out to Kaiser.

I'd love to have some, she said. Please.

It was the first time Kaiser had heard her speak with something like sincerity. Sebastian took the bottle from Kaiser and expertly removed the cork and poured his mother a couple inches of pinot noir in a clean cup. She took a grateful drink, her throat working, one gulp, two.

Jesus, Mom! Don't fucking chug it!

Callie lowered the cup and smiled at Kaiser, her eyes dewy with moisture and gratitude. When she raised her cigarette to her mouth, he could see that her yellowed teeth had already taken on a pink hue.

It's delicious, she said. The best wine I've ever had.

Of course it is, Sebastian said. You usually drink shit.

Great pajamas, Kaiser said.

Callie stood and gave him an awkward, shaky, sideways model-pose. Though her body told a story of age and abuse, Kaiser could tell that young Callie was a stone-cold beauty.

Me and Dylan, she murmured, got these last year. It's our tradition.

More like *three* years ago, Sebastian said.

Kaiser pulled out the bottle of rum and presented it to Sebastian.

This is from Haiti, Kaiser said. Thought you might like it.

Dude! Thanks! Crack that motherfucker!

Sebastian gave him some glasses and ice and Kaiser poured them each a measure. The rum was smoky and nuanced, almost whiskey-like in its balance and character.

I've never had anything like this, Sebastian said.

Of course, Callie yelled from the other room, you usually drink *shit*!

At the end of dinner Callie dozed over the crème brûlée that Sebastian finished with an acetylene torch. It was the best meal Kaiser had ever had, and he told Sebastian so, sparking a round of high fives among the boys. They got Callie on the couch in front of the TV and then tromped up the stairs, carrying their drinks.

You gotta check this shit out, Sebastian said.

Dylan's bedroom was high-ceilinged and large, his single bed and set of drawers pushed in the corner, the bed neatly made and not a stitch of clothing or scrap of toys about. It didn't look like a child's bedroom. There were small structures covering most of the hardwood floor, built up on top of each other, creeping up the wall like festering mechanical vines, miniature devices and shapes built with popsicle sticks, matches, cardboard, paper, and glue. Some were recognizable as buildings, but most were abstract expressions of angles, vectors, negative space, most with slanting arrows and spear-like lines hitting them at a precise angle, piercing through the paper and cardboard, all oriented in the same direction. Some parts looked almost like some kind of model for a futuristic city, but most of it was so abstract and unstructured that it was hard to tell just what it was. In the opposite corner of the room, a large papier-mâché ball, painted brilliant yellow and with a light bulb inside hung from the ceiling, a nest of thin dowel rods projecting out toward the structures. It was the only light source in the room.

Kaiser bent down to examine some of the structures by his feet, steeply raked rooftops supported by spires and clear cellophane portals transfixed by thin cardboard strips. It was like the sprawling innards of some future machine, or a fantastic vision of an alien planet. Antic and cluttered, but you could sense there was some kind of byzantine order at work. The boy was channeling something metaphysical, some vision beyond himself and this world. He looked up at Dylan, who was staring at him, glassy-eyed.

You did all this?

Dylan nodded.

Kaiser turned to Sebastian.

You need to make sure this kid goes to school. To college.

I told you he's wicked smart, Sebastian said.

Kaiser got on a knee and got Dylan squared up to him. The boy went all slack-jawed and limp. Kaiser held him by his arms, gave him a little shake.

Hey, he said. Listen. Never stop doing this. You understand?

Dylan nodded, mouth open. They had put away most of the bottle of rum and Kaiser was aware that he was being too intense.

You have something inside of you, Kaiser said. Let it out.

Fuck yeah, said Sebastian. *Exactly.*

Dylan closed his mouth. Kaiser ruffled his hair and stood up.

And if you need help or supplies, *we* will get them for you. Whatever you need.

He backhanded Sebastian's chest.

That's right, bro, Sebastian said. Me and Kaiser. We got you.

Dylan looked at Kaiser, then back at his brother, unsure of what to do. Downstairs they could hear the slow intonation of Callie's snores on the couch, then Schroeder banging out the Peanuts theme song. The snowplow truck faded in the distance as it headed off toward the darkness of the lake. Dylan let out a breath, then wrapped his arms around his brother's waist, burying his face in Sebastian's stomach.

I love you, little bro, Sebastian said. More than anything in this world.

Phil found some cement nails in the garage and hammered some of his hockey socks onto the brick mantle. After Sydney stuffed Juliet's, the distended toe nearly touched the floor.

This looks kinda ridiculous, she said.

Phil was sprawled on the couch with a drink. It took him nearly an hour, but he finished assembling the Dora the Explorer dollhouse and had settled in with a jug of Stewart's eggnog, Canadian Club, and a soup bowl of ice, watching Sydney finish wrapping the presents and placing them under the tree that was ablaze with lights and great nests of silver tinsel bunched in the branches.

Guess who I saw, Phil said, down at Cliff Haven beach the other night?

Who?

Your old buddy Tom Kaiser.

She paused, just the slightest tremor, but he saw it. The house smelled like the roasted ham and sweet potatoes they had for dinner, and the kitchen sink was full of pans and dishes. Sydney had the week off, and she looked like she needed it. She was getting thinner and had pouches under her eyes. When she got home from work, she usually laid down on the couch and took a nap. Phil knew her job was stressful. She was dealing with the shit-end of Clinton County.

What was he doing there?

A college party, he said. Bonfire. Scotty and his crew took everybody out to Crab Island.

That's weird. Did you talk to him?

Nah. I was on a sled. He stayed on the beach by himself. Seemed like he was there with a couple college girls. Kinda sad, really.

She gave him a glance over her shoulder.

You were there with college students.

I'm getting paid, Phil said. Paid well. A job.

I know. But it's a weird job, Phil.

Temporary, Phil said. I got calls from a couple AHL teams. The Adirondack Flames. Albany Devils want me to come to their tryout.

You sure you want to play? I mean, you really want to play?

Phil poured himself another measure of nog from the carton. He still hadn't really thought about it. When the holidays were over, he'd have to get some more work in at the rink. Maybe Scotty and his frat shitheads could provide some bodies to bounce around.

This is like, Phil said, some counseling shit you're doing, right?

Sydney came over and sat on the edge of the sofa.

No, Phil. I just want you to be happy.

He held up his hands, his swollen knuckle joints, the fourth finger of his left hand cockeyed, the middle finger on his right a misshapen slab, dislocated last year when he got his hand caught in a facemask. Half of his fingers had been broken or fractured. The calluses on the pads of his fingers and palm still lined up, as if he held an invisible hockey stick in his hands.

Hockey is what I'm made for, he said. It's like my destiny or something.

You don't believe in destiny.

Yeah, Phil said. But I wish I did, you know?

She leaned into him and rested her head on his chest. The house was quiet, just the faint whistle of the wind in the eaves.

Those stockings look kinda ghetto, Sydney said.

She'll love it. Now open yours.

He nudged the small, wrapped box on the coffee table with his toe.

Aren't we going to do it tomorrow morning? With Juliet?

Yeah, but that's Santa. This is from me.

Sydney sat cross-legged in front of the coffee table, taking the small box in her hands. She peeled open the wrapping paper and seeing the black velvet box she paused and looked at him for a long while. Then she opened it. A string of Mikimoto pearls, creamy white and nearly translucent as she ran them through her thin fingers.

They remind me of the lake, Phil said. Like the ice, you know?

It's too much, she said. It's too expensive.

I paid for it, Phil said. Cash.

Yeah, but Phil. Look around.

What?

Jesus, Phil! Priorities?

I'm gonna get some guys in here next week to redo the bathroom. In the spring we'll get some fresh sod for the backyard. And a swing set for Jules. It's all gonna work out.

Sydney stood up and fiddled with the plastic holly vines on the mantel. He could tell she was trying not to cry. This was not how he wanted this to go, especially on Christmas Eve, and he felt desperate to make it right.

I'm sorry, he said. I'm gonna get that other stuff done. We'll have the money for it, I promise.

When she turned around, her eyes were glassy. She placed the box on the mantel among the plastic ivy. Phil stood up and came around the coffee table.

I'm trying, he said. I swear. You know I love you. I just want to be with you and Jules. That's all.

Sydney covered her face with her hands.

Syd. Please.

She opened up her hands, and her face was red and puffy and slicked with tears. She put her arms around his neck and pressed her forehead into his chest. He put his nose and lips into her hair, the faint smell of woodsmoke. He wrapped her in his arms and leaning back, he picked her up off the floor. She was so light, like she was hollow inside. Phil felt a maddening rush of something like frustration. He couldn't make it out, he couldn't make it clear. But he knew that everything he cared about, all the things that mattered, were right here.

I just wish there was a way, he said into her hair, that I could show you.

She sighed and wiped her face on his shoulder.

You don't have to show me, Phil. I know.

Sydney kissed his rough face as he carried her back into the dark bedroom, rubbing her wet cheeks on his forehead. He held her with one arm and fumbled with her pants with his other hand.

Wait.

She got her feet on the floor and pushed him back onto the bed, where he sat looking up at her, the light from the hall shining on his face. He didn't know. How could he? Sydney pulled off her shirt and kicked her pants off her ankles before peeling down her underwear. They were both warm and funky from being inside the house all day, and when they got under the covers Sydney wrapped herself around him tight, tucking her ankles under his thighs, clinging to him like a koala bear. He ran his hands over her back and legs, reaching down to cup her ass and sliding his fingers in the warm cleft. She shuddered and pressed her lips to his, mashing their faces together. She felt like something was pouring out of her, channeling into him. It was as if he soaked up all her abstract weaknesses, the frailties of the heart. A man who dealt with such brutality, such violence. It was the strength of his innocence.

The magic of belief is never more fully realized than in the face of a two-year-old on Christmas morning. Sydney's mother and her Aunt

Debbie and Uncle Albert came over with a hash brown casserole in a Pyrex pan. While Juliet babbled over her gifts Phil lounged on the couch sipping coffee and talking with Albert about ice fishing for perch.

When everyone left in the afternoon, Juliet was laying on Phil's belly, both of them stretched out asleep the couch, the TV muted. The sky was dark, but the wind had died down. The wall across the street filling the front windows almost looked like an endless field of snow. Almost.

Sydney took the small box from the ivy and opened it.

I just want to be with you and Jules.

This life. This beautiful life.

Sometime near midnight, Laurence Sterne walked down the hill toward the lake, a stack of paper held together with rubber bands under his arm and an axe resting on his shoulder. The night sky was clear, making the snow-covered landscape seem charged with luminous light. Sterne had spent the day turning out all the closets and drawers in the house looking for something. He didn't know exactly what it was, but he vaguely understood that he was hoping to find something about Sue. He was searching for some kind of article or trinket or note, anything at all, something he had never seen before. He felt that if he uncovered something new about her, some kind of secret, then she would become diminished in some way, her presence lessened. Or maybe he hoped that by finding some secret item of hers Sue would bloom anew in his memory. But other than a couple random items—a refrigerator magnet from Niagara Falls, a pamphlet from Glacier National Park, a picture of a young Sue on a grassy lakeside holding a fish—he hadn't found anything. Sue was all that she had ever seemed to be. She was the only pure and honest thing in his life.

Sterne turned to his home office and ransacked it in a kind of rage, as if he was looking for some secret item of his own. By dark, he had drunk all the bottles of wine from the basement and smoked so much weed that he felt he was on the deck of a heaving ship at sea. Then he found himself tromping down to the lake, hatless and vibrating with anger.

When he figured he was far enough out, he dumped the stack of papers, and taking the axe in both hands, he began to hack away at the ice. Sterne took wild swings, pulling it far back over his head like he was hammering a railroad spike, the heavy blade throwing up showers of shards. After a while he paused and examined the hole. He had cut a crater the size of a manhole about a foot deep, but still no water.

Silence. It was like the whole world had gone quiet. It was Christmas Eve.

Sterne went back to work with the axe, but after a dozen more whacks his hands and arms were burning, and his breath tore at his throat. How fucking thick was this stuff? He got on his knees and stuffed the stack of papers, the complete manuscript of *The Sun & the Sublime*, into the hole, then took a flash drive out of his pocket and dropped it in too. He would sweep the broken ice and snow into the hole, covering the papers, and it would freeze and by the spring thaw it would be torn to confetti by the seismic forces of the ice.

What would Sue say about this? He knew. And she would be right. He had emailed copies to himself over the years, and he would be able to recover it from the hard drive on his computer. This wouldn't rid him of anything. He covered his face with his hands, feeling humiliated and naked in the blank gaze of the ice.

Then he remembered he had his lighter, so he lit the manuscript on fire. As soon as the papers caught fire the gusting wind began to peel off pages, pulling them out of the hole and sending them tumbling. He stood and watched the burning sheets drifting like flaming leaves across the lake.

This is when he saw the shadow under the ice, a massive black shape spreading south.

Is this how it happens? he thought. Is this true madness? The dark shape accelerated, then veered to the right to come directly toward him. Pages burned and flapped in the hole, and he thought maybe he should put it out, that it, whatever it was, was being drawn toward the fire. But this was bigger than any real living thing. It was impossible. He was drunk, high, in a serious sorrow spiral, and he was out on the lake in starlight; it must be some kind of effect of wind and shadow. Then the ice bulged and lifted and as the thing came closer, the cracking of thick ice mixed with throbbing booms, and Sterne dropped the axe and ran back for the shoreline, his boots slipping until he found a trail of drifting snow for traction and then he was leaping onto shore under the pine trees, scrabbling on his knees over a log and curling up and covering his head with his arms. A sound like glass shattering, a chandelier thrown down the stairs, then a deep groan and crunch of something large settling back into the deep. And then silence.

When Sterne looked back, the small fire guttered, nearly out, a few last burning pages scattering to the north, the shape of the axe lying on the ice. Everything else was flat, still, and quiet.

LeClair arranged the covered roasting dish in the passenger seat of the Escalade. The boys were dismissed for the holiday break, and as he negotiated the road out to the farm, LeClair was mostly concerned with grease slopping out onto the leather seats. It had been a tradition since their parents died that LeClair prepared the goose and brought it out to the farm on Christmas Eve to eat with Walt. LeClair had mastered a recipe with an apple-clove brine and sea-salt scrub, one of a half-dozen things that he actually knew how to cook, along with toast and boiled eggs. Walt made a raft of vegetarian sides, green bean casserole with Chinese noodle topping, whipped sweet potatoes with marshmallows, and gelled cranberry sauce from a can. Walt also ordered a tofu goose from a vegan market in Montreal: a *Goofu*. The thing was vile looking and tasted even worse, but Emerson loved to place it on a platter with vegetable trimmings and make the brothers try it.

As Emerson grew older, she threw herself into the preparations, determined to make a festive holiday event for the two brothers whose holiday passions teetered between ambivalent and reluctant. As he knocked the car door shut with his hip, LeClair imagined, as he did every year, what the holiday would be like without Emerson. Two crusty old men staring at each other with cloudy eyes across a table in a cold house. LeClair pulled his chin down into the collar of his wool trench coat as he carried the roasting pan and shopping bags up to the front door. This was a far better thing, and he ought to be grateful. Emerson insisted they dress formal for the Christmas dinner, which made LeClair uncomfortable. Not for his own sake, but it pained him to see his older brother struggling to put together something appropriate. Walt would oil his sparse hair and wear an old white oxford shirt with mustard collar-rings, a sweater-vest from 1973, a pair of black loafers he'd bought for a funeral, and hand iron the pleats in his trousers into Escher-like disarray. The man belonged in an oil-stained Carhartt jumpsuit.

When Emerson opened the door, resplendent in a new cream-colored dress with a green ribbon belt, cream stockings, her hair pulled back and plaited in a single braid, her face scrubbed and shining, LeClair exhaled and thought, Yes, this was *so* much better.

That morning LeClair had eaten buttered rolls with hot coffee in his bed, littered with the inner sections of the Sunday *New York Times*. He felt as if a clean, warm, southern wind moved through his bones, and when Alejandro clucked his tongue in the kitchen, he only shrugged and grinned. Later, he put on his best suit and spent the day haggling with the elderly air force widows who came caning their way into his shop, clutching Ziploc bags of misshapen pearls and bent rings smuggled from the old country during the Second World War. He felt a curious kind of contentment that he hadn't felt in years. It had everything to do with Scotty Marin. While their night together was terrifying and exhilarating, the aftermath—the sheepish look on Scotty's face in the morning, the way he stumbled as he put on his clothes, how he kissed LeClair on the cheek when he left—opened up something inside of him. He was alive to the prospect of sharing his life with another person. For a long time, LeClair had seen his imagined future as the long days of a solitary soul wandering through his house, surrounded by images of different worlds, all of them distant, out of reach.

Now he had two new possible additions to this vision: young Scotty lounging in his oxford shirt and khakis on the settee, and on the wall above him, shining like an ancient icon of some fabled religious order, his *Glaucus and Scylla*.

If Walt found out, he would be furious. He warned LeClair that if he felt insecure, he would review all their financial transactions and holdings. He would see how LeClair had been selling off parcels of land and dumping mortgages over the last few years to fund his painting acquisitions. What he was paying the boys, what he was spending on them. It wouldn't take Walt long to find the towering stack of spinning plates LeClair had going, including how he was betting their future on Kaiser's ability to find a miraculous path across the border.

The fireplace was roaring and the house overheated as Emerson stacked the fire high with dry oak.

If I'm going to walk around in *this* thing, she said, indicating her dress, then it's gotta be warm in here!

LeClair could tell his brother was thrilled to see his grown daughter so forthright, so charming, and so beautiful. As LeClair mixed them all a cocktail, he watched his niece move about the room, placing things on the table, checking the stuffing balls in the oven, the way she moved with such grace, as if she was some kind of woodland sprite caught indoors. Youth itself, he was thinking. *Youth.* Every candleholder in the house was on the table and when they sat down for dinner Emerson turned the lights down and the room was lit from the blaze of the fireplace and the antic arrangement of guttering flames on the table.

I feel like I'm in the *Phantom of the Opera*, LeClair said.

Emerson took the green beans from him and tossed her braid over her shoulder. She dug into the casserole and thwacked a lump the size of a grapefruit on her plate.

I've always felt, she said, that dinner should be a dramatic event. If I had my way, I'd eat this way every night.

Walt cut a rubbery slice of Goofu with the side of his fork and popped it in his mouth. He blinked as he chewed, even though the stuff didn't need chewing.

I also think, Emerson said, that everyone should recite a short poem or make a toast or something. Wouldn't that be cool?

Such a romantic, LeClair said. Are you in love?

Emerson's eyes lowered. She smeared some mushroom gravy around the edge of her plate, then took a drink of wine.

No-o, she said in a singsong voice.

I think she is, Walt said. But E's always in love. With something or someone. It's what makes things like this—he waved his fork over the array of dishes, the bonfire of candles—happen.

I agree, LeClair said. She clearly takes after her uncle. Thank *god*.

Emerson and LeClair clinked their glasses of wine. The fire popped and shifted, knots of resin going up in gassy flares. The lines of simple dinner plates on a shelf, put there forty years ago by their mother, the heavy walnut high boy with the deep circular watermark, the kitchen counter with peeling veneers, the delicately carved clock their father got in England that hadn't worked since the 1970s.

I don't know, Walt said, who the lucky man is going to be. But I know that he will be *very* lucky.

Agreed, LeClair said, and he raised his glass, and the brothers awkwardly clinked their glasses together. When had we done that last? He couldn't remember.

Maybe there'll never be a lucky man, Emerson said. Maybe I'll travel the world solo. Maybe I'll just stay here with you guys.

That's it, LeClair said. We know the lucky man, already. There's two of 'em. They're sitting right here.

LeClair's vision blurred and before he could react a hot tear was making a track down his cheek. They both looked at him, astonished. When did he become the sentimentalist? Emerson covered her mouth with her hand, her eyes welling up. Well, he'd better finish it up right. He raised his glass again, even though it was empty.

You said you wanted toasts, LeClair said in a rush of breath. Poems, whatever. This is the best I can do, Em. Merry Christmas. I love you both.

Later, after Uncle Donnie had gone, Emerson slipped on her ski-overalls and down coat and crunched out on the back field toward the barn. The glasses of wine and Uncle Donnie's cognac made her feel a sanguine sort of contentment. Or perhaps it was that moment over dinner, when Uncle Donnie burst into tears and said he loved them all, something she had never seen him do before. She threw her head back, allowing herself to sway slightly, the pinpricks of lights slashing back and forth in a pleasant way. The wind was cutting and her face started to burn from the cold. She was drunk, but more than anything she was happy. She held herself still, opening her eyes wide and waiting, like Kaiser had told her to, waiting for the rods and cones in her eyes to adjust and gather the light. She began to discern different sizes and subtle shades of color, the cherry pink, cornflower blue, river green, the faint star-points of light, deepening into shades of gray light that she knew was a thick cloud of distant stars.

Scotty Marin was just a child. He had tried to charm her out on Crab Island and again proffered her an array of drugs, but she blew him off, standing shoulder to shoulder with her pals, who after receiving the briefing from Emerson, closed ranks against the fraternity boys. Sure, Amber ended up making out with one of his compatriots, that Cool-Mite fellow, but by one o'clock they demanded a return to the mainland, the three of them nearly passing out in the boat on the way back, exhausted by the cold, booze, weed, and vigilance.

But Kaiser was not a child, even though there was a childlike quality about him. Something terrible happened to him in Afghanistan, she knew that. Something that got him in trouble. Despite whatever horror he experienced, he seemed to retain a kind of adolescent innocence. The look on his face when she brought up the satellites. The way he drank his coffee in convulsive, furtive gulps. Holding his hand on the blanket in the amphitheater of court square. His shape on the shore of the lake as they raced away.

Then Emerson caught one, a small mote of blue half-light. She watched as the satellite bent slowly to the horizon before neatly dropping behind the mountains like a coin slipped into a pocket.

PART III

Beneath me is nothing but brightness
Like the ghost of a snowfield in summer.
As I move toward the center of the lake,
Which is also the center of the moon,
I am thinking of how I may be
The savior of one

James Dickey, "The Lifeguard"

Fool! I am the Fates' lieutenant; I act under orders.

Herman Melville, *Moby Dick*

The boy in the lake slumbered in a bed of silt. His legs were squeezed under the rusting hulk of a trawler. When the ice was solid, he sometimes lay like this for days, his ears full of the whoosh of the water shifting around him, the distant booms and squeals of the ice. Eventually, he dragged himself free and drifted upward to bump against the white ceiling of ice, crawling along the shoreline weeds until he found an opening. Sometimes this process took him an entire day. So complete was the ice, the rim of the world above.

One afternoon, he crouched in a pile of deadfall pine and watched a group of children skating in a small cove. Some had sticks and they batted a ball around the ice and others worked themselves into tight circles, moving faster, riding the melt between the blades and the ice. Each time he heard their laughter and giddy shouts it seemed to vibrate something inside his chest. He watched them until it began to grow dark, and the children slung their skates over their shoulders and walked off toward the road.

When they were gone, he crept down to the smooth space they cleared and getting down on his knees he ran his fingers across the lines and grooves they made. When he touched them, it was like he could feel their laughter through his skin.

Then the sky was black and the stars came through with their cold pricks of light and the boy knew that he needed to return to the lake. Sometimes he felt that he had always been here, crouched in the dark, holding out his arms to catch the drifting bodies as they fell. He thought there must be a beginning he had forgotten, a start to this existence. He had to believe that, if only because it meant that there might also be an end.

The Boy at the Bottom of the Lake &
Other Legends of the North Country,
Jean-Pierre Montour, 1936

KAISER

Kaiser left his car at the main road and hiked through the foot deep snow to his parents' house. In the garage, he cranked up the old F-150 with the plow attachment and made a couple passes to clear the long driveway. The snow was light, but it was going to get heavier over the next couple days, and if he didn't complete the job with the snowblower, his mother would be stuck. It wouldn't matter much to Janice, as Bill came by with groceries every week, and she had her cable TV. Janice arranged her life around PBS historical dramas and conservative news shows that screamed about mayhem and madness. Kaiser cooked her some scrambled eggs with baked beans, and they sat together in the living room, watching a turn-of-the-century London detective in a bowler solve a double murder committed with a cavalry sword. His mother took a small bite of eggs and put the plate aside. She would only talk when the commercials came on, and she spoke with a distracted air, like she was addressing some shadowy company in the room that he could not see. Janice seemed convinced that the world was collapsing around her, and that Bill was in great danger.

He can't go on like this, she said.

Bill is fine, Kaiser said. He's going to be fine.

I think of him out there on that dark highway, she said. All alone. The way people are now, the way the world is now. There's no goodness or light out there.

That's not true, Kaiser said. You shouldn't think that.

Kaiser didn't know why she was so fixated on Bill and his troubles, whatever they were. Sure, his wife was a lunatic, but they knew that a decade ago. His daughter would be heading off to college soon, and Bill had his log cabin by the stream and his patrol friends and the bowling league. His job was dangerous, but it always had been. It's true there were desperate men driving fast toward some real or imaginary release, men walking the edge of the woods along the highway with something weighty in a paper bag, men angrily smoking cigarettes outside the gas station by the border. But there had always been bad people out there in the dark.

He's worried about you, Janice said. He blames those listening stations, the Chinese number lady. He thinks you're following your father down a dark road. He says it's a dangerous delusion.

He doesn't need to worry about me, Kaiser said. You don't need to worry.

On the screen the British detective was striding across Trafalgar Square with an umbrella, stepping over puddles in his galoshes. He was being followed by a pair of men in tweed suits.

I wasn't a good mother.

That's not true, Mom.

I should have been more careful. And I blamed you. Oh, it's so horrible.

No, you didn't, Kaiser said. You never blamed me.

Oh, Tom, it's so much worse than you know.

The detective was drinking tea in a café when the men in tweed approached his table. One held a small knife behind his back. Janice squeezed his hand.

I'm so sorry, she said. I blamed you in my heart.

The snowblower was in the usual spot in the garage, covered with a tarp. A pair of headlights came across the field, bulldozing through the snow. It was Bill in his Tahoe, the emergency lights on the rack spinning. He left the engine running and the lights on as he came to a stop in the driveway.

Beat me to it, Bill said. Got oil in it?

Yeah, Kaiser said.

Bill squatted down and checked the oil anyway, fingering the idle switch.

Made an interesting catch on the Northway the other day. Somebody who said they knew you.

Oh yeah? Kaiser said.

The guy that shot your buddy in Wiggletown. Gorman? He was heading south. An easy pull because the goddamn idiot was naked. Guess what we found in the trunk?

Kaiser looked out over the lake, the faint lights of Burlington. The mad irony of the thing was that he was hoping that Gorman had got away.

Pretty good stack of money, Bill said. And a few pills. Stamped with a Fleur-de-Lis. Some special kind of Ecstasy. Hard to get but apparently everyone wants it. He said he knew you. Before what happened in Wiggletown.

I don't know that guy, Kaiser said. Never met him before.

Yeah, well, Bill said. He said a lot of crazy shit. He said that someone was going to bring a big load of the stuff over the border. Across the ice.

What? How?

That's what I said. The dude said a lot of crazy shit. He was ranting about death planets, a little boy living under the lake, end of the world kind of shit. Anyway, we remanded him for psychiatric evals and he's on his way Albany. Only a complete idiot would try something like that. The assets they've got for this section of the border, man you couldn't run a muskrat across without the feds knowing.

I bet, Kaiser said.

They stood looking at the snowblower for a few moments, shining under the glare of the neon light. Bill waved an arm toward the open garage door, the dark slot of night sky.

You still see 'em up there? You know, like you used to?

Kaiser gripped the throttle, flipped the choke switch. Kodiak wiped the snowblower down after every use. The thing was spotless.

You used to say they were telling you things, Bill said. Remember that?

Kodiak loved the clean, orderly rows the blower made when the snow was fresh and light. During a big snow, sometimes he would do the driveway several times during the night.

Are they telling you anything now?

I don't know, Kaiser said.

Bill sighed and jammed his hands in his coat pockets.

Well, I'm gonna go say hi to Mom. Everything good in there?

We had dinner, Kaiser said. She seems tired.

After Bill went inside, Kaiser rolled the snowblower out of the garage and cranked it up, the roaring engine splitting the still evening air.

The pair of Chinooks came low through a steep gorge of basalt and sandstone before climbing a thousand meters up the westward slope of a mountain scaled with snow-crusted stands of pine, the whop of the rotors banging back off the rock and reverberating in his chest. Through the porthole, Kaiser could see the mountain ridges with deep valleys where streams of whitewater flowed through mud-walled hamlets and the shadows of the helicopters sweeping over the ground until they cleared the ridge, and the unending peaks of mountains spread out before him like some vast, stony sea. The Ranger next to him, a large fellow named Wiley who carried the SOFLAM targeting laser, poked the window with a finger.

God's country, he said, adjusting the fat knot of Skoal in his lip with a burrowing tongue. *Which* gods though? That's the fucking question amirite?

He elbowed Kaiser and then after a moment turned away and spit on the floor as the pair of Chinooks dipped hard and began to shadow the terrain, every man taking hold of something as they banked and lurched.

The first Chinook came under immediate fire when it approached the drop zone. When it was a hundred meters off the plateau, a half-dozen RPGs arched out of the trees, trailing corkscrewing tubes of smoke. One rocket punched the tail section and Razor 2 fell hard on its belly then canted over a quarter turn before righting itself, the engine shrieking as the rotors chopped themselves to splinters in a cloud of snow and stone. Kaiser and the second team could see the sparking muzzle fire from the trees and rocks around the downed chopper and they watched as the team of Rangers came out into a visible sleet of lead, two men somersaulting down the ramp in a spray of blood, killed before they touched the ground. The Chinook's 7.62-mm minigun began raking the tree line, shredding the pines in explosions of white pulp but the gunner was quickly hit and the attached TACP, a man named Suarez that trained with Kaiser at Fort Bragg, came down the ramp and took four rounds to his legs and groin and was dead before they could drag him out. The remaining nine Rangers got prone on the plateau and tried to establish a perimeter and return fire. The Air Support Operations Center diverted Razor 3, so Kaiser's helicopter shuddered as the pilots backed away and pulled into a climb, banking hard to the east.

They dropped Kaiser and the dozen Rangers two kilometers down the mountain, where a company of the Tenth Mountain Division had set up temporary bunkers to monitor the valley. A captain with the Tenth was hollering at them through cupped hands from a pile of sandbags, but Kaiser and the Ranger squad ignored him and went immediately up the rocky slope toward the downed chopper, working through crevasses rimed with ice, scrabbling for handholds. As he climbed, Kaiser searched the intensely blue sky for movement and caught the thin contrail of a distant AWAC, and the faint traces of avian predators, distinct for their organic, circular geometry. In his earpiece, he heard ASOC decree no more landings in the hot zone until after nightfall.

A half hour later, they reached the landing site and the smoking hulk of Razor 2 and surviving Rangers. The valley behind them was now fully engaged and the mortar rounds began falling on the Tenth

Mountain positions at the bottom of the hill. Through his scope, Kaiser could see bands of men in the valley wearing knee-length tunics and running with mortar tubes over their shoulders, men on the roofs of the compounds with binoculars and radios. A rusty ZSU-23-4 with Soviet markings came grinding out of a clay-walled shed and began pounding the Tenth Mountain sandbag bunkers, pink tracer rounds bouncing up the mountain in antic ricochets. Kaiser crawled to a small promontory on the western edge of the landing site and wedged the satellite antennae in a rock fracture. In the valley below, the mortar rounds *whupped* and climbed, creating faint arcs of air disturbance and velocity, and when they hit the ground rings of smoke rolled like raindrops falling on a dusty table. Kaiser could see men thrown by the concussion and the insect-splay of their limbs as they came apart. The radio crackled with throttled voices shouting for airvac, extraction, angels. His heart burned with anger, and Kaiser bared his teeth and hissed like a wounded animal at the sun as it touched the silvery rim of the mountains. The village in the valley had tilled fields, a donkey cart full of grain, a battered Toyota Corolla banging down a dry riverbed. Civilians scrambling for cover. Kaiser used his compass to shoot an azimuth, feeling the quickening in his bones as the machinery in the sky circled and stacked up. The surge of power made him clack his jaws like a hypothermic reaction. It was too much. He knew he should stop. He opened the radio channel.

This is Razor 3, Kaiser said. Who's out there?

I'm right here, buddy, the radio said. This is ASOC Solar. Whaddya need?

What's in the air?

We got a full menu, my man. I've got F-14s, Strike Eagles, C-130s, B-52s, A-10s. I got spooky, JDAMs, MK-82s, 40 millimeter. Even a fucking B-2 about six minutes out.

I've got the bomb box set, Kaiser said, SOFLAM to mark.

That's cool, the radio said. We've got CAOC clearance, my man. No problem.

I've got two boxes, Kaiser said. With us in between.

Whoa, that's some crazy shit.

The B-2 first, Kaiser said. Bring it down the mountain low and over the hostiles in the valley.

Yeah, man, the radio said. Let 'em know who's coming.

Then the B-52s, Kaiser said, with two-thousand-pound JDAMs. The F-14s in pairs hit the valley with dummies, whatever else they got. I want spooky cleaning up on the mountaintop, with the A-10s coming in after.

Just give me the digits, brother.

As Kaiser started reading out the numbers, he saw the Tenth Mountain captain coming up the slope, working his way over to his position with his radio man. The mortar rounds in the valley fell with the steady precision of a kickdrum. Venus was blazing white in the purple-charcoal sky and every second more stars appeared in the firmament. Kaiser watched the men below him swarming like gnats, more emerging from doorways and trucks. They would never stop coming. He saw Tucker's grinning face, obliterated by a storm of hot metal. Only the scorching hammer of the gods could end this.

Which gods?

TAC! the captain shouted.

He was waiting with his radioman to cross an open gap, waving his hands, trying to get Kaiser's attention. Kaiser finished off the numbers to ASOC, then turned and tapped the shoulder of the Ranger to his left, who was in the prone position with the SOFLAM laser pointed down in the valley.

You see that high-walled building in the center? With the guys on the roof?

The Ranger took off his helmet and sighted through the scope.

Sparkle that target, Kaiser said.

Roger that. Laze-on.

Is that it, brother? The radio said in his ear.

Affirmative, Kaiser said. ETA?

Two minutes, tops. You sure you don't need anything else, man?

Like what?

I don't know. Like you wanna talk about something? I'm sure as hell not going anywhere.

TAC!

I gotta go, Kaiser said.

All right, man. If you say so. You better square it away righty-tighty, know what I'm saying? Cleared hot, danger close. You'll know when it's coming.

The captain started crabbing across the gap double-quick, his radio man low-crawling and pulling his set by the straps. Kaiser felt the surge of blood in his heart. He tapped the blond Ranger with the laser again.

Sparkle that fucking target.

No problem, the Ranger said. You're the reason we're here.

The Ranger winked at him again. Something about this was terribly familiar and awoke a mortal fear, deep in Kaiser's bowels. A sour taste swelled in his throat. The Tenth Mountain captain was now crouched right up in his quarter, red-faced, his breath hot.

What the *fuck* you doing, airman?

Close air support, sir, Kaiser said. I've got a full complement of ordinance coming down danger close. The grid is set, drop time less than two minutes. But we got civilians all over the place.

I don't give a shit! the captain shouted. We're taking heavy mortar fire, and I want those position suppressed now!

Sir, the radioman said, ASOC is asking if this is a clean target.

There are third country nationals in the valley, Kaiser said. You can see the vehicles.

The captain surveyed the valley and the ridgeline with the smoking Chinook, then looked at the Ranger with the laser sparkling the rooftop. He rotated around again, trying to take in the whole scene, his face blank.

Shit. You got those coordinates tight, JTAC?

Yes, sir.

The sun finally went behind the mountain and the long shadows over the valley coalesced and within seconds the air temperature dropped twenty degrees. The faint outline of an AWAC rolled above the clouds and into the darkening sky. The information was transmitted, the targets marked, the numbers locked. Kaiser could see the delicate, invisible stitching of the entire system in low earth orbit, the name they wrote in the sky.

The captain cursed and shook his head.

Stand it down, JTAC.

I can't do that, Captain.

Whaddya mean, you *can't*?

Kaiser could hear the sound of air being rended apart and then rushing back together behind him, and he turned and caught a quick cobalt gleam in the purple sky, like a black knife edge coming directly at him. It was coming.

It's too late, Kaiser said.

The captain grabbed Kaiser's harness and jerked him to his feet. A round snapped by Kaiser's ear and both men flinched.

That's a direct order, airman!

Kaiser rotated at the waist and chopped his arms down and the captain went to one knee, hanging on to a strap, trying to pull him down to the ground. They locked eyes, holding on to each other, the captain's face white with shock. Kaiser could feel it building like an extraterrestrial storm system, something strong and sure, a guiding force, something that would swing through the night like a star.

Kaiser punched him cleanly between the eyes and the captain sat down hard in the dust. The radioman had the satellite phone to his ear, staring at Kaiser.

Holy *shit!* He fucking punched the captain!

The sky began to roar like some loosed demon-seeded beast, and Kaiser felt the hammer of the gods begin to swing.

The B-2 came over the summit at five hundred feet, a shimmering triangle of darkness that created a blast of down-force that flattened the men on the plateau. It cut down the slope of the mountain, then nosed up, the afterburners sending a great torrent of light to the ground and the valley was bright like full day and every man and machine and shape in it cast sharply in raked horizontal shadows and they all heard the thin whistle and sucking vacuum sound of dropping death.

Danger close! Danger close! Oh god!

The shockwave was like a distortion in the ground, the earth rolling and dropping and then the flash of eternal light, every particle illuminated like a frozen strobe image followed by the black gouts of billowing smoke and spreading tentacles of flame like a bloody-veined eyeball in the sky and great columns of fire stabbed at the ground from the heavens churning up rock and earth and men in a circular shaft of explosive steel, the air full of the whistle and whine of compressed particles, fine dust and glittering shards and then the larger debris, chips and pieces of rock metal and bone clacking and thudding and the cries of men in pain and fear and they rolled up like pill bugs, crying and puking and clutching each other and every one of them believed they had been called home to death.

SYDNEY & PHIL

On Monday morning, Sydney dropped off Juliet at her mother's and drove into Frenchtown for some home visits. Her first stop was Calliope Trombley's place, so she loitered in the parking lot of Dunkin Donuts until eleven, drinking sugary coffee and reading a book given to her by Pastor Lyle—*The Enchiridion of Epictetus.*

Much of *Epictetus* seemed like common sense to Sydney. The world is divided into two classes of things: those that we can control and those that we cannot. It made her think of Phil. For Phil, there was only one class of things. *Nothing* was in his control, all was moved by an unseen and incompetent hand.

Sydney parked her car on the hill in front of the Trombley house. There was a worn track through the snowplow wall and up to the front door. The house next door was unoccupied, plywood tacked across the doors and windows. Across the street a couple men in their twenties wearing garish hoodies splattered with neon lettering sat on an old couch on the front porch with a Styrofoam container of chicken wings between them. They stared at her, clearly stoned into a state of disgruntled lethargy. One of men pulled a clean bone out of his wet mouth and flicked it into the front yard. Sydney drank the lukewarm dregs of her coffee and stepped out of the car. The temperature hadn't been above ten degrees in weeks. A young boy was sliding down thc hill on a skateboard without wheels, using his feet to steer. He slid sideways and tumbled over, then picking up the board he started coming back up the hill. He was wearing jeans, a sweatshirt, and an old watch cap pulled down low. When he saw her standing there he froze, then turned and started walking back down the hill.

Dylan! Sydney yelled. Dylan!

He turned around, and putting the skateboard on his shoulder, he trudged up the hill, his sneakers slipping on the packed snow and ice. His face and hands were beet red from cold and the sweatshirt hung on his thin body like a rag.

My mom's inside, Dylan said.

Okay. I'd like to talk to both of you. That cool?

He nodded and slipped through the notch in the snowplow wall and headed for the front door. It struck Sydney that Dylan was afraid of her. He must know that she could change his life in powerful ways.

The house was a wreck, and her breath steamed in the foyer. She would have to check the boiler and make sure they had heating oil. Sydney knew that the older brother was an occasional tenant in the basement and that he had an uneasy relationship with Callie. He wore some kind of monstrous headgear for an unspecified injury to his neck. She'd seen him a few weeks back lurking outside of Pizza Bono in downtown North Chazy, a nightmarish figure in a black leather jacket, the rods and bars encircling his shaved head flashing red and blue under the neon sign. But she also knew that he was gainfully employed last time she checked, working as a cook at the Stagecoach, and that he seemed to have a strong affection for Dylan.

Dylan tromped through the kitchen in his wet shoes.

Mom? The DSS lady's here!

Callie Trombley was in the living room sitting on the couch, watching Oprah with the sound muted. Her bare feet were propped on the coffee table, the skin of her feet blue and hard like marble. On the table a collection of red Solo cups. The TV was panning to various close-up shots of women jumping up and down and contorting their faces in joy, rage, or sorrow, Sydney couldn't tell.

Hello, Callie.

A flicker of the eyes, twin plumes of smoke from her nostrils.

Do you have heating oil? Have you checked the tank?

Callie flicked her ash on the carpet. Dylan stomped up the steps to the second floor.

Callie? Why is Dylan playing outside with no coat? And more importantly, why isn't he at school today?

Callie cranked her head around. She seemed to be vibrating slightly, and Sydney suspected she hadn't had her first drink yet.

Ain't no school today, Callie said.

Today's Monday. There is definitely school.

She saw a thin film of embarrassment cross Callie's face, quickly replaced with belligerence.

He said he didn't want to go. Said he was sick.

What about his coat? It's freezing out there.

Callie began searching through the collection of Solo cups on the table, likely looking for one that held the dregs of yesterday's vodka.

You can't do this, Callie. I have to mark it in the report.

Callie sat back on the couch and closed her eyes, sighing dramatically.

Okay, okay, she said. You got me. I fucked up.

I don't want to *get* you, Callie. That's not what I'm here for.

Callie shook an empty pack of Parliaments, tossed it back on the table.

I'm here to help you, Sydney said.

I'm not well, Callie said. I've been sick a long time.

What's the problem?

C'mere, she said. I wanna show you something.

Phil eased the Audi onto the grass and around the gate at the top of Greek row. In the afternoons, the row was crowded with students who lived in the houses walking to and from classes, trudging head down and swaddled with layers of wool and Gore-Tex, eating the driving wind that swept from the south off the lake. The terms of Phil's employment involved picking up Scotty at his condo in the morning, dropping him at the college for classes, hanging around in the background for the day, then taking him home. If Scotty went out in the evening, Phil would go with him. Six hundred a week cash, plus bonuses. Not as much as Dannemora, and no benefits, but the hours and environment were exceedingly better. Phil couldn't imagine why this guy would want to pay him to protect a student at Ausable College. Who was after him?

When he'd asked, Gene Marin had waved a hand, his eyes closed.

Look, I'm not going to sit here and tell you the kid's innocent. He's not. He gets himself involved in things he shouldn't. He's got a mouth on him.

So this is a bodyguard thing?

He just needs an attentive, protective friend, Marin said. Okay?

Driving the Audi was another perk. Phil was never much of a car guy. Lots of guys he played hockey with were serious gearheads, cars and sleds, running the drag races on the ice on King's Bay, some kind of bondo-emblazoned wreck in the barn or garage. Phil had only owned one car in his life: a 1990 Toyota Corolla. *It's like the anti-car*, one of his buddies told him. *It's like the opposite of everything that a car should be.* But the noise and the stink of engines bored him. He also barely had any time for such things, because from the age of six he was playing on a travel team, and by the time he reached junior high he was on a select all-star squad that played across the Northeast and Canada. His mother used to go to the games, but after she passed nobody else did. His father's world consisted of the prison and the house. Weeks went by when the old man never veered from the eighty-odd feet that separated the receiving entry and his front door, other than trips to the liquor store. His sister was too busy smoking weed and listening to Phish tapes. So from an early age Phil was bumming rides with his hockey bag and five bucks in his pocket for a burger and a Coke. He spent a lot of his youth in the back of random station wagons and vans, crammed between a couple guys he barely knew, somebody's dad up front with a map in one hand and a can of Blue in the other, checking the rear-view mirror and wondering who in the hell was this big sonaofabitch mooching rides?

Phil didn't know that driving a car could be like this; the way the black leather of the interior seemed to wrap around him like a cocoon, all of the instruments laid out before him glowing crisp orange, the responsiveness of the accelerator and the tightness of the steering. Each time he got in it, he couldn't help but think he was in the cockpit of some kind of far-future spacecraft, and when he accelerated briskly onto the Northway he imagined that the thing just might take off, climbing up over the pines and coasting over the mountains.

Playing hockey still occupied his thoughts, but only abstractly. The Albany Devils were a team he wouldn't have considered five years ago, and the prospect of a season banging around New England in a shitty bus with the Adirondack Flames was just depressing. He didn't feel like getting punched in the face anymore. But was that all? He wasn't *afraid* of getting hit. His ability as an enforcer depended on his ability to "stay in the pocket," to tuck his chin and keep his eyes up, his hands firing. Phil was known as a guy who could *hang on*. A good twist of jersey in his grip, using his weight and balance, slipping punches, angling them off helmet, pads, face, until he got the opening he needed. *Just hang on*, he told himself as the situation started to go badly for him. It worked. Phil would simply not let go until the other man was down or quit. It didn't hurt much in the moment, unless you got your nose broken, and that was more annoying than anything else with all the spraying blood and some clumsy Canadian equipment manager trying to set your nose on the bench with his nicotine-stained fingers. No, it only really hurt later, when the contusions and cuts had time to settle in and your body stopped producing the various enzymes and brain signals that told your body that everything was okay. There must be some other reason he didn't want to play.

Phil drove with one hand on the wheel and let the Audi coast down the row at ten miles per hour, the car silent except for the crunch of the fat Pirellis on the snow. He couldn't believe people would really come after Scotty. Would he fight for him? He wasn't the fucking secret service. But he did want to keep the job, so Phil figured he'd trust in his ability to defuse situations before they happened. He could be very persuasive in convincing people to not take that first, fateful swing. Every moment he was on the ice he was playing that role, quietly broadcasting to the opposing team: *you don't want to do that. Trust me, you don't.*

After the first day, Phil thought he was either going to quit or kick this kid's ass. Scotty treated him like a nuisance, instructing him to stay in the other room, to wait in the car. Phil told him what Scotty's father said, but Scotty said *fuck that old man and his bullshit.* But after a week, Scotty started to seem to like him being around, especially when his fraternity brothers caught on and welcomed Phil heartily. *It's so badass, bro! A fucking bodyguard!* When they ordered Phil to get them a drink and he told them to go fuck themselves they laughed and jumped around the room, high-fiving each other.

On campus, Phil trailed behind Scotty and his crew, and it was remarkable how the world of the college opened for them wherever they went. Nothing was ever crowded, or unpleasant, or out of reach. In the dining hall, the boys had their own table, a choice spot in the corner, held for them by some unspoken agreement. The boys glided through the student center, passing the array of conveniences and technology arrayed for their usage, and gathered in an upstairs hall in the library, which was also seemingly reserved for them, where they talked and laughed with their feet up on the table, their books scattered on the floor, some of the boys sprawled out and napping between the tall bookshelves. All his life, Phil had felt as if he was in an adversarial relationship with the world; everything was a contest, everything was *against* him. Only by competing and fighting was he able to accomplish anything. His family, schools, the town, none of these institutions were trying to help. They only tried to hold him back. But not Scotty and his boys. They glided through this buffet of options and support, with their only reaction being an annoyance that such things were cluttering up their day.

Phil parked the car in front of the house and texted Scotty that he was here. He had a paperback copy of *Islands in the Stream*, a book that Sydney said he might like, that he kept in the car. Scotty nearly always kept him waiting, sometimes for a long time, but Phil didn't really care, as he was getting paid, and he kinda liked the book, all the fishing and skin diving and rummies getting beat up. He'd have to get Sydney and Juliet down to the Florida Keys sometime, see what it's like to hook onto a black marlin. He'd never seen the Gulf of Mexico.

After an hour, Scotty got in the car with a few guys, reeking of weed.

Home, Jeeves, Scotty said, and the other guys laughed until Phil turned around in the seat and looked at them. Cool-Mite, Tripp, Stanton.

C'mon, dude, Scotty said. Just fuckin' with ya.

Scotty's lakeside condo was part of a small development, six luxury units, white concrete blocks fastened to the side of a steep hill with four hundred square feet of deck hanging over the water, two bedrooms, chunky stainless appliances, and a floor-to-ceiling shower stall in the middle of the living room like a glass elevator shaft. One wall was dominated by a large flat-screen with a chaotic semicircle of inflatable chairs, gaming consoles and controllers, headphones, turntables, mixers, amplifiers, keyboards, cables, and speaker systems. When they arrived, it was already dark, and the wind howled off the lake. Stanton got a fire going in the fireplace, and the other boys starting mixing drinks. Gene Marin didn't say shit about drinking on the job, so Phil took a glass of Scotch. They said it was eighty dollars a bottle, and while the stuff was pretty damn glorious, smoky with a sort of coffee aftertaste, it seemed absurd to pay that for a bottle of booze. The east side of the condo facing the lake was floor-to-ceiling windows, and Phil watched the wind push and pull the snow on the ice into neat, sinuous rows. The techno music started up, the real tinny, tinselly sounding stuff Scotty and his boys always played, with sober Finnish girls singing like they were hiding under the bed on a rainy afternoon. Scotty came over and stood next to him.

My dad ever talk about, like, secrets, or shit like that?

What?

Like, there's shit that goes down around here, you know?

Okay, Phil said.

Let me see your hand.

Phil held out his right hand and Scotty took hold of his wrist and traced a finger across his palm. Phil watched, confused, until he saw the thin red line, welling with blood. Scotty held up a small razor pinched between his thumb and forefinger.

Motherfucker!

Phil gripped him by the shoulders, getting a good wad of Scotty's cashmere sweater in his fists, preparing to rip it over his head.

Whoa, whoa! Phil! Dude! It's cool! Look!

Scotty held up his own hand and drew the razor across his palm.

The other boys were watching, tense, and Phil wondered for the first time if any of these guys could produce guns or other weapons. Likely, he decided.

What *the fuck* you think you're doing?

Blood pact, Scotty said.

Scotty took Phil's hand and shook it with his bloody hand.

See? Done. Cool-Mite, get the first aid kit.

What the fuck? Phil said. You gonna show me your tree house next?

You're in it, bro! Now we have a vow of secrecy.

Scotty turned to walk away but Phil reached out with his bloody hand and grabbed a handful of his hair, turning him back around.

You do something like that again I'll fucking beat the shit out of you.

I know, Scotty said. I believe it. Ow, fuck. Can you let go?

Phil looked at him for a minute, then released him. Scotty tried to smooth his hair back, but it was all sticky with blood.

Fuck, man. Now I gotta take a shower.

Fuck you, Phil said. You fucking love taking showers.

He did. Every time Phil was there Scotty had some reason to shower, which meant stripping down naked in the middle of the living room and climbing into the glass tower. The shower steamed up but remained translucent and Scotty was fond of a leisurely, attentive washing, spending a lot of time soaping up his undercarriage. Whatever. Most the things these frat boys did felt gay to him. Phil helped himself to another expensive Scotch and joined the other guys on the inflatable chairs playing *Halo* with headsets on, shit-talking in pidgin English with kids in Singapore. When they passed the bong, Phil took a hit. He hadn't smoked pot in at least a year, and he felt it immediately. The action of the game on the screen became florid and oversaturated, so instead he watched the faces of the young men as they writhed and jumped in their chairs, fingers working the buttons furiously, their eyes shining with light.

Scotty had just finished his meticulous post-shower regimen when his phone buzzed, letting him know that their visitors were arriving. He came over and shut off the Xbox and told the boys to get out.

Go take a smoke break, he said. Phil, just chill where you are, cool?

The boys piled on their jackets and went out on the deck, lighting up cigarettes in the darkness. Scotty came over and handed Phil a set of headphones.

Listen to this.

Phil put the headphones on his head and the sweeping roar of an electronic crescendo drowned out the rest of the world. Scotty said something else, but Phil just took a drink of his Scotch and smiled. Sure, he could sit here and listen to this weird-ass music. The bass felt good in his chest, and the simple repeated rhythm, urgent at first, now seemed relaxed, like gentle waves lapping the reefs of Key West.

The visitors were two Asian men dressed in black puffer jackets and with immaculately coiffed hairstyles. Both had tattoos snaking up their necks, a mixture of language characters and sinuous lizards. They sat with Scotty at the table and conferred, Scotty doing most of the talking. Outside on the deck, the boys smoked and pretended not to pay attention. Phil wasn't feeling particularly protective. Then the men and Scotty were shaking hands, and they left without incident.

He wouldn't tell Sydney. Phil knew that she was relieved he wasn't going into Dannemora, but she hated this new gig. But Sydney didn't understand the kind of money and power Gene Marin wielded. Who knows? If Phil did a good job, he might get more work. So he would do this thing with Scotty and collect the money and better things would happen. Or he'd go back to playing hockey. He tipped up his glass.

Scotty sat next to Phil and picked up the bong. It was cashed, but Scotty searched it with the lighter anyway. Phil slipped off the headphones.

Who're those guys?

Some guys that are gonna make me a shit-ton of money.

A hard knock on the balcony door, and when they looked over, they saw three moon-white bare asses, cheeks spread, pressed against the glass. Then Tripp shoved Cool-Mite, who slipped and fell down the frozen deck stairs face-first, pants around his ankles.

Why are you fucking around with this shit? Phil said.

What?

Those guys. Drug deals.

Hey, Scotty said, we have a pact, remember?

Yeah, but that doesn't mean I shouldn't tell you you're an idiot. You already have a ton of money.

My dad has money, Scotty said.

He swung his arms around, indicating the condo, the dock, the sleds parked outside.

All this shit is *his*.

You want your own shit, Phil said.

Exactly.

Callie walked into her bedroom, closing the door behind Sydney. A large, open closet disgorged clothes on the floor; a four-poster canopy bed with a wad of sheets and blankets; two greasy pillows; a clutter of shoes underfoot. There was a built-in vanity with a bench seat covered with a stack of *National Geographics*. Half the lights on the vanity were burned out or missing, but the small shelves were choked with makeup and hair care items, and the air smelled like baby powder and black mold. Callie turned around let her robe drop.

Callie, Sydney said. What's going on?

Here, she said, reaching for Sydney's hands. You need to feel.

She pulled Sydney's hands up and placed them on her breasts.

Here.

She moved Sydney's hands around, squeezing her fingers. Sydney turned her face away from Callie's ray-gun halitosis, a focused beam of ash and kerosene.

Do you feel it? Callie said.

Sydney felt the marble-size lump in the right breast, then two of them, then in the left there were several more. Now a half dozen or more, like ball bearings suspended in aspic, a constellation of nodules.

Aw fuck, that hurts, Callie said.

Sydney dropped her hands, took a step back. She closed her eyes and tried to comport her face.

How long has it been like this?

I dunno, Callie said. Couple months at least.

Jesus, Callie. Have you been to the doctor?

Doctor? How would I pay?

Callie, Sydney said. We went over this. You have vouchers for the clinic. They are in your packet. The one I gave you at the beginning of the year?

Oh hell, Callie said. I don't even know where that shit is.

When was the last time you saw it?

I told you I don't *know*.

Where's your son? Where's Sebastian?

Who knows? Somewhere off with Kaiser.

Kaiser? Tom Kaiser?

Yeah. Seb's been working with him.

Doing what?

I dunno. Something with satellites.

Satellites?

Yeah.

That doesn't make any sense, Callie. When does he get back?

I don't fucking know! Okay? He don't always stay here.

You need to call him, Sydney said. *Now.*

Sydney picked up the battered flip phone on the vanity she assumed was Callie's and handed it to her.

I'm going to take you to the hospital, she said. Put some clothes on. I'll get Dylan.

Sydney tried to run through the protocol as she went up the stairs. She wasn't supposed to directly intercede in medical situations, not without filing a report first and getting approval. But nearly every client needed direct assistance, whether it was a trip to the grocery store or someone to replace a fuse, and it was understood that such small acts of mercy could go unreported. Transportation and hospital admittance was something else, but Sydney figured this would fall under the category of an emergency.

She was due to check in on Eileen and Bianca Leroux in the afternoon, but she would have to call Kara and reschedule. She knew Kara wouldn't answer. When Sydney brought their case to Protective Services, Kara stopped communicating. Braden Tullus was still missing but Sydney was going to pass that off to his assigned caseworker. And *Tom Kaiser?*

Dylan?

She knocked on his door. Downstairs she could hear Callie banging around her closet, hopefully putting on some clothes. Dylan opened the door slightly and stuck his face in the crack.

Yes?

I need to talk to you, Sydney said. Can I come in?

He blinked at her, a lock of dark hair over his nose. The boy needed a haircut.

Or can you come out?

Yeah, he said. Can you turn around?

Sydney stepped back and turned away. There was a photograph hanging on the wall, a teenage boy swathed in a heavy sweater, perched on a sled somewhere out on the ice. It wasn't Dylan. Must be Sebastian, she figured. He had a knowing smile. No crazy headgear thing, yet.

Actually was kind of handsome. She heard the door rasping and turned around just as Dylan was closing the door behind him. In the slice of the open door, she saw a cascading jumble of shapes that seem to pour off the wall and onto the floor. It looked like a scaled-down version of some ancient Sumerian city built into a desert mountainside. *What the hell?*

Dylan closed the door and snapped the padlock on. He was already wearing his heavy coat and hat, and he had a small backpack over one shoulder. Where does he think we're going?

I'm ready, he said.

They stood there for a moment, just looking at each other. A door slammed downstairs, and Callie crossed the kitchen, murmuring something. Then Dylan's eyes were full, and his shoulders were shaking. Sydney went to one knee and took his hands in hers.

What is it? What's the matter?

You'll take it away from me, he burst out, sobbing. You'll take it.

Take it? Take what, honey?

Mom is sick, and when she goes, you'll take it all away.

Sydney took him into her arms and held him tight. He leaned into her, his wet face on her neck.

No, she whispered into his ear. I won't take anything from you. I promise.

STERNE

Laurence Sterne propped his office window open with a paperback copy of *The Collected Writings of John Ruskin* and lit a joint. The icy draft from the window carried the current of smoke around the room and into the hallway. The door was partly open, but he didn't feel like getting up to close it. Classes wouldn't start for another week, and the building was deserted anyway. Sterne was slated to teach three classes in the spring, but he didn't know what they were and didn't care. The dean offered a semester leave, but he declined. He found a half-empty bottle of Crown Royal in a drawer, given to him by a grateful student after the completion of an honors thesis. He wiped out a crusty coffee mug with his shirttail and poured a couple inches. In his pocket he found some loose hydrocodone pills. Going through the bathroom medicine cabinet at home, he found a couple bottles from Sue's knee surgery last year. The pills numbed him in a way that helped him get through the long hours of the day. He washed down two with a gulp of warm whiskey and put his feet up on the windowsill to watch the wind blowing across the quad. A student pedaled a bike along an icy sidewalk, face wrapped tight with a scarf. He drained the mug and poured another. He belched and grimaced with the burning taste that rose in his throat and brushed some mysterious brown flecks off the front his shirt. Sterne switched on the CD player and hit play. *ELO's Greatest Hits.*

Our propensity for self-deception is infinite, he thought. It will never end.

A few minutes later, Sterne heard the steps coming down the hallway. Another faculty member coming in to do some prep work, or maybe custodial staff. The joint was still on the windowsill, and he suddenly didn't remember how long he'd been in the office. He gazed, glassy-eyed, at the strewn papers, folders, and books, as if he didn't know this place. The footsteps came down the hall toward his office and it seemed inevitable to Sterne that they would stop, pause, and then the cautious, polite knock at the door. And there it was.

Yes?

The door swung open, revealing a young woman with a familiar face, a coat and scarf folded over her arm. Emerson LeClair. She of that famous last name.

Emerson, right?

Yeah. Hi.

Can I help you?

Well, she said, I was just going to the library, and I saw you in the window.

She wrinkled up her nose.

You know you can smell that, like, all the way downstairs?

She had definitely been in at least two of his classes. A good writer. Fully engaged. Earnest as hell.

Sterne picked up the joint and held it out to her.

This?

She bunched up her face in an awkward smile. Her boots were rimmed with muddy slush that was starting to melt.

Does it bother you?

Doesn't bother *me*, she said, but, like . . . you might get in trouble?

She sat down, her jacket and scarf in her lap, and looked around at the mess of the room for a moment, then back at him.

So, she said. Is everything . . . okay?

Sterne put the joint in his teeth and lit it, working it with pursed lips until it was burning.

Just doing some reorganizing, he said, blowing out a thick cloud of smoke.

He handed her the joint and she took it off his fingers like a seasoned pro.

Umm, can I at least close the door?

She closed the door, then sat down and hit the joint and passed it back to him, turning her head to exhale into a stack of graded exams. Her wool sweater was twisted around one side, and she worked it straight. Why was she here? Sterne suddenly felt empty, his heart a wind-scoured field. He didn't really care about anything. He closed his eyes for a moment, letting the darkness settle. He spoke with his eyes shut.

Emerson, he said. Have you ever been in love?

I . . . think so?

I'm talking about a truly religious experience, Sterne said. Not like one time you did mushrooms with your buddies. I mean a real triumph of the holy. When the earth splits open, exploding hearts fill the sky and you have visions of the infinite in a bucket of water. You ever had that?

Her voice came back to him out of the black, like it was drifting through space.

I'm not sure.

Then you have never been in love.

When he opened his eyes, she was still there, her lips slightly chapped, the hollow of her throat rolling as she swallowed. He felt the power in the room, how it emanated from him in concentric waves, like something mathematical, compounded and expanding. Sterne stood up, holding the desk for support, then walked behind Emerson to the door and flipped the light switch off. The half-light from the window cast everything with a dull, metallic sheen.

Stand up, he said.

Emerson stood, looking over her shoulder at him. He couldn't keep her face steady, but she wasn't afraid, he was sure of it.

Put your hands on the shelf, he said.

She turned slowly, facing the bookcase, and Sterne took her wrists and placed her hands on the shelf.

Move your feet back.

Sterne moved behind her, his hands hovering just over the contours of her body. He moved them down over the rough wool of her sweater to her jeans and the gentle swell of her hips.

Dr. Sterne?

He moved his hands back up, over the narrowness of her waist. He wanted to build to something, to increase the pressure, to grip her slender body in his hands and crush some part of her. Something terrible was about to happen. He looked up and saw she had turned her head toward the window. A tear was tracking down the skin of her cheek.

My god. My god!

Sterne backed away, bumping into the desk and flailing for a moment, nearly falling over his chair. He steadied himself and watched the young woman take her hands off the shelf, turn around slowly, hugging herself.

I just wanted to say I'm sorry, she said.

Sterne sat in his chair and gazed up at her, his mouth open. He was gasping for breath. It was like he couldn't get any air.

For what happened to Dr. Jansky, she said. Your wife.

The radiator under the window began knocking as the pipes warmed, and the room suddenly seemed dark as night. Sterne moved nearer to the window, to be in the light. It was like he was awakening from a curious nightmare, something incomprehensible. Emerson brushed her hair back with her hands, picked up her coat and scarf. She turned and walked to the door.

A minute later he was in the faculty parking lot struggling with the keys to the Rover. He gunned the engine and bumped over the curb, smashing through a plow wall of muddy snow.

Sue.

When he turned onto his street, he saw a car idling in front of his house, an old Volkswagen with a man sitting behind the wheel. Sterne turned into the driveway, and while he waited for the garage door to open, he saw the man get out of the car and walk up behind him. He was wearing a tight-fitting leather jacket, dark pants, sunglasses. Sterne had seen this man before, somewhere. This couldn't be about what happened in his office, could it? Not this soon. The man followed his car into the garage. In the side-view mirror he could see the leather jacket, both hands in his pockets. Sterne shut off the Rover and opened the door.

He was tall and broad-shouldered, wearing black boots with ornate buckles. A heart-shaped face with a pointed chin. He took a hand out of his pocket and Sterne flinched but he was just holding out a piece of paper.

I'm here to take you to the airport, Dr. Sterne.

Sterne took the paper. A plane ticket to Dallas–Fort Worth. Leaving that afternoon. Sterne stood there looking at him, holding the ticket in his hand. *Fort Worth! The goddamn Turner!*

You're with Donnie LeClair?

The man took off his sunglasses and checked his watch. He was wearing black leather driving gloves. He didn't belong here, Sterne thought.

You've got about thirty minutes to pack, the man said.

Wait, Sterne said. I . . . I don't think I can do this anymore. I'll return the money.

The man shook his head.

It isn't a matter of money, Dr. Sterne. We're going to Burlington and you're going to get on that plane. C'mon, I'll help you.

He walked past Sterne and opened the door that led into the kitchen.

Where's your bedroom? Your suitcase?

Sterne went down the hall to his bedroom and went to his closet and opened the door.

You don't understand, Sterne said. Some terrible things have happened.

The man stood next to him and surveyed the closet. He smelled of soap and leather and his jacket creaked with each small movement of his arms. They both stood there for a moment, staring at the shirts and suits, the folded sweaters, the rows of shoes on a shelf. *Glaucus and Scylla*. Why did he ever care? What did it matter?

I heard about what happened to your wife, the man said. I'm sorry.

Yeah, Sterne said. Well. Here you are, anyway. And I gotta go to Texas to look at a fucking painting. Do you even know why?

You're a professor of art history, the man said. Your expertise is valuable.

No, Sterne said. It's not.

After a moment, the man reached up and took down the suitcase from the top shelf and dropped it on the bed. He unzipped it and threw it open, then started opening some dresser drawers. He first opened the side with Sue's things, paused, closed it, opened the other side, and started tossing socks, underwear, and undershirts into the suitcase. Sterne realized where he had seen him before, in LeClair's courtyard that first day he saw the Turner, sitting on the bench in the snow. The tableau of fear.

If I refuse, Sterne said, are you gonna do something to me?

I'm here to help you, he said.

Who are you? Why are you doing this?

The man paused, putting his hands on the top of the dresser, checking his watch again, then looking at his fingertips. The room was silent except for the low hum of the central heating. Sue's bathrobe hung on the back of the bathroom door.

I know something about this, the man said. My little sister went through the ice when I was a boy. I was pulling her on a sled. I left her. I could have saved her. I could have pulled her out. She was four years old.

Sterne felt helpless, a kind of complete, terrible weakness for the second time that day.

Did you see it? Sterne asked. That . . . thing. Under the ice?

The man turned back to Sterne. His face was dark, a deep crease in his forehead, his mouth open slightly. He suddenly looked much younger, innocent, like a small boy.

You did, Sterne said. You *saw* it. It took her. That thing took my wife!

But it was gone, the look on his face, replaced with that strange blankness. The face of the man who sat in the atrium filling with snow. He stepped to the closet, pulled out a couple suits on hangers, and pushed them into Sterne's chest.

You need to get packed, Dr. Sterne. We leave in ten minutes.

KAISER

When he got back from the Burlington airport, Emerson LeClair was sitting in the hallway outside his apartment. He hadn't seen her since the night of the beach bonfire party, when she took off with Scotty Marin. He wasn't sure if Scotty had seen him, but he figured he'd told Emerson about the incident at the restaurant, the reason he and his boys were so confrontational at the Dry Dock. Beating up a college kid would make Kaiser look like a dangerous fool. Then why she was here? Was she angry? Emerson was slumped over, her face tucked in the collar of her coat, wool cap pulled low, a puddle of dirty water under her boots. She got to her feet and came toward him, opening her arms and embracing him hard, her face on his neck. Kaiser put his arms around her and after a moment she shuddered and began to cry.

What is it? he said. What's wrong?

She snuffled and lifted her head, their faces close. She was searching his face with her eyes. There was the slightly skunky smell of weed on her.

Can we go inside? she said. Please?

Inside the apartment, he took off his coat and hat and hung them in the closet, but Emerson kept her coat on, walking around the table with the radio set, fingering cables, tapping dials, looking at his graph paper pads where he hand-recorded the transmissions. The kitchen sink was full of glasses and bowls, and the floor was dusty. Kaiser realized that no one else—other than LeClair when he brought the clothes—had been in his apartment. He felt uncomfortable and ashamed. Nothing on the walls, no real personal items of any kind, the stock furniture of a furnished room, the tangle of cords across the floor, and the pile of his radio equipment. He gestured to the sofa and took a seat in the armchair, but she just stood with her hands in her jacket pockets, swaying slightly, looking with glassy eyes at the open closet full of dark clothes and LeClair's accessory matrix sheet taped to the wall. The trainyard boomed as the boxcars engaged and wheels screamed with weight and force.

Kaiser had a lot of work to do. The weather was setting up perfectly and everything would have to start tonight, with the run happening in the early morning darkness. Dr. Sterne was supposed to go to Texas before everything happened, but that couldn't be helped now. After all the waiting, now it came in a rush.

What're you doing? Emerson said.

She swung an arm at the closet, the radio set.

I mean what is all this? What the hell are you *doing* here?

I don't understand, Kaiser said.

What are you trying to *do*?

I'm not trying to do anything, he said.

Why are you here? Why did you come back?

My father was having open-heart surgery, he said. I wanted to come back home. And I had nowhere else to go.

She raised her arms and let them fall to her sides, biting her lip as more tears rolled down her face.

This is all so fucked up, she said. Everything is so fucked up.

No, he said, it's not.

You don't even know, she said. You don't *know*.

You're right. I don't.

I want you to hold me, she said.

Kaiser got up, unsure, but it didn't matter as she came to him and clutched the back of his neck and drew his head down and kissed him. Softly at first and then she was smashing their slick faces together and pressing her body against him, an arm around his lower back to bring their pelvises together. Something stirred in the deep recesses of his reptile brain. Part of him wanted to hang on, to bring her even closer. But that part of him was a glimmer of something that tailed away into the dark. Kaiser put his hands on her shoulders and pushed her gently away.

Wait, he said.

Her mouth was hanging open, her lips red and swollen.

Why?

I didn't know, he said. That you wanted . . .

You didn't *know*?

Her eyes closed and she spoke evenly through gritted teeth.

Bullshit, she said. You're either a liar or a dumbass. What was all that shit with the satellites? The party? Why are you doing these things?

Because you were nice, Kaiser said. You were nice to me.

So what's wrong with me?

Nothing, he said. You're an amazing young woman.

That's it? You think you're too old for me?

No.

Is it because you work for my uncle?

Your uncle?

Oh my god. Are you kidding me?

Donnie LeClair is your uncle?

Kaiser didn't know what it was until that moment, maybe something about the way she was standing in her damp boots, her coat askew, the sorrow in her face. Kaiser thought about Donnie sitting in his enormous room chock-full of landscapes. How did he not know? He was standing right there, right next to them both. What else was he so blatantly ignorant of? He thought about the wreckage of Laurence Sterne in the airport security line, the slump of his shoulders, a man who lost his wife to the same darkness that took his little sister. Kaiser had never told anyone about the dark shape under the ice, the size of a mythical whale, the impossible speed. But Sterne knew. He *saw* it.

What the fuck happened to you over there? she said. What did you do in Afghanistan? You kill someone? You kill a child or something? What?

There was a man, Kaiser said. A soldier, a Ranger. He was killed right in front of me. It got into my head and then later I did something. A lot of people died. It was a mistake. I can't really talk about it.

What?

I'm sorry, Kaiser said. I know it sounds crazy.

Emerson covered her face with her hands.

I'm such an idiot, she said. It's like . . . I don't know. I'm gonna go now.

She wiped her face on the sleeve of her coat and heaved a big sigh, then turned and walked out the door. Kaiser watched her go. He knew that this was a terrible mistake on his part, and he felt a strange hollowness spreading inside of him. What had he done? How could he fix this?

Honesty. He would tell her everything, about Afghanistan and her Uncle Donnie and the plan, the Chinese number lady, his sister and the darkness under the ice, all of it. It might be enough. But when he got to the hallway, she was already gone, the outside door closed. He went down the stairs and threw the door open.

Emerson was standing outside in the bright glare of the snow-covered square, talking to another woman in a long jacket. Kaiser shaded his eyes as both women turned and looked at him. Sydney Beauchamp.

Tom?

Sydney. Hey.

I gotta go, Emerson said, pulling on her hat and reaching deep in her coat pockets she walked across the street.

You sure you're okay? Sydney called after her.

Emerson raised a hand and kept walking across the empty square toward the Artful Dodger. Sydney shrugged and sighed a little jet of sparkling vapor. The courthouse shone yellow white, and the air was so still Kaiser could hear the faint tinkling sound of water freezing in a billion permutations all around them. Snow was coming. Sydney turned back to him, an awkward smile on her face. He was struck again how thin she was, her worn eyes, but otherwise she still looked like a senior in high school, about to head off to college. Across the street, a battered Subaru was idling, the shadow of a woman sitting in the front passenger seat. Kaiser could see the woman raise a red Solo cup to her lips. In the back seat a smaller shape, motionless. Callie and Dylan.

I know her from the coffee shop, Kaiser said. She's a little upset.

Let me guess, Sydney said. You have no idea what she's upset about?

There was some kind of confusion, Kaiser said. I mean, she didn't tell me—

Sydney waved a mitten.

Forget it, none of my business, just giving you a hard time. I'm surprised we haven't run into each other more. North Chazy isn't that big of a town.

I've sorta been lying low, Kaiser said.

I'll bet, she said. Hey, one of my clients mentioned you. That's why I came by.

Kaiser swallowed. He was due to pick up Sebastian from the Dry Dock to go over the particulars of the run tonight. Sydney had her head cocked slightly to the side. He must look agitated. He nodded and tried to smile.

You know the Trombley's? Sydney said. Callie Trombley? She said her son Sebastian is working with you?

Oh, right. Yeah.

So you know him? You work together?

Sorta, Kaiser said.

Doing what?

Debt collection. For Mr. LeClair.

Was *he* the guy, Sydney said, that got shot by that preacher in Wiggletown? That was you guys?

Yeah.

Damn. You know where I might find him?

I'm not sure. But I should see him pretty soon.

Sydney pulled one of her gloves off with her teeth and fumbled through her bag, locating a business card.

Give him this, she said, and tell him he needs to call me right away, okay? Thanks. So, how's it being back in this lousy town? Same old stuff?

It's a bit different.

Sydney sniffed and put her face into the wind.

I guess. Crazy Chazy.

Hey, Kaiser said. I want to say I'm sorry.

For what?

For the way I left, Kaiser said. For not writing you back.

You wrote me a couple times.

I should have explained myself better, he said.

Some things you can't explain, right? And we were just kids then. I mean, I got a three-year-old daughter! Can you believe that?

Yeah. That's amazing.

She *is* amazing. Juliet is the best thing that's ever happened to me. But listen, I gotta go. My number is there on the card. That other stuff, that's in the past. Ancient history, you know?

Sydney turned on her heel and crossed the square toward the idling Subaru, trailing a plume of breath like a white feather.

Sebastian was crouched in the back doorway of the Dry Dock wearing a long black trench coat and fingerless gloves, smoking a cigarette. When Kaiser stopped the car in front of him, he grinned and flicked his cigarette butt at Kaiser's window. Kaiser cut the engine and rolled down the window.

What're you supposed to be?

Sebastian stood up and stretched, lacing his fingers together and bringing them over his halo-head. Under the jacket he was wearing his "Catch and Release All Finless Brown Trout" shirt, the chest area splotched with rust-red blood stains and flecked with small holes.

I'm the dark screamer, bro, he said. The midnight ice bird.

Jesus, Kaiser said. You look like an idiot.

Dude, Sebastian said, you realize you roll around this town looking like a motherfucking bouncer at a Soviet disco?

When he got in the car Kaiser could see the man was fucked up. His eyes were bulging and topped with a shiny meniscus, the pupils flexing hard in the bright snow glare. Sebastian yawned, the bolts in his halo squawking as his jaw stretched, and he leaned over to turn up the radio, which was playing an old Joe Jackson cassette. Kaiser turned it back down.

You understand what you're about to do?

Yeah, Sebastian said. I'm gonna do a screamer run towing a fucking crate of product.

Don't you think you ought to be sober?

Sebastian pulled out a B&H 100 and was bringing it up to his lips when Kaiser smacked in out of his hand.

Dude, *chill*, Sebastian said. That was my last B&H!

You got to get your shit together.

Bro, I got it. I've done all kinds of sled runs in all kinds of conditions. I'm talking mentally, physically, emotionally, and meteorologically. I'm good. Just a little Fleur-de-Lis.

You fucking idiot, Kaiser said.

I'm tuned in, Sebastian said. I'm gonna be moving the product on the outside and moving it on the *inside*. Or is it *in* the inside? I'm talking about synergy. Or kismet? I always forget what that fucking means.

I don't think *synergy* is a real word, Kaiser said.

Sure it is. The president uses it on TV all the time.

Sebastian spread his fingers and thumped them across the dashboard like he was playing the piano part during the bridge of "Look Sharp."

I'm in a heightened state of awareness, he said. I can see the world the way a dog smells it. I'm pulling in olfactory information through my *eyeballs*. My brain is processing multiple sensory inputs, you know what I'm saying? I can see things that aren't even there, the ghost traces left behind, the thing yet to arrive.

Forget about all that shit, Kaiser said. Just drive the sled.

Sebastian tapped his halo bars with his knuckles.

I got the whole run up here, he said. I don't even need my eyes, bro. I could cut 'em out and still make Point Au Fer in ten minutes.

You have anything electronic on you? Your phone?

Nah, bro. I got nothin'. Just like you said.

Kaiser pulled out the black Musto survival suit from the duffel bag in the back seat, along with some Gore-Tex mittens and Smith goggles with a ventilated black plastic face shield. The Polaris sled at Gerard's warehouse had a 1656cc four-stroke that put out 200-plus horsepower. Sebastian could reach ninety miles an hour in less than eight seconds, even towing 250 pounds.

You're gonna have to put this on, Kaiser said. Wedge it through the bars or something. Now the weather is stacking up faster than predicted, so we are going to need to go at three fifteen. Got it?

Yeah, man. You got anything to drink in here?

Kaiser handed him a bottle of water and opened the glovebox and pulled out a small flat metal box the size of a cigarette lighter. He took a pair of needle-nose pliers from the center console and cranked a knob on one end of the box, causing a light green diode to blink. He reached inside the survival suit and slipped the device in the interior pocket and rezipped it and sealed it with a watertight adhesive strip.

I've set it to broadcast a very low-frequency signal, something regular scanners won't pick up.

Where'd you get *that* fucking thing, man?

Radio Shack, Kaiser said.

Tight!

Kaiser reached into his jacket pocket and took out a GPS locator with capped wires hanging out the back. He turned it on and watched the grayscale screen till he picked up the signal. Then he wedged a steel thermos of hot coffee and a fresh pack of B&H 100s in the leg cargo pocket of the Musto suit.

So you remember the route?

Sure, Sebastian said. Chill at Gerard's place, then hook up the package, take the sled northeast across the cornfields to the Lacolle River, two miles east until the little marina. Then I'm on the ice going south in the middle of the lake, following the sightline of Windmill Point across the border to the drop just off Point Au Fer. Fishing shanty with a blue tin roof. Tomorrow night I'm buying at the Dry Dock.

What if something unusual happens?

I take off on the sled, follow the plan.

If you go early, Kaiser said, or late, you'll fuck it up. You'll miss the window.

Got it. Three fifteen.

You got a watch?

Nope.

Jesus fucking Christ.

Kaiser pulled up his sleeve and unclasped the silver Breitling with the inlaid bezel and hand-wound timers. He liked the watch; it was maybe his favorite thing LeClair had given him. He set the alarm timer, then handed it to Sebastian.

When the alarm goes off, Kaiser said, you hook it up and go. You got that? Come out of the marina fast, and once you get pointed south get it going wide open, okay? The weather is going to be shit. Follow the landmarks we talked about. Don't slow down.

Snowflakes were falling on the windshield in heavy clumps, like fleshy white insects. The National Weather Service was predicting heavy snow, more than thirty inches of accumulation. Sebastian repositioned himself in the seat, his halo scraping the ceiling of the Volkswagen.

Listen, Kaiser said. Somebody who works for DSS told me they want to talk to you.

About what?

About Dylan and Callie. Said you need to go home. You know what that's about?

Probably, Sebastian said. I'll handle it when I get back. Then Dylan and I are outta here.

The Northway crossing was a dozen cars deep in all three lanes, but there was a designated special lane for law enforcement.

You go in the regular lanes, Bill said, in this piece of shit? You'll be in secondary in thirty seconds, emptying your pockets while they x-ray the car.

The lunch rush was normal for the crossing, as the best poutine in Quebec was a couple miles away at the 202 intersection, a greasy place called Cantine du Poulet. Despite the name, they didn't sell any chicken, just flimsy burgers and paper cartons of poutine made with hand-cut french fries, squeaky cheese curds, and steaming brown gravy ladled over the top. Kaiser and Bill used to go to the Cantine regularly when they were in high school, back when you didn't need a passport. When they got to the booth, the Canadian agent took their passports and looked over the rattling Volkswagen.

Nice ride, Bill, he said.

Bill slapped Kaiser on the arm with the back of his hand.

This piece of shit is *his*. Gustave, this is my little brother, Tommy.

Yeah, Gustave said, Tom Kaiser. Heard about you.

Each booth was manned by a single guard, with another standing outside with an extension pole with a mirror to check the undercarriage. By the main building a Canadian officer sat on a bench holding a German shepherd on a chain. Kaiser had never been in secondary before, where you went when the border guards brought you inside, but everybody knew it was an unpleasant experience. He also knew the powerful x-ray scanners at the American side of the crossing could spot a loose marble in the gas tank of a tractor trailer. Or a single pill under your seat. Gustave swiped the passports and handed them back to Kaiser.

Whatcha up to?

Headed to the Cantine, Bill said. Little brother wants some poutine.

Bring me one?

You got it.

The Cantine was part of an old gas station, a plank building surrounded by flat fields stubbled with cornstalks. After they got their food at the counter Kaiser picked out a two-top and sat facing the window. Bill carried the tray, two double orders of poutine, burgers, two large sodas, and sat in the seat across from him.

I was in the basement of the house the other day, Bill said. Noticed the radio was gone. You have it?

Yeah.

You still recording those stations? That Chinese number lady?

Yeah.

Bill sawed into his carton of poutine with a plastic knife and stuffed a forkful into his mouth.

Mom said you've been up at the old cabin? What're you doin' up there?

Just messing around, Kaiser said. Checking out the antennae array.

Kaiser lifted a fork of dripping potatoes. The line at the counter was growing and cars crept through the parking lot in the slanting curtains of snow. His Volkswagen was pointed nose-in to the restaurant just outside the window, which was dripping with condensation. Bill wiped his forehead with his wrist. He picked up a french fry and poked it at Kaiser's face.

You been paying the back taxes on the farm?

Yeah.

Business with LeClair must be good.

Through the window, Kaiser saw Gerard get out of an old Toyota sedan across the parking lot. He was wearing a long parka with a fur-lined hood cinched in a tight circle, like a walking periscope. La Herrisson sat behind the wheel, his lumpish, bearded face obscured by the frost on the windows, a hand on the wheel, his arm in a plaster cast to the shoulder.

It's not like I have anything else to spend money on, Kaiser said.

Gerard skirted a passing car and walked to the back of Kaiser's Volkswagen. He stood by the trunk, meeting Kaiser's eye through the window. Kaiser looked down and stirred his poutine.

I'm gonna get a refill, Bill said.

I'll get it, Kaiser said, standing up quickly and taking his cup.

On the way to the soda machine, Kaiser took a couple deep breaths. He topped off Bill's drink. On his way back to the table he could see

Gerard had opened the trunk. Bill was wiping up excess gravy with a french fry, and just over his shoulder, Kaiser watched the tall form of Sebastian and his halo-head, wearing the black Musto survival suit, unfolding himself out of the trunk and stepping into the snowy lot. Gerard closed the trunk softly and the two men jogged across the lot, disappearing into the gusting snow.

This was Kaiser's idea, an added risk on the front end but a way to confuse the evidence afterward if they were detected. The first thing US law enforcement would do is inspect the checkpoint data to see who had been across in that area, and who hadn't come back through. Sebastian was so recognizable already, and trying to come through the crossing with the survival suit and gear would be an obvious red flag. But smuggle him over with a cop in the car, and they'd be waved right through. After the drop, Sebastian would drive the sled into storage in King's Bay with an airtight New York alibi and there would be no discernable record of him having been in Canada at all.

Bill was watching him with a curious look in his eye.

Everything okay, man?

Kaiser set the drink down in front of him and stirred his mostly untouched poutine.

The numbers changed, Kaiser said. The Chinese number lady.

So?

They hadn't changed in forty years, Kaiser said. All the time Kodiak was tracking her, always the same sequence. Six numbers, all from one to twenty. The number sequence dropped to five the week Kodiak died.

Yeah? You saying it's connected? That's crazy.

I don't know. But it went down to four the same week that professor at the college disappeared. Just before Christmas?

Bill tossed his fork on the tray, sat back, and spread out his hands.

You don't even know where this number lady is, right? How could she *possibly* know about Kodiak, or that professor?

Kaiser shrugged and balled up his used napkins.

You gotta let that shit go, Bill said. I know we've been over this, but really what is the fucking point? What's it got to do with you, or us?

I don't know, Kaiser said.

It seems like you are *trying* to make it mean something.

Yeah. Maybe.

People are dying out there, Bill said, all the time. They found a guy last night. Braden Tullus. Some kind of pedophile, lived out at the White Pines. He was way out in the middle of the ice near the border, on foot, apparently alone. Poor fucker had fallen through and got enough of a grip to hang on, but the ice refroze around him. His head, arms, and shoulders above the ice. Had to cut his body out with a saw. Nobody knows what he was doing out there. You understand? I'm trying to say that sometimes there is no *reason* for it. Bad things happen. Real evil out there, operating randomly in the world. There isn't someone or something controlling everything.

Dad didn't believe that, Kaiser said.

Kodiak let that number lady shit burn in his head for too long. You obsess about something long enough and it'll become real to you, as real as anything else. Dad let this shit torment him for decades. Now you're doing it too.

Kaiser tried to eat a forkful of fries, but it tasted like sand in his mouth. He felt the closeness of the other people around him in the crowded restaurant, the greasy floor, the stinking breath of mouths opening and closing.

And you can't keep doing collections for LeClair, Bill said. You know what happens to guys who work in collections? They get popped, end up doing time or worse. You just can't have that many confrontations without shit going wrong. And LeClair is mixed up in some shady shit. You don't even know, believe me.

He's just a weird guy who owns property and likes to collect paintings.

Well, Bill said, none of my business until it is. Let's pack it up, I gotta split.

Bill eased his large body around the table, gathering their poutine containers and cups in one hand.

I need to get in line to pick something up for the boys at the border, he said.

Let me get it, Kaiser said. My treat.

EMERSON

When Alejandro opened the door, Emerson's hair was uncovered and wild and her face shining with frozen tears. He brought her to the study in front of the fire, taking her coat and boots and firing up the teakettle before calling up the stairs to LeClair that his niece was here. She sat in the big wingback chair, slouched with her head resting to the side, squeezing the cold out of her red hands, watching the fire.

LeClair came down the stairs in a dark blue pinstripe suit, fastening his mother-of-pearl cuff links. He was preparing to go somewhere, she thought, and he seemed nervous. But still there was a lit flame of compassion in his face, and she felt momentarily buoyed by love from her uncle who seemed to love no one else in this world. They embraced in the middle of the room.

I've got a meeting in Montreal, he said. What's wrong?

Don't go, she said.

Why?

Something bad is happening.

The fire snapped and hissed in the fireplace. She could feel his body tense and relax, a decision being made.

What? What's happening?

I can't explain it, Emerson said. But it's like I can't trust anyone. Nobody is telling me the truth.

She gripped his sleeves and pushed back, looking him in the face. He was trying hard to give her a comforting look. She wanted to shake him.

These men who work for you, she said. I don't think you know who they are, what they do.

LeClair arched an eyebrow in genuine surprise.

They prey on people, she said.

What? Who?

She sat heavily on the couch and leaned back, closing her eyes. She was bone-aching tired and weary of crying.

No, really, LeClair said. What happened? Did someone do something to you?

LeClair took out a handkerchief and wiped the smeared tears off his lapels. He glanced at the wall clock.

Em, he said, everything is going to change, soon. Everything will be better. I'll be back tomorrow, and we'll talk about it. You look exhausted.

She closed her eyes. She was drifting off. She needed to lay down.

I promise, he said. Tomorrow, we will make it all right.

You're wrong, she said blindly into the dense air of the study, into the crowded conversation of paintings, into the patterned weave of his suit. He was leaving and somehow, she knew that he wasn't coming back.

I don't think it's over, Emerson said. Something terrible is going to happen.

Nothing terrible is going to happen, LeClair said. Not to me, not to anyone.

Emerson left her bike in the front yard of the Slaughterhouse, leaning against a lumpy snowman, half formed and already coated with six inches of fresh snow. The house was dark, many of her roommates either asleep or out somewhere, but her window was half lit by the reading lamp she left on beside her bed. She felt refreshed by the two-hour nap she took on her uncle's couch after he left for Montreal. When she awoke, Alejandro was waiting with a plate of scones, sliced apples, and a mug of cinnamon tea. She ate it all, then wandered around the room for a bit, sipping her tea, looking at the paintings, scratching the Constable behind his ears, who stood at attention before her like he had been assigned to mark her movements.

As she stood in the snow looking up at her bedroom window, she heard a knocking sound and saw that Matthew the English major was sitting on the porch couch, wrapped in a blanket and knocking his pipe out on the railing. He had a small stack of books next to him with a tin cup balanced on top. The streetlight reflected off his glasses, giving him a glowing, eyeless visage, rounded out by his patchy beard. The man was desperately trying, she thought. He was living in the skin of someone else, the writer that he wanted to be. She realized that this was something they shared. They were both pretending. They regarded each other for a few moments, listening to the gentle tap of the falling snowflakes, then he gave her a small smile and lifted the blanket, inviting her in. It only took her a few seconds to decide what to do.

In her room she went through her desk drawer until she found the Altoids tin and the wax paper inside containing two pills adorned with blue Fleur-de-Lis. She swallowed one and rinsed her face in the sink, pulling her hair back tight in a ponytail, checking her face for blemishes, brushing her teeth. She picked up her headphones. Her clothes were rumpled, smelling of woodsmoke and sweat.

When she opened the door to Jud's room, he was on the floor in his sleeping bag, head propped up on an old couch cushion, the copper tray of incense and candles at his feet and a joint smoldering in an ashtray. The floor speakers in the corners of the room beat softly with the opening bars of Yazoo's "Only You":

Looking from a window above,
it's like a story of love.

She knew he was playing it for her, even when she wasn't there. Jud sat up, pleased and smiling. She put on her headphones and motioned for Jud to do the same. Closing the door behind her, Emerson held out her hand, the pill on her open palm.

LECLAIR

LeClair checked himself into the Auberge Bonaparte and waited in the bar. It was past eight o'clock and he was starving, but he didn't want to be cramming smoked salmon with truffle oil into his face-hole when Montagne's emissary arrived, so he stuck with the gimlets. He texted Emerson to make sure she was okay but got no response. The deal was going down earlier than anticipated because of the incoming heavy weather, so he didn't have time find out what was troubling her. Some of the people who worked for him tried to prey on her? Who? He could hardly believe someone would dare such a thing. The unknown love, the man who burned in her eyes at Christmas, perhaps? Whoever it was, he would find out. He would deal with the matter.

A young couple sat in the window seat and an attractive man down the bar with salty blond hair and a blue blazer was reading a book. In the narrow streets of the old city, the snow came down sideways, moving down Rue Saint Paul like a white river. LeClair was grateful they didn't put him up at the Westin or the W or some other corporate office complex. He was licking the frosted sugar off the rim of his glass when the man down the bar turned and addressed him.

Avez-vous lu des romans en français?

He held up the book cover: *Voyage au bout de la Nuit.* LeClair couldn't help noticing the handsome features of this man: the patrician nose, the careful symmetry of his eyes and brow, the swept hair, thinning at the temples, faded crow's-feet, the look of a man who should be carrying a sail bag, leaping from the deck of a rigged sloop with a wool sweater tied around his waist.

No, LeClair said. I'm afraid I don't. Not much in English either.

Dommage, the man said. To experience Celine in his native tongue is a special kind of journey.

I'll have to check it out, LeClair said.

The man stood and walked over to LeClair, flat-front khakis rolled up at the bottom, and sure enough, worn boat shoes. The brass buttons on his blue blazer and the crisp, open collar spoke of ivy-walled boarding schools and summers on the stony beaches of Saint Tropez. He could have been thirty years old or fifty. He held out his hand and they shook with a somber formality, using the time to explore each other's faces with a frankness that snapped a flag in LeClair's mind.

Shall we go? he said, gesturing to the door. Are you hungry?

LeClair looked at the blowing snow outside the door. A long dark car was idling, wreathed in swirling exhaust.

Yes, I am, LeClair said.

The car headed south into Griffintown, stopping at an innocuous bistro on Rue Barre. The driver, an enormous man in a fur cap, opened the door for LeClair. The bistro was empty save a couple pensioners huddled up with cups of tea and deep bowls of dark soup. They sat at a table by the window, and he ordered for them both, two-dozen Malpaques oysters, a couple bowls of cioppino, and gin martinis made with sweet vermouth. Looking at this hale and vigorous man across from him, LeClair thought that if this was how he was to spend his time during the drop, then this deal was sweeter than he had hoped. It was strange that he didn't give his name, but after the oysters and a round of martinis, it didn't seem to matter. He talked about French writers and postmodern prose styles, subjects that barely interested LeClair, but it mattered little when his shirt collar flexed and LeClair got a glimpse of the tanned hollow of his collarbones, the way his hands lay upon the table, holding an empty oyster shell, the pale half-moons of his manicured fingers. The cioppino was peppery and warmed him against the chilly draft in the bistro, and his dinner companion insisted that they heft the bowls to drain the last dregs of the rich broth. When the final piece of bread was buttered and eaten, the last swallow of the second round of martinis down his gullet, the big man with the fur cap appeared from the shadows with their coats and they were bundled out into the snow and into the car.

I think now, the man said, would be a good time to give me your phone.

LeClair took out his cell phone and handed it over. The man casually flipped through the calls and voicemails, his lips pursed, before slipping it into his jacket pocket. He shot his cuffs to check his watch, a chunky silver Rolex Submariner. LeClair didn't like this part of the deal, but Montagne said it was part of their security arrangement. LeClair also wanted to have Dr. Sterne's verification that the Fort Worth *Glaucus and Scylla* was a fake before the operation started, but that couldn't be helped now. Sterne's flight was earlier this afternoon; he was probably arriving in Fort Worth at that moment. Hopefully he would call with good news before the deal was done.

D'accord, the man said. I think we should proceed.

He reached into his coat pocket and pulled out a small wax paper packet. There were four pills inside, each inscribed with a Fleur-de-Lis of various color: red, blue, green, and yellow.

I recommend the blue, he said. Though many enjoy the yellow. It has a soft tone, like a summer afternoon with a spaniel in your lap. The red, well . . .

No thanks, LeClair said, not my thing.

For a few moments they both watched the snow whisk over the windshield in the glimmering streetlights. They weren't in the old city anymore, and LeClair realized he had no idea where they were, or where they were going. The man shifted over in the seat, sidling up next to

LeClair. He gestured with his other hand, as if to indicate the street, the city, the snow.

You have to fulfill your end, Donnie. Your role in this little production.

The car slowed and the driver pulled to the curb, put the car in park, and turned his head so that he regarded LeClair with one eye. He had small eyes set deep in flat cheeks, the narrow lips of an amphibian.

Can you tell me where we're going?

We will have a couple drinks, he said, perhaps enjoy a show, and then I will return you to your hotel.

That's it?

We have about eight hours to kill, Donnie. By the time you finish your coffee and *oreilles de crisse* in the morning, everything will be finished.

You know my name, LeClair said. But I don't know yours.

He gave LeClair a sleepy smile, pulling deep creases in his tanned face. He offered the pills.

D'abord, vous choisissez.

The driver rolled his neck, popping vertebrae, then unsnapped his seat belt and began to open his door. LeClair snatched the red pill out of the wax packet and popped it into his mouth.

That was an interesting choice.

He reached into the door compartment and handed LeClair a bottle of water, then took the blue and yellow pill and popped them both. The driver fastened his seat belt, turned back to the steering wheel, and put the car in gear.

Il est vivant cet homme, he said to the driver. *Je ne m'attendais pas a ça!*

LeClair gulped the water and checked his watch and tried to mentally etch the time into his memory. Nine fifty-six. Call it ten. He needed to keep track. The driver smoothly accelerated, passing through a row of warehouse yards stacked with shipping containers hulking under blazing security lights. Must be near the river, he thought. He felt the little pill travel down his throat, disintegrating as it fell, until it faded to nothing.

Emerson was right, he thought. It isn't over. Something was happening.

Your name, LeClair said.

The man put his hand on the back of LeClair's neck, a familiar gesture, and LeClair was flooded with a momentary feeling of longing and regret.

Boucher, he said.

They went to a cocktail party at a rooftop penthouse overlooking Parc du Mont-Royal. Boucher introduced him to a slate of beautiful and elegant men and women who immediately broke into flawless English, such is the way of the Quebecois. After a few difficult exchanges of small talk, LeClair wandered off by himself, gnawing half-heartedly on a shish taouk skewer, and watched the rounded hill of Mont-Royal through the floor-to-ceiling windows, a stubble of trees dusted white, the lights of Chalet du Mont-Royal blinking. Dr. Sterne had better come through with that call, he thought. Kaiser said he looked like shit when he took him to the airport.

With every passing minute, LeClair was becoming increasingly alarmed by the three-piece jazz combo in the corner that seemed to be playing songs specifically for him, songs that reflected his state of mind. The way the trumpet player blatantly pointed the golden bell of his horn at LeClair as they launched into "Smoke Gets in Your Eyes." When the melody eased in, LeClair felt like a fish on the end of a line. It was uncanny. It wasn't paranoia, rather a feeling of shared experience, a communal conduit. It was a kind of connection, a pleasant one. But he couldn't shake what Emerson had said to him. Something was off. There was a danger, but it seemed distant and subtle, pushed to the periphery by the blazing force of love building in his body.

So this was what the kids are crowing about, he thought.

LeClair went to the bathroom and drank a glass of water. His face looked pleasant and unperturbed. He had to remind himself that he *was.* He locked himself in a bathroom stall and took out the disposable cell phone he had strapped to his ankle. He picked up the phone on his way to Montreal because of Emerson's plaintive appeal back at the house; she was convinced something terrible was going to happen. He fired off a text to Kaiser:

Something is off can you go to
G's place to check

He strapped the phone back on his ankle and gave himself a reassuring smile in the mirror. Kaiser was eminently capable of handling the situation, if there was any real problem.

Boucher moved through the crowd and LeClair had never seen a man kissed so earnestly and so often by men and women alike. He watched as Boucher held a small group rapt with an anecdote in French, his arm around the swollen waist of an aging socialite with a heavy strand of pearls knotted between her breasts. Everyone laughed, and raised a glass, and LeClair was struck for a moment by the resemblance to Scotty Marin, a man in the zenith of his appeal, and he thought about Scotty waiting in the fishing shanty at dawn, the first rays lighting up his eyes, that noble brow.

Boucher excused himself from the group and stepped away, pulling a phone out of his pocket—LeClair's phone. The call from Dr. Sterne? LeClair suddenly had the horrifying thought that it might be his brother or even worse, Emerson. What would Boucher say to them? How would he possibly explain this? Boucher turned away and spoke into the phone, then listening for a bit, then said a few more words, nodding his head. Then he put the phone back in his pocket. He straightened his lapels and turned quickly, catching LeClair staring at him. He held out his hands in a sort of *well, what are you going to do?* gesture. LeClair hadn't even really considered what would happen if Sterne said the Berrellez painting in Fort Worth was the real one. What recourse would he have anyway? Boucher came across the room to him with his tanned face creased with that wide, antic grin.

Time to move on, Boucher said. We have another appointment.

The driver appeared from nowhere and handed them their coats. The jazz trio eased into "These Foolish Things" and LeClair didn't want to leave. He wanted to sit across the room and look into the golden bell of the trumpet player and wait for the end of all things. Boucher held up the phone. A text from Emerson on the dim gray screen:

it's like a story of love.

Does that mean something to you? Boucher said.

Yes, LeClair said. I think so.

He could feel the vibrating lips of the trumpet player in his ear. The valves pulsing, fluttering, massaging his heart.

Boucher put his arm around him.

A romantic, Boucher said. We are a lot alike, *mon ami*.

Boucher ushered him to the door, ignoring the salutations of various groups of people as they passed. LeClair couldn't help inhaling his scent of seasoned leather, red wine, and salt. He knew he should be concerned about the painting. He should be concerned about this fragile, complex set of arrangements that all had to come together like some kind of DNA helix out of the primordial ooze. But mostly he wanted to nuzzle in the nape of Boucher's neck, to whisper confidentially in his ear, to hold hands as they walked through the snows of Mont-Royal. He wanted love, he thought. A story of love. Why couldn't he have it?

I got something to show you, Boucher said, that you're *really* going to like.

KAISER

There was too much remaining physical evidence. The equipment in the cabin on the mountain, the antennae array, the scanners and boards, the laptop, it all had to be destroyed.

Kaiser changed into a layer of silk thermals under the Italian wool tactical pants, navy cable sweater, and Gore-Tex storm shell. He put a pair of collapsible snowshoes and crampons in his pack along with water, flashlight, nylon rope. He erased all the calls on his cell phone.

He gunned the Volkswagen up the switchbacks, his headlights flashing across the stands of fir blanketed with snow. There was a single set of fresh tire tracks and Kaiser kept his front wheels in the ruts, but it was slow going. This was putting him behind schedule. He white-knuckled the steering wheel, snarling at the windshield in frustration. When the car finally bogged down on a steep section, he backed out and got turned around, facing down the mountain. He cinched his gear, strapped on the snowshoes, and hit the woods at a dead run, high-stepping through he drifts, the spaces between the trees aglow with snow-light. The smell of woodsmoke in the air. About a half mile off he was coming up the faint trace of the old logging road when he saw the trees tipped in gold, the winking and flashing of something over the top of the butte. Something was burning. Kaiser circled away to the west, coming at the cabin plateau from the shadow of the mountain.

The cabin was engulfed in flames, the tower burning like a torch, sparks and smoke trailing off to the west. A man stood with his back to Kaiser, watching the buildings burn. A tall, broad man in a watch cap, heavy parka. Something about the slope of his shoulders, the length of his arms made Kaiser think of a hockey player. The clearing was lit like a snow globe, the snowflakes seeming to descend in slow motion, the figure, structures, and trees like plastic toys. Was it Phil Herring? But why?

Then Kaiser thought of the data on that hard drive, the unmistakable evidence that something was under the ice. The dark spot. Something that was making people disappear. Now all that evidence was gone. Nobody would ever believe that this thing was real.

Kaiser's phone vibrated, signaling a text message. He took it out and read the message from LeClair. *Fuck.* He needed to hurry.

He reached under his coat and snapped the baton out of the holster, circling to the right, approaching the man from an angle, stepping quickly and closing the distance. He flicked the baton open. The fire roared as the wind whipped across the clearing. When Kaiser was nearly in range, the man whipped his head around and going into his parka he drew a heavy revolver and leveled it at Kaiser's chest.

Bill.

His brother's eyes were glazed and his arm swayed slightly.

What the fuck happened to the cabin?

Bill exhaled heavily and lowered the gun, closing his eyes, the snow falling on his face. Bill was drunk.

I warned you, Tom, he said in a barely restrained voice. I told you.

Listen, Kaiser said, I need to—

—I don't want to hear it! Bill shouted. It's over!

Kaiser held out a hand and started to speak, but Bill put out a straight left like a piston that closed Kaiser's eye, then hooked him hard in the temple with a right hand. Kaiser crumpled and went down into the snow, the reverberating roar of a bonfire in his head.

You understand? Bill said. It's done!

Kaiser got to his feet, holding a handful of snow over his eye. He could feel the swelling coming up around the orbital bone.

All those years, Bill said. All that stupid shit with the numbers, the goddamn Chinese lady. Tortured Dad his whole life. Mom too. Not anymore.

Kaiser checked his watch. He was a half hour behind schedule.

Okay, Kaiser said. I get it. You're right.

Bill patted his pockets and glanced toward the fire.

Man, I'm sorry I hit you, Bill said. I was just . . . I don't know.

I gotta go, Kaiser said. I'll call you later.

What? Where you going?

I'll explain when I call. I promise.

Kaiser turned and started sprinting down the mountain.

LECLAIR

When the car stopped, the snow was falling steadily and Boucher opened up a green-striped golf umbrella for LeClair. They shuffled over the curb to the sidewalk in front of a long brick building with a set of metal doors but no windows or sign. A man in a black ankle-length down coat and watch cap was standing by one of the doors. LeClair felt increasingly euphoric but controlled. Maybe this was it? It wasn't so bad, quite pleasurable, actually. Why did he take the red one? Was that just a mistake or was he trying to impress Boucher? Regardless, he held together the collar of jacket and tried to steady his breathing. He would put his feet into the ground like taproots, he would anchor himself and fight this thing, whatever it sprung on him. Except for the love. For Boucher and his fellow man. That part was already pinioned to his brain.

The Gauntlet, Boucher said. There aren't many places like this left.

After Boucher gave the man at the door a roll of cash, they were ushered through into a kind of vestibule with another steel door and a coat check off to one side manned by a lopsided old man in a tracksuit with a milky eye. Another man in a dark suit and an earpiece gestured and LeClair and Boucher followed him down a passage with cement walls, then down a set of stairs to a large room with a square bar in the center, dim argon lights hanging from the ceiling by long chains, and Joy Division's "Incubation" thumping at terrifying decibels. A scattering of people stood around in various states of dress, from business attire to a man wearing only a set of black ropes around his torso and legs. Boucher left him standing there to consult with one of the patrons sitting in a booth in the corner, so LeClair stood very still, trying to appear as if he was at ease, but the thumping bassline of the music began to feel like it was burrowing inside and disrupting his heartbeat with a ghostly hand. Above the hanging lights, something writhed in the dark like an enormous spider, and when his eyes adjusted to the dim lighting LeClair could see that it was a naked young woman, suspended from the ceiling by four cables attached to wrist and ankle, struggling frantically, her muscular body shimmering with exertion. Her mouth was covered with tape and her face was streaked with mascara tears and she caught LeClair's eye and give him a hard, pleading look. No one else there seemed to notice her. LeClair felt something rotten gather in his stomach and his mouth began to water. He looked around, trying to determine where the bathroom was when the nausea passed just as swiftly as it came and Boucher came back grinning and carrying a small wooden box under his arm.

They went through another door with heavy rubber seals like a commercial freezer, which led to a small theater space, a short proscenium stage with a seating area with small tables and booths along the back wall. The carnival tones of "Everything Counts" by Depeche Mode. On the stage, a naked man was hanging from the ceiling by a large leather collar around his neck, his toes just barely touching the floor, his hands tied behind his back. He was blindfolded and gagged with a black rubber ball that contorted his jaw into a mournful grin. An older woman in a billowing white caftan strode onto the stage, a riding crop in her hand.

Boucher guided him to a booth stitched with red vinyl and a waiter brought a frosted bottle of vodka, a bowl of lemon wedges, a bucket of ice, and two short glasses. An acrid, metallic smoke was in the air and in the darkness, LeClair could see a few other shadows sitting at the tables, several of them smoking something through long steel pipes, the glittering flash of a lighter sparking. Boucher grinned and shot his cuffs, his white oxford shirt glowing.

Just in time, he said.

Boucher opened the wooden box and took out a small glass bottle with a foil-sealed top. He placed this on a small dish in front of him along with a slice of lemon, then took out a small notebook and pen and laid it beside the dish. The hanging man on stage began to spasm, legs kicking, before going still, apparently passed out. LeClair looked away.

Boucher nodded at him thoughtfully, as if some thought was conveyed between them, then perforated the foil cap on the little bottle with a fingernail and stuck the opening into his right nostril. He closed his eyes and took a big snort, his head going back. After a moment his head snapped down and his eyes were wild and seizing the pen with a flourish, he wrote something down on the pad and then gave LeClair a toothy grin.

Let me ask you a question, he said. What is the most beautiful thing about the suffering of others? What makes the spectacle majestic, sublime?

I don't think it's beautiful, LeClair said.

Cela n'a pas d'allure, Boucher said. You are familiar with the vagaries of aesthetic values. You have pondered representations of the beautiful.

Maybe, LeClair said, realizing he was expected to play along, it has something to do with the juxtapositions. Pleasure and pain. Beauty and horror. Life and death.

No, Boucher said. That's a reasonable assertion but, no. It's the manifestation of the code of the great Roman Stoics. The source of all possible joy comes from our ability to reconcile what we can control with what we cannot. And to subvert this alignment represents the greatest power of discipline you can witness. Save suicide, of course. All the great philosophers were sadomasochists of one kind or another. It's the best opportunity to see their logical proofs made concrete.

LeClair took a sip of vodka. Boucher pushed the small bottle closer to LeClair.

Avail yourself of this, he said. *Attache ta tuque!*

LeClair picked up the bottle, brought it carefully toward his nose, and took a cautionary sniff. Immediately dry, hot air seared his nostrils and rushed to his brain, inducing an immediate euphoria that was dizzying for a moment, but then he found himself smiling, leaning back in the booth, the room charged with antic possibility. The stage show seemed to telescope away from him like a distant cartoon and when he looked at Boucher they both laughed and Boucher reached over and took his hand, squeezing his fingers. Onstage, they were dragging the unconscious man behind the curtain.

That's why so many spooks, Boucher said, are into this shit. Black baggers, bang and burners, danglers, any type of operator. They've got the streak in them.

LeClair was buckled over with laughter.

What the hell are you talking about? he said. Are you like some kind of spy or something?

Perhaps?

The whole scene seemed incredibly funny, and LeClair squeezed his hand back and he genuinely liked Boucher. He was wrong to doubt his intentions. It really was just a ruse, wasn't it? All of it? A big joke, a production, a play for fools. He took another slight sniff off the bottle and immediately blasted off.

Right? Boucher said. Maybe the FBI?

CIA, said LeClair.

Or the DEA?

LeClair slapped the table and collapsed into him, both of them laughing and pushing on each other like siblings in the back seat of the family station wagon, LeClair relishing the give of his body, the muscles of his arm and shoulder. That scent on his skin that brought to mind the mid-Atlantic trade winds filling big-bellied white sails.

What *is* this stuff? LeClair said.

Popper, Boucher said. In the common parlance. Surprised you aren't familiar.

What's it doing?

The usual, Boucher said. But it'll give us the proper dilation, which will make the next act a bit easier.

LeClair put the bottle down. He was still laughing, but it didn't feel like laughter.

Boucher was holding both of his hands, tenderly, like a parent might a child's hands. The effects of the popper were fading fast, and with it came a new kind of shaking fear, cold and razor sharp.

Dilation?

Of the anus, Boucher said.

He put his arm around LeClair, pulling him in tight, like teammates.

I'm sorry, Donnie, he said, but you are about to get *fucked.*

LeClair had a choking knot in his throat, looking at the now-empty stage. He had put them all in terrible danger. His brother, Emerson. Scotty. And for what?

I wanna stop, LeClair said. I don't want to do this anymore.

You know we can't do that, Boucher said. *Alea iacta est.* We will see it through.

He sniffed and shot his cuffs again to consult his watch, then made a note on the pad.

Listen, he said. I want to tell you about something I read recently. Using powerful radio-telescopes we have observed and been able to verify a black hole near the center of our galaxy with a mass a million times that of our sun. Now, orbiting this vast, dense creature is a giant star, *many* times larger than our own sun, moving at about 2 percent of the speed of light, which is at least twelve million miles per hour! *C'est vrai!* This star roars through space in a tight circle chained by extreme gravitational forces, on the very edge of the event horizon, where time stops.

LeClair wiped his face with his sleeve and tried to steady himself, both hands on the table. Boucher poured them both another measure of vodka.

Now, I know, Boucher said, that it is hard to conceive and hold the idea of something this large moving at this speed. It seems to defy the natural order of things as we observe them here on this planet! But what I am saying to you is that it is necessary to do so, if we intend to live an honest life.

What do you want? LeClair said.

Want? We already have everything!

He ticked off the items on the fingers of one hand.

We have the product. We have the painting. We have the route across the ice. We have all your compatriots. And now we have *you.*

LeClair closed his eyes again.

Please don't, LeClair said. Nobody else needs to get hurt. I'm the only one.

Boucher snorted.

You poor fucking sod! You are worried about Scott Marin? Was he your boy?

No, LeClair said. How . . . he's not part of this.

Please, let me stop you. This is embarrassing.

He's just a student at the college, LeClair said. He sometimes works for me—

Yes, yes, Boucher said, we know all this. Scott reached out to *us*. He'll be there on the ice to receive the package. This was *his* idea! *Un garcon ambitieux!*

LeClair coughed and vomited, a heavy gout of vodka and shellfish spilling over the table. Boucher leaped to his feet to rescue his notebook, the bottle, and the wooden box. He laughed like LeClair was a small child getting sick at a carnival after too much cotton candy.

Scotty.

LeClair crawled out of the booth onto the floor, gulping for air. His throat and nose burned with gastric juices, and he convulsed violently several more times. Someone put a hand under his armpit and hauled him up and walked him out the rubber-sealed door and through a crowd of people milling around in the dark and down a short hallway where he was shoved through a swinging door into a dank bathroom lit with blacklights. LeClair steadied himself against the sink counter, retching. Something was pounding through the floor in a regular, metronomic pace, like some kind of devilish machinery, making the counter vibrate. When he raised his head and looked in the mirror, he saw a disembodied, emaciated, hollow-eyed skull floating in the dark. The pounding noise was coming from the row of stalls that stretched off into the dark, the door of the third stall rattling with each violent percussion. Someone was smashing the door repeatedly from the inside, as if trying to escape. LeClair staggered into the nearest stall and locked the door. The toilet was pristine white, a gleaming offertory, and he bent over it for a few moments, spitting and clearing his throat before putting a foot on the rim and taking out the disposable cell phone strapped to his ankle. He powered it up and waited for a signal. The pounding noise slowed, and after a few climactic percussive thumps, went silent. LeClair put his hand over the screen and held his breath. Small scraping sounds, the toilet paper roll, tearing paper. A text would be found in the call records; it would be deciphered and tracked. What should he say? Whomever he texted would be implicated. They might also be saved. Not Scotty. No, he wouldn't warn *him*. Only one of them might survive whatever was happening. Montagne said he would come for everyone, including Emerson. He fired off a text to Kaiser:

My niece Emerson lives in the Slaughterhouse
you must protect her.

A metal rattle and catch and a stall door opened. He heard the sound of unsteady feet, shuffling, one man, perhaps with a limp? Two people? LeClair huddled over the screen, one foot still on the toilet. He was shivering, his eyes closed. Montagne's people would know Kaiser's secret route across the border. They could exploit it, again and again. Maybe he could at least deny them that.

Call it off stop the screamer.

Then he heard the sound of the door, the wall of music blasting, voices, something murmured, then the door closing.

LeClair typed another text to Kaiser.

They are going to take everything and everyone. All of us.

Then more footsteps, an easy gait—someone must have come in the same time the other man left?

Donnie?

A hard rap on his stall door. Boucher.

Everything come out okay, petit copain?

He rapped again. LeClair typed out one more text, then eased the toilet tank lid up and slid the phone in the water. As he lowered the lid, he flushed the toilet and dropped the seat.

Yes, he said. Just a minute.

Save Emerson.

JANSKY & STERNE

Laurence Sterne didn't realize he was still wearing his sunglasses until the woman at the car rental counter mentioned it.

Nice shades, she said. You look ready for Texas.

A young Hispanic woman wearing a tight Hertz polo. Sterne had his wallet on the counter and was stuffing his ID and credit cards into the slots. He wanted a Land Rover, but they didn't have any, so he rented the most expensive car they had, a Lexus convertible. He took the stack of rental papers and wadded them into a ball in his fist. The Hertz lady was already checking her phone for messages, popping her gum.

Hope you enjoy your stay in the Dallas–Fort Worth Metroplex!

Sterne stepped out into the sunshine, the temperature about sixty degrees, his carry-on bag slung over his shoulder and a bag of toiletries in his hand that he purchased in a terminal convenience store. He didn't really remember getting on the plane. But he did remember popping two hydrocodone and washing it down with a double Crown Royal before Kaiser walked him to security.

Good luck, Professor, Kaiser said. This will all be over soon.

The rental car was a milky pearl gray, sleek and rounded like a seal, with crème leather interior. He got out on the highway to Fort Worth and punched the gas, the wind roaring in the cockpit of the coupe and his rental papers thrashing around in the footwell. The sun felt hard on his skin as he pushed the car up past eighty. He'd never been to Texas before, and was shocked when the highway was lined not with grassy fields and lowing cattle but rather never-ending strip malls, billboards, and big-box store complexes, every possible chain restaurant in several permutations, soft-core-strip-club chicken wings and sports joints, amusement parks that stretched for whole miles with sinuous steel roller coasters, free-fall towers, high-altitude swings that arched over the highway, waterparks with blue water-slide shafts gathered up in tubular knots, a two-mile banked oval NASCAR speedway with lines of blocky RVs clogging the exits, professional baseball ballparks rising up in faux brick horseshoes tricked out in red-white-and-blue bunting, vast gas station-bar-b-que joints with their own petting zoos and child care. Billboards for products, politics, prayers; paper and electronic, digital pictures of smiling faces hawking car insurance morphing into aborted fetuses and hotline numbers.

Sterne arrived at the Berellez residence in Fort Worth as the sun was setting. It was the kind of neighborhood with small artificial lakes behind brick walls topped with pikes, monogrammed wrought-iron gates, swiveling security cameras, and elaborate but tasteful displays of Christmas lights arranged by crews of illegal Mexicans. He poured some water into his hands and smoothed back his hair. In the rear-view mirror, his eyes were fractal veined. He popped another hydrocodone, washing it down with warm whiskey.

He had arranged the visit on the basis of an academic study he was doing and received an enthusiastic response from the Berellez family. The Berellez house was a spread of white concrete blocks meandering over a three-acre lot, split-levels and glass walls overlooking a flagstone garden and infinity pool with a four-step waterfall. Carmen Berellez opened the door, a sweet-faced woman in her midthirties wearing a TCU sweatshirt and tight jeans. Her husband, Manny, was a partner in the biggest law firm in the DFW Metroplex and she was on the board at the Kimbell, Amon-Carter, and the DMA. Just a couple of kids from Frio County with immigrant parents. Sterne was several hours late.

Well, she said. You just missed dinner. Enchiladas con mole.

Sorry about that, Sterne said.

Family recipe. I cook it for six hours. Tell me what you are working on again?

While she took him through the main foyer Sterne gave her the short spiel about *The Sun & the Sublime.* She handed him a glass of sparkling water and he could see her sniff the air, catching his fetid aroma. He stepped back and chugged the water, ravenous with thirst. The house, Carmen told him, was designed by a famous Dallas architect specifically to feature their collection of paintings. The paintings, mainly modern pieces with a couple minor masters thrown in, were tastefully spaced, nothing like LeClair's cluttered mess.

The nineteenth century lives in here, Carmen said, leading him into a square room with giant angular skylights. She had a chair and side table set up in front of *Glaucus and Scylla* with some writing paper and a single white rose in a vase. Sterne set his briefcase on the table and opened it. A bottle of Pepto-Bismol, half a tuna sandwich, a wad of dirty paper napkins, four airplane bottles of Canadian whiskey, a box of Q-tips. He didn't even have a pen. He closed the case.

The painting is all I need, he said.

You'll likely want to look at the other pieces in this gallery, she said. We have a few loans you might find interesting.

He nodded in a thoughtful manner, thinking absolutely nothing. He didn't want to look at any of it.

Well then, she said, I'll leave you to it. Call if you need anything.

Sterne sat in the chair facing the painting and loosened his tie. He looked at the painting in a vague, unfocused way for a few more minutes, then got up and took it off the wall and sat back down with it on his lap. He ran a forefinger over the faint ripples of paint, the woven texture of the canvas, circling the signature in the corner with his thumb. Time passed.

She was running from him, a final look back as he crouched in the dark cave, his face bunched in anger and remorse. He remembered the lecture on *Glaucus and Scylla* by Dr. Rosen more than a decade ago—which he paraphrased for *The Sun & the Sublime*:

> *This moment, the heartbroken old god in his grief, the terror of the maiden, is what Turner has chosen to depict. The moment of realization, that she is lost, and he will never be whole. He will never have her.*

Sterne put the painting back on the wall and took out his phone. Whatever he said wouldn't matter. Perhaps LeClair would be out a decent chunk of money. But he would go on filling his house with landscapes, he would have his family and his friends and ultimately this decision would be a little consequence, a fragment in the history of a life. The rest of them had a minor role to play. It was LeClair who pulled the strings. If he hadn't been called to his house that day, if he hadn't come drooling to his knee like a sycophantic hound, then perhaps Sue would be still here. It was LeClair who threatened him, who gave him no choice in the matter.

In that moment Sterne decided that if there was a god, then he was a cruel and ignorant being. Or if it was some expression of evil, then the forces of good were powerless against it. The ancient Carthaginians understood this. Their worship was an attempt to assuage the vengeful and capricious god of man, to offer him sacrifice to slake his thirst for blood. But where was the furnace, where the noble martyrs?

He punched the phone number and walked the circuit of the room as it was ringing, glancing at the passing paintings until he came to a medium-sized canvas with a bright slash of white light down the center, bleeding red and orange in the upper section, into the sky. He stopped and stepped closer to the painting until his eyes were full of the canvas, all the color at once.

Yes? the man said.

The original is here, Sterne said. The other painting is a forgery. It's worthless.

I see, the man said. That is unfortunate.

Mr. LeClair is a liar, Sterne said. He should not be trusted.

D'accord.

A storm-tossed sea with a ship foundering, leaving behind a trail of struggling bodies, the dead and the drowning in the dark, pitiless sea.

That thing under the ice, Sterne said. It took her.

Through the phone he could hear the sounds of people talking in French, some kind of music in the background. The gentle draw of his breathing. Night was falling. The wispy whitecaps rolled above murky shadows beneath the surface.

It's coming for me, Sterne said. Do you understand?

Bien sur, the man said.

Night was falling and the ship was sailing away, forever. A leg thrust high out of the water, a black chain around the ankle. The man on the phone sighed.

Mon vieil ami. You know what must be done.

KAISER

Kaiser got through the Canadian border without incident, a knowing nod from the guard whose name he couldn't remember from their poutine run. The turnoff to the gravel road that led to Gerard's warehouse was marked by a faint set of tire tracks, now covered by a couple fresh inches of snow. The dark clouds hung so low in the sky they seemed to be resting on the tops of the pine trees, and when his car entered the forest, the visibility dropped to almost nothing except the blurry fingers of his headlights and the security floodlights of Gerard's warehouse glowing through the trees in the distance.

When he got to the gate, Kaiser stopped the car and cut the headlights. There was a truck in the front yard, a dark SUV, parked at an angle with tracks indicating a high-speed approach. They'd driven through the chain-link fence, tearing out a twenty-foot section, part of which was still caught in the front wheel. Kaiser did a slow four-point turn and got the nose of his car pointing back toward the main road and got out, walking around the circle of light from the floodlights and into the darkness by the tree line. He could see the light burning in Gerard's office window. The faint hum of machinery coming from the main warehouse area. A mess of tracks around the SUV and leading to the open security cage and front door. Nothing moved.

After ten minutes, Kaiser left the tree line and walked through the gap in the fence and approached the SUV. He came around the front fender and almost tripped on the body of a man in a shell suit curled up on his side, a light dusting of snow piled along the ridges of his body. His arms were wrapped around his faintly smoking torso, the snow around him a wet, red slush. By the way the snow was disturbed around his legs Kaiser could tell he'd kicked for a few minutes while he bled out. Kaiser crouched and slipped the baton into his hand and waited, watching the window and doorway. He reached over and pushed the body with the baton just enough to see a slice of his face. It was a man he'd never seen before, Asian, with sinuous dragon tattoos on his neck. Around the body a dozen small holes in the snow were trailing wisps of heat vapor. Spent cartridges. A shootout.

Another man lay athwart the doorway of the warehouse, flat on his back, one arm in a plaster cast, his heavy beard clotted with thick skeins of dark blood. La Herrisson had been shot several times in the face. The half-open door behind him was pocked with bullet holes and spattered with a fine red mist. The Luger was in the snow and Kaiser could tell the poor bastard had probably instinctively gone for the pistol with his right hand when the shooting started. A confusion of bloody footprints led down the hall to the open warehouse door where the orange light pulsed. He eased Gerard's office door open. The same stack of greasy papers, folders, takeout containers from the Cantina, the cut-glass ashtray holding a bouquet of butts, the smeared bulletproof glass, the video monitors blank. Down the hall he could hear the faint sounds of voices, shouting, two men, maybe three, and behind that a steady thump and thrum of some kind of machinery. An orange light was pulsing down the hall from the emergency light over the open back door. Kaiser walked in past the Geoid-Sfera satellite, still crouched on the floor like a giant spider, down the central row of shelves toward the back door. A boom box–style radio was just outside the door, LED lights flickering. A small man wearing a watch cap lay face down in the snow beside it, the snow stained dark around him, one arm extended toward the dark woods. The sound Kaiser was hearing was not machinery, it was music. A song that he knew.

The back field was luridly lit by the security floodlights thick with falling snow. Several sets of tracks led from the dead man out to where two enormous men in black shell suits were taking large overhead swings with a shovel and spade at something on the ground. A man wearing a suit. Both men were blubbering as they hacked away, their faces slick with tears and snot.

Though his face was obliterated, Kaiser recognized the tattered suit coat as Gerard's. The two men sobbed and moaned as they swung the tools like a tired railroad gang, the sickening crunch of bone and tendon. There was no sign of Sebastian. Kaiser crouched by the body of the small man by the door. In a back pocket he found a Velcro wallet, like something a child would carry. Spider-Man. Inside a couple wadded singles and a thick stack of crisp Canadian one-hundred-dollar bills with the band still around them. A receipt for gas at a station outside Montreal. A Clinton County library card: Jake Lavoie. The Lavoie brothers, LeClair's collection men that he replaced. Lunatics for hire. Like him.

One of the twins lurched around, swinging a rope of snot from his nose. He brandished the shovel, the blade smeared with blood, and took a step toward Kaiser.

Don't fucking touch him! he bellowed.

Kaiser stood and held out his hands, dropping the wallet, still holding the library card between his fingers.

The other brother turned, panting, leaning on the hoe. His face was ash white, his head leaning to one side. This one had been shot in the side of the neck, a ragged black hole that pumped blood down the front of his shell suit. He looked like he could barely stand.

Who the fuck are you? he slurred.

I'm nobody, Kaiser said.

The first brother hefted the shovel, regripping the shaft with his bare hands.

No, he said, you're somebody.

Kaiser stepped out away from the doorway and snapped out the collapsible baton. As the man came toward him, holding the shovel across his hips like a hockey stick, there was no recognition of the baton and Kaiser knew this was a dead-end job for all of them. When he got closer and brought the shovel back over his shoulder, Kaiser took two quick-skipping steps forward and whipped him across the face with the baton, splitting his cheek from eye socket to chin. Lavoie faltered, crying out and using one hand to cover up his face, and Kaiser brought the baton across his wrist still holding the shovel, snapping his radius bone with an audible pop. He dropped the shovel and went to one knee. There was a blur of movement to his right and Kaiser went toward it, stepping inside the distance of the other Lavoie brother's swing and took the handle of the hoe across his outside shoulder blade, knocking him off his feet. He fell to his hands and knees in the snow, baton still in his fist, scrambling for traction, getting to his feet and ducking as the hoe came whistling around in a vicious arc and then Kaiser snapped the baton in a short backhand across his temple, the knock of skull bone and a flying tuft of hair and the white-faced brother took a step back, his eyes closed, the black hole in his neck gaping like an open mouth, and fell backward like he was going over a cliff.

The hammer of the gods will drive our ships to
new lands,
To fight the horde, singing and crying: Valhalla,
I am coming!

Kaiser turned just as the horrid bloody visage of the first Lavoie brother came at him, a diving bodycheck driving him onto his stomach and flattening him in the snow with Lavoie on top of him. Kaiser took a blow to the back of the head and when he heard the howl, he knew it was the broken arm and he turned under the man and grabbed the shattered wrist and twisted, rolling him over and getting onto his back. Kaiser wedged his forearm under his chin and got his baton hand up and behind his head and hooked both heels under the man's legs, spreading him out face down. Kaiser felt the rubbery texture of his windpipe against his forearm as he sunk the choke in tight and Lavoie began torquing his body from side to side and Kaiser clung to the big man, mashing his face into the back of his head, his sweaty hair in his teeth.

He heard the rasp of metal on snow, and he looked up to see the other Lavoie brother getting to his feet again, using the hoe to steady himself, the left side of his head and face a sheet of glistening vermilion. He took an uncertain step toward Kaiser, then heaved a big sigh, spraying a mist of blood through his lips like some kind of weary ghoulish night-breed. He raised the hoe, bringing it back over his shoulder and setting his feet. The man under Kaiser began to spasm violently, and when the standing Lavoie brother began his wide swing, Kaiser waited till the last moment before rolling over. With a wet crunch the hoe blade hacked a neat wedge out of the brother's forehead and nose, taking a decent portion of his frontal lobe with it, a divot of bone and flesh with a stringy tail describing a short parabola in the air before falling into the snow. Lavoie shrieked and released the hoe on the follow-through and it went whipping off end over end toward the darkness of the trees.

Kaiser rolled the body off him and got to his feet, holding out the baton, as the other brother stood there swaying, hands on his head, moaning. He took a step toward his disfigured brother and then went to his knees, his eyes rolling up and his head bobbing. The bullet wound on his neck was blackened with frost and the stream of blood came in slow spurts. Kaiser backed up and edged around him, taking in the fence line and the trees, the warehouse, the bodies in the yard. The roiling sky above like an underground sea, moving north. They were up there, beyond the clouds, the delicate invisible guidewires stretching to earth. He could feel their energy, the intent, but he couldn't see them. So much darkness.

He went to Gerard's body, but it was too hideous to look at. What happened to Sebastian? Walking the perimeter, he found a set of snowmobile tracks headed off to the north through the woods, maybe an inch of fresh snow on them. Sebastian must have taken off when the shooting started. There was no way to follow or find him through the forest on foot, especially in a blizzard. Kaiser stared at the dark woods and the trail getting fainter every second as the snow came down. Seb would be waiting by the abandoned marina for the alarm signal, the sled turned off and hidden in an old boat shed. He would complete the run. At the signal he would crank the sled up and fire out onto the ice, turn due south and floor it, not stopping till he was at the drop site. That is what Kaiser told him to do.

When he turned back to the warehouse, the second Lavoie brother was slumped forward, still on his knees, his breath coming in quick panting gasps like a small dog. Then his head went to his chest, his hands opened up, and he fell face down into the bloody slush of snow.

Four numbers left, and now four more dead men. Was it finally over?

Kaiser stood by his car and calling LeClair's cell. If he could get back through the border, get the GPS locater working, he might have a chance to intercept Sebastian before he got to the pickup spot. There would be no way to get to LeClair in Montreal.

As he stood there holding the phone LeClair's texts came through.

My niece Emerson lives in the
Slaughterhouse you must protect her.

Call it off stop the screamer.

They are going to take everything and
everyone. All of us.

Save Emerson.

After midnight, the smaller border stations shut down. The only way into the US was the big Northway crossing. Doug LaChance swiped his passport into the computer and a minute later Kaiser was in Secondary while they ran the Volkswagen through the x-ray imaging machine. Kaiser had used snow to rub the blood off his face, neck, and gloves, but his eye was swollen and there were stains that he couldn't get off his clothes. He told them that he'd been to Montreal and got into an altercation with an unknown man on the street. He hadn't reported it to the police because there were no serious injuries and the man ran off into the night, so he decided just to return home. They brought him to a small infirmary with a Homeland Security paramedic and Kaiser complied with their request for a strip search. The paramedic whistled at the crimson welt across his shoulder blade, just beginning to purple, then scraped a few samples of the dried blood on his shirt and collarbone for DNA testing, took pictures of the wounds from multiple angles. An ICE officer brought him to a holding room, bare white walls, a card table and folding chairs, gave him a couple ibuprofen, a bottle of water, and a bag of chips. A tinted window for observation and cameras in the corners of the ceiling. They left him there for thirty minutes.

The interviewing ICE officer was named Martine, a guy who graduated from North Chazy High School a couple years after Kaiser. They had played on the basketball team together, Martine a little round kid with no left hand who rode the bench, but Kaiser remembered him. He had gained more weight since high school, his face pink and sweaty as he gripped Kaiser's hand with enthusiasm.

Tom Kaiser! Martine. You remember me?

Yeah, from basketball.

Those were the days, eh? You ever miss it?

Kaiser exhaled and looked around the white room. The gears on the cameras whirred, the only sound save Martine's heavy nose-breathing. He checked his watch.

Nope.

Yeah, I hear you, Martine said. Sometimes I do, but I hear you.

Martine slid a folder across the table.

Take a look, he said. Let me know if there is some mistake or anything missing.

Kaiser opened the folder and glanced at the printed reports. His passport picture and information and a spreadsheet of his entries and exits for the last few months. The next page had surveillance photos from several border locations, Kaiser in his car, copies of his passport, his face. Close-ups of his injuries, the dried blood, the baton. A transcript of the interview, his story, the itemized contents of his phone, personal items on his person and in his car. Kaiser closed the folder and slid it back.

You know, Martine said, most everybody ends up in secondary eventually. I'm surprised this is your first time! I was in secondary *twice* back in high school. Once at the reservation crossing, and once right here. We were coming back from a Canadiens game, too many beers. But you've been gone a while, right? Did a tour overseas?

Kaiser nodded.

Martine opened the bag of chips on the table. Sour cream and onion. He ate a couple and proffered the bag to Kaiser. He wiped the corner of his mouth with his finger and thumb and then opened the file again.

The weird thing is, he said, your military record is incomplete.

He sorted through the papers, selected a couple Department of Defense forms.

Like, there's almost two years unaccounted for. That's weird, right? I mean, even for special forces?

Kaiser could barely focus on the man or what he was saying. His body wanted desperately to shut down. *Emerson.*

I mean, Martine said, *I've* certainly never seen that before. And my supervisor doesn't know what to make of it either.

He licked the salt off his fingers and held up his hands.

I'm just saying it's weird, that's all. Martine pulled out Kaiser's cell phone and put it on the table, his hand resting on it.

Can we just talk about the missing part for a minute?

Kaiser bit down on his tongue with his molars and his eyes shimmered and he blinked and wiped away tears with his shirt cuff. This was taking too long. Martine ate the last chips from the bag, then crumpled it up and chucked it across the room at a wastebasket, missing by several feet.

Also kinda weird that your phone is empty.

Am I under arrest?

No, no, nothing like that, Martine said. You are free to go. It just looks a bit odd, you know?

Martine took his hand off the phone and sat back in the chair.

Kaiser looked at the phone for a moment, searching his memory for something lost, a remembered sweetness, some moment of genuine kindness. He closed his eyes, sending his message into the night, where the secret machines skimmed the edge of space.

The Slaughterhouse had a single light on in an upstairs window. The curtains were closed, no cars out front or in the driveway. Kaiser parked down the street and approached through the neighbor's yard. It was still snowing, heavy, clustered flakes that accumulated quickly. The town of North Chazy was dead quiet, no one on the roads, no voices, no machines, just the soft pat of falling snow.

There was a young man sitting on the front porch, smoking a pipe. He looked somewhat familiar, like someone Kaiser had seen in the Artful Dodger perhaps, a student most likely. He sat with a blanket around his legs and waist, the wan streetlight reflecting off his glasses. Kaiser went around back but the door was locked so he came up to the side of the front porch. He silently cursed himself for not going back at his apartment for the .357. Kaiser checked his watch. Too much time. *Fucking Martine.* His face abrasions throbbed with heat, and he took a couple deep breaths. If something happened to Emerson, he would never be able to forgive himself, or LeClair, for setting all this into motion. He had to move fast. The man on the porch hadn't moved, the pipe still clenched in his jaws. Then Kaiser noticed the pipe was not lit, and there was something unnatural about the way the man held himself so rigid and upright. His breath came out in fast little jets of vapor, and his face looked wet. His exposed feet were bare and blue.

Kaiser held the baton behind his back and stepped out of the shadow of the house. The man didn't seem to see him until he was at the front steps, and by then Kaiser could see he was terrified, his eyes round and staring, his cheeks wet with tears. He moved his head slightly and gaped at Kaiser. There was blood spattered across his neck. Kaiser stood there for a moment, the snow gathering on his shoulders. He regripped the baton, measured the steps. He could hear the faint echo of a voice, coming from inside the house. It sounded like someone giving a speech in a language other than English.

The young man moved under the blanket, his arms coming up, and Kaiser vaulted up the steps, the baton ready. The man froze again, opening his mouth in a silent gasp. Kaiser lowered his arm. There was a dark circle of sticky blood around his feet. They locked eyes for another minute and Kaiser could see the life ebbing out of him. He nodded, and the young man slowly brought his hand out from under the blanket. He held up one shaking finger, then pointed to the room above him.

Inside the house, the voice came clearly from the upstairs bedroom, directly above the entrance. The lights in the foyer were off. The upstairs hall was dark, save the light shining under the bedroom door. Kaiser went up the stairs and stood against the wall, listening. Someone inside the room was reciting something, like a sermon, in a language he didn't recognize. He slowly turned the doorknob with his fingertips. It was unlocked. She could be in there, right now. They could be doing something to her. She could be dead already. He started a countdown in his head, trying to visualize his entry. A toilet flushed, the next door down the hall, then the sound of running water. Kaiser flattened himself against the wall, the baton behind his back. When the bathroom door opened, a young Filipino woman came out in a bathrobe, her hair wrapped in a towel. She went the other way down the hall, opening another door and going inside. There were other people here. Regular people. Civilians. They didn't know what was happening.

Kaiser opened the door and slipped into the room, closing it quickly behind him. The speaking voice was from a vintage record player, something Kaiser now recognized as an Irish accent, or something similar. The voice was reciting a poem. Emerson's bed was centered against the big front windows, and to one side were bookshelves made of cinder blocks and boards next to an old leather recliner. On the side table there was a large bouquet of white lilies in a cut-glass vase with a red bow tied around it.

A man sat in the chair with a book in his lap, the floor lamp next to him the only light in the room. He had obviously been reading. He smiled at Kaiser, a broad, toothy grin,. He was an attractive man with a thick head of blond hair, his skin tanned and lined like he'd just come in from a round of golf. He wore khakis and a blazer with a golden crest, tasseled boat shoes. He seemed young and old at the same time. He held up the book. *The Plague* by Albert Camus.

Our girl has some taste, he said. In novels, at least. The rest . . . is un peu minable. But she is young.

Kaiser could not exactly place this man's face, that grin. The heavy French accent.

What are you doing here? Kaiser asked.

The man eased himself out of the chair and replaced the Camus on the bookshelf. He ran his finger along a couple other titles, frowning. Kaiser gripped the baton that he held down along his leg. This man hadn't seemed to notice it, or maybe he just didn't care.

I'm waiting for *her*, of course, the man said.

He thrust his hands in his pockets and smiled, rocking on his heels. The recording of the man reading poetry reached the end, the needle bumping along for a moment, then the auto-return raised the arm and returned it to the start position. He picked up the record and spun it between his fingers.

Are you a fan of this kind of poetry? I find it . . . *autoritaire*, too much, you know? Such wailing and flailing about. Did you know there is a record like this, made of solid gold, that is right now traveling through space at seventeen kilometers per second, going farther than any object made by man?

Kaiser took a few slow steps, looking around the room. There was nobody else in the apartment. He wanted to close the distance with this man, but he didn't want to draw attention to it. Again, the man didn't notice or seem to care.

Voyager One, Kaiser said. Carl Sagan. Everybody knows that. You should leave.

I'll wait for our friend.

He smiled, his broad white teeth flashing. The light in the room seemed to dim somehow, and Kaiser felt a sudden weakness ripple through is body. Sweat rivered down his face and the baton felt heavy and clumsy in his hand. The man placed the record on the player and pushed the start button. He returned to the chair, and lifting the tails of his blazer took a seat, crossing his legs. He lifted the bouquet of lilies off the table and held them on his lap, running his fingers lightly across the open mouths of the flowers.

Donc. Let's see if this Welshman has *anything interéssant* to say.

And death shall have no dominion.
Dead men naked they shall be one

Here we go, the man said. Now we are getting somewhere!

Why are you doing this? Kaiser said.

My brother, if you had a million years, you wouldn't understand, and it wouldn't matter.

He put his face into the flowers and inhaled deeply.

Vous savez, the gift of cut flowers is such a powerful expression because they will die, very soon. What can you do? Put them in a nice vase, give them water and light, perhaps stroke a stamen or two at midnight. They will die without knowing that they meant anything. *C'est vraiment dommage.* But for us, terror and confusion is the ruling principle of the sublime. There is no beauty in this world without it. And that is why I am here.

What's your name? Kaiser said.

They call me Boucher. And you are the one they call Kaiser, *non*? We have a mutual friend, Monsieur LeClair.

He sat back and smiled.

I was just with Monsieur LeClair in Montreal.

When his blazer gapped Kaiser could see a bloom of blood across his crisply starched white oxford shirt. The boy on the porch. Or Donnie?

Boucher put his right hand to his face and sniffed his fingers. His sleepy, half-lidded eyes looking steady at Kaiser seemed to soften, as if he was about to burst into tears.

Un moment délicieux.

Boucher opened his mouth and still holding Kaiser's gaze, delicately touched the tip of each finger to the pink dart of his tongue. He smiled, his body seeming to vibrate with anticipation.

Now it is *her* turn.

Kaiser knocked the arm off the record; the Welshman's voice cut with a ghastly shriek. Boucher put the flowers back on the table and sat back in the chair, hands folded neatly on his lap.

Careful or you will wake the others. That would be *bad* for them. Then we will make this place *un véritable abattoir*—

Kaiser came at him with a snapping backhand swing of the baton, but Boucher was lightning quick and raising a hand he caught it across his forearm. He sprang out of the chair with a snarl, unsheathing a long knife from behind his back. His easy smile was gone, and the color of his face was changing, going mottled purple. His knife was smeared with dried blood. He lunged at Kaiser, the blade angling toward his groin. Kaiser sidestepped and brought the baton down like a hammer across the back of his head, snapping the baton in two pieces. Boucher went to one knee with a grunt, then looked up and gave Kaiser a smile. That blow should have killed him, Kaiser thought.

Alors, voici comment nous allons procéder.

Kaiser swung for his face, but Boucher ducked and came under the arm with the knife, sinking it into Kaiser's side. In a rush of pain and horror, Kaiser dropped the broken baton and grabbed Boucher's wrist with both hands, pulling the knife out, then kicked him in the face with his bootheel. Boucher grabbed his leg, and they went to the floor, grappling over the knife, four hands knotted around it. Kaiser got a grip on the handle and twisted it hard, cutting into his palm, completely severing two fingers from Boucher's hand. In a frenzy of fear, Kaiser rolled on top of him and still holding the knife began crashing elbows into his face. Boucher's visage was a wreck of blood and saliva. Kaiser straddled him and got the knife turned down, the point catching the tab collar on Boucher's shirt, and he leaned on the knife with all his weight. Boucher spat black strings of blood into Kaiser's face. Lifting a fist, Kaiser hammered the end of the knife handle, once, twice, until it punctured Boucher's neck between the clavicle and shoulder, the next blow driving it in further, and Boucher's strength finally wavered. Using all his weight, Kaiser pushed the knife deep into his upper chest, then wrenched the knife from side to side, cracking rib bones and churning the organs. Boucher's eyes went wide and a gush of blood poured out of his mouth.

Kaiser rolled off him, clutching the wound in his side. He could feel the pulse of his heart in his fingers, ribbons of blood running down his sleeve.

He lay there, listening to the silence of the house.

SYDNEY & PHIL

A pair of sleds with matching blue and gold trim sat parked outside an ice fishing shanty just northeast of Point Au Fer, New York. No wind, dark sky, and the temperature below zero, the heavy snow coming straight down in streams like water. The door to the shanty was sealed with a couple feet of fresh snowdrifts, and they had to dig it out before they could yank it open. Inside the shanty there was a locked cooler, folding chairs, a rod case, a rusted bait bucket, and other assorted ice fishing gear. Scotty Marin hefted a gas-powered ice auger with ten-inch boron blades while Phil lit a propane lamp. On the New York shore, a yelping dog sent his complaint into the black morning. The lake boomed as the ice warped and shifted.

A few minutes later, they heard the wail of motors coming from the north. The first lines of light from over the Green Mountains revealed a line of men on snowmobiles coming toward them, their shadows stretching all the way to the New York shore. Phil watched the phalanx of sleds, rooster tails of sparkling ice cascading behind the machines, the men wrapped tight in helmets, goggles, black one-piece shell suits, hunched over the handlebars, blasting through drifts that rippled over them like white smoke. Four men. Scotty slapped him on the back.

Time to get *paid*, bro! Scotty said.

When they got to the emergency room parking lot, Callie began to panic, insisting that they go back to the house. After a tearful half hour, Sydney got her checked in with the help of her friend Brett, who came down from the blood lab. Brett got on the phone with the state to get the paperwork squared away while Sydney plied Dylan with all the packs of peanut butter crackers and M&M's she had in her coat pockets. Dylan sat in the waiting room wearing his coat and backpack, staring at the floor, eating the food with robotic precision. Next to him, a young man in a trench coat slept in a chair, his head bowed to his chest, his foot covered in a dirty wad of gauze and tape. Brett hung up the phone and waved Sydney over.

Whaddya gonna do? Brett asked her.

A nurse stapled a thick sheaf of papers and handed it to Sydney. The place smelled like bleach and cigarettes. The steady atonal beeping of invisible equipment.

I don't know, Sydney said. I just want everything to stop for a moment. I just want a minute to rest.

Hey, listen, Brett said, I guess I'm leaving town.

What? Where?

Outta here. Colorado.

What? Why?

I can get a job at one of the resorts, Brett said, get a free ski pass. My cousin says there's lots of jobs and that the guy-to-girl ratio is like ten to one. For real.

Sydney felt another stone placed in her hands. She never imagined Brett leaving. Maybe that was the problem. Brett cocked her head and sighed and took Sydney in her arms.

I'm excited about this, she said. Be happy for me.

I know, Sydney said. I am.

Behind the curtains of the processing area, a baby started screaming, a throaty, guttural roar of violation. It was nearly morning, a few hours till daybreak. Brett squeezed her tighter.

I love you, Syd, she said. You're a good person.

Sydney got Dylan buckled in the car and drove back to Frenchtown, inching her way in the heavy snowfall. She was technically violating protocol, but she couldn't bear the thought of bringing him to CPS. He would be sent to a temporary foster home, and Callie might never get him back. Sydney would keep him with her until she could figure out what to do. If Callie was seriously sick, if it was cancer, then she wouldn't have much choice. But maybe it wasn't. Maybe she would be okay and in a couple days they could be back home, carrying on in their usual dysfunctional way. Where was the goddamn brother, Sebastian? Off with Kaiser, Callie said, doing some kind of "science" work in the mountains? What the fuck was Kaiser doing? First the shooting, the shady job with LeClair, then this mysterious shit with Sebastian?

Her phone buzzed in her jacket pocket and when she saw the number she pulled over to take the call. It was Kara Leroux's number. Sydney was still overdue on checking up on Eileen and Bianca. A court date had already been set for removal of the girls and termination of parental rights. Saul had disappeared.

Kara's voice was clotted and angry. She was crying.

Oh, you shouldn't of done it, she said. Now it's all over.

Kara, please tell me what's happening. Where are you?

Saul's gone, she said. You did this.

That's not fair, Sydney said. You know what Saul did to Bianca.

You don't get it. You fucking *stupid* woman.

The phone was muffled for moment as if Kara was holding her hand over it. She coughed a few times.

Hello? Kara? Tell me where you are. Where are the girls?

The red one, Kara said. That was a mistake. Shouldn't have taken the red one. Oh, god. It got him. That thing out there.

What are you talking about? Where are the girls?

They went under, Kara said. That thing under the ice took them.

Kara, stay where you are I'll—

Kara hung up. Sydney put the phone down on the dashboard. She was maybe a mile away from Saul and Kara's house. In the back seat, Dylan was leaning against the door, watching her.

I'm gonna make a stop, Sydney said. I need you to stay in the car.

The house was dark when she pulled up, but Kara's car was in the driveway, covered in deep snowdrifts. A thin stream of smoke issued from the stovepipe. The west windows of the house were covered with plywood, and the others by ragged plastic sheeting. She knocked on the door, hard. She heard the rustling of feet, something that sounded like a whisper. She stepped off the porch and went around the side of the house. The plastic sheeting on the bay window in the dining room was torn and Sydney was able to get a look inside. It was dark, but she could see a flicker of firelight, perhaps the woodstove, and vague shapes on the floor like furniture covered with blankets. She knocked on the glass and that's when she saw the spread of hair on the floor. A little girl's head of hair.

No, she thought. Not this.

Sydney scrambled back around to the front door. She took hold of the metal railing and kicked the lock with the heel of her boot again and again until the deadbolt busted through the hollow-core door. She pushed the door open and stepped inside into darkness.

Kara? Hello?

The snow-light from the doorway fell on the stairwell and to the right in the darkness, she could see the flickering light and the dark shapes on the floor. There was a small potbellied stove in the center of the room and arrayed around it, ragged shapes of cardboard and piles of blankets. The air was thick with woodsmoke and the temperature barely above freezing. The head of hair she saw through the window was gone, but Sydney caught a glimpse of a small hand pulling a blanket edge.

Kara? Are you here? It's Sydney Beauchamp, from DSS.

The blankets moved and Bianca popped her head out, her face streaked with soot.

Miss Sydney? she whispered.

Sydney knelt on the floor and uncovered the sisters inside a nest of blankets, Bianca spooning her little sister Eileen, who kept her face hidden in the crook of her arm. Both girls were wearing multiple layers of mismatched clothing. They were surrounded by piles of clothes and pieces of furniture that they were using to feed the woodstove. Both girls were shaking with cold and the tips of Bianca's fingers and earlobes were blackened with frostbite.

Where's your mother?

Bianca shook her head.

Sydney took Eileen in her arms, a tiny scarecrow in an old wool sweater. She tried to pry her arms away from her face.

Eileen, she said. Let me see you. What's the matter?

Leave me alone, Eileen said in a strange voice.

Eileen's ear was grossly swollen and cracked, blackened with frost, and when she pulled her arm away, she could see that the girl's nose had been broken, the bridge split and canted sideways, her nostrils clotted with dried blood. Her cheekbone was oddly sunken and the skin yellow and blistering. Sydney felt herself drop away, as if she was rising up, leaving her body below, and she saw the three of them arrayed there among the blankets and clothes. She was thinking about that day in her office: *He choked her but then she came back to life!* and then she saw Callie in the hospital laying supine under a machine, her chest heaving as she sobbed, her x-rays on the light board, the loose crowd of stars spread on a field of black.

What will become of us?

Eileen was crying, but no tears came, the breath coming fast through her lips.

Please, don't, she whispered. Please don't take us away.

The sled drivers casually unsnapped their suit straps, stamping their boots on the ice. A tall man wearing wire-rim glasses and three young Vietnamese men with the same neck tattoos and long coiffed hair as the guys at Scotty's place. This was some kind of drug deal, but Scotty hadn't brought anything. No money, drugs, or bags. The men on the sleds didn't seem to have anything either. So what was the transaction here? Phil looked at Scotty and a glimpse of something harrowing crossed the boy's face.

The man in glasses nodded at them, slapping his gloves across his thigh. He certainly didn't look like a drug dealer, more like a nineteenth-century schoolteacher.

Fellas, Scotty said. This was not the plan.

A rolling *whump* of ice plates shifting in the distance. The Vietnamese guys cranking their necks around, checking out the shoreline, the south end of the lake.

Where's the package? Scotty said.

The schoolteacher held out his hands.

Let's go inside and I'll explain, he said in a heavy Quebecois accent. Apologies for the confusion.

The schoolteacher and two of the men followed them into the shanty and arranged themselves opposite Scotty and Phil, the open floor hatches and old, frozen-over ice holes between them. The schoolteacher lit a cigarette and parked it in his cracked lips, appraising Phil. All of them were sizing him up, trying to figure out what he was, what he was going to do.

Are you Montagne? Scotty asked the schoolteacher. I want to talk to him.

He shook his head, an apologetic look on his face.

We had a plan, Scotty said. That we agreed to.

The schoolteacher nodded.

We were told it would be one guy, not four, Scotty said. Where's the package?

Phil could tell by his voice that Scotty was genuinely scared, something he'd never heard before. This was all going wrong. He considered the distances. The space was small and confined, which was to his advantage.

I understand, the schoolteacher said. I am here to make things right.

There was a pause and they all just looked dumbly at one another and then in one smooth motion the schoolteacher pulled a small black pistol out of his parka and shot Scotty in the kneecap. The sharp clap of the report and the spray of bone and cartilage and Scotty went down, howling, holding the knee that burst like a blooming rose.

The schoolteacher was still pointing the gun at Scotty, a sad look on his face, the gunshot reverberating through the ice under their feet. The other two guys were reaching into their pockets. Phil knew this was his chance. But he froze. And the next moment it was too late; the other men had pistols out, their black eyes pointing at him.

Fuck! Scotty screamed.

He was sitting with his back against the wall, his face defiant, enraged. He reached in his jacket pocket, but the schoolteacher kicked him in the face with his boot, snapping his head back against the wallboard and Scotty dropped his phone and fell over on his side, hands over his face, just a few inches from Phil's feet. He shrieked in a high, plaintive voice.

Phil!

The schoolteacher and the other two men looked at Phil, seeming to wait for him to reply. He shrugged and held out his hands. The schoolteacher smiled and flicked his cigarette in Scotty's face and then one of the Asian guys pocketed his gun and hauled up the ice auger from the corner, and straddling the opening in the boards, he flipped the choke and yanked the starter. The schoolteacher started rummaging through the shelves and the cupboard in the corner, tossing items out onto the floor: canvas gloves, a spool of heavy gauge fishing line, empty beer cans, a paperback thriller, a couple perch tip-ups. The other man kept his pistol pointed at Phil's face. The ice was thick but working the big auger in a circular pattern they cut a big hole about twenty inches across, all the way to the edges of the floorboards. They were all sweating now and one of the Asian guys opened the window, the other man wiping his brow on his sleeve as he wrestled the auger out of the slushy hole. Scotty moaned and held his hands over his eye, his other eye blinking a steady stream of pink tears. His leg sticking to the floor of the shanty in a pool of frozen blood. The schoolteacher checked his watch. Then, stepping over the hole, he grabbed Scotty by the hair and began wrapping loops of the fishing line around his neck.

What the fuck? Scotty gurgled, trying to get his fingers under the line and the schoolteacher stamped on his knee, making the boy scream. Then they wrapped the line around Phil's wrists a dozen times. The shanty was hazy and drifting and Phil felt sleepy. Maybe it was the smoke from the auger, but he knew that it was something else. Not fear, or dread, or some kind of consideration of mortality; it was like his mind would not let him consider these things, even though he knew he should.

Why? Phil asked.

The schoolteacher patted Phil on the shoulder, almost apologetically.

The bullet needs a body, he said.

But Phil didn't hear it. He was engaged in a desperate sort of mind's eye imagining of Sydney and Juliet, the three of them sitting on the dusty floor rug in front of the fireplace, his daughter pulling plastic horses out of her stocking, his stupid distended hockey sock, the shared feeling of contentment and love at that moment. He would not have another chance. This fact stunned him into insensibility, and all he saw was the ice dust floating in the air, the tail of the dragon disappearing behind a man's ear, his face blank as stone, and Scotty's moans and writhing like some faraway dream. He thought about carrying Juliet into her bedroom after her bath, the shape and weight of her in his arms. He wanted to hold his arms like that again because he knew he would feel her ghost weight, he might be able to take that with him.

Then they pushed the generator into the hole, and as it sank, Phil could see the line attached, whispering against the ice, and Scotty Marin was jerked headfirst through the hole into the water. With his head and shoulders submerged he caught the edge with one hand and spreading his legs in a kind of sprawling handstand Scotty tried to hold himself there, but they kicked his fingers off the ice and his body slipped in, disappearing in the milky slush. Phil stared at the hole, unable to fully understand what he was seeing. Then the line snapped tight on Phil's wrists, and he went to his knees, leaning back against the weight, the line a hard angle into the water. He got a foot on a board edge and thought that he might be able to hold Scotty there. But the schoolteacher pistol-whipped the back of his head and Phil went dark for a second, falling forward, his hands and arms going into the hole, the upper part of his face smashing into the ice, his shoulders on the edges, his bulk keeping him from falling through the hole. Phil tried to lift himself, his forehead on the ice and arching his back, but the weight on the line was like an immovable object. He could see down into the hole, his arms underwater and his purple hands swollen unrecognizably, the thin line trailing off into the deep. About twenty feet down, the pale face of Scotty Marin, his mouth in an astonished circle. Phil's hands were like dumb clods of flesh and Scotty's struggles made his arms twitch and swing like a rod with a pike on the line. Phil tried to lift himself again, but the weight was too much. Then the line was still, and Phil knew that Scotty was done. He heard the roaring sound of engines all around him and he closed his eyes, shuddering with the shock of it all, still not yet dawning on him. It was like he was anchored to the very center of the earth.

Don't let go, he thought. Just hold on.

Sydney brought the girls to the hospital, where she was met by her DSS supervisor and the police. When she checked her phone, she had a few frantic texts from Brett: *Get over here—Callie is going ballistic!*

When they tried to sedate her Callie had exploded and fought with the staff for a good half hour until they were able to poke her with a syringe of lorazepam. When Sydney came in Callie was sleeping, her arms and legs secured by restraints. One of the orderlies had a vicious bite wound on his arm and Callie had apparently struck a nurse in the face with an IV stand, splitting her forehead open. Now this, too, was a police matter. While Callie slept fitfully, jerking in the restraints, Sydney stood by the bed, steaming in her damp coat, while the police and the hospital legal team discussed the charges. Sydney couldn't follow the conversation, but it was clear Callie was in real trouble. They repeatedly used the phrase "termination of parental rights." Then her supervisor was there, calmly explaining to Sydney that DSS would be reassigning her, taking her off the Trombley case. She needed to take a break, a rest. Sydney nodded. Her body ached and her eyes kept filling with tears. She couldn't stop thinking about the image of Eileen's shattered face, the way the girls clutched each other, refusing to let go, till the very end.

She would have to tell Dylan. He wouldn't be going back home; he wasn't going to be with his mother anymore. Kara Leroux was right: Sydney had ruined everything. She had done the one thing she promised him she wouldn't do.

When they arrived, Juliet was sitting at the kitchen counter of her grandmother's house in Dannemora, eating a cup of lemon yogurt. Her grandmother was playing "Für Elise" on the piano, the bright notes clattering around the room. There was bread in the toaster, butter and jelly on the table. A half-finished puzzle on the coffee table. Juliet eyed Dylan warily for a moment, then ran to Sydney with open arms. Sydney picked her up and held her, holding her tight until her daughter began to squirm and struggle. The gray cat ran across the keys of the piano, seeking shelter from the stranger, and her mother clucked her tongue and began to make another pot of coffee.

Mommy, I want to show you something!

Dylan sat at the counter, still wearing his coat and backpack. Her mother put a plate of buttered toast and a glass of juice in front of him.

This is Dylan, Sydney said. He's going to stay with us for a little bit.

She sat on the couch and unwound her scarf, Juliet at her knee. The puzzle on the table was a picture of a painting, an ocean scene at night, with a three-masted ship plunging through the dark waves, carrying a smoldering cauldron of fire.

The gray cat sat in the windowsill, watching with sleepy eyes, reaching out a paw to touch the invisible threads by which her life, too, was held.

EMERSON

Emerson lay on the left side of the bed, her head half under the damp pillow. She thumbed the earphones off and opened one eye. The window shade glowing vermilion, her clothes on the dusty floor, the sink on the wall with a toothbrush in a glass. The house was quiet. She heard the crunch of footsteps in the snow, a few solitary cars creeping by on Main Street. There was a man sleeping next to her, also naked. She could smell his sour, oniony funk, and his left arm was across her hip. This is how it happens, she thought.

Emerson curled up on her side, pulling Jud's arm around her shoulders, and tried to fall into a half-remembered dream, a hopeful memory; the brush of her mother's hair across her face, barefoot steps on the gravelly beach, sunlight shining on the thrashing elms, the sound of the lake gently lapping at the shore. It was almost enough.

And then the screaming started.

STERNE

Laurence Sterne stood at a boardwalk taco stand in Port Aransas, Texas, a breakfast taco in one hand, watching the pounding ocean roll up the beach of dark sand. Light was emerging on the eastern horizon and the seagulls were squawking and wheeling over the boardwalk, alighting on the trash cans, nodding at each other with greedy, black eyes. A teenage boy rode by on a bicycle, weaving side to side. The chorizo grease had soaked through the wax paper in his hand and Sterne dropped the taco, *slap*, on the cement floor. In his other hand, he had a plastic bag from a hobby shop in Seguin. Tejano music rattled from an old speaker on the counter next to a bowl of plastic flowers.

Hey, buddy!

Sterne turned and regarded the man behind the counter, a squinting, sunblasted stump in a Dallas Cowboys baseball hat.

You gonna pick that up?

Sterne looked dumbly at the taco on the floor, then lurched toward the bathroom.

Amigo! Buddy!

Sterne locked the bathroom door and took off his jacket. The sink was gutted with rust, but the mirror was intact. He reached into the bag and took out a liter of Jack Daniel's, half empty, and set it on the sink. Then he pulled out a small wooden box and laid this on the shelf below the mirror. Sterne unscrewed the bottle and took a deep drink, his throat working once, twice, then he upended the rest of the bottle over his face and head. It was warm and burned his scalp. Something rose in his throat, and he retched in the sink, his body convulsing, hands gripping the fixtures. Sterne opened the wooden box containing a set of X-Acto knives, three steel shafts and eight cutting blades of different shapes. He selected a sharp triangular angle and attached the blade with a twist. He wiped the hair back from his forehead and stretched the skin around his eyes with his fingers.

He checked his watch. He mouthed the word in the mirror.

He watched his mouth purse and round out the syllables, his tongue pointing upward, then snapping down like a fish. He settled the blade in his hand, then pulled his eyelid straight out, taught, the delicate stitching of veins, the way the world shimmered around the edges. Then he said it out loud.

Moloch.

Moloch.

LECLAIR

Donnie LeClair crawled in darkness across the floor of his room in the Auberge Bonaparte, the heavy drapes pulled tight over the tall windows. He heard the distant tinkle of breakfast service, a truck downshifting on the brick streets sealed in snow. He found the leather case, then crawled into the bathroom, easing the door shut and engaging the lock. He flipped the light switch, and the fluorescents flickered, a strobe image of a small, middle-aged man in his underwear crouching at the sink, holding up a hand to shield his eyes. LeClair sank to his knees and slowly worked the zipper on the bag. He took out the painting, encased in a heavy layer of bubble wrap and duct tape. He held it up, but the picture was obscured through the plastic, just a faint wash of color.

LeClair stood on shaky legs and glancing in the mirror he saw the raw abrasions on his face and the crotch of his underwear crusted with dark blood. LeClair looked away and tried to stifle a sob as the night began to reassemble in his memory. He heard what sounded like padding of feet on the floor, the shuffling of clothes. Someone was in the hall outside his room. LeClair slipped the painting back in the case.

KAISER

Court square in downtown North Chazy was still and quiet. Kaiser paused at the corner of his building, but the snow in his doorway was unblemished. He leaned against the gray brick, hands in his coat pockets. For a few moments he listened to the distant rumble of plows on the interstate. When he moved to the door, he left a puddle of blood in the melted snow.

In his apartment, Kaiser flipped the power switch to the ham radio set, and as the old vacuum tubes warmed up, he went into the kitchen and took out a large garbage bag. He stripped off his leather overcoat, his boots, pants, and gloves, then peeled off his blood-soaked shirt. The wound was stanched with a washrag from Emerson's apartment, tied tight around his stomach with his cashmere scarf. The flow of blood had mostly stopped, so he left it alone. He used paper towels to wipe flecks of dried blood off his midsection, neck, and collarbone, stuffing them in the garbage.

He searched through his gear bag for the extra GPS locator. It took a few minutes, but the signal came up, the blinking dot just across the border. About three hundred meters from the New York shore of his parents' farm. Sebastian should have been at the drop site hours ago, but instead he was he was stopped at the anomaly, right in the dark spot.

Kaiser sat at the table in front of the ICOM 735 HF as the readouts came to life and the meter-wands flickered and waved: volts, amperes, transmission. He checked his watch, six fifty-eight Eastern Standard Time. Kaiser dialed in the frequency and put on the headphones. A waterfall of static. Thirty seconds.

He was weak. His hands ashy white and trembling on the dials.

Ten seconds.

The pop and hum of an open channel, bouncing off a half-dozen satellites and relays on the other side of the earth. He eyed the dark closet full of clothes hanging like ghostly sentinels.

Her voice rang out like the clatter of stones on a beach.

Good morning! Are you ready? Now we begin:

Twelve. Four. Nine. Sixteen. Six. Two.

May these numbers serve you well in this life!

The snowfall was so heavy that the long driveway up to his parents' house was impassable, and he had to leave his car near the road. He trudged through the drifts across the field, angling to the lakeshore, one hand pressing on the wound. When he paused to rest, he felt the blood trickling down his leg and filling his boot. The pain had stopped, but he knew if he fell, he would not be able to get up.

Why did the numbers come back? What did it mean?

As he came down the hill, Kaiser could make out a faint glimmer of something out on the ice, like a satellite in the dark sky but in negative image. The ghost of a snowfield in summer. He looked back up to the lights of his parents' house, the front porch, the living room, the upstairs bedroom. He thought of his mother in her bed, perhaps just stirring or making her way downstairs for coffee, looking out the broad front windows at the blizzard that obscured the lake. Wondering at the unmarked landscape, so pure and clean the world must seem filled with light.

Kaiser paused at the lake edge, then stepped out onto ice, beneath him nothing but darkness and cold and the eternal fall. His boot was full of blood, and he left a line of red boot prints on the ice as he limped toward what was waiting for him.

Then he heard a voice; it wasn't Sebastian, but it was a voice he knew. The dark glimmer spangled through the falling snow, an oscillating stain, a murky starburst. It drew him on. He kept walking. The ice quivered under his feet as the darkness roused; he could feel the black shape spreading in all directions. A young voice, calling to him in sorrow, over the dark heart of the lake. The child of water that he lost.

The boy at the bottom of the lake sat in the rusting hulk of a fishing shanty that lay on a dune of silt. The thickness of the ice and heavy snowfall made the depths of the lake especially murky, but the boy knew that if he sat still for long hours his eyes would adjust. His gaze was drawn to a spot on the ice overhead, some distance away. He could tell that some mortal struggle was being enacted.

He never understood how he knew this, the same way he knew to rise in the evenings and walk the woods, the same he knew to find a place in the dim bottom to sleep, the way he knew that he had been here forever.

The boy rose and began shuffling through the knee-deep silt making his way to the falling star. He was surprised to find it was a man, tall and angular, coming with arms outstretched like a diver. A shining crown on his head sent shafts of silver light piercing through the darkness. The boy caught him with both arms and laid him on thc bottom. The light from the metal crown that encircled his head dimmed and the boy touched the smooth dome of his head, the angle of his strong jaw. This man was surely a king among men.

As the light faded the boy began to cover the body with the black mud of the lake bottom.

The Boy at the Bottom of the Lake &
Other Legends of the North Country,
Jean-Pierre Montour, 1936

EPILOGUE

In the end, the boys came for him.

The boys flowed across the border like water with passports and cash, the boys surged down the streets of Montreal, through the hallways of the Auberge Bonaparte, and burst into the hotel room with their blue jackets and duck boots and a packed suitcase. The boys picked him up and carried him; the boys wrapped him in blankets and took him outside to the fleet of SUVs lined up on the street. The boys ferried him to the airport, the boys handing him ibuprofen, spring water, granola bars. Alejandro wiped his face with a warm towel, patiently explaining to him what could not be written down. The boys arranged flights and connections and visas and money transfers from their secret chapter bank accounts and worldwide connections. The boys put him on a plane with fresh socks, moisturizer, inflatable neck pillow, a vial of Ambien, and a pair of first-class seats. When LeClair awoke, he was in Madrid and a man was holding a sign that said "Bryan Ferry" in the baggage claim and he was whisked through customs with perfunctory stamps and then, in a battered van driven by Alejandro's cousin, he traveled south through the mountains. He dozed and arrived at night at an abandoned mountain villa near Paloma Baja, across the Strait of Gibraltar from Tangiers, and he was led to dark room with a wooden pallet with homespun blankets. When he awoke, the sun was shining through the window and a woman was frying fish and rice in a skillet in the kitchen. Out the back door a wide veranda made of stacked slate overlooked the pounding Atlantic as it rushed around the corner of Europe, Gibraltar, spilling in the Mediterranean.

The boys were gone.

A little more than a year later, LeClair was standing on the veranda as the battered van came up the drive again and stopped in a cloud of dust. The door opened and Emerson climbed out with a backpack and a book in one hand, her hair in a thick braid. After graduation, she moved to Paris for the summer and then enrolled in graduate school at King's College London. Every month, a package arrived from her father and money was wired to her bank account. In the early spring she was on holiday in the beach town of San Rafael, France, when she received a postcard. The picture: *Sunset, Lake George, New York*, by Jasper Francis Cropsey. No name or address, just a string of numbers. It took Emerson only a couple minutes to determine they were coordinates.

When her uncle disappeared in Montreal, the fraternity filled the house with flowers. Neither the boys nor Walt ever let on that Donnie was still alive, hidden away on the coast of Spain.

Now Donnie looked thinner and older, his skin ruddy from sun and sea wind. They held each other for a long time. Then he led her up to the villa with the unrelenting view of the Atlantic, the bright skies and clean air, and inside the four small rooms with sandstone walls all painted white, all as blank as a field of fresh snow.

In a closet in the bedroom, leaning against the wall on the floor behind his boots, there was a small, wrapped painting, layered with dust.

The body was discovered drifting on a sandbar. A local shopkeeper claimed that early in the morning a man mutilated his face in his bathroom before staggering, bloody and screaming, out to the beach and into the water, but when the body was found it was covered with blue crabs that had eaten most of the flesh from the face and head. It was several weeks before the body was identified as Laurence Sterne of North Chazy, New York.

When Sydney walked in the door, her mother and Juliet were playing on the floor in the square of light from the sun. The walls were painted a faint rose color, giving the room a warm hue, and the smoke stains on the ceiling were gone. A hockey game on the television in the family room. The boxes from last night's Chinese takeout on the coffee table mixed with a set of plastic farm animals and chapter books. Juliet ran over to her, holding out her hand.

For you, Mommy.

A fortune cookie, the little folded orange ones, like mollusks without a shell. Sydney tried to smile. She was exhausted and wanted to sleep, but she dropped her bag on the floor and lifted the little girl up, surprised once again by how much she had grown.

When Callie's cancer tests came back negative, the woman sobbed on her shoulder for an hour, telling Sydney over and over how sorry she was. In the late spring, Sydney petitioned the state and got Dylan accepted into a special arts program in Saratoga Springs, a school for gifted children. Callie got a job in a local coffee shop, and so far had been able to hold off her drinking till the afternoon. Her first parental rights hearing was coming up and the lawyer was hopeful. Dylan was finally beginning to emerge from the deep well of sorrow. His older brother was still considered missing, though most people knew he was gone. Dylan still believed he was alive, that he would return to their apartment in Saratoga Springs and find Sebastian in the kitchen, something popping in a skillet, gripping a slotted spoon, the mad grin on his face, his halo shining.

Juliet tore off the cookie wrapper, breaking it open with her small fingers and handing the little slip of paper to Sydney.

Tell me, she said. Your fortune!

Sydney read it aloud: *There is nothing so dark and terrible that cannot be cured with goodness and light.*

Juliet furrowed her brow, crunching on the cookie.

What does that mean?

Sydney shrugged and flipped the paper over and read the other side.

Please enjoy your Lucky Numbers!

12 8 3 16 7 11

May these numbers bring you joy and good fortune!

The little girl led her mother into the family room, where her father was sitting on the couch, waiting for them. Juliet dove into his chest, wrapping her arms around his neck. Phil had been half dozing, watching the Canadiens torch the Rangers for three goals in the first period. On the floor was his set of prosthetic arms, each tipped with a curved hook that he used to buzz people in and out of the visitors' area from his desk in the Clinton County Correctional Facility, Dannemora, New York. Juliet called the prosthetics his *robot hands*. Phil rarely wore them at home. Because when he held his daughter, when he wrapped what was left of his arms around her, it still felt like they were all there. It was as if he could feel his hands on her thin shoulders, her rib cage, like he could run his fingers through her hair again.

Sydney stood in the doorway, smiling. He could see that she was exhausted. He would put on the hooks and make dinner; he would persuade her to go to bed early. He would bathe Juliet, dress her in her pajamas, and read stories as they lay together in her small bed.

Daddy, Juliet whispered into his ear. Daddy.

What?

Hold me tighter, she said.

He squeezed, encircling her in his arms. The sharp slap of the puck and the cheer from the television, Sydney taking off her coat, dumping the leftovers in the trash. The day was nearly over.

I love you, he said. I love you more than anything in this world.

She settled herself into him, murmuring into his neck.

Don't let me go.

ACKNOWLEDGMENTS

I am thankful for my time in the North Country and Plattsburgh, and all the fine people I met there. Special thanks to Roland and Phil for letting me join their sailing crews, which changed my life. Thank you to the Marlowe family for their hospitality during my research and for taking me out on the ice for ice fishing and sled races, plus drinks and conversation in their garage.

This book contains names, places, and situations both real and imagined, drawn from my own life experiences, research, and stories I heard during my time in the North Country and after. It is not intended to portray any specific person, organization, or place. The epigraphs by Jean Pierre Montour about the boy under the lake are a complete fabrication.

There are places where the extremes of geography, weather, and history seem to make the normal barriers between our world and the metaphysical realm seem thin, unsubstantial, and confused. To me the North Country is such a place. It is a difficult, unforgiving environment, peopled by some of the most generous, honest, and determined people I have known. This story is intended to honor these people.

I would like to thank my generous readers, Seth Tucker, Susan White Norman, Julianna Baggott, Ray Balestri, Mike Mannon, as well as my editors William Boggess, Lydia Rogue, Josie Woodbridge, and all the fine folks at Blackstone. I remain indebted to my agent Alex Glass of

Glass Literary Management for continuing to believe in my work. I would like to thank all my colleagues at the University of Mississippi English Department and MFA program. Most of all I thank my wife, Stacy, and my family, for being patient and humoring me in this mad escapade that took more than a decade to complete.